Lady Gallant

by

Gini Rifkin

Lady Gallant

COPYRIGHT © 2009 by Virginia Rifkin

Cover Art by *Nicola Martinez*

The Wild Rose Press
PO Box 708
Adams Basin, NY 14410-0706
Visit us at www.thewildrosepress.com

Publishing History
First English Tea Rose Edition, 2010
Print ISBN 1-60154-679-3

Published in the United States of America

Dedication

In memory of all those who have gone on ahead
to mark the trail and light the welcoming fires.

Dedicated to the amazing women who have
come into my life by birth, marriage, and destiny.

With gratitude once again
to Amanda Barnett and The Wild Rose Press.

War has always fascinated me. I don't mean the tactical maneuvering of whole armies by famous generals—movements of such magnitude are quite beyond my imagination. I have in mind the real essence of war—the killing.

~Leo Tolstoy, *The Raid*

Chapter One
The Ottoman Empire, November 1854

The laws of the Universe did not supersede the laws of Man. At least not here thought Garrick Allen, not in the Crimea. Here there was no order to the Cosmos. Here there was no Karmic justice meted out by Divine Intelligence.

Shoulders hunched against the morning breeze, he studied the barren hills and plains of Turkey. Desolation glared back, defiant and unblinking. Thankfully, the vision no longer clawed a bloody path across his soul. Surviving five months in Hell did that to a man. It hardened him to the sight and smell of death. Death that hung in the air like a poisonous fog. Death that haunted his memories by day and his dreams by night.

Abandoning the grim view, Garrick headed for the Day Sergeant's Office. Unlike the scenery, his thoughts were not so easily dismissed and as he sidestepped a broken-down lorry, he came to the conclusion that there was no Supreme Intervention in the Crimea because God wanted neither the credit nor the blame for such abomination. This was strictly Man's doing, Man's ultimate folly. And it seemed frightfully instinctual this thing called War.

A familiar din interrupted his reverie, and he

slowed his pace. The ramshackle dock up ahead was the usual beehive of ineffectual activity. Anxious to avoid the noisy muddle, he altered course and angled inland away from the spit of pebbly sand that constituted the beach. The nearby road would also be crowded but in the long run, the route should prove to be less disruptive. And today, disruption was to be avoided at all cost. Today, nothing would deter him from his mission; not the war-engine, not the plight of the troops—in truth not even the edicts of the Queen.

"The truth indeed," he scoffed. Truth was always the first victim of war and few seemed to mourn its passing. Especially not the antiquated Majors and Generals who orchestrated this catastrophic soiree. These Grand Old Boys fought today's war with yesterday's strategies, all for a cause the world had long ago forgotten.

He sighed. Thoughts of the "truth" had once stirred him to lofty contemplation. Now the word inspired sadness and try as he might, he could barely recall the face of this old companion. Yet, "truth" was the very basis of the dispatches he and his colleagues relayed back to *The Times* in London. Dispatches he wrote with as much accuracy as was humanly possible. Dispatches he hoped were not swayed by the deplorable personal circumstances in which he found himself or by the overt threats aimed at him by the military. Threats, he might add, that were issued with far greater enthusiasm and regularity than food and clothing to the soldiers.

Head down he trudged on. The road proved deceptively difficult to navigate, and his knee-high boots were soon spattered with mud the color of dark taffy. Had it rained last night? How had he missed the occurrence? It seemed he never slept but rather he spent hour after endless hour lying in the darkness staring up at the nothingness that surrounded them all. Staring, wondering, and feeling so terribly alone until the dark void finally consumed him and he felt just as empty on the inside as this wretched corner of the world was on the outside.

Hazarding a glance to the right, he studied the discarded humanity that littered the countryside. More than the truth had been abandoned here. A few feet beyond the edge of the waterlogged road, a young British infantryman sat shivering—propped up against an empty salt-pork barrel. The lad sought to raise his canteen to his mouth but he shook so violently the simple endeavor was not to be accomplished. Instead, the liquid sloshed about and spilled uselessly down the front of his threadbare uniform. Only the memory of clean cold water reached the boy's parched lips.

Garrick stopped to assist the fellow. Then not expecting nor wanting a "thank you", he continued on his way.

At times, he wondered which was the more difficult task, keeping the truth alive or the cholera-stricken soldiers. Both suffered equally. He supposed there was little enough he could do directly for the common soldier, but he still possessed the means to accommodate the much-maligned truth. And wouldn't championing one victim of the war help to save the other? Who could say? Without the tools of his trade, it was all pure supposition and theory. Which was precisely why today, short of taking it out of someone's hide, he was determined to procure the items he needed. After all, it had been several weeks since he had been promised a tent, a lamp, his own ration of coffee, and paper...precious paper. How the devil was he supposed to write a newspaper column without paper?

Determination mounting with every step, he walked on. Finally, the commandeered military shanty he sought wavered into view. He eyed the line already established before the ramshackle structure and his enthusiasm dissipated along with the last vestiges of chill morning air. Apparently, several other men had awakened this morning with high hopes of obtaining custom. *Buck up old boy*, he chastised. The imminent call to mess would route the majority of soldiers preceding him and he was still a step or two ahead of the bewildered masses spewing forth from the newly arrived ships. Besides, something about this day felt special to him. It was akin to the feeling he got when he knew a lead story was about to break, and although the war was masterful at dulling one's emotions, his intuition had survived unscathed and today it was telling him to keep his nose to the wind.

Bolstered by his own rhetoric, Garrick took his place in the queue and retrieved a half-smoked cheroot from the inside pocket of his worn leather coat. Carefully lighting the precious stub, he savored the taste and breathed deeply of the aroma. A pleasurable sensation twisted through him momentarily brightening his mood. A man could tolerate living on half rations and he had reconciled himself to the fact that his luggage, "mysteriously" lost in military transit, would never be recovered but he was running short of smokes. That was entirely unacceptable. Thank heaven the Turks still had plenty of whiskey.

"Hey, Mr. Allen," a gravely-voiced soldier called out, "you seen young Paddy lately?"

Garrick glanced up and shook his head. "Not since the skirmish at MacKenzie's farm," he replied.

"Well hold a good thought for the lad," the man said, as he hurried on, "with any luck he might make it back."

Luck? Garrick gave the small cigar two quick puffs to keep it lit then angled his worn wolf-skin cap further back upon his brow. A snort of sarcasm escaped his lungs along with the smoke he'd been holding. He'd long ago given up on luck or trying to be optimistic or philosophical about the situation here. He just reported what he saw, as honestly and professionally as possible. Clamping his teeth down on the cheroot, he shoved his hands into his pockets. Damn but he hated this war. Why had he volunteered to come here?

****

The steamer *Vectis* had been docked for nearly three hours, yet Nurse Josephine Posey's stomach continued to heave. Trying her best not to vomit over the rail, she took another calming breath and tugged at the neckline of her blouse.

In the wee small hours before dawn, she had shivered with the damp and cold and her woolen suit had seemed an appropriate choice. Now, as the cool morning breeze died a silent death and the Turkish sun took command of the sky, the fabric she wore itched mercilessly and a trickle of sweat ran down between her breasts.

Fighting the urge to wriggle and scratch, she gritted her teeth and silently observed the thirty-nine other women on the foredeck who had come to the Crimea to care for England's finest. Each woman appeared as miserable as she, yet nary-a-one issued a complaint and neither did Josie. Like them, she had sought this impasse of her own free will. If conditions here were not to her liking, she had no one to blame other than herself. Besides, her situation would most assuredly improve once she was ashore.

On second thought, why should it? Their entire journey from London to Scutari had been one disaster following upon the heels of another. The Channel crossing had been unusually rough, nearly capsizing the packet to Boulogne and while traveling overland to Paris and Marseilles, they had endured cramped quarters with little food and no clean water. Mercifully reaching the south of France, they had boarded the last vessel heading for the Mediterranean and a sorry little boat it had been. Gale-force winds had dashed and pummeled the converted mail carrier across the roiling sea. Then the engines had quit and the listing craft had shipped water at a fearful rate, transforming the dimly lit hold into a dank airless prison of seasick women.

She grabbed the rail to steady herself as her graphic recollections fueled new whitecaps of nausea. Then darker memories bobbed to the surface and the queasiness in her midsection gave way to an aching in her heart. When power had finally been restored to their floundering transport, they had come up lost. The Captain, poor fellow, saw only one course of action. Sorrowfully, he established their route by following the trail of debris and dead bodies cast off by the ships preceding them. Men were dying before they even reached the battlefields. Would she be just as helpless to save them here?

No, she must not even entertain such an idea. It was bad form to give up before she'd even begun. Yet, not one single happenstance had occurred to give her cause for optimism. Only a fool would expect things to improve and perhaps that was exactly what she was. Perhaps her parents had been correct and she should not have come here after all.

Forcing the dismal possibility aside, she again contemplated the throng of women who stood upon the deck. This time she was afforded a glimpse of her friend's comforting face. Gemma, dear Gemma, who remained cheerful even in the most dire of circumstances. If only her companion were here at her side, but the nurses had been instructed to exit the steamer alphabetically, regardless of group and that meant her childhood cohort was positioned further back in the pack and seemingly a world away.

Gemma grinned and waved. The tiny blue-eyed blonde was nearly unflappable, with a gift for attracting men that was most alarming but never boring. Gemma beguiled and entranced men with ease and claimed they reasoned only with their private parts. Josie had never been able to play such games but it unerringly worked for Gemma.

Josie smiled and waved back. They were such opposites. Take the day they had left home for example. Half of the men in the county had appeared to give Gemma an appropriate send off and Gemma had taken it all in stride, acting as if she expected nothing less. No one had been there to see Josie off and she had not expected more.

Yes, this tedious morning would have progressed more quickly and more pleasantly with Gemma's humorous commentary to distract them. But it was too late for disobeying instructions and maneuvering into a new position, just as it was too late for second thoughts or for turning back.

As if giving credence to her practical thinking, the queue advanced at a more energetic pace. Josie struggled beneath the weight of the two valises she carried and nudged a small trunk along with the boot-toe of her right foot. Then obliged to endure another halt, she set down her burden and pressed a handkerchief to her cheeks and forehead.

Craning her neck for a better view, she spied the bustling wharf, and her enthusiasm was reborn. Unfortunately, it was also short lived and her spirits plummeted to a new low as she spotted a bloated horse carcass floating and bobbing beside the gangplank. Poor beast. With unseeing eyes, he stared up at her and with his lips curled in death, his great yellow-white teeth were locked in a perpetual grin.

Tears slipped down her cheeks to mingle with her sweat. Even the dead mocked her for coming here. Dear Lord, what had she gotten herself into? Where were the jubilant soldiers? Where was the patriotism and glory of war? She had understood that conditions here were harsh, but she had not expected them to be desperate. She should have taken *The Times* articles to heart. They had not minimized the horror that now surrounded her, nor had they whitewashed the suffering. Yet in keeping with so many others back home, she had assumed the accounts were exaggerated for the purpose of selling more copies. They had all been terribly mistaken

She squared her shoulders and blotted away her tears with the back of her hand. She was not prone to crying, another theatric Gemma found useful when dealing with men. Being strong was Josie's forte, and it had seen her through many struggles in life. She could only pray that her strength was equal to what lay before her now.

The line of nurses again quickened into life, and stepping up to the processing table, Josie handed her transit papers to the deck officer. He shuffled through a sheaf of documents then marked off his ledger in what seemed a dozen places. Not bothering to ask for her permission, two nearby soldiers snatched up her luggage and threw open the latches. Her cheeks burned with embarrassment as they unceremoniously pawed through her belongings.

She had a penchant for rather worldly underclothing. A bit of lace and a wisp of silk made her feel pretty and feminine beneath her stiff and prudish clothes—not an easy task for a woman of her height and outspoken personality. More importantly, this luxury had amused and delighted Phillip. A secret smile tugged at her lips. She could do that now, on occasion, smile in the face of her grief. Yet, the remembrance of her dearly departed remained a tricky proposition. Memories were like diamonds, brilliant and priceless, yet jagged and hard enough to cut glass. It hadn't taken long for her to realize that recollections were to be evoked with caution and great consideration for their handmaiden could be cruel sorrow as well as sweet comfort.

Voices cleaved through her private musings.

"Hey Robbie," one soldier chortled, holding up a beribboned camisole for all the world to see. "How'd ya like to be bandaged up in one of these?"

Mortified, she snatched the garment from his grasp and shoved it back into the trunk. These unmentionables had been for Phillip's eyes only and to honor that memory she continued to wear such trifles. Now she paid the price of ridicule for the wayward indulgence of keeping the past alive.

"The show is over gentlemen." She dropped the lid closed on one of the men's hand. "I am here to tend the wounded, not spy for the Russians. You'll find no mortar shells nor confidential papers amongst my things."

The second man guffawed and allowed her to pass. "See the Day Sergeant dockside," he directed.

Her shoulders slumped. Not another checkpoint. "But I am not under the jurisdiction of the British Army," she protested.

"Don't matter," he flatly informed her. "Be they Colonel or camp-follower if they passes through this port, they sees the Day Sergeant dockside. I suggest you do the same."

Resigned to her fate and luggage in tow, she grappled her way down the gangplank, all the while averting her gaze from the dead horse and the miasma that rose upward from it. As she blessedly reached terra firma, she felt a tug on her skirt.

"You need help lady?" a little voice piped up.

She glanced down into the angelic face of a small Turkish boy.

"It's gonna be a hot one," he said solemnly and wiped the back of his hand across his brow. Every inch of him not covered with clothing was streaked with dirt and sweat, and his big brown eyes returned her stare with a wisdom no child should have. "I know the best places to stay," he added conspiratorially, "only the finest rooms and the richest men."

Saints above, the boy had mistaken her for a prostitute. She didn't know whether to laugh or cry. "I'm a nurse," she explained, "and I am afraid I shall be assigned quarters much less exciting than the ones you have to offer."

At first, the lad appeared disappointed. Then his bright smile returned. "I will help you anyway," he offered enthusiastically.

Well why not? Regardless of his small stature and limited age, she had a feeling the lad was frightfully well acquainted with the immediate area. "Thank you," she said, "might you know where the Day Sergeant is stationed?"

"Sure, lady, this way. Fortune smiles upon you," he added, as he wrestled her small trunk up off the ground and onto his shoulders. "They have just given first call. The line is much shorter now." The boy momentarily swayed under the weight of her luggage, then finding his "sea legs" he confidently led the way.

Skirting the confused throng of women milling about the dock, he expertly guided her to a dilapidated hut where several men of various rank and condition stood in attendance. Not daring to wait for Gemma, she secured a place in the line. The lad staggered to a halt and deposited her trunk upon the rocky shore. Josie eased her valises to the ground as well and handed him a half-crown.

Grasping the coin with small grubby fingers, he instinctively raised the token to his mouth, biting down upon it to make sure it was real. Eyes wide he found his voice, "Thank you, lady." Then with a whoop and a holler, he disappeared into a nearby covey of dark-eyed children.

"You're going to spoil the little fellow and make it difficult on the rest of us," the man in front of her gruffly pointed out. "That's more money then he normally earns in a week."

"It shouldn't be," Josie defended. "He looks half-starved, and his clothes are in tatters."

"Why should he be any different than the rest of us?"

Startled by the man's biting comment, Josie studied him more closely. The cut of his jaw and the planes of his cheeks were obscured by a shadowy beard, but the potential of a ruggedly handsome face seemed to lurk beneath the stubble. His attire, on the other hand, was as hard-bitten as his attitude. He wore an odd-looking leather coat sporting fringes across the shoulders and his brown woolen trousers, stretched tight over long lean legs, were tucked into very muddy, knee-high black boots. A cap, made from some poor unrecognizable dead animal perched upon his head, covering the majority of his untamed dark hair. She had to concede that the preponderance of his clothes, although cleaner than the boy's, were frayed beyond repair, and he appeared as if he truly could use a hot meal.

Her gaze meandered back upward and crashed headfirst into his, and the lonely haunted expression in the man's dusky green eyes sent a shiver down her spine. He appeared more forlorn than the child who had assisted her. At least the lad had been cheerful and accommodating. Reminded of the man's rudeness and criticism, Josie made to step around him. "Excuse me," she said edging closer to the office.

Extending his arm, he blocked her forward progress. "I beg your pardon, madam. Pretty or not you'll have to wait your turn." With the air of a hooligan, he looked her up and down. The loneliness in his eyes transformed into a rakish glint, and the slight curl of his lip stretched into a sarcastic smile.

Such blatant insolence ignited Josie's temper and anger burned upon her cheeks. "I have been on that wretched boat for weeks on end," she gritted. "I must procure the sanctity of a room."

"It's a ship, not a boat," he casually corrected, "and I don't care if you were born and raised on the foredeck. You've only just arrived. I've been in Turkey five months and I'm not giving up my place in line."

Tired and frustrated, Josie was at a loss for words—an unusual condition for her. As she groped for an appropriate response, Gemma strolled up fresh as a morning rose in May. An entourage of uniformed men followed in her wake, carrying her luggage. She glided to a halt. The men, as if delivering treasure to the feet of a princess, grandly deposited the baggage on the ground before her.

"Thank you ever so much," Gemma purred. "Each and every one of you has won a special place in my heart. I could not possibly have managed without your assistance." She simpered and smiled and batted her lashes. The soldiers puffed out their chests and grinned like schoolboys, then reluctantly wandered off to attend to their real duties.

Josie smirked. This condescending donkey's backside blocking their path would not be so smug now that Gemma had arrived. Leaning close to her friend so as not to be overheard, Josie explained the situation then watched in silent expectation as Gemma sized up their quarry.

"Kind, sir," the little blonde began. "Would you mind terribly if we preceded you in line? I do believe I feel faint." Employing her best damsel-in-distress demeanor, Gemma artfully freed a button at the neck of her blouse then she sighed and pressed a lace hankie to her temple. "If I could but secure my room assignment," she added, "so I might tuck in and rest for a bit, it would greatly improve my condition."

"Feeling faint are you?" the man replied, with great solemnity. "Perhaps the most beneficial course of action would be for you to assume a seated position with your head between your knees."

Gemma's eyes widened and her mouth dropped open. Josie had never seen the girl in a fluster before. To cover her confusion, Gemma launched into one of her crying spells. Josie stepped forward and put her arm around Gemma's quaking shoulders. "That was most ungentlemanly," she accused.

"If I am not willing to relinquish my place in line for God nor the Queen, a chit of a girl, no matter how remarkably curvaceous, shan't accomplish the task."

To Josie's amazement, Gemma produced fake tears at an even more incredible rate. "Well it's hardly fair of you to reduce the poor thing to crying," Josie argued.

"Fair?" The man reared back as if struck a physical blow, then his heated gaze pinned her in place. "If you're looking for fair, madam, you've come to the bloody wrong place."

He doffed his hat and his hair dipped forward, lending an even more rakehell appearance to his demeanor. "Now if you will pardon me, ladies, I believe I am wanted inside." Turning and without so much as a backward glance, he leisurely strode into the office.

Josie studied his broad shoulders and

swaggering walk. This handsome wastrel piqued her curiosity.

He was the first man she had encountered who seemed resistant to Gemma's charms.

Despite his rude demeanor, she rather fancied that.

"...one would believe that the sick and the wounded cease to be men when they can no longer be soldiers."
~Pierre Francois Percy, Fr. Military Surgeon

Chapter Two
The Barrack Hospital, Scutari

For weeks on end, the nurses had begged to be admitted to the wards but their pleas had fallen upon deaf ears. Now their demands had been met, their prayers had been answered, and heaven help her, Josie wished she were anyplace else on earth.

"We are the first to be granted such an honor and responsibility," Miss Nightingale extolled. "And if our efforts here are to be taken seriously and we are not to be the last as well as the first, we must attain our goals despite the impediments before us. Hear me well, Ladies. The very future of nursing depends upon our ability to prove wrong all who would see us fail."

Unfortunately for the nurses, the British Army topped their list of adversaries. The military did not tolerate anyone who disrupted the regimental flow of Army life, and this ruthless hypothesis included the sick and the wounded as well as those who cared for them. In addition, the medical staff had not requested that the women come here, and by gad they'd be damned if they would admit to needing their services.

Until now.

Following the battle of Inkerman, all logic had changed. That day of infamy, remembered by some as a military victory and by others as a nightmare of unparalleled slaughter, had taken a heavy toll on the Allied Army. So it was in the midst of these overwhelming conditions that the nurses were finally given leave to tend the wounded. Yet, even in the face of such dire circumstances, all was not forgiven nor forgotten. True to form, the doctors continued their overt exhibitions of condescension, and a general atmosphere of ridicule and intolerance prevailed throughout the hospital.

Remarkably, through it all, Miss Nightingale remained confident of their success, and standing tall in the midst of her circle of followers, she calmly met each fearful and wide-eyed gaze with a steely-eyed and direct one of her own. "Never to know that you are beaten is the way to victory," she encouraged. A deceptively simple statement from an obviously complex woman. How many battles, Josie wondered, had this woman fought in order to advance the concepts of nursing to where they were today? How many more obstacles loomed ahead for this selfless lady and their scorned profession?

"My faith in you is unshakable," their leader continued, "and I am sure you shall each endeavor to persevere."

"Persevere in killing ourselves most likely," Gemma whispered in Josie's ear. Today, even her friend seemed doubtful of their ability to conquer what lay before them. And who could blame her as one appalling scene after another overwhelmed their senses.

Josie swallowed hard. Her gaze drifted from the face of one wounded soldier to the next. So far, not one of the near seven hundred patients had bandied words or remarks with any of the women. Nor had she heard any complaints. Both were bad signs.

As if to contradict her observations, she felt the fleeting pressure of a large hand upon her thigh. Evidently, one lad still harbored a delinquent thought or two. She turned, intent on putting the soldier gently in his place, but the words died in her throat as she stared into the face of an older man with only respect in his eyes.

The patient was bandaged from head to foot, and the wrappings prevented him from sitting up or moving freely. Her thigh had been the only part of her he could reach with his trembling hand.

He breathed heavily and worked his mouth, as if even the act of speaking was too much for him. "Praise be," he rasped, with a noticeable burr, "and thank ye for coming, lassie. You and all the fine ladies."

Mustering a smile, Josie tucked the threadbare blanket more snugly about the old soldier. If only she could stay and talk with the man, or merely sit beside him and hold his hand, but the band of women had already moved on, and she had no choice but to follow. "Try and rest," she advised and lightly touched his arm. "We shall return on the morrow to help in earnest."

Averting her face, so the old soldier would not see the tears that burned in the back of her eyes, she forced herself from his bedside. Vision blurred, she exited the ward too quickly and crashed into a broken down gurney—carelessly discarded beside the door. Oh for goodness sake, she fumed. Since leaving home, she felt bruised and battered at every turn, both physically and mentally. Shoving the contraption out of her way as if it had purposely lain in wait for her, she struggled onward. But the condition of the corridor merely added insult to her injury. The narrow passageway was a jumble of steamer trunks, defective equipment, and overflow patients, and simply traversing the hallway resembled running a gauntlet.

Pushing and winding her way through the clutter, she headed for the second floor bathing chambers. Then her breath caught in her throat as she stepped around a soldier whose shirt was stiff with his own blood. Lice shimmered on the bare mattress upon which he lay, and a furry rat scurried from beneath his bed to a hidey-hole in the nearby wall. As if preparing to fight a flesh and blood enemy, Josie clenched her hands into fists and silently vowed that the ward given into her care would never look nor smell like this one.

As she hurried along, it became obvious that none of the rooms were properly ventilated, and the archaic latrines were unable to appropriately function under such unrelenting conditions. The sanitation system at the old Turkish military barrack spilled lethargically into the sea, and a foul odor was blown back in their faces by the onshore breeze. The desire for a more favorable wind direction would be added to her evening prayers.

At the upstairs antechamber, she rejoined the nurses but any attempt to hear what was being discussed at the front of the class proved futile. In frustration, she wandered away from the cluster of women, halted before an open window, and leaned her forehead against the marble framework. The coolness trapped by the chiseled stone proved a welcome panacea for the dull ache that throbbed in her temples. Her gaze, restless as her mood, drifted downward to the outer courtyard and to the men crowded around the main entrance. Amidst scavenging dogs and wailing cries of pain, the injured soldiers lingered in mournful disarray, waiting, ever waiting, for the mortally wounded to die and give up their cots.

She wrung her hands and felt helpless in the face of such overwhelming anguish. This was all terribly wrong. Surely the lack of rations, clothing, and common daily necessities was a temporary oversight...a simple mistake.

"Psst. Josie," Gemma signaled. "It's time for us to go. Miss Nightingale has given out the assignments for the remainder of the morning."

Josie levered away from the window and eagerly followed the group out of the bleak facility and into the outdoor storage area. Even more gladly, she focused her attention on their mindless task of inventorying the stockpile of Miss Nightingale's medical supplies. As she toiled, visions of what she had just witnessed harried her mind and her stomach revolted and twisted into a knot. The next time she visited the wards she would fare better. Now that she knew what to expect, she would be properly prepared to ingest another dose of the misery that awaited there. Until then, she must apply herself to the chore at hand. For now, she would not think about what she had just seen, at least not in too great a detail.

"Many of Miss Nightingale's provisions have traveled poorly," Gemma commented, her voice echoing up from behind the wall of canvas bags and trunks that hid her from view.

"Indeed," Josie agreed, as she re-labeled another box. "What isn't identified incorrectly seems to be ruined by rot and mildew from the ocean voyage. At least we've clean linen for bandages and sufficient tow with which to tend wounds."

"How could Miss "N" have known that the Army would refuse to relinquish supplies to us?" Gemma asked.

"The same way she knew we would need to set up our own kitchens and laundry," Josie pointed out. "She plans for the unthinkable. That's what makes her so amazing."

"She is wonderful," Gemma agreed.

The awe in the girl's voice surprised Josie. There were few people whom Gemma truly admired and her respect and esteem for their leader, or Miss "N" as Gemma had dubbed her, was quite a compliment.

"Too bad the same cannot be said for the Army," Gemma added with distain. "An amazing blend of too much pride and too little efficiency and it all leads to more suffering for the lads."

"Yes, "Josie agreed, "'tis Bedlam here with no one in charge and every man for himself. I dare say things will change now that Miss Nightingale has been given leave to act." Cataloguing the last of the items from the wooden crate, Josie gathered them into her arms. "I'd best take this assortment to the storeroom."

Gemma peered from behind her little fortress of supplies. "Don't get lost," she teased.

The tower of boxes precariously balanced in her arms, Josie wended a path to the door which led inside. Gaining entrance, she rounded the far corner only to collide with a force as immovable as a wall. The supplies tumbled from her grasp, and a few of the fragile items shattered upon impact.

"Oh bother," she exclaimed, as a strong hand reached out to steady her. "Must you go charging about like a bull in a pasture?" she accused. Glancing up, she regretted her angry words. The man gripping her arm was tall and dashing with blue eyes that burned with the look of curiosity.

"I would have employed more care," he said, "had I known someone as lovely as yourself occupied the meadow." His sensuous mouth slanted upward in a mocking smile, and releasing her arm he stooped to retrieve one of the boxes. It clinked with the disheartening sound of broken glass.

"Frightfully sorry," he grimaced and handed it back to her.

"Oh this is dreadful," she declared. "Those were the only graduated flasks and stopper bottles to survive the journey."

"I shall purchase you a new set straight away,"

he offered. "Where might I send for replacements?"

"I'm afraid it's not quite as simple as that. In London we waited two months for these bottles. Heaven only knows how long it will take to have another compliment shipped this distance."

"It's all a matter of knowing the right people. I promise you an alternate set within the month."

She smiled at this man's cocky enthusiasm and shifted her gaze to encompass his full countenance. His clothes were well tailored and stylish with no missing buttons and no frayed edges, and he was clean-shaven, smelling of lavender soap and talc. He appeared to fare quite nicely here, avoiding the hardships that most others incurred. She was relieved to know not all the men about were as dubious and ill-mannered as the scurrilous fellow she had met on the docks when she had first arrived.

"Been here long?" the man asked, breaking in upon her thoughts.

Unaccustomed to answering casual queries from strangers, Josie hesitated. "Might I know with whom I am speaking?"

"Yes, of course. Forgive me." He bowed with a flourish. "I am Danford Harrison Smythe, T.G." He straightened and slid his thumbs beneath the lapels of his fine coat. "Been here since the beginning."

"T.G.?"

"Traveling Gentleman. Here at my own expense, as it were. Just had to see firsthand what was going on and of course I want to help the lads in any way I can."

"I see," Josie said, although she didn't see at all. Why anyone would come here out of curiosity was beyond her ken. It sounded like base amusement for the idle rich—reminiscent of the lords and ladies in centuries past who frequented asylums for entertainment. On the contrary, Mr. Smythe seemed sincere in his offer to help.

"I'm Nurse Josephine Posey."

"Ah yes." He sobered. "I heard that a flock of angels-of-mercy had arrived. I'm afraid you will have more to contend with here than broken instruments."

Miss Nightingale's speech echoed in the back of Josie's mind. "The conditions are a bit frightful, but we shall manage nicely as long as the Cossacks are kept at bay."

"'Tis the British Army more likely to give you trouble than the Russians," he said knowingly.

"There's a wee bit of truth to that," she admitted. "Several of the higher-ups have cast a jaundiced eye in our direction. But we shan't be deterred so easily," she added brightly knowing full well the value of keeping up appearance.

A strange little smile pulled at Mr. Smythe's mouth, then he glanced down at the remainder of supplies at his feet. "May I offer my assistance with these?"

"Oh...yes...thank you." Before the man could renege upon the offer to subject himself to common labor, Josie shoved the box into his hands, retrieved the rest, piled them into his arms, and ushered him along the corridor. "I'm afraid the collision was as much my fault as yours," she conceded.

"No, no," he protested as they rounded another turn. "I accept full blame and responsibility. Wouldn't want you getting in Dutch with your superiors."

With a murmur of thanks, Josie pushed open the door to the storage area assigned to Miss Nightingale. The room was cold and damp and dimly lit and it reminded her of a mausoleum. Shaking off the peculiar notion, she proceeded further into the unfamiliar chamber and then turned to help Mr. Smythe settle the jumble of supplies upon one of the empty tables. Their hands touched. His were large and obviously strong but they were also soft and well manicured and for some reason that bothered her.

He took a step back and lounged against the nearby wall, arms folded across his chest.

Josie busied herself arranging the stores with their labels facing forward. Glancing up, she caught the stranger's bold gaze as it roamed lazily over her form. His raised brow of approval added a lusty aura to his features. Mr. Smythe radiated a brashness that threatened to overwhelm his charm. Feeling suddenly awkward, she fumbled the last of the cartons.

"Where must I send for those much needed glass instruments?" he asked, as he lowered his arms and levered away from the wall.

"The address is here on the box." She pointed to the lettering stenciled upon the small wooden crate. He did not look where she indicated, but rather his gaze lingered upon her lips. In truth, he seemed not to notice the address at all.

Heat climbed into her cheeks. "I really should be getting along," she said, hoping to make a quick exit.

Mr. Smythe caught her upper arm and held her in place. "A pleasure to have met you, Nurse Posey." He eased his grip slightly then leisurely drew his thumb back and forth across the stiff fabric of her uniform sleeve. "Please inform me immediately if I can be of any further assistance to you or your cause." The brilliance of his eyes was compelling, and her pulse quickened with unexpected excitement.

"I'll keep your offer in mind, Mr. Smythe."

He smiled but made no attempt to release her.

Heart pounding, she pulled free of his grasp, stepped around him, and hurried out the door. A burst of boyish laughter tumbled along in her wake. Although undeniably handsome, Danford Harrison Smythe was also a somewhat unsettling individual.

Nearly at a run, she retraced her steps to the safety of the unloading area and Gemma's reassuring presence.

"And what have you been up to?" her friend asked, as she glanced up from her task. "You're all flushed and fidgety."

"Me? Why nothing, of course," Josie lied. Gemma would tease her for days if she knew a man had flustered her. "It must be the heat," she added as an excuse. "Even the weather here is unfathomable. Freezing all night and blistering hot during the day. I just grow accustomed to one condition when the other descends upon me."

Gemma agreed and nodded toward the fuming black clouds gathered overhead. "It could be worse. It could be raining." Before her voice faded to silence, thunder rumbled across the sky and great drops of icy water splashed down onto Josie's face and chest. "I told you," Gemma shrieked, as they dashed for cover beneath the overhang, "this is definitely worse."

Pressed against the outside wall, Josie glanced down and eyed the one size fits all grey dress and worsted jacket she had been issued as her uniform. To her dismay, she watched as the red embroidered words Scutari Hospital streaked into the white Holland scarf around her shoulders. Fashioned in haste, the scarlet threads had not been properly set prior to being put to needle. Now the dampened lettering blurred and ran as if written in blood.

She shivered and huddled closer to Gemma, and the full impact of how terribly far from home they were seemed nearly suffocating. Oh, why had she come here? She could be at home right now, safely cosseted in her parent's splendid parlor with bright flames dancing in the fireplace, more logs waiting upon the hearth. But such comfort came at a very high price. Along with enjoying such luxury and contentment, she would be obliged to suffer yet another of her mother's chastising lectures or one of father's opinionated tirades. She sighed wearily. Had her behavior and beliefs truly been so unreasonable and unacceptable? She supposed keeping company with George Elliot hadn't helped her situation. Championing the woman's articles in the *Westminster Review* seemed to have been the last straw. Following that incident, the emotional storms raging about Penmarrow had left Josie feeling more cold and lonely than the storm she braved at present.

No, she countered, by coming here she had chosen correctly—perhaps not wisely, but correctly.

As the rain scoured the world around her, Josie willed it to wash her mind free of self recrimination. Dwelling upon the past was a painful and demanding journey and today she did not have the energy to spare for such a dubious indulgence. It was best to allow the present to command her attention, and in this exotic land of extremes, it was easy enough to be intrigued by all that she saw or heard or tasted. The Ottoman Empire was truly a strange country, full of strange notions, and yet most of the time it intrigued rather than frightened her.

"What irony," she said, garnering a questioning glance from Gemma. "We have traveled thousands of miles," she explained, "and have come to reside amongst a people who grant women few if any liberties, only to finally be given the independence we had so desperately sought at home."

"Sounds a rather deceptively easy accomplishment when you put it that way," Gemma, objected. "Of course you left out the "good gracious, we're in the middle of a bloody big war," part. That makes it all a bit more difficult."

"Are you frightened, Gemma?" she asked over the din of the rain drumming down upon the eaves.

"I was," her friend admitted, "until we toured the wards this morning. Now I'm too angry to be afraid."

"Angry at whom?" Josie pressed.

"I'm not even sure," Gemma confessed. "I'm angry at the Cossacks for shooting our lads, and I'm angry at the British generals who order our soldiers to their deaths. So many are mere boys never destined to be grown men."

"Thank goodness."

Gemma shot her a startled look.

"I mean," she amended, "I worried I was the only one stripped of all emotion other than incredulous outrage. But it's good we're here, Gemma. We can help. We can make a difference."

Gemma reached for Josie's hand. "We can die trying," her friend said, with a cynical little smile.

****

The storm ceased as abruptly as it had begun. The clouds thinned, the sky brightened, and a rooster crowed as if he thought it was the break of day. Across the compound, their group leader signaled that the girls should come inside. Josie gave Gemma a nudge, and together they ducked between the icy drops of water that lingered and plopped down from the overhang. Side by side, they ran to higher ground.

"While you were gone with your supplies," Gemma spoke between breaths, "I heard that the permanent assignments have been posted." Never missing a step, the tiny blonde clasped her hands in a show of reverence and cast her eyes heavenward. "Please, Lord, spare me from the night watch."

"Yes, it would definitely play havoc with your social life," Josie teased.

"Don't be so quick to scold. I know for certain it is not your favorite shift either."

Gemma was right, third watch was an emotional

26

nightmare. Too many people died in the twilight hours. It seemed as if they fought all through the night just to see one more day, but come the first blush of dawn, they relaxed their guard. Then death rode them down swiftly and Josie took the loss of her patients personally. She waged a war in the Crimea too, but it was not a human enemy she sought to quell.

Second watch was her preference. By afternoon the hustle and bustle of the day had usually subsided, and although the Government warned against proselytizing, a nurse could unobtrusively tend to the spiritual needs of her patients as well as the physical. In the evening, there was more time for talk and the nurturing of the soul. And preparing supper and putting the sick to bed for the night was like answering a call as old as motherhood.

Reaching the entry hall, they paused to scan the newly posted roster. The dressers and orderlies were to be burdened with the night duty into the morning. That was a blessing, but all nurses were to work throughout the day and into the early evening. So much for fretting over rotating shifts. At least she and Gemma had been assigned to the Barrack Hospital, the same building where their sleeping quarters were located. The living arrangements were less favorable, but they would be spared the daily half-mile walk to and from the General Hospital.

Hungry to the point of being famished, they maneuvered the narrow flight of stairs that led to their somber little room. More than food awaited them there. During the torrential rainstorm, water had leaked in through window casings and the cracks in the walls. It pooled on the floor and meandered in all directions.

They looked at one another, shook their heads, and managed weak smiles. Nothing would induce them to give up the sanctuary of the tiny room they shared. It was much more acceptable than the space allocated to some of the nurses. The Sellonites had accommodations previously commandeered to contain a captured Russian general. The prisoner had died only two days prior to the arrival of the good Sisters and rumor had it, his ghostly aura still lingered in the room along with a scattering of his white hairs.

So it was without complaint that they labored to push all of their possessions to the dry area in the center of the tiny chamber. Then securing a few loose planks atop the accumulated pile, they christened the heap a table and sat down to share a late frugal lunch of sour bread and tea. The brew had been delivered in a huge copper basin with no milk and only brown sugar to sweeten it, yet after such a morning as this, the Queen's tea served in Minton China could not have tasted more divine.

Following this meager repast, they retraced their steps down to the sitting area which had been appropriated for religious services and lectures. Here Miss Nightingale, again sang their praises and their individual duties were discussed in greater depth. Josie was assigned forty patients, and being as anxious as any young soldier to "rush to battle", she longed to go to them immediately. She was exasperated at being told to wait, and she was abominably tired of helplessly watching her longed for tomorrows turn into unused yesterdays.

"In conclusion," Miss Nightingale added, "I have one final announcement. Mr. Garrick Allen, special correspondent from *The Times*, seeks to interview three members of our group, one from each division. The following people have been selected. Sarah Anne of the Sellonites, Sister Mary Margaret of the Sisters of Charity, and the professional nurses shall be represented by Miss Posey."

Josie sat bolt upright.

"Of all the luck," Gemma squealed as she clutched Josie's arm. "Everyone at home will be reading about you."

That was exactly what troubled Josie. With her family's name plastered across the hallowed pages of the most prestigious newspaper in England, it would intensify the outrage and shame her parents felt regarding her chosen profession. Yet how could she refuse to be interviewed? She couldn't and that meant carefully choosing her words and concentrating on the glorious and patriotic side of the war.

****

Seated before the walk-in closet that now served as Mr. Allen's office, Josie tapped her fingertips upon the arm of the chair and rehearsed what she might say. To her misfortune, she was the last of the three women to be interviewed; which gave her exceedingly too much time to worry over the situation. Loosening her jacket, she took a deep breath to ease her apprehension.

What would Mr. Allen be like? His exposé regarding the French, who employed the best system of caring for the sick and wounded, had prompted the British government to back Miss Nightingale's bid to come to the Crimea. And it was due to the newspaper's outspoken editorials that nearly twenty-nine thousand pounds had been raised to support the effort. But on occasion, Mr. Allen and his associates wrote shocking articles questioning the skill of the commanders here. Some of his dispatches' were disrespectful at best and treasonable at worst.

If only he wouldn't twist her words to fit his causes.

The second interview concluded, Sister Mary Margaret came out of the office and motioned that she should go in. Weighed down by dread, Josie forced herself to her feet and buttoned her jacket and smoothed out her skirt. The beating of her heart quickened as she crossed the short distance to the partially open door.

She peered inside. A tall lanky man sat wedged behind a small desk. He held a pen poised above a watermarked scrap of parchment and with head bent, his posture spoke of serious intent. Her gaze settled upon his hands. They were large and gently tapered like a sculptor's or a painter's, yet they were callused and smudged with ink. Not at all, like the blunt and amazingly clean hands of Mr. Danford Harrison Smythe, T.G.

"I shall be with you momentarily," Mr. Allen muttered. Without glancing up, he set the pen aside and raked his fingers through his hair. The action appeared to be one of habit rather than any serious attempt at curtailing his unruly dark mane.

Wait a moment... That hair looked familiar. Josie's gaze narrowed, and she studied the remainder of the room more closely. A worn fringed jacket hung on a wall peg and a ratty fur cap lay abandoned on a nearby cabinet.

Oh damn. She fought the urge to turn and run. It was *him.*

"Forward, the Light Brigade!"
Was there a man dismayed?
Not though the soldier knew
Someone had blundered:
　　　~Tennyson, *The Charge of the Light Brigade*

Chapter Three

"Please be seated," Garrick directed, not bothering to look up. The words on the paper blurred and swam before his eyes, and he forced himself to focus upon what he had just written. Lord above, he was tired. It must be months now since he'd had a decent night's sleep, and the last thing he wanted was to interview a bunch of righteous nuns and stiff-backed old maids who behaved as if they were all saints in the making.

Unfortunately, Shamus, his editor wanted a story on human interest rather than one on the human condition, so that's what he would get. Besides, it was the publisher, John Delane, who doled out the assignments and even Garrick's esteemed colleague, William Russell, acquiesced to the man who ran *The Times*. Still, this entire scheme sounded crazy and doomed to failure.

What, he wondered, could so few women possibly think to accomplish in the midst of such overwhelming odds? Caring for the sick and wounded at Scutari would be equivalent to sweeping the sand from the seashore. They needed a full battalion of nurses to achieve such an objective, not a small group of women barely large enough to form a proper garden party.

He reached for another sheet of paper. The

rustle of a lady's skirt caught his attention, and from the corner of his eye he saw a slim gray-clad figure settle into the only other chair in the room. He glanced up and bit back a curse. It was her—the dark-eyed girl who had tried to maneuver her way ahead of him in line a few weeks ago. He'd hoped never to see her again and face the necessity of having to apologize for being such a cad. Conversely, he hadn't appreciated playing the straight-man to a pair of flamboyant females. Perhaps she had forgiven the incident.

"So we meet again," he indulged her with one of his rare smiles.

"Not by choice," she clarified.

His gaze swept over her, taking in every detail. She appeared younger and more vulnerable today, and her too-large uniform made her look like a little girl playing dress up. The glare she knifed his way, however, was womanly enough.

She gave a toss of her head and the frilly white cap, meant to contain her hair, slipped to one side. Several chestnut tendrils escaped the lacy confines, softening her image, and the jaunty angle of the bonnet became alluring rather than prudish. Hell, it was downright seductive. She was even more attractive then he remembered.

He met her reproachful stare and held it. This was going to be a fascinating interview. "I'm sorry we started off on the wrong foot the other day. I was mad at the world not you. Don't take it personally."

She arched her brows. "Do you frequently challenge the world?"

"Unfortunately, yes."

"Then I suggest you arm yourself with something more formidable than a pen."

"Don't underestimate the power of the written word," he countered. "Besides, guns leave little room for arbitration." A chill snaked across his shoulders, and a haunting memory rose up from the dark forgotten corner in his mind.

The young woman leaned forward. "You look rather pale. Are you ill?"

Garrick was surprised by the compassion in her voice. "It's nothing serious. I have some medicine on hand that will set me to rights quickly enough." He reached for the bottle of liquor in the top left-hand drawer then checked the impulse and rested his arm back upon the desk. What he really needed was a hot bath, a home-cooked meal, and a decent bed. Then he would be his old self again, able to keep his personal demons dead and buried where they belonged.

He smoothed the wrinkles from the ragged paper and picked up his pen. He might as well get this over with. "May I have your name please?"

"Nurse Posey."

"Your Christian name is Nurse? How intuitive of your parents."

"My Christian name is Josephine," she said crossly.

He sighed in resignation. So much for breaking the ice with a little humor. Obviously, the woman had no appreciation for the absurd.

"And my parents had nothing to do with my being a nurse," she added quietly.

At her tone and wistful expression, the reporter in him smelled a story. Glancing down he studied the name he'd just scrawled on the paper. Josephine Posey, it seemed somehow familiar. Then he clenched his jaw to squelch the laughter that threatened to erupt deep inside of him. Good God. Her name was Josie Posey.

"Where are you from?" he asked, struggling to keep his voice normal.

"It is where I am that is important," she countered, with a defiant tilt of her chin. Her cap slid another half-degree to the side. "Have I said something that amuses you, Mr. Allen?"

"No, of course not, Nurse Posey."

Her name and the precarious angle of her headgear were too much for him. He tried to replace his strangled laugh with a cough but it came out a sputter. There were so few things lately that struck him as humorous. She stared back at him with righteous indignation, apparently unaware of the picture she created. Unexpectedly her expression crumpled and she clasped her hands together tightly in her lap.

He cleared his throat and contrived a more somber demeanor. He hadn't meant to hurt her feelings. "What do you wish to accomplish here?" he asked.

At that question her face brightened. "We are here to aid in the recovery of the wounded, so that they might quickly return to the frontlines and the glory of battle."

He stared at her. Was she jesting? Could she possibly be so naive? The glow of determination in her eyes and the resolute set of her Cupid's-bow mouth assured him that she was not "Who told you there was glory in war?" he asked.

"Why no one had to tell me, it has always been so. Poets write about it, and composers immortalize it in music."

"I'll wager none of those particular artistes' carried a weapon or charged into the thick of it by wading through a sea of dead comrades. Or perhaps those other wars were different. I can assure you there is no glory in the Crimea. Here, there is only needless death and pointless suffering."

She drew back in her chair, as far as possible, as if she feared his shocking ideas might be contagious. "But it is treason against the crown not to support the Queen in her campaign."

"It is treason against God and nature to condone senseless killing." He knew his voice was too loud but he didn't care. Where had Florence Nightingale found this little flag-waver? "Have you heard of the ill-fated battle of Balaclava?" he asked. "No doubt the maimed results await you at the hospital."

A wary expression sharpened her features. "We were told of the brave charge of the Light Brigade if that is to what you refer. With great valor and daring those men rode into battle and fought against all odds."

"Arrogant personalities and gross miscommunication ordered those trusting soldiers to their doom," Garrick countered. "It seems only Lord Tennyson saw through the veil of deception when he captured the true essence of the event in verse. Six hundred and seventy-three men went into that valley and far too many failed to return. That blunder was not only against all odds, it was against all logic."

"Oh, and let us not forget the "glorious victory" they call the battle of Inkerman," he added, the words tumbling from his brain to his mouth without pausing for editing or revision. "Thank heavens we had the Minie and ammunition to spare, for 'twas the stalwart soldiers and the rifles they carried that saved the day in that battle—not the generals."

She opened her mouth to speak then clamped it shut without uttering a word. Apparently she would not be baited into an argument, but neither did she cower beneath his brusque manner. He admired both her good sense and courage.

"Is this part of the interview?" she finally asked.

"No, not really," he exhaled deeply. He was doing it again—trying to change the world one person at a time. Just write the dispatch, he reminded himself. He grazed one hand across his cheek, and the stubble of beard scraped against his palm and fingers. One of these days, he really must remember to shave.

"Your parents are no doubt proud of you," he said, trying to reach her on a more personal level. "What do they think of your dedication to helping the sick and wounded?"

A troubled expression flickered across Nurse Posey's face and she stood so abruptly the chair she vacated nearly toppled to one side. "It is quite late Mr. Allen, and I must be up at dawn on the morrow. Might we conclude our discussion at another time?"

Garrick was taken off guard by her quick show of retreat. He didn't know why, but the idea of her walking out the door gnawed a little hollow place in the pit of his stomach. He found Nurse Josephine Posey intriguing in spite of, or perhaps because of, her naiveté.

Trying to regain control of the situation, he rose and studied her luminous brown eyes. They were pensive and trusting to a fatal degree. Suddenly he wished he knew how to paint. She would be a vision captured on canvas. So soft and innocent. Such a contrast to all the hard mean horror that surrounded him of late. He gave a little shake of his head. *Easy old boy*, he silently cautioned. *You're getting sentimental.*

The girl stepped to the door, wrapped her hand around the knob, then hesitated and turned back toward him. "Perhaps," she suggested, "the rest of your interview with me could be approached from a different perspective. Afford me a week to settle into my routine then accompany me on the ward. You could see firsthand what we nurses are really all about."

Strangely relieved that he was to be given a second opportunity to know her, he nodded. "Why not?" he said, then thinking he was far more eager than he should be to tour the squalor of the wards, he glanced away. "I'm sure I could set aside a few moments to spend with you."

She studied him thoughtfully. "If you accept my offer, you must stay long enough to complete at least one set of patient rounds."

"You drive a hard bargain."

"Did you expect less?"

"Not really," he admitted and stepped closer to her. "I accept your offer. We shall meet again in one week's time." Not wishing her to return to her quarters with her hat out of kilter, he boldly reached up and set it to rights. All these human-interest stories he was forced to write were making him soft.

"Thank you," she tugged the unruly bit of fabric more securely into place. "This cap has a mind of its own."

"Hovering upon your brow," he muttered, "I am somehow not surprised."

"What?"

"Oh nothing. Good evening, Nurse Posey. I look forward to our next engagement."

"Good evening, Mr. Allen."

He watched the girl walk away, and a whisper of her perfume lingered to remind him of a Cotswold garden in spring. Her light step belied any hint of fatigue, and although her ill-fitting uniform confused the issue, he suspected a rather nice figure lurked beneath the yards of wool. Just seeing her would be good medicine for the men in hospital.

As she disappeared around a corner, Garrick closed the door and leaned back against the panel of wood. Nurse Josie Posey. What a myriad of images those words conjured. What was it like to be young and optimistic? He tried to remember but couldn't, and it made him feel older than his thirty-four years.

He crossed the room, slumped down into his chair, and liberated his "medicine" from the desk drawer. Uncorking the bottle with a practiced hand, he downed a throat-burning mouthful of Ankara Gold, then gasped as the Turkish alternative to Scotch whiskey seared a path all the way to his gut.

What in Hades was someone like Nurse Posey doing here? Judging from her speech and manners, she was well educated and if her smooth manicured hands were any indication of her lifestyle, she had never suffered financially. Most professional nurses spouted tales of hard luck or hid sordid pasts. She didn't seem to fit the mold. Exactly what was her story? Newsworthy or not, he decided he would make it his business to find out. He also made a bet with himself as to how long it would take for the surrounding circumstances to wear her down to a disillusioned shell. The war-beast consumed stalwart men on a daily basis, one little girl could hardly expect to conquer the dragon. Still the image of her being defeated wouldn't form in his mind and he was glad. Garrick didn't really want to see her that way, he was just afraid that it was inevitable.

A yawn caught him by surprise and he scrubbed a hand across his face. He should go to bed, then a grossly vivid image of his temporary sleeping quarters came to mind. The room was cold, damp, noisy, and bug ridden—a combination of wretched circumstances that transformed the act of sleeping from a sought after pleasure into a necessary evil. Regardless, he must get some rest. Tomorrow it was back to the frontlines, back to the nebulous edge of sanity. Of course he yearned to be where the action was. What news correspondent worth his salt didn't? At least now he had a picture of Nurse Posey to carry in his mind. It would give him something new upon which to dwell. Something to dull the pain and sorrow that was so uncaringly spawned and nurtured by war.

Braving a second swallow of whiskey, Garrick allowed his thoughts to roam unfettered. They beat a hasty path straight to England and with deep longing, he recalled the calm of the cool countryside and the gay bustle of the bright cities.

How could the people of Great Britain not realize the dark horror they had unleashed in this part of the world? Fathers, husbands, and sons were dying here by the score. An image of Nurse Posey flashed through his mind. *And now they had dared to send their daughters.*

Theirs not to make reply,
Theirs not to reason why,
Theirs but to do or die:
   ~Tennyson, *The Charge of the Light Brigade*

Chapter Four

Her brain still muddled with sleep, Josie traversed the now familiar path between the Barrack kitchen and the north wing of the hospital.

It was cold again this morning, and the frigid air, relentless in nature, wormed its way between the many layers of clothing she wore. Finally, it breached the last cotton barrier, penetrating her skin and seeping into her very bones.

Provoked by the assault of this unseen foe, she tightened her grip on the caldron she toted and quickened her pace. The new cadence disrupted her rhythm, sending the large kettle crashing into her leg with greater regularity. Gritting her teeth, she kept moving. Heavy and cumbersome though the vessel might be, she did not rue the unwieldy burden. It contained beef tea, one of the few comestibles available to help fill the perpetually empty bellies of her patients. And at least the puffs of steam escaping the ill-fitting lid kept one of her bare hands from freezing. During her first week in Turkey, she had given away every pair of gloves in her possession. At the time, it had seemed the compassionate thing to do.

Minding the convoluted path, she hurried on. Was it especially dreary this morning? The land appeared encased in a sad and ghostly pall as if Mother Nature, too, was tired and disillusioned, for 'twas with a weary hand that she painted the dawn.

As the trail leveled off, she hazarded a glance at the road that wound past the hospital. Thin horses with dull shaggy coats coughed and wheezed their way up the hill toward town, and the men who led the beasts appeared equally as drawn and listless. Their once bright uniforms were tattered and dusty, and it was most alarming to realize that such cruel hardship could be wrought in such a short span of time. She recalled the soldiers back home in Benfleet harbor as they prepared to come to the Crimea. Each had appeared fearless and eager to fight for their country's ideals. They were ready to win the honors that foreign duty could afford a man of courage. But the soldiers tramping along the muddy avenue below were mere shadows of those men so far away. No gaily-dressed infantry paraded in proud formation, and no cavalryman on a high stepping-steed sought to capture the attention of a pretty woman's eye.

How long before she looked and felt the same? How long before the human suffering swallowed *her* up?

With a shiver of dread rather than cold, she circumvented an icy puddle and reminded herself that achievement was not measured by a clock or a ruler. She must seize the moment and not worry about the weeks and months and years. If she conquered each day in turn, she could not be defeated. This was her new rule to live by—her mantra. At least it had become so—ever since the ill-fated day she had dared to question the surgeon as to why they had no blankets, nor meat, nor even shirts for the men to wear. What a grand mistake that had been. In no uncertain terms, she had been told not to wonder why but to make do with what was on hand and not complain. That was when she realized that the horrible conditions surrounding her were not temporary, they were routine and enduring. That was when she realized it was every bit as costly in time and energy to worry over the future as it was to worry over the past. It was more logical to concern oneself with simply surviving the day. Yet it wasn't for herself she worried long into the night when she should have been asleep, it was for "her boys".

That is how she had begun to think of her patients... "her boys." The battlefield demanded their unquestioning bravery, it claimed the stamina and courage of men, but on her ward they could be prankish, or homesick, or sorrowful if they chose. They could be the young lads they actually were, and for a brief passage of time, she would fight their battles for them.

Entering the hospital, she schooled her expression into a mask of cheerfulness and negotiating the perpetual clutter of the hallway, she pushed through the double doors that cordoned off the small section of purgatory she guarded so fiercely.

As her gaze swept the room, her steps faltered. Something was terribly wrong. Her breath stalled in her chest, and her smile withered into a desperate frown. Every bed was empty. Had they all perished in the night? Although it seemed highly improbable, the possibility careened through her mind.

She squinted and peered deeper into the dark recesses of the freezing room. As her eyes adjusted to the early morning gloom, the hazy outline of the wounded soldiers began to appear. She gave a sigh of relief. There they were, huddled around the wood stove, holding onto one another as they fought to stave off the deadly cold of December. Two patients lay curled on the floor amongst the cinders and wood chips, and one man, like a tired old plow horse, slept leaning upright against the wall.

Abandoning the beef tea by the entryway, she

hurried forward.

Only the promise of heat radiated from the blackened sides of the pitiful little stove and peeking through the open grate, she saw it held nothing but ash.

Where was the morning allotment of wood? Not even a stick of kindling lay waiting to be burned. Keeping her anger in check she coaxed the soldiers to their cots. They grimaced but not a whimper nor moan did she hear as they assisted one another back to bed. 'Twas a cruel impasse that forced a man to choose between the pain of getting up and seeking heat, or the pain of being frozen stiff if he remained where he was. Her patients drew upon wells of fortitude of which she could not even conceive.

An icy draft poured across her shoulders and turning 'round, she discovered they had lost another pane in the mullioned window. Grabbing up a torn and useless pillowcase, she scrambled onto a chair, knotted the fabric into a ball, and shoved it into the opening. As if angry at her interference, the frigid wind gave one final disgruntled growl before it admitted defeat. She stepped down from the chair and brushed the snow from the beds that lay beneath the casement. Her poor boys. In England, she had seen farm animals treated with more pity.

"Mose," she called and glanced over her shoulder. "Mose, I need help." Where was the lad? Henry Moses Stillwell, nicknamed Mose, was the youngest orderly in the lot. But he was also the most kind and caring. At least he usually was.

Rubbing his eyes and stifling a yawn, the gangly youth stepped from behind a tattered three-wing screen. His hair was a riot of spikes. "Mornin' Nurse Posey," he mumbled.

"Mose," she scolded, "you know you are not to sleep on duty. The fire is out and there is no wood at the ready. You really must be more attentive."

Mose hung his head and distress creased his brow. "I'm sorry," he apologized. "They had me up all day yesterday unloading the supply ship, and I ain't had no sleep since Tuesday....-"

His chin trembled, and Josie knew he was exhausted. "Oh, Mose, I am the one who is sorry. I did not mean to fuss at you. I know you work twice as hard as anyone here." She patted his shoulder, and the lines of worry usually reserved for adults eased from his young features.

"Was any of the Army transport allocated to the hospital?" she dared to ask. As she awaited the boy's response, she curbed the feeling of expectation that sprang to life with her words. In the Crimea, hope was also in limited supply, it didn't do to indulge in the emotion too readily or too frivolously.

"There was one box marked for us, ma'am," Mose claimed, "but instead of medical supplies it was filled with used quill tips and chipped prisms."

"Quill tips and prisms?"

He nodded.

She groaned.

The War Office in England made an abomination of the crucial task of executing purchase orders, and the purveyors over here followed suit by fouling up the distribution of the few shipments that arrived properly filled and intact. It was a hideous situation, and she shuddered to think what the trenches were like. Did they need ammunition as much as they needed everything else?

"Prisms and quill tips," she repeated in wonder. "Perhaps we could write to the Russians and politely ask them to surrender." Her teasing brought a halfhearted smile to Mose's much too somber face.

"When next you see the purveyor," she instructed, "tell him if no one claims the shipment we will accept it. Although it escapes me at the moment, I know we shall think of some purpose for the odd assortment. Perhaps we can use the lot for barter. Now go wash up Mose and then please distribute the beef tea. Remember to place the cups where the patients can reach them."

"Yes, ma'am. And I'm sorry about the wood."

"We shall manage," she reassured, without any idea as to how.

Mose blushed furiously under her scrutiny, then turned to follow her orders. On occasion he seemed so vulnerable and confused as if he were fed up with being a boy, yet mystified at how to proceed with being a man. When he became all tongue-tied and clumsy, like a youth suffering his first crush, it was difficult to know how to approach the lad. Yet she would not trade him for the world.

Many of the nurses endured orderlies and dressers who were rough and untrustworthy, ones who had gained their appointment by default; because they were unfit for any other duty. Mose was different. It was true he had lied his way into the army, but when his correct age of fourteen had come to light he had begged to remain. He seemed to have no family and eventually everyone forgot about sending him home. The Army being full up for drummer boys, Mose had been assigned to the task of tending the wounded. It was a perfect fit. Yes, Mose was here to stay, and Josie was glad to have him.

After making sure the last patient was back in bed, she glanced nervously at the door and quickly organized her equipment tray. Dr. Dennison was due to make his morning rounds, and he harbored a foul enough disposition when the ward was not in turmoil. As if summoned by her concern, the dreaded man rounded the corner issuing orders before she even knew he was upon her.

"Nurse Posey," he thundered, startling one

extremely ill patient to wakefulness.

"Yes, doctor," she said brightly, as the words *"keep your voice down you brutish jackanapes"* battled for freedom in the back of her throat.

"Assist me with this man's leg," he ordered.

The doctor stood beside Old Paul Wiggins' bed. Pauly was barely twenty-four years old, but since he was currently the eldest soldier in her ward the affectionate and honorable term "old" had been bestowed upon him by the other patients.

Josie stepped to the bed and gently removed the outer dressing wrapped around the calf of Pauly's left leg. His lance wound had festered. It was mean looking with a red streak advancing upward toward his thigh. She knew the gash had gone bad, and the poison was spreading through his blood. It would probably cost him his leg if not his life. She also knew what excruciating pain the slightest touch caused him.

"Hurry it up, nurse," the doctor groused. Impatiently he brushed aside her hands and tore at the last layer of dressing.

Old Pauly blanched, and Josie grabbed his hand in an attempt to comfort him. Never had she seen a more callous doctor. She realized the physicians here were overworked and overwhelmed by what they could not cure nor put a stop to, but unlike some of the doctors, this man labored without compassion nor human kindness and heavenly Father 'twas not the fault of her brave stoic boys.

"Where is the probe I ordered?" Dr. Dennison growled.

"You did not sign the requisition, sir." Josie liberated the slip from her pocket and offered up the order form that had been rudely thrown back in her face yesterday by the purchasing department.

"Well why the damn didn't you remind me?" he stormed.

"I was not here when you filled it out. At your direction I was procuring a pot of hot tea for you."

"Making tea is all you women are good for," he muttered.

Josie's cheeks burned with anger and humiliation. As if warning her not to speak Pauly's grip tightened upon her hand. The other patients averted their eyes pretending they could not hear the dressing-down she was receiving.

The doctor properly completed the order slip and shoved it under her nose. "See that it is filled today," he ordered.

"Yes, doctor," she said with all the meekness she could stomach. "Would you sign the diet roll as well, please," she added. In for a penny in for a pound. How much angrier could he get?

"Your patients already receive more food than any other ward. What am I suppose to tell my superiors when they ask why I sanction such foolishness."

"Tell them that decent food is medicine in itself. Tell them that since these men have been receiving more to eat this ward has had the highest recovery rate at the Barrack Hospital.

"Three weeks is hardly duration enough upon which to base a scientific theory," he scoffed. "You'll have to do better than that."

Josie's indignation at groveling for food pushed her beyond good sense. "Then tell them that if they were not such overfed pompous asses they would not have to ask such a question."

The room fell silent, and she felt the pulse jump in her neck. Oh mercy, what had she done? It would do no good to alienate the only man who could help her patients.

"I'm sorry," she apologized, but the apoplexy that mottled Dr. Dennison's cheeks did not fade.

"Perhaps you would like to donate your own

supper," he threatened. "I assure you, it can be arranged."

"She already saves half for us," one patient declared under his breath.

Doctor Dennison spun around to face the men. "Who said that?" he demanded.

"I did," Mose volunteered.

"No, it was, me," a nearby patient insisted.

"No me," another chimed in.

Soon every man in the ward was admitting to having spoken.

"Silence," the doctor shouted over the din of confessions. "Another such outburst and you will all go to half-rations."

Josie's mouth went dry, and her hands began to sweat. She had pushed too hard. She had made things worse rather than better.

"You had best watch your step around here, Nurse Posey. If I were not mustering out at the end of the week, I would follow up on this incident to the hilt. As it is, a report to Miss Nightingale shall be forth coming." The doctor tossed the orders-for-the-day in her general direction and stalked from the ward.

Frustration and regret churned in her stomach as she bent to retrieve the scattered papers from the floor. When would she learn that charging straight ahead was not always the best way to conquer an enemy? Straightening to her full height, she shoved the clutch of written orders into her pocket and silently turned her attention to redressing Pauly's leg.

Murmurs of appreciation for her efforts rippled through the men as they told her not to worry. God bless them, they were suffering untold pain yet they worried over her as much as she worried over them. They had even stood up for her at the risk of making their own condition more miserable. She pressed her lips together to stop their quivering. Her boys were brave in so many different ways. To her, each one was a hero.

"A man dies," Pauly said, without preamble.

"What?"

She glanced at Pauly's face and was relieved to discover that he was not in the throes of delirium, but rather he was telling one of his amusing tales. The soldiers who were able drew closer to hear the story.

"A man dies," Old Pauly repeated, "and he's up in heaven waiting in a very long queue for supper. Now he's right put off about having to wait as he imagined heaven would be much nicer than this.

"Suddenly, an impeccably dressed man with a long white beard pushes his way past everyone else. This fancy gent is wearing spectacles and carrying a small black reticule. Without so much as a by your leave, he shoves his way right up to the head of the line. 'What's all this,' the newly arrived man says to the fellow at his side, 'just who does he think he is?'

'Oh, him?" came the reply, "that's God, but he thinks he's a doctor.'"

Silence floated in the air. Then the hang-time spent, laughter exploded from every corner of the room. Old Pauly's story was just what they needed and for one blessed moment, the dismal high-arched chamber rang with merriment.

Suppressing her laughter and portraying a show of mock sternness, Josie shushed the men and ordered them back to their cots. Then as she finished tying off Pauly's dressing, her indignation and anger cooled and the freezing temperature in the ward again made its presence known. She had forgotten to ask the doctor for a special wood allotment. The next regular delivery would not be until tonight. That would never do.

As she washed and stowed her equipment, she

wracked her brain for a solution to their dilemma and a daring idea darted into her mind. "Watch over the men," she ordered Mose. "You are not to leave them unattended for any reason or anyone. I shall only be gone a short while."

Mose's expression proclaimed his concern, but he held his tongue and simply nodded.

Josie seized an empty laundry bag and bustled from the room. A thrill of anticipation danced down her spine. The Military had their way of doing things and she had hers.

The Army frowned upon those who reasoned or acted independently, especially if they happened to be women, but she hadn't achieved her goals in life by being conventional or by taking the safe route. She was here to tend to her patients' needs and if that meant appropriating wood to keep them from freezing, then so be it.

With forced nonchalance she passed through the adjoining wards, and wishing to avoid any probing questions, she spoke only briefly to the nuns and other nurses. Reaching a deteriorated section of the building where Turkish carpenters and glaziers labored, she paused beside the tool-crib and eyed the hammers. Just as she was about to help herself to one of the implements, the man in charge spotted her and headed in her direction. He was burly, yet tall, and his long-legged strides made short work of the distance that separated them.

"Bono," Josie used the Turkish word to show appreciation or delight. Then recalling Gemma's tactics, she threw in her best *beguiling* smile.

The overseer halted at her side. Apparently the smile worked for he returned it in kind and happily jabbered away while pointing to various pieces of architecture. She did not understand a word he said, but while he was distracted by his own enthusiasm, she slid a wooden mallet from the nearby jumble of tools and concealed it within the folds of the laundry pouch.

"Bono, bono," she repeated and slowly backed away.

He bowed and waved goodheartedly, and she appeased her conscience by silently promising to return the stolen property as soon as possible. Unless of course she was caught, then there would be more to worry about than a simple charge of petty theft. A warning in the back of her mind insisted she was courting disaster, but she forged onward to the most sacred part of the Barrack Hospital, the Doctors' Quarters.

"Nurse Posey?"

She froze in her tracks. The voice that called to her sounded familiar but she could not place it. Turning, she came face to face with Danford Harrison Smythe, T.G. He was impeccably attired in a buff jacket and matching trousers and his shirt was starched and clean. There was not even a spec of dust on his boots.

Hoping she did not look as guilty as she felt, she clutched the concealed mallet closer to her chest as she waited for him to speak.

Danford stared at the canvas pouch, a curious tilt to his head.

She wanted to melt into a puddle and slip through a crack in the floor.

"Do you frequently visit the doctors' inner-sanctum?" Danford asked. His gaze washed over her, and his blue eyes gleamed at what vision she could only hazard a guess.

"Certainly not. I believed it to be a shortcut to the Apothecary." The lie popped out before she could stop it. She could have told him the truth but the idea of confiding in Danford made her nervous. She wished he would go away so she might get on with her wayward mission. "What are you doing here?"

she countered, realizing that he too had little reason to be in this area.

"Why I've come to see how you are faring since your arrival."

"How kind," she said, although it seemed odd that he would search for her in an area where he seemed so surprised to find her.

"I've ordered your equipment," he informed her, taking a step closer. "I expect delivery any week now."

"Thank you. It's very generous of you."

"Nonsense. What good are personal contacts and money if you do not make use of them? I had a few markers I didn't mind calling in."

Danford's words evoked a sour taste in her mouth. She did not cheriesh being obligated to anyone, personally or professionally. "You really should not have gone to so much trouble."

"For you...anything." He reached up and poked a wayward curl back beneath her cap.

Intuitively she drew away from him. Danford's touch was rather too forceful, as if he were more accustomed to taking than sharing, and the flattering words that flowed from his lips with such practiced ease did not seem to come from his heart.

"I really must retrieve the medicine from the pharmacy."

"Yes of course. You'll want to go by way of the west wing I imagine." He stepped aside to let her pass. "'Til we meet again," he added, in a manner that sounded more like a dismissal than polite banter.

She nodded her goodbye.

Run, run, run....the words screamed through her brain, but she forced her pace to a slow steady walk. Finally reaching the connecting annex, she slipped between the oaken doors that led to the west wing and with a sigh of relief, she took refuge behind them. She was not really very good at subterfuge and game playing. Perhaps this was not the brightest of ideas after all.

Easing open one of the doors she peeked through the crack. Smythe was gone. She glanced down the hall in the opposite direction and indecision tore at her. She should abandon this crazy notion and return to her ward. Then her doubts were burned away by the searing memory of her patients shivering around the wood stove. She really had no choice. Re-entering the hallway, she hurried to the grand stairway that led to the second floor Doctors' Quarters.

The architectural display was reminiscent of the sweeping staircase that graced The Hotel Carlyle in London. But it was not the beauty of the wood nor the artistic accomplishment that held her attention. Josie admired the gleaming banister with a newly acquired and unique appreciation. She viewed the entire world with a different slant since coming to Turkey.

Tightly gripping the mallet, she gave one of the spindles a good whack. It broke loose at the top. Unfortunately, the noise created echoed around the deserted landing like a death knell. She cringed and waited. No one stirred. So far so good and time was of the essence. All of her attention focused upon the task at hand, she tapped and loosened and unscrewed every other baluster all the way to the next floor. By the time she reached the top, her hands felt raw, and her back ached from bending over. She flexed and stretched her muscles and wished she could rest for a moment, but fear of being caught took precedent. She backed down the steps and shoved each dismantled wooden dowel, one at a time, into the laundry bag. They were solid oak, they'd burn for hours.

"Need any help?"

With a yelp of surprise, Josie straightened and spun around. Her feet tangled in the frayed carpeting on the bottom step, and her arms flailed as she reached for something to break her fall. The bag of spindles crashed to the floor, and the image of Garrick Allen flashed before her.

A horrified expression contorted his features as he rushed forward to gather her into his arms. Tightening his grip, he cradled her head against his shoulder, and she felt the solid musculature of his back as she instinctively wrapped her arms around him and came to rest against his broad chest.

"Don't be afraid," he said. "I've got you."

She immediately regained her footing and there was no need for him to continue to hold her, but she didn't resist. Instead, she relaxed against him and surrendered to his offer of support. As she savored the strength of his form, an avalanche of loneliness crushed in on her. It had been a long time since a man had held her in a strong embrace or since anyone at all had held her with such concern. She had forgotten how good it felt.

The musky man scent of Garrick filled her nostrils, making her reel, and the fiery need that surged through her midsection brought her to her senses. "You may release me now," she said, the words catching in her throat.

"I could but I don't want to."

"But I insist."

"You do?"

She pushed against Garrick's broad chest, breathless at the resistance she met. "Yes, please," she whispered.

He relaxed his hold, leaned back, and studied her face. As his expression softened, a quirky little smile teased one corner of his mouth. He lowered his arms to his sides, and she clutched at the banister and stared back at him.

He was clean-shaven today and minus the shadowy façade, the bold contours of his face were clearly revealed. Strong angular cheekbones gave him an aura of determination, and rugged but not rough-hewn, Garrick Allen was an unconventionally handsome man. Did he meet adversity head on as he chiseled his way through life? Everything about him appeared to match that concept, everything except his mouth. It was a contradiction even unto itself.

Pleasingly full, his bottom lip promised laughter and sensuous pleasure. But the upper one, thinner and straighter, proclaimed sorrow suffered. The desire to trace the outline of Garrick's tempting mouth tingled on her fingertips. She balled her hands into fists to keep from answering the wicked urge.

His lips parted and her gaze darted upward and tangled with his. From beneath eyebrows that scowled more often than not, his expression seemed to call to her, and his pensive stare made her all shivery inside. Josie couldn't explain why, but Mr. Allen's eyes disturbed the far reaches of her soul.

"It's been three weeks," she said, "I was afraid you had forgotten me, I mean our interview." Suddenly she felt all school-girlish and lightheaded as if she had just tasted her first kiss.

"I told you I'd come back."

"Yes," she admitted, "regardless of your other shortcomings, you did seem the type of man to keep a promise."

He studied her expression. "Thank you, I think. I would have returned in a more timely manner but the Russians had us pinned down at the Redan, north of the Quarries. By the time we were able to push on, the trenches had turned to quagmire, and the going was slow."

"You were at the frontlines?"

"I *was* sent here to cover the war," he pointed

out.

"Yes, of course, but I gathered from your articles and our brief discussion that you do not support the effort."

"My personal feelings are beside the point. It's my duty to seek out the truth. And that elusive quality exists at the vanguard. Only regret exists in the wake of combat."

"Do you pursue all your stories with such heated emotion?"

He glanced away. "Don't mistake thoroughness for enthusiasm. It's just a job."

She didn't believe him for a moment. The furrow of his brow said he worried about the world, and the strong curve of his jaw convinced her that he wanted to solve the problems that hounded him.

Garrick's eyes darkened as his gaze returned to her face. "Why was Smythe sniffing around here?" he asked.

The sudden shift in conversation took Josie by surprise. Had Garrick been watching her? "Doesn't he have a right to be here?" she challenged.

"With enough money, a man can buy the right to just about anything."

She thought of her own inheritance. A large portion of the money left to her by her Aunt had been spent to purchase her career in nursing. In a field of endeavor that was frowned upon by her parents and everyone else in their social circle, she had been forced to use her influence and wealth to transform the unconventional into the acceptable. She had defied many people to buy her dream, but she had done nothing wrong.

"Money can be used for good or ill," she said.

"That kind of a statement usually comes from someone who has plenty of it to spend."

Was he trying to make her feel guilty for being financially solvent? Such tactics wouldn't work with her. She'd fought that battle before too. "And your attitude generally comes from someone who does not."

"Touché," Garrick grinned.

When Mr. Allen smiled, the alteration of his face was remarkable, but the transformation was fleeting. It was as if the man did not smile frequently enough for his features to be comfortable with the metamorphosis. Why did sadness seem so much more at home on his countenance?

The sound of footsteps approaching broke her contemplation. Josie tensed and stared down at the canvas bag of wooden spindles that lay at her feet. If she were caught, she could be harshly punished—perhaps even dismissed and sent home in disgrace.

Near dizzy with panic she turned first one way then the other.

Garrick retrieved the laundry bag and shoved it beneath one arm. "This way," he said as he grasped her wrist, "come with me."

Too frightened to protest, she willingly followed as he dragged her into a small cedar cupboard beneath the staircase. Tossing the bundle onto the floor, Garrick reached behind her and pulled the door shut. They were plunged into total darkness.

Twisting around to find the door, she accidentally backed into Garrick. His breath whispered across the nape of her neck, and the heat from his body wrapped around her like a fevered caress

"Mr. Allen, I must protest," she admonished, as she fumbled for the doorknob.

Garrick gripped her arms from behind. "Keep still," he growled and jerked her back against his chest.

At his commanding tone, she fell silent, afraid to move.

Then she heard the voices.

With blind faith each one fought.
Precious freedom, they sought,
And their courage shall not go unsung.
~Garrick Allen, Special Correspondent,
The Times

Chapter Five

Concealed within the tiny cupboard, Garrick fought to assign faces to the two men he could hear just beyond the door. Then his hips made contact with Nurse Posey's backside and his thoughts veered off in another direction. Veered off...hell, they plummeted over a cliff.

With a silent curse, he released her arms and concentrated harder. One of the men was Danford Smythe—he was sure of that. But the other voice, although definitely British, was unfamiliar to him.

Josie's softness pressed back against him. Garrick clenched his jaw, fighting to ignore her sweet womanly scent and the quick, fearful, panting way she breathed. Then he gave up trying to reason and just listened.

"I'll set up the meeting as soon as possible," Smythe said. "Did you bring the money?"

"Yes," the second man replied, "in rouples and kopecks as you requested."

"Excellent. It's most inconvenient but obvious why our contacts do not wish to be paid in English pounds or French francs."

Garrick heard the rustle of cloth and the jingling of coins.

"I'll inform you when the maps and documents have been delivered," Smythe said.

"Shall we meet here again?"

"No." Danford's reply came sharp and immediate. "There are too many people about lately. I'll get a message to you regarding where and when."

"Very good, old boy. Oh, by the by, General Harker at Headquarters sends his regards. He says in your own way, you're doing as much for the war effort as any soldier."

Danford emitted a snort of what could only pass as sarcastic amusement. "It's nice to know my participation is so construed. Keep watch for my missive. I'll send it by means of the usual courier."

Two sets of footsteps echoed in opposite directions.

As the sounds faded to silence, Garrick relaxed. He regretted not being able to follow Danford. Then Josie twisted around to face him and he decided he didn't really care.

"Was that Mr. Smythe?" she whispered, her cap brushing against his cheek.

"It sounded like him."

"But what was he discussing?"

"I don't know." It was only a partial lie. Garrick knew Smythe was up to something clandestine, but he wasn't exactly sure what it might be.

"I think he's a spy," Josie said.

Nurse Posey was a quick study, but Garrick resented the excitement in her voice. Why did women always seem attracted to bounders and adventurers? "Whatever Mr. Smythe is up to," he warned, "it's probably no good and you would do well to give him a wide berth."

Nurse Posey remained silent, and as much as he was enjoying the company and solitude of the cupboard, Garrick decided he'd best vacate the premises before Josie asked more questions and before he surrendered to his sudden impulse to kiss her.

Bending, he searched for and found the drawstring on the canvas bag. As he straightened, the cord unknotted and slipped through his fingers and the wood crashed to the floor. Josie lurched forward and stepped on his foot. He gasped in pain. She jerked backward at the sound, her raised knee catching him just below the groin. He reached around her to open the door, but his other foot slipped on one of the spindles and arms wide and hands splayed he careened forward and pinned her between his chest and the cedar-scented wall of the tiny cupboard

The air rushed from her lungs in a soft breath that teased his ear and one side of his neck. Made bold by the pitch darkness, he pressed closer and savored the hidden softness that lay beneath the rough wool of her uniform. He lowered his head and instinctively found her lips and an odd feeling of comfort intertwined with the hot craving that raced through his veins.

He shifted his hands to frame her face. She tasted so good. Sweet and delicious and fresh baked. He wanted to nibble at her and consume her essence one little bite at a time. Her struggles ceased and to his surprise and delight, she kissed him back and wrapped her arms around his neck.

She fit so perfectly against him, as if she were made just for his embrace.

Desire flared, fueling need and passion, and the thought of slipping his hand beneath Nurse Posey's uniform tore a ragged groan from him. He slid one hand from her face to follow the impulse, and as he trailed his fingers downward, her shoulder trembled beneath his touch.

"Oh, my," she gasped.

The innocence in her voice somehow slogged its way into his desire soaked brain and it brought him up short. What was he doing? He wrenched away, breathing hard. Damn, she was probably a virgin. He had become too accustomed to the Turkish delights that worked the backstreets of Varna.

"Forgive me," he said, his voice resonating in their dark little haven. "I believe the lack of air in here has affected my reasoning." The quiet roared in his ears, yet he could still hear her rapid needful breaths. Why didn't she say something?

"Nurse Posey? Are you all right?"

"Yes," she whispered.

"Open the door."

As if fleeing for her life, she spun around and kicked a spindle upward into his anklebone thus adding to the bruises she had already inflicted. The woman could defeat the Russians single-handedly if she could but get them one at a time into a cupboard.

The door squeaked open. Light flooded into the chamber. He squinted then glanced at Josie. Her cheeks were flushed and her lips were pouty and bruised.

Eyes wide she stared up at him. He couldn't tell if she was scared, confused, or surprised. He suspected it was a combination of all three. At least she wasn't yelling at him. Anxious to avoid such a fate he nudged her out the door and gathered the wood back into the bag.

As he turned to face her, she opened her mouth as if to speak. Then a more pronounced blush colored her cheeks, and she licked her lips and glanced away.

"We had best make haste," he advised. Handing her the pouch, he ushered her down the hall. "I take it you had some purpose in gathering these."

"I stole them," she openly confessed, head held high.

"I assumed as much," he said, and decided he liked Nurse Posey all the more with the fire of rebellion in her eyes.

"You won't tell will you?" Her step faltered and he tightened his grip on her elbow.

"Are they for a good cause?" he asked and cringed at the bleeding heart sound of his own words.

"We've run out of firewood on the ward," she explained. "I've fought too hard to keep my patients alive to watch them freeze to death."

Guileless courage and naïve wisdom. "Sounds reasonable to me," he agreed.

Her shoulders relaxed, and a tentative smile curved the edges of her lips. It appeared Nurse Posey was tougher than she appeared...and felt...and not above a little pilfering when the need suited her cause. She wasn't bad at kissing either.

As they approached the construction area, she slowed her pace.

"The mallet," she explained, pulling the wooden hammer from the bag. "I must return it."

Great, a thief with a conscience. "You just defaced a hand-carved grand staircase and you're worried about a two drachma hammer?"

"The Turks are not to blame for the fuel shortage."

Again, her logic was a bit off center but he couldn't argue with her principles. "Don't stop," he muttered. He slid the hammer from her hand and tossed it in the general direction of a bucket of nails. "Never return to the scene of the crime," he instructed and hurried her along.

"You sound as if you've had some experience with such dealings."

"And you sound as if you haven't. Keep moving."

As they reached the sick ward, Garrick felt out of place. He hung back, allowing Josie to enter alone. She held up the packet of wood and received a resounding cheer from her patients. For some reason pride kicked at Garrick's stomach. He tried to ignore the feeling, pretending it was merely peptic distress following last evening's night on the town.

"Start a fire quickly," Josie advised, as she entrusted the wood to the orderly, "and keep the rest of the spindles out of sight." The lad grinned, gazed at her with adoring eyes, and carted the oak dowels over to the stove.

Garrick lounged against the doorjamb and considered the cavernous room. So this was where Nurse Posey labored. The cold, drafty, high-ceiling chamber reminded him of a Norman feasting hall. On his right, a series of arched windows ran half the length of the room. On his left, a sparse assortment of ramshackle wardrobes were lined up in accordance to height. The entire area was well organized and neat as a pin, just as he would have expected. The walls appeared recently scrubbed and whitewashed, yet this vast room was somehow serene in its bleakness.

He glanced up over his shoulder. A bundle of dried flowers had been nailed above the door. Actually, it was a composite of prickly weeds that contained only the occasional withered bloom and a few frayed pieces of lavender ribbon. He was sure Josie had crucified the bough into place. Who else would be idealistic enough to expect such a forlorn bouquet to drive away the despair that hid in the shadows and crept along the baseboards?

Stepping further into the ward, he turned around full circle. The four rows of cots and the men who occupied them were dwarfed by the grand cathedral-like room, yet the spirit embodied within those soldiers remained undiminished. He studied their faces. Each maimed and disabled man returned Garrick's perusal with hard-won pride and silent dignity. With such courage they must have fought, giving their all, sacrificing their youth.

was it just for the key
to the church by the sea
that men died so brave and so young?

Retrieving his leather bound journal and a stubby pencil from his coat pocket, Garrick jotted the words down before they could flee his mind. Those were the lines he needed to finish his poem. It was sadly fitting that the missing stanza should be inspired by the expressions on the faces of these heroic men.

"Are you ready?" Josie asked.

"Ready for what?" he countered, as all manner of possibilities teased his imagination.

"You were to follow me on the ward for the article," she prompted.

"Oh, quite right. Lead on," he straightened to his full height. She was tall for a girl; tall and lithe, and she was a glory to watch from behind. Observing Josie in action he was captivated by her skill and stamina. Battle courage glowed in her eyes, and with back straight and shoulders squared, she wielded her bandage scissors and tray of supplies as if they were a sword and buckler.

Efficient, but unhurried, she kept up a lively banter with each of her patients, but she also listened attentively to their questions and concerns. Her hands fluttered over the wounds she tended and the fevered brows she soothed, and her graceful movements elicited a reassuring calmness.

Stepping up to the next patient she pressed her fingers to the man's wrist and studied the rise and fall of his chest. Then her gaze flickered the length of him. She removed the pillow from beneath his bent knees and a more healthy color circulated into his feet as she elevated his lower legs.

"Eating well?" she asked.

He nodded.

"And how many trips to the latrine since

yesterday?"

"Seven or eight...of any importance," he said weakly. "It's beginning to wear on me more then my wounds."

"I understand," she said and patted his hand. "I'll see that you receive an extra glass of negus tonight."

Garrick had been here long enough to know cholera when he saw it. The disease was killing more soldiers than the Russians. "A hot toddy won't cure his ills," he said, out of the corner of his mouth as they moved on.

"I realize that," she replied, in equally hushed tones. "I worked with cholera in the Bowbelles district and in Edinburgh. But such meager palliatives are all I have to offer."

As Josie crossed through a shaft of late afternoon sunlight, the white scarf around her shoulders brightened to an ethereal glow. The image of a female Saint he'd seen in a children's book flittered through his mind and the idea for the theme of his article began to form. Yes, that was it. He would compare the nurses to Joan of Arc. After all, they were women battling against all odds in unrelenting conditions. The story was sure to bring tears to Shamus' eyes. His editor was hardheaded but softhearted.

As Josie progressed from cot to cot, she used her foot to nudge along the bucket used for soiled bandages. The uneven surface of the stone floor transformed moving the bin into an exasperation and the going was awkward at best. In the margin of the paper upon which he made notes, Garrick drew a little picture to remind him later of her dilemma.

Keeping pace at her side, he flexed his shoulders. Before long, his joints felt stiff and his legs ached from standing on the cold damp stone floor. "How many times a day must you do this?" he asked.

"Only two or three," she said with amazing cheerfulness. "Depending on supplies and the doctor's orders of course." As she spoke, she replaced the oilskin strapping that bound the nearly healed stump of the amputated leg she dressed. "Take heart," she added. "We've only one more patient to see. He's newly arrived from the front with a saber wound to the thigh. He was asleep earlier or I would have tended to him straight away."

Garrick followed her to the bedside and grimaced at the sight of the injured man. Layered in dirt from head to foot, the man appeared as dark-skinned as the Turks. His hair was matted and twisted into tufts and now awake he rolled his eyes in pain.

"I'm, Nurse Posey," she said, by way of introduction, as she peeled back the dirty rag-of-a-bandage from the man's leg. A battalion of maggots roamed about on the festering wound.

Garrick choked back an obscenity, but Josie didn't hesitate nor did she wrinkle her nose at the odor that followed upon the heels of the visual horror.

"Such foolishness," she chided, as she bunched up the covers so the man could not see the wound. "They keep these poor boys in the lines until their conditions are too advanced for the field facility, then they ship them to us for a miracle cure." She paused and smiled at the soldier. "Fortunately we've a few miracles left."

The fear eased from the soldier's face, and he relaxed his head and shoulders back against the lumpy mound that passed as a pillow.

A knot formed in Garrick's stomach, and although he pitied the poor patient, it was all he could do not to turn away. How did she survive this day after day?

Using a bit of tow, Josie swatted the majority of mealy worms off of the glistening wound and onto the floor. Then she employed a pitcher of water and rinsed the remainder away neatly catching the runoff in a kidney-shaped basin pressed against the patient's thigh.

"Would you mind?" she nodded at the floor.

"What?"

"Step on them. We've enough mouths to feed."

Garrick stared down at the plump rice-like pellets that wriggled frantically about at his feet. Well he supposed it must be done, but he was not anxious to be the one to do it. He didn't even like putting worms on hooks for fishing.

"Please," she persisted. "I can't stand to kill bugs, even the most disgusting of them. Mose usually does it for me but he's gone to fetch clean water."

Garrick studied her face. How could he refuse? When she gazed up at him with an expression of such need, he felt ready to slay a dragon for her.

Rustling the pages of his journal in an attempt to obliterate any sickening sound, he stepped forward and crushed the disease carrying wretches. He felt them pop and smear beneath the leather sole of his boot.

"Slimy little buggers ain't they mate?" the patient said, as he peered over the side of his cot. "You missed one."

Damn. He dispatched the lone survivor and scraped the bottom of his boot on the ridge of a stone.

"Well done, laddie," the man, said with a shaky smile. "You been at this long?" he added.

"It seems like a lifetime."

"I know what you mean."

"Thank you, Mr. Allen," Josie spoke over her shoulder as she turned to empty the basin.

"Blimey. You're that reporter fella," the patient said, as he looked Garrick up and down.

Garrick reached out and shook the man's hand. "Yes," he admitted, noting that the conversation seemed to take the soldier's mind off his pain.

"I'm Davey Willis, Coldstream Guards. Heard about your piece on Lord Cardigan. He had the ague for days after readin' that one."

"It was all true," Garrick defended.

"That's what usually sticks worst in a man's craw," the old man admitted. "But don't you be printin' nothin' bad about Lord Lucan," the soldier cautioned. "He's one of the good ones. Even eats the same rations as his men."

Yes, Garrick acknowledged with a sigh, if only George Charles Bingham, the 3rd Earl of Lucan, possessed an aptitude for command equal to the strength of his stomach.

Josie returned to scrub and dress Davey's crudely sewn lacerations. Garrick sidestepped out of her way closer to the head of the bed. He scrutinized the man and realized with a bit of a shock that he had yet to ask any of the soldiers what they believed they were fighting for. He had asked the Generals, and the Ministers of Parliament, and by way of his column he had even dared to petition Her Majesty the Queen. But he hadn't actually put the question to the men who risked the most.

He peeked sideways at Josie. There was no time like the present. "Just what is it you're fighting for in the Crimea?" he asked the wounded man.

The soldier screwed up his face in thought. "Why I'm fightin' for the Queen," he answered proudly.

"But isn't that *who* you are fighting for, Davey, not why?"

"Well, sometimes I'm not so sure meself what we're doing here," he admitted in hushed tones. "It gets confusin' to be sure. In the last war, we was allied with the Russians fighting the French. Now we're allied with the French fightin' the Russians. I guess we're tryin' to stop the Muscovites from taking over the world." He shrugged. "Whatever the reason it must be important. If it weren't they wouldn't send so many of us here to die."

Josie tugged on Garrick's sleeve and pulled him aside. "Don't distress my patients with senseless prattle or engage them in treasonous conversation," she warned.

In truth Garrick was surprised she had waited this long before interrupting. "Oh sorry, Nurse Posey, I didn't mean to offer this man anything so damnable as a chance to freely express his own opinion."

She straightened and her eyes narrowed. "Just don't misquote him or get him into trouble with his superiors," she said. "All of my patients are loyal lads. They fight because England has asked them to, but now they're hurt and their minds are tired as well as their bodies. I'll not have them battling wits with you, any more than I would allow them to physically battle on the field." Not waiting for a reply, she stepped back to the man's side.

Garrick couldn't help but smile. Nurse Posey guarded her charges like a tigress with cubs. If only she would direct all that enthusiasm toward stopping the war rather than supporting it. He knew she was bright enough to grasp the concept, but she couldn't quite distinguish the dancer from the dance. She was still captivated by the aria sung so sweetly by the Queen and Parliament. Garrick was afraid it would be a good long while before the finale was conducted and the curtain came down.

Completing the treatment, Josie drew the covers over the man's legs and hips and tucked him in good and proper. "Rest a bit," she said. "Then Mose will help you to wash up."

Nurse Posey's protective outburst had brought a rosy glow to her cheeks and a sparkle to her eyes, and Garrick recalled the hungry kisses they had shared in the dark cupboard. Had her face glowed then with passion of another kind?

Her gaze met his and she took a quick shuddering breath as if she too recalled the encounter. "Perhaps, Mr. Allen, we should conduct the remainder of our interview elsewhere."

Without waiting for his response, she grabbed up her tray and crossed the room to an alcove furnished with a small lopsided table and two mismatched chairs.

Garrick turned, intent on following, but Davey reached out and grabbed his arm.

"Nice meetin' you, Mr. Allen," he said. His voice remained calm with nary a quiver, but loneliness screamed from the soldier's eyes. "Tell the people back home we ain't forgot them."

"I will," Garrick promised. He patted the man's hand and slipped free of his grasp. "And they won't forget you either," he reassured, his gaze sweeping the room, "not a single one of you. I'll see to that." And somehow, he would. Somehow, he'd make known the truth about the conditions here. Conditions no man should be made to suffer.

Deep in thought, he strode the length of the room and settled into the chair across from Josie. The orderly he had seen earlier hurried forward and stationed himself at their side.

"Yes, Mose," Nurse Posey acknowledged, "is there something you needed?"

The lad made no attempt to hide his disapproval as he scowled at Garrick. "No, Ma'am. I don't need nothin'. I just wanted to make sure everything was all right with you."

"All right with me?" Josie glanced up in seeming

confusion then her features relaxed. "Oh, I see. Yes, of course. Everything is fine. But thank you for your concern. I always feel much safer knowing you are here to help me should the need arise."

Mose's expression melted into that of a lovesick pup's and he stared at the floor and shifted his weight from one foot to the other. The young swain was enamored of Nurse Posey, and he apparently fancied himself her protector.

The image of an adolescent boy defending a grown woman was a haunting memory in Garrick's past. It was difficult being young, and harder still to be governed by a world in which you were granted no power or voice.

Nurse Posey rolled another bandage and the simple repetitive motion was near spellbinding to watch. Mesmerized, Garrick twisted a discarded scrap of linen in his hands. Then without meaning to or wanting to, he remembered that night so long ago that had transformed his young life forever. What had prompted this mawkish recollection? Perhaps the earlier vision of Josie on the stairway as she toppled from that bottom step. The sight of her falling, the sight of her desperately reaching out for help. Lost in his recollections, he continued to toy with the soft tails of cloth.

"Mose," Josie said. "Have you no chores to see to?"

At the sound of Nurse Posey's voice, Garrick jerked the strip of fabric into a knot, and his attention snapped back to the present.

"No, ma'am," the boy answered. "Not at this particular time." Like a sentry on duty, he clasped his hands behind his back and stared straight ahead. Garrick couldn't blame the lad for being attracted to Nurse Posey, and he suspected Mose would remain in position ad infinitum unless instructed to do otherwise.

"Well, if you've nothing else to see to, please take the bucket of soiled bandages to the burial detail," Josie requested. Garrick breathed a sigh of relief. "And inform them," she instructed, "that I shall be watching and they are not to dump the lot into the sea to save their shoveling arms. If they have a pyre of suitable proportion, they may burn it. Otherwise they know the orders, far away and deep as possible."

"Yes, ma'am," the boy answered respectfully. "I'll be trimmin' the wicks and lightin' the lamps as soon as I return. Unless you need more light now," he offered, with a sideways glance at Garrick. Mose was wise beyond his years.

"Later will suit, Mose. Thank you. And when you are through you must rest for a bit before night watch. I'll wake you when it's time."

With obvious reluctance the boy ambled off to follow orders, and as Garrick returned his attention to Josie, his gaze settled upon her hands. They were a fascination to him. Whether she smoothed a sheet or cleaned the most gruesome of wounds, her movements embodied a tranquil quality that was almost hypnotic. How ironic that he should find such a sense of peace watching her roll bandages for the victims of war.

Relaxing more fully in his chair, he folded his arms across his chest and stretched out his legs. His left foot brushed against hers, coming to rest nestled beside her instep. She did not glance up nor acknowledge the intimacy; neither did she move her foot away.

As they sat quietly, the early evening shadows slanted across the room and an odd contentment simmered in the back of his mind. He enjoyed the twilight when the universe was drawn in charcoals and dark pastels. No garish bright colors to distract the eye or confound the brain. The world, with all its truth and lies, existed only in black and white and comforting shades of gray.

Josie's hands suddenly stilled. "Why do you not support the war?" she blurted.

Garrick jerked upright and hastily sorted through the heated anti-war rhetoric that sprung to the ready in the back of his mind. "War is the great deceiver," he began tentatively. "It promises glory but yields sorrow. And even when it is over, no one truly wins, for all concerned have fallen victim to the madness that turns man against man."

She stared at him in silence as if she weighed each of his words. "So in your eyes there is never an acceptable reason to fight?"

"There will always be a reason for war as long as it remains more profitable than peace. But the only true good is in its ending, and even then those who survive must find absolution for the killing."

"But what if it is all done in the name of religion?"

"By the Saints, woman," he said with a start. "That is the oldest, and oddly enough the most irreverent, excuse in the book. History has proven that concept frequently enough. Besides, in this instance, free-rein of the Black Sea and the trade route to India is much more important to the French and the British than freedom of religion or Man's salvation."

"But did not Czar Nicholas demand the Turkish Sultan relinquish the keys to the Church of the Nativity. And did not Louis Napoleon demand the same right along with the privilege of the French to place a silver star on Christ's birthplace in Bethlehem? Those sound like religious motives to me."

"Yes," he conceded, "that is factual information as far as it goes. But unwilling or unable to choose between the two sides, the Turkish Porte said yes to everyone involved. Rather than establishing peace, his actions incited circumstances beyond his control. Russia soon sought a warm-water port with access to the Mediterranean and that maneuver challenged Britain's supremacy on the seas. And later, when the Muscovites began occupying Wallachia and Moldavia, we had no choice but to rally around the Turks."

Nurse Posey stared past him, her expression contemplative. He could almost see the wheels turning in her mind as she sorted through the information he had heaped upon her.

"But what interest did the French have in joining the fray?" she asked.

"During all this mayhem," he explained, "the French economy was failing, and the people's disquiet for their leader was rising. So Louis Napoleon devised a plan to politically consolidate his position and increase national pride by declaring a second empire."

"So," she reasoned aloud, "the French pulled themselves up by the bootstraps and shrugging off their shame of losing at Waterloo, they joined forces with us and now they can claim equal footing with Britain."

He nodded and smiled at her. She had a surprisingly keen mind for military strategy.

"But how," she asked, "how did it come to this? Didn't the Turks defeat the Russians at Silistria, and didn't the Russians retreat further into their own territory?"

"Again, yes," he agreed enthusiastically "but now Turkey has become the 'Sick Man of Europe' and both Russia and Great Britain see expansionism as the cure." He was proud of himself for using terms relative to her profession.

"It sounds like a case of the cure being worse than the disease," she replied. "Would it not have been more prudent at this point for Britain to simply return home?"

"Prudent, yes," he admitted, "but honor and glory do strange things to people and neither side had laid claim to or acquired enough of those accolades."

"But why attack the Crimean peninsula located four days away by sea? "

"The Russian stronghold at Sevastopol is symbolic as well as strategic. Whoever commands Fort Nicholas holds sway over the Black Sea, and in effect, control of the Bosporus and the Dardanelles. Besides, once the war began in earnest, it became a military matter rather than a political campaign and there was no turning back."

Sadness troubled her expression. "So we are helping the Turks, a people long persecuted by these Cossacks." She uttered this statement as if still seeking a reason for the unreasonable nature of war.

"On the more noble side that's true," he admitted. "To be honest, it doesn't really matter to me why we're here. But I believe if you make the commitment to go to war, you must do so with a unified front, well developed plans of attack, and soldiers who are well fed and well equipped."

He glanced up. Was she still listening? She didn't appear to have succumbed to the glassy-eyed far away look that most people assumed in the face of his speeches.

"But how does one stop the wheels of war? The soldiers cannot refuse to fight lest they be accused of cowardice or desertion."

"The voice of protest must come from the people," he said, as the familiar fireball of rebellion burned in his stomach hotter than a shot of Ankara Gold. "There must be heard a hue and cry that Parliament, nay the Queen herself, cannot refuse to listen to. A government with no support for its war will soon turn to peace."

Josie chewed pensively on her lower lip and this time her gaze tiptoed around the ward and over the still forms of her sleeping patients. "But the Queen does not heed the call, therefore we must continue to support her, for she loves her people and Britain."

"As do I," he defended. "But sometimes you have to love your country enough to point out its shortcomings. Sometimes you have to want something badly enough to defy logic, good advice, and even the feelings of those around you. Do you understand what I mean?"

She nodded. An expression of anguished crossed her face, and her hands came to rest next to his on the table. He had seen that look before, at their first meeting, when he had mentioned her parents.

Boldly, he reached out and cradled one of Josie's hands and a wanting he had never before experienced sharpened his senses. The room seemed brighter, and he felt like a man awakened from a dream. He squeezed his eyes shut, opened them again, and stared at her face. He was behaving more besotted than Mose. Lips parted and dark eyes searching, Josie returned his gaze.

What was the matter with him? If hard pressed he couldn't even say what it was about this girl that attracted him. He didn't generally favor brunettes and he certainly wasn't here to educate virgins. He liked his women wise to the arts and with no strings attached.

She gently withdrew her hand, leaving his feeling cold and empty. He wasn't looking for any complications in his life and nothing had happened to change that rationale. Nothing, he admitted with sudden annoyance, except his meeting Nurse Josie Posey.

*Change is certain. Peace is followed by
Disturbances; the departure of evil men by their
return.*

~Percy Bysshe Shelley

Chapter Six

Bold as brass, Danford Harrison Smythe stepped across the threshold of Ayah Sophia. He had done the devil's bidding everywhere else, why not on hallowed ground? Besides, this ornate house of worship had been granted no special dispensation. Man's self-wrought destruction and the hellish storms conjured by the Black Sea had been given free reign here. It was Satan, not God, who held this country by the throat.

He glanced around. Winter sunlight, pale and weak, tripped and fell through the missing sections of the arched roof. The meager light held no heat. It could not even melt the snow that drifted in through a hole in the wall. And it reflected dimly off the heaps of party-colored shards now reduced to mere memories of the brilliant stained-glass windows they had once formed.

Ah well, he mused, as long as the majority of prayers were said amongst the smoke and chaos of the battlefields, perhaps the need for churches was moot.

Seeking a more advantageous place of concealment, Danford kicked the rubble from his path, and strode down the center aisle. His footfalls echoed loudly in the oppressive tomb-like silence. He shuddered. The resonance reminded one of exploding mortar shells and the din of cannon fire. What a dreadful recollection. He hadn't stayed long at the front. There was no profit to be had there, and it offered far too many discomforts for a man of his discerning taste.

Ascending the steps to the altar, he wedged his body behind the lattice of the chancel. As he settled in for the wait, the hair on the nape of his neck prickled. Was he being watched? He glanced up over his shoulder. Several figures returned his stare, but they were faces created by the few remaining mosaics that clung with desperation to the cathedral wall at his back. The crucifixion scene was the main event, but the image of Christ was pock-marked by bullet holes, his body scarred many times beyond the seven original wounds. Could the gold leaf employed on some of the tiles be melted down and rendered into a more useful form? How ironic if the mosaic Messiah were to be sacrificed again to save his people.

He shrugged and glanced away. Religion. What folly. Money and power were the gods he worshipped, and he would never have enough of what those icons promised. That was the reason he had come to the Crimea. Why else would he choose to set foot in this disgusting and desolate land? Why else would he seek to mingle with filthy cutthroats as he pursued relationships with rabble not fit to shine his boots? Fortunately, the upheaval of war generated side profits of relatively suitable proportion, and these amusing interludes would keep him occupied until his true mission here could be accomplished.

A scuffling noise sent Danford's thoughts scurrying back to the present. He slid his hand inside his greatcoat and settled his fingers around the reassuring butt of the revolver nestled inside his pocket.

A lone figure stood at the entryway of the

church. The man's face was obscured by a fur hat and the turned up collar of his bear-coat. Slowly, and with caution, the stranger crossed the nave. Then with one foot tentatively place upon the bottom step of the altar, he hesitated.

Come along, just a little closer, Danford silently urged and slipped the pistol free.

As if inspired by the unheard plea, the man resumed his advance. He traversed the sanctum and positioned himself only inches away, his back to the chancel.

Danford shoved the muzzle of his gun through the latticework and pressed the cold steel up against the back of the man's skull. "What are the pass words?" he growled and cocked back the hammer.

"*Sukin sin*," the stranger cursed.

"Not even close," Danford chided. He recognized the man's voice. They had sent Vlad. "I would be well within my rights to shoot you for an imposter."

"Big Ben never sleeps," Vlad sputtered.

"Ghastly choice wasn't it," Danford said cheerily, as he eased the hammer down and returned the Colt revolver to its place of concealment. "It was the best I could do on short notice," he explained, "and our superiors expect such furtive nonsense."

The Cossack exhaled with relief. "You have brought the money?" he questioned over his shoulder.

"Yes."

"In rouples?"

"Of course." Danford stepped from behind the enclosure to face the Russian. "Where are the maps and documents?"

The man groped about in the lining of his coat and liberated a roll of papers crudely bound in soft leather. Danford retrieved a bag of coins from his own pocket. The pouch was lighter now. He always quoted England double the fee requested by his

Russian informers, then he appropriated half as compensation for carrying charges and hazardous duty pay. He held out the amended offering. Vlad followed suit. The pouch of money and bundle of papers exchanged hands at precisely the same moment.

The Russian jerked open the ties and peered inside the bag, and his eyes brightened. It was always refreshing to do business with a man motivated by simple greed.

Not bothering to look at the documents and diagrams, Danford tucked them under his arm. He could care less about the authenticity of the procured merchandise. That was the British Army's problem—not his. This was strictly a business transaction. And tomorrow it would be business again as usual when he met with a different Russian and gave him English goods in exchange for furs and caviar. The British Army hadn't arranged that particular meeting. Should he feel regret? He didn't. They were all great blundering fools. England should make up her mind as to who her allies were to be, and Russia should not be so avaricious and opportunistic.

Vlad secreted away the money. "It may be some time before we contact you again," he cautioned. "With the weather growing worse day by day our generals are content to bide their time by the fire. We Russians have the advantage there. We know the land and we are well entrenched. Why should we hurry in winning the war?"

Danford knew Vlad was bluffing. The Russians were reportedly losing men by the thousands even before they reached the front. Their supply-line crossed from the heartland through over 230 miles of the most treacherous inhospitable land known to man, and it was taking a grave toll on the Cossacks. "Are you so sure you will win?" Danford asked.

"It makes no difference to me who wins," Vlad admitted. "With the money you have given me, I am prepared to follow the victor regardless of who he might be."

"Yes, to the victor go the spoils. But I've no intentions of waiting until the war is over and neither have you."

A sly smile backslid across Vlad's face. "Comrade, I think you lack as many scruples as I."

"Probably more, which you may wish to bear in mind. And I am not your comrade."

The smile withered.

Danford was here to make money not friends. On the other hand, it was a poor business tactic to offend the customer. "Perhaps all this nonsense will soon be over," he soothed. "Then such things will not matter."

Vlad's smile revitalized and he produced a silver flask. "To the upcoming New Year and free enterprise," he downed a shot of liquor. "Svoboda."

Danford accepted Vlad's offer to join him, and overriding the urge to rudely wipe the lip of the flask on the cuff of his shirt, he savored a generous sampling of the expensive vodka. Here was one Russian who knew how to live. "To the imminent New Year," he concurred, "and to high priced trading in the wages of sin." He returned the flask.

Their business concluded, Vlad left by the front door, and a few moments later Danford slipped out the back.

As the gloaming deepened, he was forced to slow his pace. Even in broad daylight the forest trail leading to the wharf was inhospitable, now in the dark it bordered upon the treacherous. Yet he dare not risk being seen on the main road. Stumbling on a patch of uneven ground he cursed Garrick Allen. It was the "Newsboy's" presence that forced Danford to skirt the city like a common thief. On two previous occasions, Danford had spotted the nosy *Times* correspondent frequenting Pasha Johnny's, a notorious drinking establishment in Constantinople. Mr. Allen was a distinct pain in the ass. Why didn't he stay at the front where he belonged?

Finally reaching the docks, Danford gained passage on the next caique bound for Scutari. To his good fortune, the Bosphorus was calm and the crossing was quick and uneventful. The seventeen mile long waterway was less than one thousand yards wide, yet there were occasions when the brackish bit of water was absurdly hazardous and near impossible to navigate.

As they came to port near the Barrack Hospital, an image of Nurse Posey pricked at Danford's mind as well as his manhood. What had she been engaged in the other day while sneaking about the Doctors' Quarters? He could read faces, especially a female's, and she'd been up to something. A woman with a mystery—all the more entertaining. He was drawn to intrigue. Girls who gave in easily could be had for a song, there was no challenge there. It was the prim high-minded ones he enjoyed corrupting. He would dress Nurse Posey in furs and ply her with fine wine and then toy with her at his leisure. He knew how to find a person's weakness and desire, and if he put his mind to it, he'd have his way with her before the year was out.

With that in mind he quickened his step. She certainly was a sweet morsel. Could she be a virgin? That would be an additional benefit. They were so much easier to work with. They had few expectations and if properly schooled even fewer inhibitions.

Ascending the hospital stairs two at a time, he tried to recall Nurse Posey's Christian name but couldn't. Well no matter. First names were for long term relationships. He just wanted to be the first in and the first out. But how was he to capture Nurse Posey's heart and bring her to her knees? She hadn't seemed impressed with his efforts at replacing her silly glass equipment. She was different from most women, and seemed to have a mind of her own. She would be a challenge to be sure.

He paused at the door to her ward and stashed the leather-wrapped bundle. A cursory glance about the dim chamber revealed the usual gloom and suffering. It left him untouched. Life wasn't easy, and it was harder for some than others. With nary a concern for the injured men, he ducked into the shadows to secretly observe Nurse Posey.

She bent over a soldier and spooned gruel into his mouth, and he could barely suppress a groan as she angled her backside in his direction. Soon all that would be his to savor. Just look at her, she was a jewel amongst cobbles. Why did she waste her beauty and youth on the wretched dregs of the world? The old and ugly could serve them as well.

As she straightened, he strode forward and took the empty bowl from her hand. Setting it aside, he grasped her wrist and pulled her into a dim alcove.

"What on earth do you think you are doing?" she sputtered.

He shoved his hands inside his pockets, although what he really wanted was to plant them flat against the wall on either side of her. Resisting the urge to trap her in place by straddling his legs outside of hers, he simply lounged to one side still managing to successfully block her exit.

She pushed at his chest. "Step aside at once, Mr. Smythe" she demanded. "Without doubt, sir, you are the most forward man I have ever encountered."

"Will you promise not to run away this time?"

"I don't know what you mean."

"You seemed rather in a hurry when last we spoke," he said, and studied her mouth. Did her lips tremble? "I hear a bit of mischief was perpetrated near the Doctors' Quarters on the very day I saw you there. Just a coincidence I suppose."

"Of course it was." She glared at him defiantly, her head held high. What a little hellion. She'd be a tiger in bed. Danford watched the rapid rise and fall of her chest, and imagined the young firm body that waited for him beneath that starched linen and rough wool. Filled with a stabbing need, it was all he could do not to give in to the urge to take her right there against the wall.

He leaned forward. Her gaze turned wide-eyed and she pressed back closer to the wall. Don't push too hard he reminded himself. Taking a step back, he changed the subject hoping to catch her off guard.

"I've come to ask you to dinner."

"Dinner?"

"Yes. You remember dinner. The evening meal they make a mockery of around here. I promise you haute cuisine, French wine, charming conversation, and unabashed adoration."

"Absolutely not."

"Why? Have you plans for the opera or a soiree of a more grand nature?"

"No, of course not, but..."

"There you see. You've no proper excuse at all."

"But being proper is the point indeed. I cannot spend the evening with you without a chaperone. Besides we nurses are not allowed out in the evening unless we travel in pairs."

"I'll manage that," he reassured. "And if you were bold enough to leave your home and travel here, I dare say you are woman enough to keep me in line. I promise to live up to my reputation...as a gentleman," he clarified and added his best little-boy smile.

She smiled in return. Good, she was weakening.

"Trust me," he coaxed.

"I shouldn't."

"But surely you deserve one evening of light-hearted diversion. I shall pamper you in every way."

He could feel her on the brink of accepting. She was hooked but not in the net. He must sweeten the offer. "I couldn't help but notice your patients lack many basic necessities." He shook his head sadly and coated his next words with practiced sympathy. "You know I have influence with the purchasing department. If you join me for dinner we could discuss the procurement of more comforts for the lads."

As she glanced around the ward, Danford knew he had discovered her Achilles' heel. She would do anything for her charges, and unless he was mistaken for England. At times patriotism did have its uses.

"Yes, all right," she agreed as she searched his face. "As long as it would be more of a business discussion rather than a dinner engagement."

"We shall call it whatever you wish," he said smugly. "Which evening best accommodates your schedule?"

"Saturday."

"Then Saturday it is. May I call for you at seven?"

"Yes. At the north tower. Martha, our housemother, will fetch me."

Danford captured her hand and kissed the back of it and the desire for much more stirred in his belly. He hadn't had a decent woman in a very long time. Waiting would be agony. But Saturday was only two days away, and when he finally had her, he planned to make up for lost time.

"Good evening then, Nurse Posey. I shall make all the necessary arrangements—including permission with your superiors."

She slid her small hand from his. "Good evening,

Mr. Smythe. Your concern for the sick and wounded is greatly appreciated. God shall reward you for your kind intentions."

Danford didn't give a damn what God had planned, but he did expect a reward. "One does what one can," he said, affecting an expression of humility. It felt downright painful. "I shall be counting the hours."

Retrieving his parcel at the door, he left the ward. Luck was with him tonight. Perhaps he could scare up a game of Monte.

****

Exhausted Josie crawled into bed, but sleep would not come. She tossed and turned, then lay staring up at the ceiling—seeing first one unknown monster and then another in the blurry watermark that leered down from above. She should not have accepted Danford's invitation. Ruing the decision, she punched at her pillow and rooted around trying to find a more comfortable position.

"You'd best tell me what's wrong," Gemma whispered, "or we shall both be up all night."

"Oh dear, I'm sorry I woke you," Josie said. "I cannot sleep."

"I know that you goose. Tell me why."

"I'm not very adept at handling men."

The straw rustled in the mattress beside her as Gemma sat up. "Did you see Mr. Allen again since your interview?" her friend asked, her voice raised an octave with excitement.

"No," Josie admitted and was surprised to find that such a small word could foster such a feeling of emptiness. "'Tis Danford Smythe that concerns me," she added. "He's asked to see me on Saturday for dinner."

"You've two suitors at once?" Gemma bounced up and down. "This is wonderful."

"Control yourself, Gemma, they are hardly my

suitors. They are merely acquaintances of short duration and I know very little regarding either of them."

"Then why do you worry so?"

"Danford is handsome and wealthy, but I'm not attracted to him. I'm only being nice to him for what he promises to provide for my patients."

"I still don't see the problem."

"It's against all my principles. It's underhanded and unkind."

"Contrary to what we've been led to believe, I think it was actually Adam who gave Eve the apple, and men have been leading women astray ever since," Gemma insisted. "So turn-about is fair play. And what makes you so sure he's not using you as well. No doubt he wants something in return for his good deeds, and I'll wager it's more than a smile."

"But he promised our meeting would be platonic and strictly business."

"Funny business most likely."

"If you think that is so, I must cancel the engagement."

"You will not," Gemma protested. "Tomorrow, I shall instruct you on how to spend an evening with a man and while never allowing him to touch you, leave him thinking he has had the most satisfying night of his life. It's simple as child's play."

"Small comfort there, since I was never very good at Red Rover or hoops."

"And who taught you those games?" Gemma reminded.

"No one. I learned them on my own."

"Ah, therein lies your problem. If you want to play like an expert you must learn from an expert."

"Then I shall most certainly be in good hands, Gemma. But you know my past, I can lay claim to only one true romance and that ended in a loss too great to dwell upon. "

"I know." Gemma reached out and touched Josie's shoulder. "You are like a sister to me. I'll not see you hurt. Just follow my advice and all will go well. Now go to sleep," she instructed, and lying back down she snuggled beneath her covers. "A clear head is one of the best weapons against the male species. When it comes to women, men rarely think with their brains and that lends us the advantage."

"Yes, 'tis true," Josie admitted, "a man's intelligence seems to diminish inversely proportionate to the size of a woman's attributes."

"Now you've got it." Gemma chuckled. "Good night, Josie."

"Good night, Gemma."

Burrowing into the lumpy mattress, Josie closed her eyes and sought escape in the calming blackness. Then an image of Garrick Allen abruptly filled the void, driving away her impending serenity. Her cheeks grew hot, as she remembered his kisses and the feel of his body along the length of hers. In the darkness of the little cedar cupboard, she had shamelessly kissed him back and it had been exhilarating.

She skimmed her hand across her breast. Garrick had touched her there. He had wanted to do more. She had felt it in his manner and heard it in his urgent breathing. As the possibility of what he could have done skittered through her mind, a ripple of pleasure erupted in the pit of her stomach and dipped lower. His caresses had excited the womanly needs in her body, and his gallant efforts in helping her to hide had appealed to the little girl in her heart.

What an amazing mixture of qualities he possessed. Opposed to the war, he still readily fought for the needs of the soldiers. And while he obviously loved his country, he boldly questioned the Queen's policies. Without doubt, he was a man of unconventional philosophies. Unfortunately, the latter condition was to be feared as well as admired. Josie knew firsthand that non-conformity was a hard fashion to wear. Unorthodox views could get them both into trouble and in that department, she needed no help by association.

She sighed. Their interview on the ward had not been what she had expected nor dreaded. Garrick had actually seemed interested in her duties, offering no ridicule or condemnation of her chosen profession. And she had enjoyed simply sitting and talking with him. She recalled his sad eyes and sensuous lower lip, and the memory of him left her feeling all weak as if she were made of warm pudding.

Languid with musings of Garrick, she again drifted toward sleep, and this time even the notion of meeting with Danford Harrison Smythe, T.G. did not break the spell. Besides, who was she to deny Danford the opportunity of showing his concern for the soldiers or his support for the war effort? Although bold to a fault, Mr. Smythe seemed a man of reasonable character. He was wealthy and dashing and most probably a spy. Yet, there was no fascination about him. He didn't set her heart to pounding and her knees to quaking the way that Mr. Allen did.

She had behaved most wantonly with Garrick. A delightful twinge of girlish wickedness streaked through her, and she smiled into the darkness.

Stolen kisses—what a lovely secret to keep.

Love looks not with the eyes, but with the mind;
And therefore is winged Cupid painted blind.
  ~Shakespeare, *A Midsummer Night's Dream*

Chapter Seven

"Bloody Hell." Pain shot through Garrick's hand and up his arm, as the hammer he wielded glanced off the targeted nail and struck his thumb. "It's too cold for such nonsense," he groused, his words frozen into puffs of white vapor.

Frustrated, he tossed the mallet aside and shoved his hands inside his jacket. Carpentry was definitely not his forte, but then neither was rummaging through the cast off odds and ends scattered about the abandoned buildings of Scutari. Of course, he'd had little else to do this afternoon so why not freeze his backside off in a rundown deserted barn? Shamus had not telegraphed any new assignments, and the medical review he was scheduled to cover at the General Hospital would not begin until this evening.

With a grimace he studied his thumb. Blood seeped sluggishly beneath the nail, and it throbbed unmercifully. He'd best take a well earned break. Carefully, he fished a crooked and slightly damp cheroot from his pocket and managed to light it with deep draws and only two precious matches. Smoke billowed around his head, and in an attempt to stave off the cold, he ambled about the sagging three-sided enclosure—idly turning over pieces of rubble with the toe of his boot.

A rotted floorboard tumbled sideways. His eyes narrowed as he bent over for a closer look at the object half buried beneath the debris. Bile churned in his stomach and rose to his throat as he reached toward it...as he brushed dirt and twigs away from the small arm and hand...as he wrapped his fingers around the cold and brittle flesh.

Tremors became shudders then he exhaled with relief. Thank the Lord. It was only a doll. A simple child's toy. Sheepishly he clutched it to his chest and leaned against a post.

"Mama."

He jumped at the unexpected sound, and even though it was the product of a mechanism built into the doll, the single word tore at Garrick. The bond between a mother and child was as holy as this war was hellish, and in his mind he could not reconcile the innocence of this toy with the corruption that surrounded it. Birth represented humanity's finest hour, blessed with hope and possibility. Needless death was the darkest hour—ravaged by finality and dreams lost.

He contemplated the sweet face of the porcelain and cloth infant, and a great sadness overwhelmed him. Just in time, he checked the unexpected moisture that threatened to spill from his eyes. Long ago he had schooled himself against sentimentality. It was no longer even a conscious effort, it was instinctive, a matter of survival. And it had always gotten him through the bad times. But today was different. His emotions were too near the surface to be ignored. Like everyone else, he was tired beyond belief, and the weather, so dreary of late, ate away at his defenses more successfully than the Black Sea eroded the rocky shore.

Gaining control of his thoughts, he rubbed a smudge of dirt from the doll's tiny turned-up nose and shook the dried leaves from the matted hair. Did a little girl mourn its loss? Or did the doll mourn the loss of the child?

He set the toy beneath a protected eave and turning away from the life-like eyes, he stared down at the jumble of boards, nails, and mismatched wheels he'd been working on. Then he gave a quick glance over his shoulder. Maybe the child would get a new doll for Christmas.

Christmas, the season of brotherly love. He took a long draw on the cheroot and exhaled slowly. As the holiday season drew near, the war activity lessened. On the day he had left the peninsula, a temporary truce had been called to allow the dead and wounded to be cleared from the battlefield. Shoulder to shoulder, the Russians and British had scoured the hills near Malakoff and the Little Redan, and as they searched for their own they assisted one another with litters and stretchers. They had even jested and traded smokes as if they were compatriots rather than enemies.

Two hours later, the white flag had come down, and the guns at Fort Nicholas had once again belched fire and shot. The thunder of the cannons and the screams of the newly injured mingled to create a familiar sad chorus, the unsettling refrains echoing across the frozen plateaus. Joy to the world.

He lounged against the rail fence and contemplated life through the billowing smoke of his cheroot. He wasn't opposed to a people or a country fighting for what was good and just, yet war confounded Garrick more completely than any other human condition. It killed the young and haunted the old, and like a living creature War thrived on the very doom and destruction that it wrought. And from what he'd experienced, it seemed high ideals and the best of intentions quickly bled to death on the battlefield beside the wounded soldier.

Growing cold with inactivity, he ground the lit end of the cheroot against a board, dropped what remained of the smoke back into his pocket, and resumed pacing. This war was going on much too long, but he didn't know how to stop it, didn't know how to save his sanity and give the world back its own. He was trying his damnedest to show them the truth. Why did they refuse to see?

He patted his side pocket and the reassuring crinkle of paper soothed his unease. It was the first draft of the article he had written about Josie and the other nurses. He had already telegraphed the final version to London, and he intended to present this copy to Josie along with the gift he was building. Would she approve of the story? Her opinion was important to him, although he had never before much cared how others judged his work. He was a good journalist, one of the best, and he didn't need someone else's praise to tell him what he already knew.

Until recently, seeking acceptance had never been his style. For that reason alone, he supposed he should stay away from Josie. But she was like opium, intoxicating and addictive. She was an oasis of calm and beauty in a desert of fury and destruction. And there was another reason he had to see her again, perhaps the most important reason of all. Last evening he'd had a dream about her. That was another first. He never had nice dreams, nor did he have erotic dreams. He shared the darkness with only one repetitive nightmare. A demon recollection that reduced him to raw emotion and basic instincts. A grotesque re-enactment of real life that left him gasping for breath as it catapulted him back to wakefulness.

This new dream, therefore, was a welcome diversion. But it was also disturbing because Josie was responsible. He could not think straight in her presence nor concentrate on his job in her absence and now, even when he slept, she altered the normal pattern of his life. Was it a change for the better? It put him off to think she had such a far reaching influence over him. It was unsettling—yet exciting.

As her image drifted through his mind, he shrugged off his doubt and contemplation, and with renewed enthusiasm, he grabbed up the hammer and nails and resumed the attack on his uncooperative construction project. Two hours later, he smiled down at the lopsided little trolley, proud beyond belief that it rolled easily along the rocky ground without losing a wheel or tipping over.

Grabbing up the asymmetrical apparatus, he tucked it under his arm, bent into the wind, and struck out for the Barrack Hospital. As he ambled along, an odd desire to whistle slid through him. He clenched his jaw and crushed the impulse. He hadn't whistled since he was a wee lad. The habit seemed rather witless and irritating, and he couldn't imagine what prompted him to such foolishness.

"Hey, Allen, wait up."

Garrick stopped short and glanced back to see William Russell hurrying along the path. Thank heaven for Mr. Russell. Here was a man to be admired. As a reporter he was relentless but not ruthless, and as a fellow human being Garrick enjoyed his company immensely. And, he recalled with a grin, when the Army had *lost* the supplies sent over by *The Times,* it was Russell who had taught them all how to concoct ink out of gunpowder.

"The Medical Conference has been pushed up," Russell informed him. "It starts in twenty minutes."

"Twenty minutes. That's a bit of a surprise."

"Isn't it though" Russell agreed. "I think it was done deliberately—the plan being that we reporters would miss the event entirely. Obviously, the articles we've written in the past have not set well with the medical staff. Now they have no choice but to respond to our charges and I think they're running scared. I can barely wait to hear them explain why the jackleg conditions here are killing more British soldiers then the efforts of the Russians. I think they intended to plead their case behind our backs and out of ear shot."

"Less chance of being asked any embarrassing questions that way I would imagine," Garrick said. "How did you hear of the rescheduling?" Russell's ability to ferret out information was uncanny.

The other man smiled. "Robbie Wilson has been chatting up a nurse at the General Hospital. She got wind of the schedule change and passed the information along to him. The boy has a way with the ladies don't you know."

"I heard 'twas the girl having her way with Robbie," Garrick chuckled. "Apparently she's already sweet talked him out of every farthing he can get his hands on."

"You may have a point," Russell conceded, with a rumble of hearty laughter. "This time Wilson may have met his match."

"Perhaps we'd best have a serious talk with the boy," Garrick muttered, as his own infatuation with Josie came to mind.

"Not me," Russell said, holding up his hands in protest. "I'm a big fan of love and romance. Don't know what I'd do without my family, and I thank the powers that be every day for my dear Mary. I love that woman so much sometimes it hurts."

Garrick envied Russell. The big Irish bear of a man did indeed project a contented aura whenever he spoke of his wife and the brood of children they shared.

"Have you seen Fenton?" Russell asked, breaking in on Garrick's musings. "Old Roger won't want to miss this opportunity. A picture is worth a thousand words or so he keeps reminding me."

"Haven't seen him today," Garrick said, trying to remember when and where he'd last seen the field photographer, "but I'll keep an eye out for him."

"Good enough," Russell said. "I'll commandeer a place up front for us. The seating should be plentiful enough as I doubt we'll have any competition from the *Morning Herald* or the *Daily News.*"

"I take it our competitive counterparts are still holed up across the sea," Garrick said.

"Yes, quite. The one reporter is living onboard the *Caradoc*. He only comes ashore now and then, usually long after a battle has been fought. And the other has taken refuge upon another ship and never comes ashore at all. Bad show on their part but to our advantage. See you there," he added over his shoulder and sauntered off.

For a moment Garrick stood immobilized by indecision. He dare not miss this gathering of the Sawbones Bourgeoisie. But that would mean postponing his visit until this evening and tracking Josie down at her dormitory where the nurses were housed.

As the journalist in him regained control, he admitted he should postpone seeing her indefinitely. She was just a nice overly idealistic young woman who should mean nothing to him. He shouldn't get involved. He'd made it a cardinal rule never to become embroiled in the lives of the people upon whom he reported. But in all honesty, it was already too late. Josie had resurrected a part of him that he had forgotten existed. She had reawakened the corner of his heart that nurtured whimsy and advocated true caring. Why these last few weeks, he had almost bordered on being happy. Of course he wasn't a damn bit certain he liked the feeling.

Reaching a decision, he stepped to the remnants of a collapsed stone wall, placed the pull-cart on dry ground behind it, and threw several handfuls of withered grapevine over the top. He shouldn't be gone long and he could easily retrieve his *masterpiece of construction* later.

As he strode down the path Russell had taken, the memory of Josie stealing banister spindles from the doctors' staircase entered his mind and he smiled. She was the most prim and proper bandit he'd ever come across. A devilish rascal with the face of an angel. Then his smile faded as quickly as it had appeared.

Courageous or not, he had a feeling Nurse Posey needed looking after.

****

Josie felt as if she prepared for her execution rather than an evening of gaiety.

True to her word, Gemma had schooled her on the fundamental elements of the feminine mystique, but knowing the theory behind swimming did not ensure ones survival in deep water. As in most things, it was experience that counted, and on that score she was sadly lacking and felt no more confidence tonight than two days ago. If only Gemma hadn't already gone off with the other girls on her own evening of adventure. There might have been time for a last minute review.

Her nerves on edge, she smoothed the skirt of her dark green jersey dress. It was her most daring frock, with a draped neckline and a fitted bodice that hugged her every curve. Perhaps she should wear something less provocative. If it were Garrick with whom she was having dinner, her choice of clothing would not be an issue. He didn't seem the kind of man to require calculated coquettishness and game playing. With him, she could be herself, speak her mind, explore the evening unafraid.

"Nurse Posey."

She jumped as the leaden tones of the housekeeper penetrated the door like iron spikes. "Yes," she called back.

"A gentleman here to see you. He's at the front

97

portal."

"Thank you. I'll be there directly." She checked her pocket watch. It was barely six-thirty. Danford was early. Her hand shook as she clicked the watch cover back into place. Her ordeal was to begin ahead of schedule.

Wrapped in unwavering resolve and her serviceable wool cape, she marched from the room to meet her fate. If she could just get through this evening, she promised God that in the future she would steer clear of Danford Smythe. Still, a wee bit of excitement mingled with her dread. After all, she had never before dined with a spy.

Easing the front door open, she peered out, and the first thing she noticed was a pair of muddy black boots. It couldn't be Danford. Her gaze soared upward on wings of hope, and she immediately recognized the long-legged lean physique before her. It was Garrick. What was he doing here? Suddenly she felt lighthearted and no longer weary.

"May I come in?" he asked. He knocked the dirt from his footwear as if he were quite sure she would say yes, and the Saints preserve her, he was right. "Yes, of course," she breathed, barely above a whisper, then stood aside to accommodate his request.

He stepped forward out of the shadows. The light spilling forth from the foyer illuminated the ragged regimental cap he wore in place of the usual fur covering. The hat was cocked at a most unmilitary-like angle, and it appeared Mr. Allen had torn the insignia from the crown thus proclaiming his independent status. With his dark hair contained beneath the headgear, it lent a youthful vulnerability to his clean-shaven features.

As Garrick ambled past, she noticed a rope led from his hand to an odd little wagon that trailed along behind him. Leaving the door ajar, she stared at the miniature lorry as it teetered along on uneven wheels.

He turned to face her. "It's for you," he explained and handed her the twisted hemp as if it were the leash to a dog.

She stared at it in amusement. "But, what does it do?" she said and glanced up at him.

The sparkle in his eyes dimmed slightly, and he seemed crestfallen at her question.

"It's to hold the bucket you kick around the ward three times a day. The theory being, if it were mobilized you would have an easier go of it. I suppose it was rather a silly idea."

Josie stared down at the contraption and tears blurred the image. *Silly*, no it was wonderful. No one had ever championed her cause. Her profession usually inspired scorn and ridicule, and not even her parents understood what she was trying to accomplish. Yet, this man, a person she hardly knew, had thought to improve her daily struggle to care for the sick. A painful lump rose in her throat as she once more studied the gift. Gripping the lead, she paced back and forth across the foyer. The homely contrivance followed in her wake like a faithful pet. By the look of the thing and Garrick's blackened thumbnail, she gathered he had built it himself.

"You are a genius." She proclaimed and smiled up at him. "And very thoughtful. Thank you."

"You're most welcome." A shy half smile played upon his lips as if he were embarrassed by her gratitude. "Treat it gently," he added. "'Twas beginners luck. I do not think I could build another."

"It shall receive my greatest consideration, and I shall be the envy of all the nurses." She crossed the foyer to the cupboard. "For safekeeping, I'd best stow this treasure until morning. I can hardly wait to put it to use." She secreted the invention away, and as she straightened and turned, she came face to face with Garrick.

Why did he keep staring at her? Nervous under his scrutiny, she cleared her throat and touched her fingertips to her cheek. Had her rouge gone spotty or her kohl smeared?

Daring to meet his gaze, she toyed with the buttons on her cloak. If only he could see past her dowdy wool cape to the forest green gown she wore. The color matched his eyes, and the softness of the fabric caressed her skin with a gentleness that she imagined only his touch could rival.

Garrick drew the cap from his head, and his hair tumbled free to frame his face. "You look lovely tonight," he said.

Their gazes intertwined like summer ivy, and she could almost feel the heat and solid flesh of him. He looked untamed and dangerous. Why didn't he kiss her? He had been bold enough before when they were hidden in the cupboard beneath the stairs. Breathless with anticipation, she willed him to take her into his arms. He leaned closer as if to comply, closer as if to fulfill the wayward desires that might be possessing him as well.

"Good of you to keep the lady entertained until my arrival, Newsboy. You can take your leave now."

Josie jumped and spun around.

Danford stood in the open doorway. He eyed her outer attire and frowned. "Or did you forget our engagement this evening?"

Garrick's shoulders stiffened and his mouth hardened into a flat line. "Maybe she's changed her mind, Smythe. It is a woman's prerogative."

Josie glanced from one man to the other—aching to beg off the prior dinner appointment. She'd much rather stay here with Garrick. But it would only delay the inevitable and she wanted to get her meeting with Danford over and done with tonight.

After all, a promise given was a promise kept.

Ignoring her presence, the men aimed smoldering glares at one another. She felt as if she had turned invisible, and her independent streak surfaced with abandon. This was her decision to make—not theirs. She'd not be treated like general merchandise, and she'd not be swayed nor bullied by any man.

"The business we have to discuss is very important to me, Mr. Smythe," she said. "I see no reason to change our plans."

An expression of sneering triumph transformed Danford's face.

She turned toward Garrick. "Thank you for the gift, Mr. Allen. Your kind consideration is truly appreciated." He didn't smile and the haunted quality she'd seen in his eyes on the first day they met had returned. "Please come by the ward and view it under working conditions," she added. Didn't he realize how desperately she wished to see him again?

"I'll do that," he said evenly. The muscles along his cheek twitched. "You're playing with fire you know."

Before she could respond, Danford took her arm and all but dragged her toward the door. Suppressing an unreasonable urge to reach out to Garrick, she focused her attention on the path ahead.

Without slowing their pace, Danford propelled her down the steps and toward a bright yellow araba that waited in the drive. The odd little carriage was gaudy and plush, the nicest one she had seen since arriving in Turkey. The conveyance even had all of its doors. Danford settled her into the coach and climbed in beside her. "Drive on," he called out and sharply rapped on the side of the coach.

The man up top whipped the team into action.

Josie jerked back against the seat. In a panic, she struggled upright and craned her neck to glance back at the Barrack tower. The golden aura of lamplight that marked the entryway wavered as Garrick stepped to the threshold. His broad-shouldered silhouette filled the framework. Then as the coach sped away into the night, Garrick's image disappeared from view and a cold dread filled her heart. She felt scared and lonely, as if she had just stepped out onto very thin ice. Facing forward, she drew the fur lap robe over her knees and wedged it between herself and Danford.

He inched closer. "Thank you for keeping our engagement."

Her mouth went dry, and she had to swallow before she could speak. "I promised I would," she whispered and silently damned honor for being a coldhearted master.

The araba hit a rut and tossed her sideways against Danford. He slid his arm around her shoulders to steady her, but the heat of his body was smothering rather than a comfort. It was all she could do not to strain back away from him.

What was the matter with her? A two-year-old child could not act more petulant or contrary. Danford had done nothing to incur her disfavor. On the contrary, she was the one using him. Perhaps it was guilt that soured her disposition. With forced determination she relaxed against the seat. Whatever the source of her discontent she had best collect herself. The manner in which she comported herself this evening could mean a great deal to her boys.

The road to the city lay just up ahead, and off to their right, stood the reassuring outline of several large establishments. Like beacons of safety, a soothing glow radiated from the collection of buildings. The bright gaiety of the town would soon renew her frame of mind. Then she would not feel so disheartened.

But the driver did not slow their pace. How could they possibly negotiate the upcoming turn? Confused, she leaned forward and stared out the window. The carriage went all the faster, and the avenue that marked the boundary of the city limits disappeared in a blur as they plunged into the silent isolation of the countryside. Mistakenly she had assumed they were going to an eatery in the city. A noisy well-lit café filled with boisterous locals and British doctors and generals. She had even anticipated crossing paths with Gemma and the other nurses.

Her heart quivered in her chest like a caged bird. "Where are you taking me?" she insisted

"To a private residence," Danford casually informed her.

Stunned by this revelation, she fell silent and an ominous feeling crushed in on her. In a fit of anger and panic she considered leaping from the vehicle. Then she shook her head to dispel the notion. She was not prone to flights of fancy nor hysteria but the wheels kept churning and churning like a unholy litany, a grim warning, a harbinger of doom. And the repetitive sound filled her mind to bursting—leaving no room for logic and reason. *"You're playing with fire you know."* Garrick's words taunted, adding to the jumble of confusion that clouded her thinking.

How many miles had they gone? Time seemed suspended. It was as if they traveled down a murky tunnel that had no end. Just as she prayed they would reach their destination, thus ending the agony of anticipation, the coach skidded to a halt at the front gate of a large villa. Perhaps there was a party in progress and other people waited inside.

Danford stepped down and turned to assist her.

She hesitated. A few moments ago she could not

wait to escape the coach, now she drew back into its shell of protection. What was she to do? As a precaution, she had brought along enough money to pay her way back from town, but it was not enough to cover the cost of rescue from this distant outpost.

"Shall we go inside?" Danford coaxed.

Ignoring his hand, she studied the manor house that loomed up behind him. The stucco walls curved outward in exotic bulbous shapes, and the terra cotta roof wound upward into minarets. The doors and windows were girded by twisted wrought iron bars. Their pointy barbed ends reminded her of the devil's tail. Such black grillwork would be equally useful at keeping someone in as well as out, and the unease that cloaked the structure seemed to come from more than just its foreign design.

A peacock strutted across the walled courtyard. His sudden and mournful cry shattered the quiet and set her in motion. Angry at being given little choice in the matter, she threw back the lap robe and with as much grace as possible, single-handedly alighted from the awkward conveyance.

As if nothing were amiss, Danford escorted her through the outer gate and across the portico. The sound of the araba driving away echoed back from the street, and a new fear gripped her stomach. She had made yet another error by assuming the conveyance was to await their bidding for the return trip.

The palatial home was dimly lit and suspiciously quiet. "Who lives here?" she asked holding her ground.

"These are my weekend quarters," Danford explained, as he unlocked and opened the door. Grasping her elbow he ushered her into the house. "For an outrageous fee the magistrate was more than happy to lease his home to me."

She crossed into the main living area. The room

was an unfettered collection of furniture which reflected a catchall of cultures. A Chinese armoire stood sentinel on her left, while a Dutch china hutch begged for attention on the right. Italian fabric cloaked the windows and mismatched chairs squatted hither and yon upon the thick Persian carpet. The furnishings were plentiful, but no other guests could be seen or heard.

"Won't you sit down?" Danford offered, with a sweep of his arm.

Josie's instincts homed in on the sturdy wingback chair near the fireplace. She took to its sanctuary and studied the room in more detail.

Nearby, a secluded alcove accommodated a small table. Beautifully set for dinner, it spilled over with gleaming china and silver. Light from the candelabrums bathed the nook in an intimate soft glow. It looked perfect, almost too good to be true. Josie retreated further into the refuge of her chair, and despite the roaring fire in the hearth, she snuggled her cloak closer about her body.

As she stared at the flames, anger surfaced to override her concern. This was most improper. How could Danford presume to bring her here? Of course, she had not bothered to ask their destination in advance.

With a dull pop, Danford freed the cork from a bottle of champagne. Filling two crystal goblets, he leaned closer and handed one to her. Did his smile border upon a leer?

"About the supplies for my patients," she began.

"Later," he insisted, as he took a step back and rested one arm upon the mantelpiece. "Let me enjoy your beauty and charm without corrupting the moment with mercenary transactions."

Uncomfortable under his steady gaze, she took one tiny sip of wine. Well, perhaps a second taste would not hurt, or maybe a third sampling.

Suddenly her glass was half empty. The heady drink eluded her empty stomach and went straight to her head. Flushed with the strength of the spirits, she slipped free of her cape.

Danford's eyes widened as her costume was revealed, and the flickering firelight lent an allure to his countenance that was normally absent. He appeared more handsome and less imposing. Could it be she had judged him too harshly? He had acted the gentleman so far and if he truly were a British spy, he risked much to aid his country.

A tentative calm settled over her, but the spell was abruptly shattered as Danford set aside his glass and clapped his hands twice in quick succession. Two young Turkish boys responded to the summons. Each labored under the weight of a silver tray laden with food.

"Shall we dine?" Danford asked.

The aroma of food wafted closer. "I am famished," she admitted and rose to take the chair he held for her at the table.

Steaming dishes of fresh vegetables, homemade bread, and several types of meat occupied every available inch of table space. It was fare fit for royalty. Spies ate well.

She savored a rich juicy bite of roast boar. It had been ever so long since she had consumed a meal that consisted of anything more grand than stringy beef and boiled potatoes. She wanted to taste everything at once and feel the juices run down her chin. She wanted to twist off big chunks of hot bread and drench them in butter. An unreasonable craving for each dish coursed through her body. Mercy, she gasped in a deep breath. The overpowering opulence entranced her as if the devil himself had come to tempt her.

Glancing up she caught Danford staring at her. He sat back leisurely in his chair. A sly gleam in his eyes, his lips stretched into a smile of satisfaction. His plate remained untouched as if eating was the farthest thing from his mind and the oddness of that fact jogged her into thinking more clearly. Recalling the meager rations the soldiers would eat this night, she now found it hard to swallow. The roast lost is appeal, and the profusion of food before her seemed decadent and immoral. Sorrow now spiced every dish, and she pushed back her plate unable to take another bite.

Resting her hands in her lap, she chastised herself for not being farsighted enough to wear a dress with large pockets rather than one with a low neckline. The least she could have done was bring back some of this bounty to the others.

"Is something wrong?" Danford asked.

"No," she said, with a wistful smile. "It's wonderful. I'm just not as hungry as I thought I was."

"I know what's missing." He nodded toward the serving lads. "We must have flowers for the lady."

The two boys grinned and scurried from the room—returning swiftly with arm-loads of roses and lilies. They laid them in her lap and piled them beside her until she was cloaked in their heady fragrance.

"Where did you find the glory of spring in the middle of December?" she asked, overwhelmed by the lavishness of such a gift.

"I have my ways," Danford said. He rose from his chair and dismissed the servants. "You could be surrounded by such luxury every day," he crooned. He retrieved a dark bundle from a nearby divan and circled the table to stand at her back. "All this could be yours and more."

Cool silk slid across Josie's neck and shoulders, followed by the weighty embrace of a fur coat. As she glanced down, her cheek brushed against the soft lapel, and she was captivated by the sensuous touch of the magnificent sable. Cosseted in the cocoon of fur, Josie was momentarily bewitched. She wanted to be cherieshed and spoiled. She longed to feel pretty and desirable. But not with Danford. It was Garrick's image that filled her mind's eye and tempted her heart. He was the one with whom she wished to share such an intimate atmosphere of romance.

Angling forward, she raised her arms and liberated herself from the confines of the coat.

In a cat-quick movement, Danford gripped her shoulders from behind and jerked her back against the chair. Her head slammed against his hard-muscled torso. She struggled in his grasp and kicked her feet out in front of her. "Please stop. You're hurting me."

"Truly, that is the last thing I wish to do," Danford said, as he edged one hand over her collarbone and downward to the curve of her breast. The heat of his hand marked a path through the thin fabric of her dress, and the chair creaked as he pushed against it from behind.

"Stop this at once," she demanded and strained forward. She gasped for a breath but only the fragrance of the flowers filled her lungs, and she choked on the sickeningly sweet smell.

"We could be so good together," he continued—ignoring her plea. "I'll make it well worth your while." Remaining at her back, he leaned down over her and kissed one side of her neck.

She stiffened in disbelief. Had she heard him correctly? Did he think she would give herself to him in exchange for money? "I came here tonight to seek comforts for my patients," she reminded him, "not to indulge in an assignation."

"You shall have what I promised," he said, "if you are willing to make a trade." He straightened to his full height as his hand dropped a few inches lower.

Gemma had been right. Nothing came for free. But Josie wasn't about to barter with her body—not even for the needs of her patients. They had endured much worse for Queen and country, but she was not as brave as they were, and she knew they would never expect or demand such a sacrifice from her.

She wrenched free, scrambled from the chair, and put as much distance between herself and Danford as the alcove would allow. "You care nothing for the soldiers," she accused, as she whirled around to face him. "You would use their suffering to appease your lust. What kind of man are you?"

"The kind who makes his own rules," Danford said calmly as he stepped from behind the chair. "The kind who takes what he wants." He reached out and lifted her chin forcing her to gaze into his eyes. "And I want you."

His expression was filled with cunning. It reminded her of a wolf's and she felt like a lamb chop.

She jerked away from his hand, her anger leaping beyond control. Words tumbled headlong from her lips. "You talk about wanting? Look past the walls of your chateau. Most of us are lucky to get what we need, let alone what we want."

"I'm not concerned with everyone else," Danford waved his hand as if he could dismiss the rest of the world. "Forget that disgusting sham of a hospital and the wretches who grovel there. You're better than they are."

She blinked at his callousness and studied him more closely.

"Stay here with me," he continued. "I'll buy you anything you want. I'll see to your needs and teach you how to properly pleasure a man. I'll be gentle the first time."

She opened her mouth in astonishment, and the heat of her ire rose another degree. The insufferable ass assumed she had never been with a man. "I don't need lessons from you in the art of making love," she spat. "And if you are so anxious to part with your money, spend it on the soldiers."

"I could invest every farthing I have on those misfits and nothing would change," he sneered, "except that I would become as poor and pathetic as they are. With or without my help they'll continue to suffer. The war ensures that."

"If you have so little concern for the men and the Queen's cause why are you a spy?"

Danford's eyes narrowed, and his cheeks grew ruddy. "That's a very dangerous accusation to toss about so lightly."

Josie gasped at her own indiscretion. As if in slow motion she stepped backward around the table and chairs. It seemed a good idea to keep the furniture between herself and Danford. He appeared angry, but he made no move other than to clench and unclench his jaw.

His complexion slowly faded to a more normal hue. "What makes you think I'm a spy?" he countered. His voice now held only the barest trace of interest.

Damn, she hadn't meant to broach the subject but now she had little choice but to back up her statement. Would an altered rendition of the truth seem plausible?

"I accidentally heard you talking to someone about maps and kopeks and Russian contacts."

"How extraordinary. And when was this?"

"The day we met near the Doctors' Quarters. After we parted company, I returned to...ah....look for a purchase order I had dropped. I didn't mean to listen."

"Were you alone?"

She didn't want to keep lying but she dare not implicate Garrick. "No one else saw you," Josie reassured him. It was the truth. Secreted away in the closet neither she nor Garrick had actually seen Danford.

"If I were a spy," he said with a raised brow. "Would you expect me to admit to it?"

"No, I suppose not."

But he was a spy. Of that she had no doubt. Danford's statements were ambiguous enough, but his initial reaction to her blunder had given him away.

"I'll tell you this much," he speared her in place with a steely-eyed stare. "There are spies in every dark corner of Turkey and the Crimea, and little girls like you should be very careful of the company they keep. Even your reporter friend has been accused of aiding the Russians by reporting statistics and other useful information in his news column."

"He wouldn't." Without pause Josie defended Garrick. She hardly knew anything about the man, but her heart told her he was not a turncoat. Beneath Garrick's indifferent exterior he cared deeply. She knew he did, she'd seen it in his eyes. "He wouldn't," she repeated barely above a whisper.

"People are rarely what they seem, Nurse Posey."

"Does that include you, Mr. Smythe?"

"Of course. It even includes you."

"Me. What do you imply?"

"When you dressed tonight, did you take special pains to make yourself desirable? Did you perfume and powder your tender white skin to please yourself or to entice me into giving you what you want?"

The hot flush of embarrassment wound through her as she returned Danford's stare. He was correct. She had expected her appearance would encourage his generosity.

"You are a hypocrite, my dear. You came here because you wanted something and you were willing to use my attraction to you to gain it. Yet, you are incensed by my proposal."

"I expected the price of your assistance to be tempered by your integrity."

"Costs always escalate during wartime." He splayed his hands and shrugged his shoulders as if there were no way around it.

She raised her chin a notch. "I'm afraid your price is too high and we've nothing further to discuss."

"But of course we do," he corrected. "You were about to explain to me why you would rather work yourself to the bone in a disgusting atmosphere of pestilence rather than allowing me to pamper you in lavish luxury."

What a low opinion he must have of her. He imagined her character so shallow she would gratefully jump at his offer. He believed she would disregard all the rules that governed her life just for the material comforts and extravagances he could provide. The man was arrogant to the highest degree, and he had an incredibly grand notion of his powers of persuasion.

"If you do not already understand my position on the matter," she said, "no amount of discussion will help. Please take me back to my quarters."

"The araba won't return until morning. I'm afraid we're stranded here without transportation."

Fear and annoyance licked at the back of her mind, but she'd be damned if she'd give him the satisfaction of seeing her alarm. She stood taller. "Surely you have a mount."

"He went lame yesterday. Take advantage of our situation," Danford urged. "Spend just one night in my arms. By morning I doubt you will wish to return to the hellish nightmare of the hospital."

He certainly was an egotistical blackguard, she'd give him that. "I insist on leaving now, Mr. Smythe, or does T.G. really stand for terrorizing girls?"

He gave a burst of cruel laughter. "You'll have to walk back," he said with a cocky smile. "Alone. It's a very long way and the sky threatened rain earlier this evening."

He was taunting her, trying to frighten her into staying. Surely, he would give in if she called his bluff.

Stalking away from the man she had unwisely trusted, she grabbed up her woolen cloak, jerked it across her shoulders, and yanked up the cowl. Danford remained silent. In a last ditch effort and a final display of bravado, she wrenched open the door and stepped out into the night. Of its own accord, the door to the chateau slowly creaked shut.

She waited in the dark, but no sound issued forth from the house.

****

Making no attempt to follow the girl, Danford stood and stared at the black obelisk. Then with a growl of discontent, he reached down and rearranged the suddenly uncomfortable fit of his trousers.

One had to admit, Nurse Posey had guts. No doubt, the teasing little bitch would return shortly when she realized how dangerous it was to be wandering alone in the night. Perhaps he should have tried harder to keep her here, willing or not. In this desolate area, he could have sequestered her for a week and no one would know. But that would cause too many questions. After all, she wasn't some local whore with no one to worry over her. If she turned up missing, every patient at the Barrack Hospital—plus a brigade of nuns and nurses would be looking for her.

Lost to his reflections, he wandered over to the table and sat down in one of the chairs. It had surprised the hell out of him that she had discovered he was a *spy*. Was she smart enough to keep the revelation to herself? If not, that information could prove very unhealthy for her. Even the remarkable Nurse Posey would not sway him from his true purpose here. No woman on earth was worth the fortune he sought.

He refilled his champagne glass and leisurely lit a cigar as he awaited the girl's return. Then he gave a burst of laconic laughter. The hallow sound arched through the empty room and shattered like fragile glass against the far wall. Nurse Posey was an interesting dilemma. What was he to do with her? He didn't know whether to kiss her or kill her.

She had resembled Little Red Riding Hood as she flounced out the door. She'd best beware of the big bad wolf and the other demons that roamed in the night.

A hero is no braver than an ordinary man,
but he is brave five minutes longer.
~Ralph Waldo Emerson

Chapter Eight

Josie remained unmoving. Not a sound came from the chateau. Danford was actually going to allow her walk away into the night. Had there ever been a man more devoid of human kindness?

Well so be it. It required more than a brisk evening constitutional to intimidate her. At home, while visiting the sick, she had fended for herself on the backstreets of White Chapel. Could this be any worse?

Bolstered by stubborn ire, she abandoned the shelter of the house and stepped out onto the patio. Shoulders back and head high, she marched across the dimly lit courtyard. Then her shoe snagged on the uneven flagstones and bravado turned to indignation as she fought to stay upright. Arms flailing, she recovered her footing if not her pride and as she sought her bearings in the center of the patio, an eerie feeling crept down her spine. She wasn't alone. Someone lurked nearby.

A shadow loomed out of the darkness and careened in her direction. Heart pounding, she fled toward the garden gate. The scraping noise at her back grew louder—closer. Whoever it was, they were gaining ground. Blindly she hurtled through the open portal, her shoulder grazing the rough brick wall. Then she spun around, grabbed the wrought iron gate and slammed it shut.

A frenzy of grand plumage crashed up against

the barrier, and a scaly clawed foot snaked out between the bars slashing at the hem of her gown, neatly shredding the green jersey.

A sob, then a laugh, escaped her. A peacock. Only a silly peacock. "Get away this instant you demented fowl." She stamped her foot, angry at the bird for frightening her and angry at herself for so easily falling prey to a bump in the night.

She must lock the gate. Where was the hasp? There didn't appear to be one, yet, if she were to loosen her grip the gate would swing open and the enraged creature would be on her in seconds. Extending her right foot, she nudged a nearby stone up against the ironwork. There, she smiled in triumph. The feathered fury was neatly trapped.

Through the bars, the peacock jabbed and pecked at the rock. He postured and bristled and challenged the world. Why was the bird in such a tizzy? Stepping back, she glanced around. Nothing unusual caught her eye. Of course a mere few yards from the house it was frightfully dark and intimidating. Anything could be lurking in the shadows.

Thinking to return to the chateau, she edged one step forward. The peacock rose to the defense. Tail splayed in magnificent fury, he scratched at the ground like a bull about to charge. Going back did not appear to be an option. Besides, she would rather take her chances with the unknown than with Danford.

Facing the situation with pragmatism, if not enthusiasm, she set off down the dirt road. It curved to the left and disappeared into the night. The lights of the town—barely visible upon the horizon—twinkled like stars and seemed just as far away. She studied the sky in search of the real constellations, but clouds blotted out all celestial radiance including that of the moon. There would be no offer of comfort from that quarter.

Irritated with herself and her predicament, she snared her cape about her shoulders and trudged on. She certainly had made a muddle of things. What had possibly made her think she could handle a man like Danford Smythe? Gemma gave her far too much credit. She should have heeded Garrick's advice and not gone near Danford.

Garrick, she mused, dear, Garrick. Oh dear Garrick indeed. He was probably no better than any other man, and right now she loathed them all. It was men who started these horrid wars, and men who had to be foolishly brave and fight and die in them. And it was men who thought a woman's place was in the home—preferably in bed.

Men... They were all show and strutting egos like that silly peacock. A little razzle-dazzle display and then they attacked. Danford assumed she would be impressed with a big house, an extravagant fur, and an over abundance of food and flowers. But bigger wasn't always better and more could be too much.

Josie wanted a man she could admire for who he was, not for what he could buy. She was not some dusky jewel to be acquired and admired at the owner's convenience. She had a brain, ideas of her own, and goals she wished to attain. Philip had understood. He had encouraged her to try her wings, then he would stand nearby ready to catch her should she fly too high. Her mother warned she would never again find a man to tolerate such preposterous notions. And perhaps mother had been correct. Perhaps it wasn't possible to find magic twice in one lifetime. Regardless, she was not about to relinquish her dreams nor compromise her integrity for any man—even if it meant spending the rest of her life alone.

Bolstered by her anger, she forged onward and a

fat raindrop hit her square on the nose. Wonderful. Upholding one's principals could be a cold and lonely proposition. Securing her hood she quickened her pace. Lightning knifed across the sky, and sharp pebbles dug into the soft leather of her shoes. She winced. These were her best slippers and to what ends she had chosen to wear them tonight she couldn't remember. They certainly were not suitable for a trek through the countryside.

Wet and tired after only a short distance, she sought a temporary respite beneath a fir tree. The trip hadn't seemed half this far in the araba. She leaned against the rough bark of the trunk and fought to gather her strength, but even the pine soaked fragrance that surrounded her could not revive her energy.

Then the leaves rustled in the dense forest to her right. She stiffened and peered through the darkness. Had that horrid bird gotten loose? In retrospect, she supposed if he'd really wanted to, he could easily have flown up and over the garden wall.

There it was again, the same noise, but now from a different direction.

Josie levered away from the pine tree and forced her body back into motion. The surrounding woods had turned sinister. Trees that had offered kind shelter now seemed to loom down over the road, their bony twisted limbs reaching out for her with ill intent.

Lightning again betrayed the darkness. She glanced about. Several sets of glowing eyes watched back from the underbrush. So that was why the peacock had been so agitated and aggressive. There were wild dogs in the area tonight. These wolf-like Turkish mongrels menaced the countryside and could tear a horse to pieces in a matter of minutes.

The threatening sounds of the dogs grew closer and more distinct. She could hear them snarling and snapping at one another, and the image of slavering jaws and glistening fangs bit into the back of her mind.

What was she to do? Escape by running was out of the question, which left refuge the only course of action. She searched for a sturdy tree with branches low enough to climb, but before she found a likely candidate, the hounds abandoned the cover of the forest. Heads down and hackles raised they slunk closer.

She froze, the taste of terror sharp upon on her tongue. A whimper died in her throat. The lead canine curled back his lips to reveal teeth as slick and white as ivory. He stared at her—his gaze never wavering. Mesmerized by the gleam in his golden eyes, Josie stared back. She was afraid to blink, afraid to swallow, afraid to make any move, no matter how small. Her heart pounded in her chest, yet no blood seemed to be reaching her brain, and she was so light headed she felt faint.

Without warning, the feral hound sprang forward.

She screamed and drew her cloak tightly about her body. Like a shroud, she thought, dear Lord, just like a shroud. One arm raised to protect her face— she blindly kicked out at the mongrel.

The other animals drew closer, and the din of vicious growls roared through her mind. Then all rational thought was obliterated, leaving only the sound of her own screams ringing in her ears. A second dog bumped her from behind. Her knees began to buckle. She was going to die. As her last whisper of hope slipped away, a spine chilling banshee-like yowl overshadowed the hellish clamor made by the hounds.

The dogs fell back in unison.

Josie straightened and glanced from beneath the protective crook of her upraised arm.

A man on horseback galloped toward her, the misty darkness coiling around him. Yelling and cursing he thundered past. With an angry yowl, the pack of dogs scattered.

Reining in hard, the stranger circled his mount for another pass. His face was a dim blur, but to Josie he seemed a glorious knight, his white charger never wavering. This time, as he drew near, he slowed the pace of the animal he rode and reached out for her. Inspired by the one bold hound that rushed forward to nip at her heels, she leaped up into the arms of her unknown champion.

****

Garrick strained sideways and caught Josie around the waist. She was heavier than she looked.

He gritted his teeth and dragged her upward to sit sideways before him. As she collapsed against his chest, he dug his heels into the ribs of the bony white mule. The frightened animal sprinted forward like a thoroughbred. The murderous canines regrouped for another attack.

Garrick glanced at Josie. Why did she feel so limp in his arms? Had he been too late? Was she injured or worse?

"Josie, are you all right?"

"Garrick?" She sniffed and hiccupped like a small child and levered away from him. Her troubled brown eyes turned wide with wonder. "It is you. Oh thank you for saving me from those horrid beasts." She slid her arms around his neck and nuzzled her face against his shoulder and for one crazy moment, he felt like some kind of hero. But the danger was far from over.

He eyed the mongrels vying for position in their wake. The mule, a brave but old mount, was already tiring. Fright would only sustain it for so long.

"We're not out of peril yet," he warned. "Hold on tight." He loosened his grip on Josie and drew his revolver. "Keep your head down and don't be frightened. I'm going to fire my pistol."

He twisted around to take aim. The thought of killing even a feral hound made his stomach churn, but he cocked the hammer back on the gun, gritted his teeth, and squeezed the trigger. One dog yelped and collapsed on the road. Garrick shuddered as he watched the remainder of the snarling horde group around their fallen comrade. Did they seek to console it or consume it?

Holstering the revolver, he faced forward and settled his arm around Josie. The feel of her in his embrace helped to dispel his unease, and as the hue and cry of the wild dogs faded, he slowed the wheezing mule to a walk.

"How did you know where I was?" Josie asked, as she clung to the front of his coat.

"I followed you."

"What?" She stiffened in his arms like wet leather in January.

"When you left the hospital, I rounded up this half-starved mule, and I followed you. But I couldn't keep up. Finally I spotted the araba you'd taken as it returned to the town. I bribed and bullied the driver until he told me where you were."

"Well really," she said, in what sounded like a huff. "You just naturally assumed I couldn't take care of myself."

The mule stumbled over a rock and as she clutched Garrick's thigh, a frown was added to the stubborn purse of her lips. "When first I saw you tonight," she said, "I envisioned you as a gallant knight on a great white charger. I see I severely missed the mark on both accounts."

Garrick roared with laughter. He had just saved her from being eaten alive, and she was peevish and ill tempered because he had dared to follow her. Now there was gratitude for you. "My mount and I may not live up to your medieval expectations," he defended, "but we were good enough to save your prim and proper ass from becoming a late night repast."

Eye's wide Josie appeared shocked by his crudity. Then she sputtered and erupted into a throaty laugh of her own. For a moment he was afraid she might become hysterical. "I'm sorry," she gasped for breath. "You're quite right. I'm still so frightened, I'm not thinking clearly." She reached over to scratch the scrawny neck of the mule. "Your steed is magnificent, and you are more valiant than any warrior from days of yore."

Excitement and fear glowed in Josie's eyes, and with her face framed by the dark cowl, her skin seemed as white as the porcelain doll he had found earlier today. She felt almost as fragile in his arms.

Suddenly furious, Garrick reined in the mule. "Damn it, Josie, how could you be so foolish as to go off alone with Smythe?"

Her expression of adoration crumpled. She began to shake and when she parted her lips as if to speak, no sound came out. He stared at her mouth and recalled the searing kisses they had previously shared. He wanted to know that fire again. With one sure movement, he crushed her to his chest and covered her mouth with his.

He needed to feel her solid and safe in his arms, and he needed to drown himself in the taste and texture of her being. But most of all, he needed something to drive away the vision of her being savaged by wild dogs. She had almost been killed—right before his eyes, and the idea of anything happening to her made him feel out of control in a way he had never experienced before.

With a small whimper, Josie returned his kiss. He traced her inviting lips with his tongue and the taste of her made him hungry for more. She edged closer. Her hip pressed against his straddled thighs, arousing the part of him that drove his need higher and higher.

As the rain pattered down softly, he tightened one arm around her shoulders and shifted his other hand to rest at her waist. The reins slipped through his fingers, and the mule jerked into motion—the slow ambling pace seductive and hedonistic in its see/saw rhythm. With each step the beast took, Josie rocked sideways up against him, driving him wild, driving him to want what he knew he should not even contemplate.

He slid his fingers inside her cape, then upward along her midriff. Her dress glided smoothly beneath his calloused palm, and he marveled at how large his hand felt caressing her delicate form. The firmness of her ribs culminated in the softness of her breasts, and he was captivated by the contrast. She eased back, ending their kiss but in exchange offered him an unimpeded path to what he had been seeking.

Breaching the draped edges of her neckline, he brushed his hand against her skin. She was like warm silk beneath his rain-cooled fingers. The lace of her camisole beckoned him on, and he dipped deeper into the gossamer folds, deeper into the hidden realm she offered. The feel of Josie's body cloaked him with fever.

She lightly skimmed her fingers across the waistband of his trousers, then boldly grazed her hand down the front of his body. He pressed closer, fully aroused and wanting more. As she toyed with a button, he groaned and nearly lost control, and he half expected the cold rain trickling down the inside of his collar to turn to steam as it ran down his neck and across his chest.

As if to match the need that racked his body, the wind grew untamed. He hunched one shoulder against the onslaught to shield Josie, but she didn't seem to notice as she wound the fingers of her other hand in the hair at the nape of his neck and moaned open-mouthed against his cheek.

An unbound wanting for human contact in this most inhumane of times raged in Garrick. Their kisses turned hungry, near desperate, and lost in a cadence of uninhibited need—they reached out to one another. As lightning flashed across the heavens, it felt as if it seared a path straight through his body. His blood was on fire, and now even the freezing rain could not diminish the heat that smoldered in his belly.

Then Josie's murmurs of affection turned to sobs—her emotions obviously out of control.

With a Herculean effort he pulled away from her. A shudder racked his body, and he could barely catch his breath. Her sobs grew farther apart and less violent, and issuing a tremulous sigh she nuzzled closer. With her cheek nestled against his chest, she murmured something unintelligible then collapsed like an exhausted child.

He glanced down at the woman cradled in his arms.

"Josie?" He gave her a little jostle but got no response. Well he'd be damned if she wasn't asleep. It was just as well. He wouldn't have wanted to discuss the jumble of innuendoes that worried his mind and harried his soul. Nor did he wish to admit out loud to the lusty feelings that still gripped his body.

With the tip of his index finger he traced a raindrop from Josie's throat to her cleavage. If just the touch of her lips brought him to such delirium, what would it possibly be like to really make love to her? With an unsteady hand he straightened her dress and wrapped her cloak about her sodden clothes. They'd both be fortunate if they didn't contract pneumonia.

She snuggled closer and Garrick recognized a new loneliness deep inside of himself. He didn't like the feeling, and he knew damn well she had caused it.

What had happened to his self-control? Raw overpowering emotion was creeping into his existence, and he didn't know how or if he wanted to stop it. For a man of the world, he suddenly felt like a neophyte of life. If the situation weren't so serious it would be laughable.

He guided the mule around an abandoned pushcart.

Josie's bold enthusiasm had certainly come as a surprise. For an innocent young woman, she seemed to know her way around a man rather well. Would she regret their fevered interlude? What if she never wanted to see him again? Damn, it wasn't as if he had planned the encounter. Why should he feel guilt or concern? The woman was corrupting him. She caused him to forgo common sense and just about everything else. He was forgetting how to be rude and insensitive. And worse yet, he was beginning to care about things he had no business even thinking about, silly things like love and romance.

He clenched his jaw and stared straight ahead into the darkness—not daring to gaze upon her face.

With a touch as light as a butterfly, Josie Posey was pulling his nice safe universe apart at the seams.

O my Luve's like a red, red rose,
That's newly sprung in June:
O my Luve's like the melodie,
That's sweetly play'd in tune.

~Robert Burns (1794)

Chapter Nine

Josie opened one eye and then the other and the room slid into focus. Confronted with the rare and painful blaze of morning sun, she tried to pull the covers back over her head.

Gemma reached out to still her hands. "'Tis highly improper," the girl chastised, "to leave for an evening of entertainment with one gentleman, only to return in the arms of another. Improper," she added with a squeal of excitement, "but most intriguing."

The memory of her ride home with Garrick seeped blissfully into Josie's consciousness. The last thing she could remember was being held by Garrick as they rambled along on that poor mule. She sat bolt upright and glanced around. "Gemma, how did I get to bed?"

"As luck would have it, I was returning just as Mr. Allen delivered you to the front door. You were in a daze, hardly awake. I guided you to our room."

"Did anyone see me returning so late?"

Gemma leaned forward as if to conspire. "Just an alley cat and a mourning dove. Josie, for heaven's sake what happened?"

"I must have a cup of tea."

"The brazier is lit and the kettle's on," Gemma countered, refusing to be sidetracked. "Start talking."

Josie eased from bed and stepped around her friendly inquisitor. Bold images from the night before rushed at her from all directions. In kaleidoscope fashion, she saw flashes of Danford's ruthless leer, the snapping jaws of wild dogs, and Garrick's sensual mouth.

"Give me a moment to dress," she pleaded and crossed the room to the washstand. Grabbing up the pitcher, she filled the bowl with water. Her hands shook as she remembered being surrounded by the hellish hounds. A terrible destiny had awaited her last night, but Garrick had altered the intentions of fate by literally cheating the jaws of death. She smiled. The recollection of Garrick and what they had shared filled her with a fiery heat. Quickly donning her uniform, she shuffled her chaotic thoughts into a semblance of order. Then she sat down with a cup of much needed tea and briefed Gemma on Danford's dishonorable behavior and Garrick's heroic rescue.

"And," she quietly concluded, "Mr. Allen saved me and you know the rest."

"Do I?" Gemma asked, with a tilt of her head and a wise gleam in her eye. "Just before I led you away to bed, I noticed a most peculiar expression upon Mr. Allen's face. It seemed to alternate between dire concern and outright lustful roguishness. What did the two of you get up to on the way home?"

Josie sputtered and nearly choked on her tea. "Nothing," she croaked.

Gemma raised a brow. "And whales speak French at the bottom of the sea."

"Truly," she hedged, "I've told you everything...worth repeating."

Josie felt awkward divulging what she and Garrick had experienced in one another's arms.

Would Garrick think her a loose woman? She barely knew him, yet she had touched him and allowed him to touch her in a way reserved for lovers. Was he laughing at her right now? The next time they were together, would he expect her to surrender as easily as she had last evening?

She turned away from Gemma and fussed with the cloak that hung by her bed. Still damp, it smelled of last night's rain and reminded her of being cradled against Garrick's chest. She stroked the rough wool then twisted her fingers into the fabric.

"When are you to see him again?" Gemma asked.

Josie started and lowered her arm to her side. "See who?" she asked.

"Mr. Allen, of course. You'd best stay away from Danford."

Josie surmised she'd best stay away from Garrick too. What had come over her last night? Her behavior had been completely wanton. She couldn't blame Garrick for what had transpired. No doubt, her brazen responses had encouraged him to continue.

A flash of desire stormed her body, and Josie's cheeks burned as she recalled the feel of being lost in Garrick's embrace. "I doubt I'll be seeing either of them again," Josie answered. "There is no point to it really. Danford has gone well beyond playing the mountebank, and my heart is too newly wounded from losing Phillip to risk breaking it with Garrick. Face it Gemma, I have no luck with suitors."

"Well, perhaps you'd do well to keep an open mind. If I know anything about men, Mr. Allen will be back. I think he's quite taken with you."

"It doesn't matter, Gemma. I shan't fall in love again. Now we'd best be on our way," she took down her cloak and wrapped it around her shoulders.

"We're running frightfully behind schedule."

****

Josie arrived late at the hospital, but to her good fortune, the physician making rounds this morning was not disagreeable old Dr. Dennison. Their new surgeon, Dr. Cowper, was kindly, wise, and self-sufficient. She left him to his own devises, grabbed up her kit, and sat down to finish sewing the ticking shut on a freshly stuffed mattress-cover.

"Nurse Posey, you be lookin' pale," Mose said, as he sauntered up beside her. "You ain't sick or nothin' are you?" His brow was creased with worry.

"No, Mose," she smiled at his concern, "I'm just tired and I'm sorry to be late."

"Oh don't fret, we'll soon be makin' up for any languor we enjoy this mornin'. Rumor has it more patients are due in this afternoon. I was just about to make up more beds."

"Thank you, Mose. After that you're to catch forty winks. In these trying times even your youthful well of energy could run dry. I'll not have you take sick."

"Yes, ma'am," he said over his shoulder, "you'll get no argument from me. I'm tired down to my toes."

Josie watched Mose walk away. She had become quite fond of the tall gangly lad. For her, growing up at Penmarrow had been a lonely business. She'd had no sister with whom to share secrets and only one younger brother who never grew old enough to tease or protect her. Mose was a soothing balm for those old wounds and was fast becoming a very special person in her life.

With a twinge of sorrow, she wondered how her parents were getting on. They had not answered any of her letters, although she wrote to them every week without fail. She knew Papa did not answer out of stubbornness, and Mamma did not answer out of loyalty to Papa. Still, she'd hoped with Christmas coming their differences could be forgotten or at least put aside.

"A flower for a Posey?"

Josie jumped at the sound of Garrick's voice, then turned in her chair to face him. A tentative smile harassed his mouth, as he held out a dried up withered rose for her perusal.

"These once ruby petals have darkened to a hue more consistent with Turkish wine", he proclaimed. "But the sentiment that accompanies this cherieshed rose is bright and new and filled with wonder."

She gazed at the fragile blossom. It was flat as a Belgian crepe and tattered 'round the edges. A gossamer cobweb dangled from the tip of one perpetually curled leaf. It was a pitiful sight—yet this lonely crumpled rose and Garrick's rather overly poetic words, stirred her heart more effectively than the mountain of fresh flowers that Danford had thrust upon her.

Garrick extended his hand a few inches closer. "Please, take it," he urged.

She slid the lifeless stem from his fingers, and not wishing to meet his gaze, she studied the bloom more closely. It appeared remarkably old, as if it had been dried and safely tucked away in the first book ever printed.

"Thank you. It's...well...it's just lovely." Still she could not meet his gaze.

"Are you sorry about what happened between us last night?" he asked.

Her eyes widened until they ached and her cheeks grew hot. How could he talk about it so casually, so nonchalantly? Would he be like most men and assume that because she was a nurse she was not only loose with her favors but also unabashed when it came to discussing body parts? She remained mute unable to think of any appropriate response.

"It could be just the beginning," he said softly.

Well really. It hadn't taken him long to let her know he expected a repeat performance and more. Indignation overruled her embarrassment and her eyes narrowed as she shifted her gaze to meet his.

"Or it will never happen again," he added in a strained voice. "You must decide."

His display of integrity shoved her off balance. Perhaps she had judged him too harshly or perhaps he was the most cunning rogue of all.

She studied Garrick's face more closely. What did she really know about him? He was opinionated and cynical, and he had the most marvelous pensive green eyes she had ever seen. His usual demeanor was remote, but when he turned his gaze in her direction, she was infused with giddiness uncommon to her nature.

"Are...you...sorry?" He repeated.

She didn't know how to answer. Previously they had only traded a few harmless kisses. But last evening their passion and longing had leaped many steps beyond casual flirting. It had all happened so fast, but it hadn't seemed wrong. Was she sorry? No. She wanted more. Garrick made her feel alive and beautiful and desirable. "I liked it," she whispered.

Her answer seemed to confuse him. His brow furrowed, and he rubbed his right hand along his jaw. Cuts and abrasions marked his knuckles.

"You're hurt." Carefully setting the fragile rose aside, she gained her feet, took his hand in hers, and led him to the medicine cupboard. "What happened?"

"This morning a mutual acquaintance of ours ran into my fist."

No doubt he referred to Danford.

"But you don't even know what happened," she protested.

"It wasn't difficult to imagine," he countered.

"And owing to the fact that Smythe didn't ask why I hit him, I'd say he felt deserving."

Legs braced and shoulders squared, Garrick stood before her seemingly every inch the hero. Without even knowing all of the facts he had rushed in to defend her honor. Without question he had risen up to protect her. A vision of Garrick fighting a duel over her at dawn on the mist driven moors flashed through her mind. Oh heavens, she was beginning to think like Gemma.

She cradled Garrick's hand, cleaned the lacerations, and applied liniment to the bruises. Then as she dressed his knuckles she remembered what enchantment his touch had wrought upon her body and a stirring of pleasure glided through her. Then the pleasure turned to pain as fond memories of Phillip crowded out her dreams for a future with Garrick.

Her heart gave a weary sigh, and her inner smile hesitated and slipped away. Garrick easily fascinated and beguiled her, and like Phillip, he seemed the solitary type with deep emotions that were hard to measure. Yet unlike Phillip, Garrick didn't appear the type to settle down with only one woman.

"May I call upon you tonight, Josie?"

Her hands faltered. Other than Gemma and Nanny Everette, no one called her Josie. It sounded different on a man's lips, soft and pretty and special. Is that how he thought of her? Was she special to him?

She concentrated on tying off his bandage. Nothing would please her more than to spend time with Garrick. But after last night, she dared not trust herself alone with him. "Another steamer from the peninsula arrives today," she said, "and it brings many patients in need of care. I can make no plans for this evening or any other."

"Then you must allow me to bring you your lunch tomorrow."

She hesitated.

"We'll have a picnic," he blurted. Then an odd expression skimmed across Garrick's face as if the suggestion surprised him as much as it did her.

She chuckled at the idea. "But its winter time, we'll freeze."

"It must be temperate somewhere in the world. We shall pretend we're there."

Garrick's offer sounded innocent and playful. It would be broad daylight and there would be other people around. She smiled, and when his expression turned bright and hopeful as a child's, she met her undoing face to face.

"Yes, all right, a picnic would be lovely."

"Then I shall be here on the morrow at one o'clock if that's convenient."

"One o'clock would suit quite nicely."

Josie rested her fingertips on Garrick's forearm, reassuring herself that he was solid and real. Her world was based on logic and routine, it was how she lived her life and how she performed her duties. But Garrick confounded logic and disrupted routine, and it scared her to be plunged into a universe governed by raw passion and unfettered sensation. It was also exhilarating.

Garrick captured her hand in both of his, and his mouth compressed into a grim line. "What," he asked gruffly, "are you doing here, Nurse Posey, amidst all this chaos and insanity?"

Here with a Loaf of Bread beneath the Bough,
A Flask of Wine, a Book of Verse and Thou
Beside me singing in the Wilderness—
And Wilderness is Paradise enow.
                    ~*Rubaiyat* of Omar Khayyam

Chapter Ten

How long, Garrick wondered, before Shamus grew suspicious of dispatches that revolved solely around the hospital in Scutari and the nightlife of Constantinople? He should be back at the front, covering the war from the trenches. But for once he didn't give a damn. Today he was going to see Josie.

He glanced out the dirt-streaked window of his new accommodations. In retrospect he wished he had not suggested a picnic. They'd be lucky if today's temperature rose above freezing, but an outing had been the first thing to pop into his mind as he struggled to tempt Josie into spending part of the day with him.

Why did women love such notions? In truth, he'd rather give up his cheroots for a week than go on a picnic, but the idea had brought a smile to her lips and in the end that was all that truly mattered.

He checked his watch. It was nearly one o'clock. Snapping shut the battered gold case, he tucked the timepiece into the pocket of his wool vest, tugged on the mismatched jacket, and reached for the greatcoat that hung over a nearby chair. It felt odd not wearing his leather coat.

He glanced over at the beat up fringed moose-hide as it lay abandoned on the bed. That garment was a page from his history and it came with fond memories. A remarkable old fellow named Willy Wager had made that coat. They'd met in the Yukon Territory, a wild frontier, where you made good friends or bad enemies and for some reason there seemed nothing in between. Together they had shared many a hardship and several adventures. Then when Garrick had decided to return to London, Wanderin' Willy had bestowed the coat on him as a reminder of their friendship. He'd worn it ever since. It was dependable and comfortable, which was more than he could say about most things in life. With a smile for those days gone by, he shrugged out of his reverie and into today's more suitable attire.

As he crossed the room toward the door, his reflection jumped back at him from the fragment of mirror that still clung to one wall. He had lost weight, but he still cut a fair figure. Or did he? He took a closer look. Maybe the years were beginning to take their toll. They had all been so emotionally empty. How could such nothingness leave a mark of any substance upon a man?

Forcing himself to his full height, he yanked at the coat sleeves. The gentlemanly clothes that he had begged and borrowed were too small for his lanky frame. They restricted his movements reminding him of his childhood and wearing clothes he always outgrew long before new ones could be afforded. He touched the folds of fabric at his throat. At least the black silk cravat was sure to please her.

Turning his back on the image, he grabbed up the basket of food and left the room. Thoughts of Josie trailed along beside him. His world should not revolve around some woman, he silently argued, but heaven help him this wasn't just *some* woman—it was Josie. Recalling his life prior to meeting her, he quickened his pace and entered the hospital ward a bit too fast nearly colliding head on with Mose.

"Sorry, lad," Garrick apologized.

A scowl materialized like a fuming thundercloud and settled over the boy's face. "So you're the reason she wore her hair down today," Mose said. "Where you takin' her?" he demanded with all the concern of an over-protective father.

"If you are referring to Nurse Posey," Garrick said, "we're going on a picnic."

"That's stupid, its winter time."

"As you get older you'll learn that women sometimes like stupid stuff. And it's lucky for us men that they do, as stupidity seems to be our strong suit on far too many occasions."

Mose perused Garrick with a suspicious eye. Not an inkling of a smile ruined the perfection of his glowering expression. "For some reason seein' you brings a happiness to her eyes," he admitted.

Garrick felt pleased with this revelation, as well as sympathy for the boy. "Youth is your enemy, Mose, not me. You did realize she was bound to find someone her own age with whom to be friends?"

"I suppose," Mose said, resignation tempering his expression. "But you better not hurt her or you'll have me to answer to."

Garrick suppressed a smile. "Warning acknowledged," he said.

"I'm guessin' she's better off with you than that Danford Smythe fellow," Mose added darkly. "There's something ugly and hard about that man."

Garrick stiffened. "Has Smythe been around bothering Nurse Posey?"

"Not lately. But I seen him yesterday over to the Purveyor's office."

"Was he alone?"

"No. He was acting chums with a bloke what has a reputation for courtin' evil."

"Did you overhear anything?"

"A little, but nothing that made any sense. When I walked up they was talkin' about somebody's hands, no it was eyes, eyes that were idle. Then they seen me and got real quiet, and I didn't hear nothin' more."

"Hmm," Garrick mused. "More of the usual shady business dealings I suppose. You're smart in not trusting Mr. Smythe, Mose. Would you let me know if you see him again?"

"Sure Mr. Allen. I guess I could do that."

"Thank you. I would appreciate it. Now, if you would please, inform Nurse Posey I'm here."

Mose hesitated. "She's gonna love the cravat," he said. Then without another word, he ambled off to do Garrick's bidding.

As he waited, Garrick fiddled with the large vegetable basket that he had converted into a picnic hamper. It contained cheese, salami, black bread, a good bottle of wine, and his misplaced romantic notions. It was not haute cuisine but rather straightforward food, just as he was a straightforward man. If Josie expected extravagant fare on either count, she would be mistaken. There were no caramel sauces to sweeten the true nature of the food or the cut of his personality. Hopefully, she wouldn't be disappointed with either.

He plucked a piece of lint from the front of his coat and smoothed his lapel into place. He felt as nervous as a man about to propose marriage. Or so he imagined. Fortunately, he had never breached the walls of that institution.

At the sound of footsteps, he quickly ran his fingers through his wind tossed hair and lightly touched the place on his cheek where he had nicked himself shaving. Good, it had not gone to bleeding again. His hand hovered in mid air as he watched Josie cross the room. At that instant, she was the only part of the world that existed for him—at least the only part that mattered.

Her eyes were bright, and a hint of a blush

kissed her cheeks. She paused and stared up at him. Standing so close beside her, he noticed once again how tall she was, and he had to wonder what it would feel like to be tangled up in those lovely long arms and legs.

Josie reminded him of a young willow, tall and supple, but also tender and fragile. So far she had managed to bend before the storm of war, but she could easily succumb to the other deadly blows that life could wield. He felt a need to protect her. Perhaps even from himself.

"I've been looking forward to our picnic, Garrick," she confided.

His heart soared. She had used his Christian name, and the smile that wrapped around her words and showed in her eyes assured him she was sincere about wanting to share this time with him. He took a deep breath and tried to find his tongue. He should say something special or at least appropriate. He was so good at putting pen to paper, why was he now at a loss for words? Thankfully, he remembered the costuming he'd procured for her.

"But you are not properly dressed for a day in the broiling sun," he said. Setting the basket upon a chair, he rummaged inside and presented her with a bedraggled straw sunbonnet with a mouse hole chewed in the brim.

Josie removed her nurse's cap and carefully set it aside.

"Allow me," he offered, carefully placing the hat upon her head. The back of his hand grazed the soft skin of her cheek, and each breath she took teased across his wrist. Attempting to tie the blue ribbon into place, he turned all thumbs, and as her lips parted in a girlish giggle, his efforts became totally ineffectual.

Gently she brushed his hands aside and jauntily secured the bow off to one side of her chin. He found her all the more fetching with her face framed in shades of teal satin.

As he offered her a small battered white parasol, her pink lips puckered into a perfect little circle of surprise, and he wished he had a trunk full of clothes and paraphernalia to bestow upon her. What a delight to stand here all day just handing her unexpected items and watching her reaction.

She eased the parasol open and rested the short handle upon one shoulder. The torn material drooped down from the bent framework, partially obscuring the atrocious hat. "Where exactly are we going?" she asked, as she peeked up at him from beneath the tattered froth of white lace.

"It's a surprise," he declared, as he buttoned his coat, "and you shall need your cloak en route."

Josie closed the umbrella, handed him her cape, and turned around. He slipped the garment about her shoulders, and a hint of her perfume tantalized his senses. She smelled sweet as violets on a cool spring morn, and her hair, as it brushed across the back of his hand, felt as soft as faerie fern growing deep in the woods.

Lingering with his fingertips upon her shoulder, he smoothed away a nonexistent wrinkle from the fabric. At his touch, she inhaled softly as if with expectation, and he fought the urge to wrap his arms around her and nestle her back against his chest. He wanted to lose himself in the loops of her hair. Instead, he clenched his hand into a fist and took a step backward. He still was not ready to fall prey to his own emotions. He'd worked too hard to free himself from those irons, and he'd be damned if he'd be shackled by them again so easily.

Grabbing up the basket, he cupped Josie's elbow in his other hand and ushered her outside. The cold weather heightened the color in her cheeks, and with each step she took, he caught a glimpse of shapely ankle peeking out from beneath the raised hem of her uniform. They grappled their way across the frozen tundra, and with nary a complaint nor a misstep, she charged straight ahead over the broken boards and rotting vegetation. He could barely keep up with her.

"It's not much further," he said, hoping she would slow their pace, "just around this far corner." Bearing to the right he steered her toward a dilapidated barnyard and his little realm of make believe. "Welcome to Morocco," he said with an exaggerated bow.

Her expression seemed frozen in disbelief.

Had he just made a colossal fool of himself? Was she about to laugh in his face?

She edged closer to the stone wall to study the Persian carpet he had thrown across the crumbling barrier. Her hand fluttered over the geometric motif as if she gained comfort from the bright colors and gay pattern of the Far Eastern design.

"If you listen carefully," he said, "you can hear the chant of the dark-skinned natives cajoling their arrogant camels down dusty roads toward an awaiting oasis." Rummaging around in the pocket of his coat, he produced a large seashell. "You can even hear the ocean roar," he declared.

Eyes wide with delight, she relinquished her parasol, and then as if she were about to cradle a baby bird, she reached for the shell with both hands. Raising the conch to her ear, pure enchantment wove a smile across her face.

Taking advantage of her preoccupation with the shell, Garrick settled her atop the cushions he'd heaped upon the frozen ground. He fed more sticks to the brazier that happily burned a few feet away, then angled a section of wood fencing up against the wall. The lean-to effectively blocked the wind and created a cozy private corner. He stooped beneath the wooden slats, eased to the ground beside her, and shrugged out of his coat.

The shell still pressed to her ear, Josie glanced around.

Garrick's heart skipped a beat. Maybe this had been a crazy idea. She didn't seem very pleased with his efforts. In truth, she looked about to cry.

"You did all this for me?" she asked, finally abandoning the shell in her lap.

A sheepish smile contorted his mouth, and he nodded.

She glanced away and blinked several times. "It's wonderful," she absently traced the ruffled edge of the shell with one finger. "And warm," she added with a smile.

"Just like Morocco."

"Have you been there?"

"A few times."

"How exciting," she said, slipping free of her cape. "And to the Americas as well?"

"Yes, and Burma, and Katmandu, and New South Wales."

"But that's wonderful."

He was amused by her enthusiasm. "Is it?" he said with a shrug. "I went to those places because there was nothing to keep me at home."

"You've no family then?"

He could feel her watching as he raided the picnic basket and laid out the food. "None except Shamus my editor," he admitted, "and Shamus is married to the newspaper. It's rather a small gathering at Holidays." He glanced up in time to see her smile waver.

"Are you ever lonely?" she asked.

"I'm too busy to be lonely," he answered too quickly and more gruffly than intended.

Delving once more into the depths of the basket, he produced one chipped crystal goblet, which he handed to Josie and one tin cup which he kept for himself. Opening the wine, he poured a good measure into her glass, but as he shifted to fill the metal cup, she slid her hand across it.

"Share this glass with me," she extended the goblet.

Again, pleasantly surprised, he corked the bottle and set it aside.

"I doubt the flavor of tin will enhance the bouquet of the wine," she added, as if her suggestion to share needed some type of justification.

He reached for the crystal goblet. Their hands touched, and his gaze meandered over her. She was as pretty as a picture, and more enticing than the imaginary backdrop he had created for her, and he realized that while the food he'd procured might feed his physical hunger, it was the sight of Josie that fed his sorry soul.

He caught the tail end of one bonnet ribbon between two fingers and gently tugged. The bow loosened, and as he eased the straw hat from her head, her dark lustrous hair tumbled forward around her shoulders. She didn't make a move, not even to blink her eyes. She just stared back at him with trust and expectation, and as he watched Josie, he realized she was also a solitary person. Wounded spirits recognized their own kind.

He leaned sideways against a cushion and rested one elbow on his bent knee. "Does having a family preclude loneliness?" he asked, picking up their conversation.

She appeared taken off guard by the question, then thoughtful. He liked the way she considered her words before turning them loose.

"Not really," she admitted. "Sometimes a family can amplify the feeling of isolation.

"Alone in a crowd so to speak?" he put in.

"Yes, quite. Happiness and affection are always

just beyond your reach, and you see in sharp relief what could be but never is." She fell silent and absently plucked at the fabric of the pillow beneath her arm.

Was she wading through images of the past? Remembering herself as a little girl. He tried to picture her. "Let me guess," he angled his head to one side. "You were an only child, raised by a nanny, taught to be seen and not heard, and your father is in the...ahh...military."

"Oh my," she gave a little breath of laughter. "For a moment I feared you were clairvoyant. But father is in politics, not the military."

He mulled her name over in his mind, trying to make the connection. Josephine Posey, Josie, Joseph. "Good heavens," he sat upright. "Your father is Joseph Posey, chief minister of parliament?"

"I'm afraid so."

"But he is a staunch believer in the war. He must be proud of your efforts here."

She sat up straighter too. "He is proud of nothing associated with my profession." Woodenly she raised her chin to the defiant angle Garrick was coming to know so well.

"But how is that possible?"

"He feels my working as a nurse is beneath my station in life."

"But surely," he protested, "with the involvement of such women as Florence Nightingale and Mary Stanley, it's obvious that the medical profession has captured the attention and enthusiasm of women in good standing. Why even Sydney Herbert has rallied 'round your cause"

"The Secretary at War has been most helpful," she agreed, "but I'm afraid it is more complicated than that." She tore at a piece of bread, but did not eat it. "'Tis not merely the social stigma to which Father cannot reconcile himself. There is a personal vendetta involved."

"What happened?" he asked gently.

"You are ever the reporter," she said teasingly, avoiding the question.

"I'm not asking because questions are my stock and trade," he reassured.

"Then why?"

"Because I want to understand the world you come from."

She glanced down, and her long lashes feathered a shadow on her pale cheeks. "Very well," she said softly, following a long moment of deliberation. "When I was seven years of age, Mother was again with child. The confinement was very difficult and it ended with an even worse delivery. The baby was a boy, the son Papa always wanted. But the poor little dear was physically weak and simple-minded, and mother was injured and could never bear another child. Papa blamed the doctors and midwives for all that transpired. When the babe died a few months later, a piece of Papa died too. He suffered greatly, and now he faces a future with only me as his heir. Therefore the entire medical profession has incurred his wrath, and I am a daily reminder of the occupation that robbed him of a son."

Garrick had heard sorrow sung in nearly every corner of the world, but the tones conveyed in Josie's words struck the deepest cord. How could a father not recognize the remarkable qualities of his own child?

"But it wasn't your fault," he said, "and now you risk your life to save others. That alone should win his love and admiration. He should not judge you by someone else's mistake or the shortcomings of a burgeoning science."

"It's important for a man to have a son," she said, as if by rote. There was forgiveness in her words, but not understanding.

"It's important for a man not to let foolish emotions cloud his reasoning."

"Have you traveled that road yourself then?"

"Once upon a time I knew no other course" he admitted and recalled the raw emotions long ignored and near forgotten. Emotions such as hate, regret, revenge, and self-doubt. These villains had all lain in wait for him upon the byways of life. His path had been cluttered with these useless feelings, and they had nearly consumed him. Then he had taught himself to exist without all emotion. It made life easier, but it also exacted a heavy price. It had cost him the opposite side of the coin; love, happiness, simple pleasure, companionship. Perhaps he was the pot calling the kettle black. He was no better than Josie's father, a man haunted by the past, a man afraid to grow and change.

He grabbed up a small knife and sliced the meat and cheese, and with each downward stroke it felt as if he pared away a part of himself. Then he felt his mask of survival slip back into place, and judging by Josie's expression, he knew his eyes had turned lonely and cold and his mouth had settled back into a familiar frown. His well-honed defense tactics were infallible and unfortunately indiscriminate.

He refilled their glass and handed it back to her.

"I'm sorry," she said, her face brightening. "We should be discussing more amusing topics on our picnic, such as the cost of tea in China, or whether the current heat wave in Morocco will beat the long standing record of 1849."

She reached out to smooth his cravat, and his emotional mask frayed around the edges.

A profound urge to kiss Josie overtook him but for some reason he felt awkward, almost shy. All he wanted was to brush his lips against hers, and after what they had shared the other evening it seemed ludicrous to be hesitant. But the other night his blood had run high from the *heat of battle* and her guard had been down due to fear and exhaustion. Danger and excitement had fired their passion— prompting them to yield to one another's touch. Now in the light of day, the danger was gone. Were the feelings they had experienced gone also?

Leaning back, he hitched up one leg and tried to ease the pounding ache in his crotch. He wanted more than a kiss. He longed for Josie with a near indecent craving. But she was different, not a girl for hire who's face he would be forgiven for forgetting the next day. Not a one-night stand who would have no expectations nor lingering attachments. He refused to be responsible for Josie's feelings or for leading her astray. His gaze lingered on the curve of her cheek. She would expect some type of commitment. Her kind believed in love. His kind didn't.

With a little sigh, Josie set the wine glass aside and rearranged herself on the pillows. One of the silk cushions slipped out from beneath her, and her eyes widened in surprise. As he reached to steady her, his fingers brushed across the fabric that covered her left breast. A quick breath escaped her parted lips, and her gaze melted into his. He leaned forward and kissed her, and all his doubts and rationalized good intentions dissolved away.

She braced one hand against his thigh. A lusty yearning intoxicated his mind, and a saber of need stabbed through is gut. He must allow her to set the pace. Then her tongue playfully teased his and it seemed in another minute her pace might outdistance his.

The pillows shifted again. Josie pitched forward against his chest. He wrapped his arms around her and eased her along as they tumbled backward.

She settled lightly atop his body—the prominence of one hip raking along his loins. "Fate seems determined to keep us on a collision course," Josie said with a girlish laugh.

He trailed his hands downward, beyond her waist, to the rounded curve of her bottom. Rocking his hips upward he tried to feel her softness through the clothes that separated them. He imagined the sensation of her skin against his, with nothing between them but the heat of passion. Yet through the haze of need, sanity and decorum niggled at the back of his brain, and he knew in his heart this was neither the time nor the place to follow through with the blind hunger that gripped them.

Sliding his hands upward, he laced his fingers in Josie's hair and eased her head back until he could study her face. She gazed down at him, her expression drowsy with ardor. She smiled and leaned closer, but he continued to hold her at bay.

"What is wrong?" she asked, her lips puckered into a frown.

He choked back a laugh. "You're driving me beyond good sense again," he gasped. "Do you know how dangerously close I am to having you right here in the mud of this abandoned farmyard?"

A blush rushed into her cheeks.

Oh damn, it made her appear even more fevered and wanting.

He rolled sideways, spilling her onto the scattered pillows. Chill air slipped between them where before hot desire had served. If he gave in to his need for Josie, his whole world would change. He would be crossing the line that safely cordoned off the edges of his existence. And once beyond that line of demarcation, he might never find his way back. Worse yet he may not want to.

He leaned away from her. It was dangerous to listen to his heart rather than the cold practicality that saw him through most situations. He mustn't become accustomed to answering to impulse.

147

Instinct and logic were more dependable.

Josie prodded a nearby cushion. "At least 'tis more comfortable here than riding upon a mule," she said, with a prim little smile.

He chuckled, sat up, and drained the wineglass in one gulp. "Josie" he said, "I don't want to hurriedly make love to you. Especially not here, with one eye open watching for passers-by and voyeur livestock. I want to take my time. I want to see and taste every inch of you." A soft mewing sound escaped her lips as if the thought excited her, and he indulged himself by allowing his gaze to drift the length of her. "I want to show you that being with you means more to me than just fleeting satisfaction or a desperate aside in this god-awful war."

Josie glanced around as if coming awake from a dream. "When I'm with you I forget the war," she confessed, and inched her hand closer to his, entwining their fingers. "Only good can come from that." She glanced down and her chin quivered.

The war. He'd almost forgotten it himself. Did she realize how brave she was coming all this distance on her own without even the support of her parents? He slid his free hand into his pocket. Where was the article he'd written about her? He hadn't had a chance to show it to her Friday night when he delivered the pull-cart to her. Where was it? Tucked away in his leather coat, that's where. He'd forgotten to retrieve it when he'd changed clothes for today's outing.

How, he wondered again, could Josie's father not admire her courage and resolve? She was as gallant as any young soldier, with the refinement of a lady. A lady gallant. The near forgotten phrase screamed through his brain and took his breath away. He scrambled to his feet and hit his head on the slanted fence-board. Was she the fulfillment of a childhood promise?

Josie clambered upright at his side. "Is something wrong?"

Oh no, he realized with a sudden burst of anger, nothing was wrong. He was acting more fanciful and quixotic than a schoolboy, neglecting his work and building fantasy worlds for a woman who encroached upon his dreams. And he was setting himself up for trouble...big trouble. But nothing was wrong. Nothing at all.

He ground his teeth together and squeezed his eyes shut for a moment. "I'd best see you back to the hospital," he said averting his gaze from her mouth, "or Mose will be out hunting for you with a battalion of men." He bent and gathered up the food. "You must promise to enjoy this later and to share it with the others."

"Yes, thank you." She accepted the hamper, but seemed confused at his abrupt change of demeanor.

"I'm going away tonight," he said. Damn, he hadn't meant to just blurt out the news. "And I'm not sure I shall make it back in time for Christmas."

Her fingers tightened around the handle of the wicker basket, and her cheeks blanched white to match her knuckles. "Where are you going?"

He wrestled with the urge to confide in her, but the fewer people who knew his destination the better. In truth, he was following up on a lead about missing medical supplies and there was most likely a black market operation involved.

"I can't tell you," he said, refusing to lie to her.

She swallowed hard and blinked several times. "I'll miss you." Standing on tiptoes she whispered a kiss upon his cheek. "Please try to be here for Christmas."

He gripped her shoulders and studied every detail of her face, the tilt of her nose, the little indentation at the bow of her upper lip. By the Saints, she made him forget the past and dare to

149

dream about a future. "I'll try," he said and meant it. For him this would be the first Christmas in a great long while that held any possibility of joy. "I promise," he repeated, as much for himself as for her. He gazed into her dark eyes and jumped headfirst into their depths.

He heard the basket hit the ground with a dull thud. She threw her arms around his neck, and as her mouth settled roughly on his, a chain reaction of pure pleasure ignited in the back of his head and ripped downward through his body.

His lips lingered on hers, and he reveled in their softness. Like a moth to a flame, he was attracted to Josie, and happily he headed for the inferno—wanting the light and heat—knowing all the while it would be fatal.

He held her closer. What a bloody wonderful way to go.

"The war is popular beyond belief."
~Queen Victoria, to the king of the Belgians

Chapter Eleven

Josie stared at her hands as if they belonged to someone else. Nothing seemed real—especially not the leg she held or the person to whom it was attached. The blood was too red and the skin too pale. It was a scene from a nightmare.

The pointed teeth of the saw rasped through Pauly's thigh bone, and the vibration traveled down his leg and into her fingertips. It was the first amputation with which she had assisted.

The outline of the people around her grew fuzzy, and the sound of her own pulse roared in her ears. Fearing she might faint Josie, bit down upon her lower lip. The shock of pain brought the world back into focus. She must think of her patient not herself. Shifting her gaze to Pauly's ashen face, her heart ached with sorrow. The war had claimed another victory—at least a partial one. Sometimes it only took small bites as it whittled away pieces of men's bodies and minds, sometimes it took more.

"Keep the poor wretch still," Dr. Cowper ordered.

Mose tightened his grip on Old Pauly's shoulders.

"Should I administer more chloroform?" Josie asked

"I'd rather not," the doctor said as he adjusted the tourniquet. "We're nearly through, and it has been officially ordered, *'the less anesthesia the better'.*"

Rumor had it the Queen willingly used the drug during the delivery of her eighth child, Prince Leopold, but Dr. Sutherland, the chief of staff begrudged the use of the anesthetic for the soldiers in the Crimea. Fortunately, Dr. Cowper was more lenient than most regarding this edict, and patients were granted a modicum of forgetfulness before the real pain set in post operatively—for once the chloroform wore off, there was nothing available to ease their misery.

Their supply of opium, so desperately needed, had been snatched from their grasp when three hundred pounds of the merciful panacea was lost in the hurricane of 14th November. Having been packed under the ammunition, the opium was not off-loaded on the coast prior to the *Prince* setting off across the Black Sea. Consequently the medicine, the soldiers' winter clothing, and all hands on deck had gone down with the ship. Twenty-one other vessels had also been destroyed by the storm that day, and they had lost nearly one-month's supply of provender for the horses and the men on the peninsula. Sometimes, the weather too was their enemy.

From across the bed, the crude-mannered orderly from Ward D stared at her and smirked. He was a licentious youth with a frightful vocabulary and a rough demeanor. Today, out of necessity, Doctor Cowper had pressed him into service, and as the loutish oaf adjusted his grip on Pauly's thigh, he rubbed his hand against hers and ogled the front of her uniform. She twitched with the urge to slap his face.

With a sickening snap, the leg came free. Pauly fainted dead away, and the doctor and orderly let go leaving her holding the severed limb.

"I'll be gettin' back to me own damn ward now," the orderly declared. "It looks like you've got everything *in hand*," he added. His mean laugh trailed behind him as he strode away.

Josie swallowed hard and stared at the leg. It was much heavier than she would have expected.

Dr. Cowper glanced up from his work. "Throw it aside, nurse, and help me to cauterize the stump."

Throw it aside? On the filthy floor? Dear God it was part of another human being, part of someone for whom she'd come to care a great deal. Tears welled in her eyes. She knew the Doctor was right, but she couldn't bring herself to do it.

As the smell of burning flesh filled the air, Dr. Cowper spoke again but she could no longer make out his words. Mose stepped around from the head of the bed and eased the amputated leg from her arms. She felt ashamed that a boy, barely past childhood, had more fortitude than she. Was it true? Did she lack what it took to endure this type of work? Maybe her pampered upbringing had left her too sentimental and sensitive to be of any use.

"Wash your hands and assist with the dressing," the doctor instructed his voice kind but stern. "He's better off now and he'll thank you for it someday. Leaving it on would have cost him his life."

In a daze Josie poured water into a nearby basin. She scrubbed her hands with a fury, as if the action could remove the doubts from her mind and the sorrow from her heart. She must think of something else or scream at the horror of it all. Frantically, she gazed about the room seeking a place of visual refuge.

The small parasol leaning up against the wall caught her attention. Gratefully, she allowed her thoughts to drift to that special corner of her mind where memories of the man that made such a difference in her life were safely tucked away. She hadn't heard from Garrick since their picnic. She wanted, needed, to be with him. Just to see him would give her strength. To touch him would renew

153

her spirit and refresh her fortitude.

She relaxed and took a deep breath and recalled the extent to which he'd gone to make their outing memorable and unique. The romantic interlude was very much in contrast to the gruff demeanor he worked so hard to portray. But it was dangerous to want him. She may never see him again. He could become a casualty of war. Or he could take another path in life that would lead him far away from her. Then it would be she who became the casualty and she did not have the strength to endure another loss of the heart.

Drying her hands on a piece of clean linen, she returned to the bedside to dress and bandage Pauly's surgical wound.

"I'll check on the lad this evening," Dr. Cowper assured her. "Call me if there is any excessive bleeding or pain beyond the usual."

"Yes doctor. Thank you."

"He's young. He'll do fine. So will you." He patted her shoulder and left.

The muscles in her neck burned and she tried to massage life back into her right shoulder. She was so exhausted she could barely think straight. And she was homesick for her family and for England. It was Christmas Eve, but instead of the holiday's approach nurturing their morale it seemed to magnify their misery. Of late, the nurses and patients alike wore their emotions on their sleeve, and these fragile feelings were easily pricked to bleeding by the slightest of upsets.

Mose removed the three wing privacy screen used to shield such procedures from the other patients and stored it away. Josie elevated Pauly's stump, covered him, and wiped his face with a damp cloth. His respirations were deep and regular and his color, although not good, was much improved. Shoving a stray lock of hair back beneath her cap, she checked the mantel clock to mark the time the surgery had ended. Then a wall of fatigue crushed in on her and she sank down onto the chair at the bedside. When had she last eaten? This morning she supposed. It was past four in the afternoon. She was too tired to care. With her elbows resting on her knees, she leaned forward and cradled her throbbing head in her hands. Closing her eyes, she lost herself to the cool blackness.

Oh, where was Garrick, why hadn't he returned like he promised? She didn't even know whom to contact regarding his welfare. Not being attached to the army, he was left to his own devices for provisions as well as for his survival. She sighed. Regardless of where he chose to travel or what job he performed, he retained the status of an unchained spirit, not bound to one person, one place, or one group. Josie wished she could be more like Garrick and not weighed down by her insecurities and tripped up by the broken pieces of her heart. But most of all she wished desperately that Garrick would make it back for Christmas.

She knew he cherished his freedom and wasn't the type to stay long in a woman's life. But he certainly was the type that sweet memories were made of. Maybe that could be enough—the making of one extraordinary memory. What did she have to lose? Her past was comprised of worn and faded recollections, and living in the midst of a war did not encourage one to think too seriously about the future. The present was all she had, and it seemed crucial that she make the most of it. If she was careful, she needn't be hurt. If she kept her eyes open and protected her heart, perhaps she could enjoy the closeness that Garrick offered without suffering another emotional loss.

She leaned back in the chair and called to mind Phillip and the love they had shared. As a selfless physician, he had fought to conquer cholera but instead the disease had conquered him—without warning he had been taken from her. In the wake of his death, she had been devastated. And in the midst of that dreadful pain and personal desolation, she had been forced to re-invent her life. She'd worked hard to prove to herself and everyone else that she could make it on her own. But now she was tired of continuing on as if all were right with the world, and she was tired of being alone. Yet the possibility of again finding the unconditional love that Phillip had shown her seemed unlikely, if not impossible. Until Garrick.

Dragging herself to her feet, she paced the length of the ward. She must face the truth. Like it or not, wish it or not, fight it or not, she was falling in love with Garrick.

Garrick was such a different breed of man. He didn't condone the war, yet he was valiant and true to his country. He wasn't a soldier, yet he fought for the rights of others.

Josie had grown up with uncles who were generals and cousins who bought commissions as soon as they were of age. Being in the Queen's army and going to war was expected and edified. She had been weaned on political rhetoric and bombarded by military logic. She didn't know what to make of a man who was brave enough to question the powers that be and gentle-minded enough to champion the runts in the litters of life. Garrick seemed to think and reason for himself, forming and supporting new opinions even if they were contrary to the majority. In some ways, she felt the same about her crusade for nursing. She had fought that battle supported by few. Mamma had thrown her hands up in resignation, shaking her head in despair, declaring that Josie certainly took after late Auntie Rue.

A smile eased across Josie's lips. Dear Aunt

Ruewella. She had stunned the family by following a *debased* career as an opera singer. But along the way the woman had wisely invested in land all across Europe, and her holdings had been transformed into a fortune. It was the money Josie had inherited from Auntie Rue that had allowed her to follow the controversial path of becoming a nurse.

"Auntie Rue," she murmured. "You gave me the courage to declare my convictions and the funds to back up my words. I wish you had also enlightened me on how to live with loneliness, or how to love a man who clearly seems to cheriesh his freedom above all else."

Her smile turned bittersweet. She was sure Auntie Rue would have approved of Garrick. He had magic. The kind her Aunt would have understood and appreciated.

Footsteps echoed in the ward. Hoping it was Garrick, she turned toward the sound—a song in her heart. Unfortunately it was Danford who approached and she wished only to run, but there was no where to go. Shoulders squared she stood her ground.

The faded yellow and purple bruise beneath Danford's eye bore witness to his altercation with Garrick. For a man averse to fighting, Mr. Allen seemed rather skilled at fisticuffs.

"I owe you a profound apology," Danford began, as he reached her side.

"You don't owe me anything."

"I'm here to extend a peace offering," he persisted. "I never meant any harm to come to you."

Josie glanced about for Mose and wished for once that her smitten young orderly would interrupt her private conversation. He seemed to have no compulsion about doing so when Garrick was around.

"I don't want anything from you," Josie

sidestepped away from him.

"It's for the men as well as for you."

Emotional blackmail again. It wasn't very creative of Danford to use the same ploy twice running. Not creative, but effective.

"What is it?" she reluctantly asked.

"A case of the finest Russian caviar that money can buy."

Caviar. She nearly laughed in Danford's face. They needed soup and arrowroot and citrus for the scurvy, not briny fish eggs. Such fare would be far too rich for these half-starved men, upsetting their digestion and worsening their debilitated state. Leave it to Danford to turn a humane gesture into a show of affluence. Or was it just another attempt to put her at a disadvantage and in his debt?

She opened her mouth intent on throwing his offer back in his face. Then she saw a potential benefit in the absurd gift. Perhaps she could barter the roe for something more practical. Not unlike Danford, several of the generals and doctors found no conflict to living high off the hog while those around them starved. It could fetch a good price in trade.

"On behalf of the men, I thank you," she said. "It will be put to the best possible use."

Danford's eyes brightened with victory.

His triumphant attitude raised her hackles, and she had an urge to tell him that his fancy fish eggs were going to be bartered for chamber pots and linen bandages. Afraid however that he might renege on the offer, she swallowed back the castigation.

He reached out and skimmed the back of his fingers along her cheek.

Caught by surprise she took a step backward. "I was taught that a gift required no recompense," she said. "If there are strings attached to yours, I'm afraid I must refuse it."

"There is no obligation." He lowered his hand and smiled. "Can't blame a chap for trying. Your beauty could incite a saint to sinning and a sinner to prayer."

"And the devil to delivering caviar."

He raised a brow as if her reasoning hit too close to home. "Do you see me as the devil?"

"I can see you cast as nothing less."

"But the devil was once an angel."

"Then more's the pity."

"Circumstances can change a being," he said, his eyes narrowing. "We all do what we must to ensure our own continuance."

"But some proceed with more compassion than others."

"Compassion has nothing to do with getting on in the world. When it comes right down to it, life is simply the business of survival and individuals, companies, and countries alike, deal exclusively in that commodity. It's all one and the same logic."

"And will you protect your trade policies as fervently as England protects hers?"

"Certainly. Life is also a war. Don't let anyone tell you differently."

"People die in wars."

"So I hear."

"That doesn't bother you?"

"What bothers me is people interfering in my transactions. Everything and everyone has a price and I'm very good at finding it."

"Everything and everyone?"

"Yes," he said as if he still harbored the idea that he could buy her as well. "It's always just a matter of time." He studied her with a practiced eye just as he had done on the first day they had met—again she felt like a piece of sculpture up for auction. Danford was truly a black-hearted mercenary.

"I'm spending the Holidays in Greece," he

announced, his voice a cross between coaxing and taunting. "Care to join me?"

Josie could not imagine what type of travesty Danford would make of Christmas.

"No I would not," she said. "Now, if you will excuse me, I really must tend to my patients."

At her dismissal Danford's smile hardened. Then it seemed to break away piece by piece—exposing the sneer waiting beneath it. "I'll have the caviar sent along tomorrow," he said coldly. "Happy Holidays." He turned and walked away, never looking back. His shadow slinked through the door after him.

Happy Holidays indeed. It seemed most unlikely that they would be. She glanced around the gloomy ward. It was obvious what they needed was a Christmas tree.

I wonder what would have come of it all
had I followed the quiet path...
instead of those noisy drums and trumpets.
~William Howard Russell

Chapter Twelve

Absence made the heart grow fonder. It also made the spirit grow reckless.

Garrick felt numb from head to toe. A blessing really, as he no longer felt the sleet, sharp as needles, driving into his face.

Head down, he clucked at his mount urging the poor beast onward. By all that was holy, what was he doing wandering about in a blizzard? And all for the sake of a woman's smile. He should have waited for the storm to pass but it was past midday already and tonight was Christmas Eve

He squinted and cursed. He could barely see the ears of his horse only three feet in front of him. This could well be the most desperate ill-advised situation he had ever dared jump into. And if his luck didn't change, it might also prove to be his last.

He peered into the crystalline void. The whole world appeared white and flat, with no definition or contour, and the harsh purity had a hypnotic effect upon him. He had been sentenced to oblivion.

Shaking his head, he tried to reclaim his rambling thoughts. A shard of ice broke loose from his hat and snaked down the inside of his collar. Shivers wracked his body until he could barely catch his breath. He could not remember ever having been so cold, not even in the mountains of Tibet. Shuddering uncontrollably, he fought to recall the places he had visited that were scorching hot. Places like the great desert of Arabia or the outback of Australia. The memories succeeded in warming his heart but not his body. Where was the damn outpost?

He'd left Varna three days ago, staying ahead of the storm until last night. The weather had caught up with him in Janibazar where he'd dared to pause and snatch a few hours sleep. But that was many miles back and what seemed a lifetime ago. Surely the Sweet Waters leading to the Golden Horn were straight ahead with Constantinople just beyond. Unless of course he had been traveling in circles.

His eyelids flickered twice, then closed, and his mind drifted into nothingness. He was floating. No, he was falling. His head snapped up as he jerked back to wakefulness. If he surrendered to sleep, he was a dead man. "Stay awake you poor dumb bastard," he shouted. With a snort of surprise, the horse tossed its head and shied to the right.

He must concentrate on something important. Anything to keep from drifting off again. A vision of Josie filled his mind. Oh no, that was worse. It made him too contented. He wanted to nuzzle her neck and lay down beside her. He wanted to cuddle her in his arms and wrap her in the comfort of his love.

Think of something else, his instincts screamed in warning.

Fighting to keep his mind on track, he reviewed the information he had uncovered in Varna. British medical and military supplies were being black marketed on a grand scale. Why should he care? He just wanted to sleep. He inhaled sharply. What else had he discovered? What else did he have to report? The War Office was so cocked up, it took them weeks, sometimes months, to discover that a particular shipment had gone missing. By then it was too late to trace the disappearance. By then the goods were long gone and so was the person who organized these ventures.

But who was the mastermind behind it all? Danford Smythe came to mind as a suitable candidate. That made his blood boil, or under present conditions, at least simmer.

Being a professional profiteer, Smythe qualified unquestionably. He must be up to something besides spying for England. He was not the type to risk life and limb for mere noble intentions, yet his ploy did offer the perfect cover. By posing as a spy, Danford was afforded numerous opportunities for traveling behind enemy lines. He could fraternize openly with the Russians and all the while England would turn a blind eye to his little excursions. Hell, they would even encourage them.

Still, the availability of supplies was unpredictable, offering only intermittent ill gotten gains. There must be something else in the works. Something even more valuable for which Danford risked all.

Garrick's eyelids drooped, and his head sagged forward. Then a cramp knotted the muscle in his left thigh. Damn. That nicely re-energized his flagging senses. He grimaced and shifted to ease the pain only to discover he could barely move. Like a man encased in mortar, he was stiff with the cold. His horse's mane was frozen into spikes that stuck out at unnatural angles, and the reins were iced solidly into place between his gloved fingers.

He felt frozen in time, as well as in place, condemned to travel the same path over and over, never arriving anywhere, never escaping the prison of this bleak infinity. He was slipping beyond logic again, slipping beyond life.

But he didn't want to die. What a quirk of fate. How many times had he not cared about seeing another sunrise? How many risks and foolhardy adventures had he purposely sought because living was either too boring or too painful? How many years had he drunk too much and lived too hard so he could forget the past, cheat the future, and exhaust the present?

By all he held dear, he wanted to survive. He wanted to make it back to Josie. What a devious coquette was this thing called love. Not logical in the least and truly without conscience or mercy. Love, a glorious malady with no cure, a most fantastic confusion, a strange chemistry that befuddled the brain and sent a man off on fantastic voyages beyond his ken and even against his will.

The sound of jangling bells interrupted his tangent of waxing poetic. Was he now hallucinating? Without preamble there it was again. The tinkling staccato danced upon the frigid air and pierced the silence with crystal clarity. It reminded him of sleigh bells, an appropriate aberration for Christmas Eve.

It couldn't be real. But the horse had heard it too, and thankfully the poor beast turned to follow the sound. Unable to move his lips, Garrick silently willed the animal onward.

****

With a sturdy thud, the tree limb crashed to the ground. Josie laid the ax aside to study her handy work. Once trimmed into shape, the branch would make a fine little Christmas tree. And although she hadn't yet had time to make decorations, she knew what needed to be done.

Happy, but exhausted by her labors, she brushed the snow aside and sank down upon the gnarled roots at the base of the cypress. Grateful, she leaned against the raspy bark of the huge evergreen and patted the trunk. "Thank you for your contribution to our holiday cheer," she said. "I trust one more missing branch will not disturb you overmuch." She had been lucky to find a tree sporting any limbs at all. Most had been ravaged months ago for firewood. The area looked like a grotesque field of twisted maypoles rather than a forest.

Sheltered from the wind, she curled into a more comfortable position. The sky was threatening to bring more snow, and the leaden clouds, riding low, scraped across the withered treetops—shreds of nimbus were left behind like wispy bits of carded wool. She inhaled deeply. The taste of winter was in the air. She could almost feel the sky wanting to snow. As she watched, flakes spiraled downward, big and soft and cottony. They tumbled and twirled like faeries waltzing on the wind. Clutching at the tree, she struggled to her feet and arms wide, she stepped from beneath the cypress to join the tiny dancers. Catching snowflakes on her tongue, she recalled figgy puddings and Yule logs and skating on the frozen pond in Belson's park near Penmarrow. Her steps turned lighthearted at the memory of those carefree early years. That was before she had developed a mind of her own and the obstinate will to follow it. That was before she had lost Phillip and struck out on her own.

Dizzily she wound to a halt and rested one forearm on the trunk of the tree. So much had changed in the last few years. Herself most of all. Head nestled against her arm she stared down the hillside toward the hospital. The recent accumulation of snow blotted out the dark muddy Turkish landscape transforming the rolling hills into a carpet of pristine white. A mantle of pale frosting, muffling all noise, making even the war sound peaceful.

War...

Why did one person or thing always have to die for another to live? She knotted her hand into a fist. It didn't make sense, but it was a fact. Perhaps in the final analysis—survival of the fittest really was the only truth. And like Nature, Man blindly upheld that philosophy with no more care and no less cruelty.

She kicked at a rock then absently made little patterns in the snow with the toe of her boot. As a little girl she had rescued ants from spider webs, only to worry later that the spiders might starve. The choices now were no less confounding and much more barbaric.

The enormity of war astounded her, and she had to fight not to lose sight of the struggle of the individual. She must keep trying to make a difference, one soldier at a time, one patient at a time. She had not made a mistake in following Miss Nightingale. This was where she belonged.

Angry at the absurdity of life, Josie grabbed the ax and the severed bough and began her trek back to the hospital. It might not be possible for her to change the world, but she could darn well fight tooth and nail for her little corner of it and that included making sure the men on Ward C had a beautiful tree for Christmas.

As she followed the snow-covered footpath a revelation spilled over her and in wondrous clarity she realized what Garrick had been subtly trying to explain to her. She finally recognized the difference between the warrior and the war. She could answer the call of the wounded soldier and wish an end to the conflict without diminishing the honor and glory of the men who fought in it.

For the first time since her arrival in Scutari, Josie felt at peace with her own conscience. Garrick had given her the means to survive here. He had shown her that she had the right to apply her logic to matters of importance beyond herself. She glanced around. Too bad only the fading twilight bore witness to her enlightenment.

As she walked, the wind sprang to life with renewed determination, and the snow began to fall in earnest. It obliterated her bright new world and transformed it into a fuzzy blur. The snow became a fury, and the wuthering in the trees reverberated in her ears and thrummed in her chest. Much to her alarm, the outline of the Barracks Hospital disappeared, and she lost all sense of direction.

Layer by layer the snow hid treacherous stumps and rocks, and it quickly accumulated on her tree branch doubling its weight. She stumbled and fell to her knees. The white powder billowed up around her like a cloud of dust, and as it settled back to the ground, it coated her eyelashes and clung to her cheeks. Snow melted through her skirt and wool stockings, soaking her knees. Her teeth chattered with the cold, and she sent a silent plea aloft asking their heavenly Father to watch over all the creatures trapped in this merciless storm.

As the wind stopped to catch its breath, the building she sought wavered back into view. She scrambled to her feet and quickly forged a path through the newly fallen snow. Twilight turned to true darkness as she reached the rear wall of the Barrack Hospital, and the storm howled again in earnest.

Knocking the snow from the branch, she stepped toward the rarely used side passage that led to her domain. As she forced open the obstinate door, it creaked with mind-grating enthusiasm. Dismayed at her fanfare of an entrance, she glanced around the dimly lit ward. No one stirred. Soft moans and gentle snores came from the patients, and Mose was nowhere in sight. She had not been found out.

Dragging the tree over the threshold, she closed the door and tiptoed across the stone floor. The cedar branch trailed along behind her with a comforting swish, and the soothing sound reminded her of

167

summer lawn parties and ladies skirts upon the grass.

She slowed her steps as she passed Old Pauly's bed. His even breathing assured her he slept undisturbed. A strong constitution had sustained him through the initial ordeal of surgery. But what would happen when he had time to consider his future, would he maintain the will to live? With only one leg, the going would be difficult for a man.

Perhaps she could tell him about Phillip. It might help, because whether a loss was physical or emotional, the pain was just as real and the future just as frightening. And although you might never *get over it*, if you were going to survive, eventually you had to *get on with it*. It was a hard lesson to learn, one upon which she was still working.

Crossing the room, she studied the other patients. The number of wounded was down, but the number of cholera victims was up. Disease, rather than Russian musket balls, had become their adversary. And a most hideous enemy it was. It lurked in every corner—waiting for the weak and the unsuspecting. She had expected the new sanitation methods, initiated by Miss Nightingale, would drive the demon back to the corner of hell it had come from. But so far, that had not been the case, and they all lived in fear of this unseen foe.

Placing the ax beside the wood stove, Josie balanced the tree branch up against the west wall and then hurried over to the nearby alcove. She lit a small lamp, removed her cape, and positioned the wing-screen to hide her activities from inquisitive eyes. Retrieving her sewing basket from the shadows, she settled into the chair and organized the materials that would become her decorations.

Her lips softened into a smile. The mis-delivered quill tips and prisms would finally be put to good use. Tonight she would utilize them to bedeck the tree. And come the dawn, their twinkling splendor would be the first thing her boys saw on Christmas morn.

****

She unraveled more red yarn from her best wool sweater and her thoughts unraveled in her mind. Where was Garrick? Was he safe from harm? Focusing her tired eyes on the old mantel clock, a stab of dejection accompanied her worry. It was nearly midnight, almost Christmas.

As she labored, the storm continued unabated, and snow laden wind lashed against the far window. The cold bitter noise magnified the depth of her loneliness and the prospect of capturing this holiday in a sweet watercolor memory gently washed away. The weather was growing worse by the hour. It would take a miracle for Garrick to make it back in time.

Barely able to keep her eyes open, she drowsily reached for a prism. Yes it would take a miracle. But then again, it was Christmas Eve.

****

Where in blue blazes was she?

As he entered the north wing of the Barrack Hospital, Garrick slowed his step but his heart continued to race. No one had seen Josie since this morning, not even Gemma, and it was after midnight.

"Mose," he shouted as he gained the corridor leading to Ward C. Damn. He wished he hadn't taken the time to thaw out and wash up after crossing paths with the perimeter guard near Scutari.

"Mose," he called again, his voice rebounding off the high ceiling and barren walls of the anteroom.

Brandishing a battered flintlock pistol, the lad he sought rounded the corner at full tilt.

"Easy, boy," Garrick advised, as he raised his

hands to show he meant no harm.

"Holy hell, Mr. Allen. The way you was a hollerin' I was sure a regiment of Cossacks was a comin' in behind you. You tryin' to wake the near dead or somethin'?"

Ignoring the boy's grim humor, Garrick grabbed Mose by the shoulders. "Where is Nurse Posey? I can't find her anywhere."

"I ain't seen her since she sneaked back in here with that pitiful bush."

Garrick released his grip. "What are you talking about?"

"Well," Mose said, "she left here this evening at the usual time, but I guess she didn't retire to her room as she came back a few hours later draggin' part of a tree with her. She was acting furtive like and lurking about, so I didn't disturb her—and eventually I figured out what she was doin'."

"And what, pray tell, was that?" It sounded like another firewood expedition to Garrick.

"She's puttin' up a Christmas tree. At least I think that's what it's supposed to be. I went to eat and ain't seen her since."

"Where's the tree?" he asked, as they entered the ward together.

"Over there against the wall. You can hardly see it now but that window across from it faces east and it'll be right noticeable in the mornin' light."

With Mose at his heels, Garrick circled the ward and advanced upon the tree. As he reached the three-winged screen, a murmur and a rustling caught his attention. Stepping closer, he peeked around the partition and the knot of anxiety in his stomach relaxed.

There she was, asleep, curled up in a chair, snug as a winkle in a shell. He felt ten years younger with relief. Her recalcitrant nurse's cap lay upon the floor, and her liberated hair drifted into soft waves that caressed her shoulders and framed her face. A hint of a smile kissed her lips, and Garrick wondered what or whom she saw in her dreams.

His gaze shifted taking in the rest of her. How had she managed to fit that long-legged figure into that chair? He guessed she appeared comfortable enough. If he moved her, she might awaken.

A jumble of yarn and quill tips lay abandoned in her lap. "Mose," he whispered, "I've a splendid idea but it will require your help." As he spoke, Garrick gently freed Josie's hands from the tangle of wool and ornaments.

****

Church bells chimed and the mellow notes billowed and tumbled through Josie's mind. She clawed her way toward wakefulness, but was too weary to open her eyes. Instead, through the foggy layers of sleep, she listened intently to the world around her. The howl of the storm was gone—replaced by a calming silence.

A kiss, gentle and unexpected grazed her temple.

"Merry Christmas, Josie."

Her eyes flickered open and like a dream come true, Garrick stood beside her. The three-winged screen was gone, and as he smiled and stepped to one side, she saw the tree.

The sky had cleared and the golden light of pre-dawn peaked through the window like the warmth of God's smile.

"Is this what you had in mind?" Garrick asked, as he laid his hand upon her shoulder.

In contrast to the whitewashed wall, her little tree was resplendent. Quill tips dangled from the branches like tiny brass icicles, and the prisms radiated rainbows and memories of Christmas past. There was even a big paper star at the top. No doubt a contribution from Garrick's precious reserve.

She turned to study his face and to savor his touch. He was really here at her side. "It's wonderful," she whispered. "You're wonderful."

"Mose accomplished most of the work," Garrick said.

The boy stepped forward and beamed with pride. "But it was Mr. Allen's idea," he was quick to point out.

Did she detect a camaraderie burgeoning between these two?

Mose gave Garrick a conspiratorial wink. "I got chores to do and the men are beginnin' to stir," he said, as he turned and ambled off.

"I was worried about you," Garrick said. "No one knew where you were." Anguish glimmered in the depths of his eyes.

He crouched down at her side, and she wriggled around in the chair to face him.

"Good," she said. "You have suffered for a mere few hours what I have endured for days. I imagined you dead one thousand times. And I knew not even in which direction to address my prayers." Tears blurred her vision, and she gripped the lapel of his beleaguered moose hide coat. Then she slipped her hands inside to brace them against the rough wool shirt that covered his hard muscled chest. It was warm and inviting beneath the outer layer of well-worn leather. Just as there was warmth beneath the hard-bitten personality of the man himself.

He slid his arms around her—his embrace tender yet reassuring. She snuggled closer, her ear against his chest. "I feared I would never see you again," she said reveling in the reassuring thumping beat of his heart.

Garrick rocked her back and forth. "Everything will be all right now," he crooned. His words echoed through her mind, and his deep rich voice calmed her fears. "I've a present for you," he declared and eased her away from his chest. Shrugging off his fringed coat, he produced a small package from one of its inner pockets.

"For me?" She shook her head in wonder. In the middle of all this disorder and turmoil, he had thought to bring her a gift.

At her hesitation he waved the package back and forth as if to entice her. "The Turks are not partial to refunds or returns," he said. "You may as well open it."

She grinned, grabbed up the gift, and tore at the brown paper wrappings with all the enthusiasm of a child. Beneath the final layer was an old wooden music box. As she tipped open the lid, the mechanism scraped into action and the song began. The melancholy waltz was unfamiliar to her but that made it all the more special, as if it had been written just for the two of them.

Feeling short of breath under his scrutiny, she focused her attention on the music box. "Thank you," she said, rewinding the apparatus, "it's lovely. But I'm afraid I've nothing to offer you in kind."

The somber hue of Garrick's eyes seemed revitalized as if a ray of sunshine had penetrated the forest-green darkness that usually prevailed there. He reached out and rested his fingertips on the back of her wrist, and his expression turned serious. "You make me forget all that's wrong in the world, Josie. No one could give me a better gift than that." As he traced little circles on her bare skin, a shiver ran up her arm and excitement sparkled through her.

He set the music box aside, and taking her by the hand, he rose and urged her to do the same. The tune echoed around her and through her as he swept her into his arms to dance.

She smiled up at him then demurely glanced away. She wished he would kiss her and hold her closer. She wanted to feel the brush of Garrick's body against hers. She wanted to taste him with her lips and run her tongue over the different textures of him.

But Garrick kept a gentleman's distance and the heat of him just beyond her reach was torture. Within the confines of the alcove, their bodies swayed and drifted in unison to the tinkling melody. A blush burned upon her cheeks, and the fluttering in her belly near drove her to distraction. She yearned for his touch in the most forbidden of places. She wanted to spend the night with Garrick, in his bed. And she wanted to wake up beside him the next morning.

She leaned closer.

He held her at arm's length.

He barely made any physical contact with her at all. It was admirable indeed that Garrick was content to spend an innocent moment simply dancing, but the ardor he stirred within her became all consuming. Soon she was obsessed with wanting to stroke his cheek. Wild unladylike desires careened through her mind, and the imaginings were not at all in keeping with Christmas reverence. Again and again, Garrick re-wound the music box and they talked and danced until she thought she must go mad. The sweet haunting melody that encased her in splendor would forever remind her of this interlude of sensual torture.

Weak-kneed she leaned closer, and this time Garrick did not resist her advance. She pressed her hips against his as she nuzzled his neck. She craved Garrick as if he were a newly discovered confection. An urge to nip at him tensed her jaw, and she pulled away short of breath.

"Slow down, Nurse Posey," Garrick warned with a wicked grin.

Josie swallowed hard and tried to collect her composure.

"Would you consider joining me for New Year's Eve?" he asked.

"But what would we do?" she questioned, although she needn't have. The spot of color that fevered his cheeks spoke volumes.

Now Garrick drew her roughly against his chest, and slanting his mouth down over hers, he kissed her until she felt faint. "We could start with something like that," he whispered against her cheek.

He leaned back, his expression smoldering.

A tingle of excitement shivered through her. "And then what?" she asked, blatantly encouraging his boldness.

Garrick stared at her lips. "Then I shall do whatever pleases my lady most, until she doth beg me to either stop or to unflaggingly continue."

Her eyes widened, and she giggled at his elaborate prose. If only it were New Year's Eve right now—this very minute. How would she ever endure the wait?

As the hum of morning activity gently intruded, she glanced over her shoulder, and the vision that met her eyes, claimed her attention and forced all other thoughts from her mind—even as it renewed her belief in the true meaning of Christmas.

Drenched in the bright morning sun, the little Christmas tree glittered as if with divine light, and all her patients were gathered around it. Some leaned on crutches, others sat on the floor. The strong bore the litters for the weak. Each was dressed in only the remnants of a uniform but the buttons were shined and those who could, stood tall and proud. An off-key rendition of Good King Wenceslaus filled the air, and she smiled up at Garrick and turned within the circle of his arms.

The soldiers' voices were strained and weak, yet Handel's Messiah sung by a choir of cherubim could not have sounded sweeter as each man exemplified the ability of the human spirit to triumph over despair. But the joyous sounds soon softened to whispers and several voices lapsed into rasping coughs.

She sobbed and leaned back against Garrick. The men were so exhausted, even being happy taxed their condition. He tightened his embrace as if to shield her from the sorrowful sight. She was sad that their little celebration would end so quickly. If only there was one more thing to mark the occasion, something special to make this day different from all the others they endured together.

Fulfilling her wish, Mose hurried forward with a bushel basket of oranges in tow. Her mouth dropped open in wonder as he ceremoniously handed out the unexpected treat.

The men hooted with joy and bit into the citrus. They ate rind and all and licked their fingers as the sweet juice ran down their chins.

Cradling three large oranges in his arm, Mose stepped to Josie's side. He handed one to her and one to Garrick. "There's another bushel in the hall," he said between mouthfuls of the third.

For a brief moment, her happiness wavered. "But where did they come from?" she asked, wondering if they were from Danford.

"I sort of found them," Mose answered.

"Sort of?" she prompted.

Mose wiped his chin on his sleeve. "A couple of days ago," he explained, "I heard tell a shipment of food had come in. But there weren't no distribution orders for the oranges, and I knew we needed them the most. I just hung around the dock until the purveyor had them throwed overboard and then I figured they was fair game."

"Oh Mose," Josie reached out and touched his cheek. "I'm so proud of you for always thinking of the men."

At her praise and attention, he blushed furiously then grinned from ear to ear.

Josie glanced around the ward, and her eyes filled with tears.

Perhaps the one redeeming quality of war was its ability to inspire profound acts of goodness and courage.

To live in hearts we leave behind is not to die
       ~Thomas Campbell, *Hallowed Ground*

Chapter Thirteen

As Josie entered the ward, her gaze snagged on the poor lackluster cypress branch. Had it only been two days since Christmas? Their festive tree had grown grotesquely withered, and the pitiful bush no longer prompted fond memories of the holiday. Rather it depicted the terminal frailty of their present condition.

The weather had worsened, and the men were dying of cholera at a fantastic rate. Some patients came and went so quickly she barely had time to learn their names or memorize their faces before the burial detail snatched them from her keeping.

With a shiver she added another log to the wood stove, closed the door, and straightened. "Mose," she called absently over her shoulder, "when you have the time strip the tree of decorations and relegate the poor thing to the stove. It warmed our hearts, now let it warm our bodies."

"Mose?" Why didn't the boy answer? She turned in search of him.

He stood across the room from her, his face flushed and his eyes overly bright. Blinking several times, he stared back at her with a questioning expression. He took a step forward—arms extended. Then he hesitated and before she could reach him, he slumped to the floor.

"Oh dear Lord," she cried as she knelt at his side. "Not Mose."

"Lend a hand," Old Pauly called from his bed.

Two soldiers, nearly recovered from their wounds, rushed forward. One grabbed Mose by the ankles and the other slid his hands beneath the boy's boney shoulders. The lad was so thin it took little effort to lift him to a nearby bed.

As Josie reached for his wrist to measure his pulse, his eyes fluttered open and grew wide with alarm. In a panic, he tried to sit up.

"It's all right," she said, as she placed her hands on his shoulders and gently urged him back against the pillow. "I'm here with you."

"Nurse Posey I don't feel so good."

"I know, Mose. You've been working much too hard."

"Sure," he said, "that's all it is." But the dread didn't leave his eyes, and they both knew he had the cholera.

"I'll send for Dr. Cowper," Josie assured him and gently covered him with a blanket.

Glancing around in dismay, she realized that she usually sent Mose to fetch the doctor. Today she must go herself and today the distance to the physicians' quarters had never seemed greater. She clenched a fold of her skirt in each hand and quickened her pace. Anger welled up inside of her. She wanted to hit something. How could God forsake Mose? He was so young, so innocent. He didn't have anything to do with the war or the killing. It wasn't fair.

"If you're looking for fair, madam, you've come to the bloody wrong place." Garrick's words from the first day they had crossed paths echoed in her mind, and she wished he were here now. There was an odd comfort in his cynicism. If he were here, he could transform her panic and anger into practical thinking. He would tell her that God created man and man created war. God was responsible for giving us free will, and man was responsible for the

consequences of using it. Garrick would make it all sound so logical.

Still, it wasn't fair.

Reaching the doctor's staircase she paused. The spindles she'd stolen had yet to be replaced, but a sentry was now stationed at a check point in front of the steps. He was a very old soldier, frail and stooped. Evidently, her assault on the banister had been viewed as a prank rather than a serious attack.

"State yer business, girl and be quick about it," he muttered.

"I must speak with Dr. Cowper," she said, "immediately."

The old man referred to his roster of names several times. With each analysis he adjusted the distance between the paper he held and his bespectacled eyes. Finally, he stabbed a gnarled finger at the document. "Here it be. He ain't in."

"Then I must see someone else."

"Impossible." Rheumy-eyed, the old soldier peered at her over the top of his wire rim glasses.

"Please, you must help me. A young boy is very ill."

"But there ain't nobody else. That's the problem. Here have a look for yourself." He held out the register.

She grasped the list and gave it a quick perusal. The names were organized into three groups, but the cryptic military abbreviations made no sense to her. "I don't understand," she said. "What does it mean?"

"This here group," he explained and pointed, "has served to the end of their duty. They're a headin' back home this very moment even though their replacements has yet to arrive. These ones are attendin' the medical confabulation at the request of the surgeon general hisself. Your Dr. Cowper being amongst them. And this third pitiful lot has got the cholera and can't even help themselves."

He gently slid the paper from her hand. "So you sees," he said, "there ain't nobody else."

"Then may I leave a message for Dr. Cowper?"

"Certainly, ma'am."

"Tell him to see Nurse Posey, in Ward C, immediately upon his return." The sentry seemed awfully old and a bit distracted. "Will you remember that?" she asked.

"My hearing is a bit off and me back is bowed, but my mind is still as sharp as a Hussar's saber point. I got it."

She smiled at his indignant tone and proud expression. "I'm sorry. I meant no disrespect. I'm sure you are a soldier equal to any task."

"That I am, lassie," he gave her a wink, "and I still know a pretty girl when I sees one too."

The old curmudgeon was flirting with her. "Thank you," she said, "now I'd best be getting along before your charm causes me to tarry longer."

"Come by any time," he called after her. "It's been down right monotonous around here since the mysterious banister incident." He chuckled and nodded toward the stairway at his back. "Even the boys at the front heard about that one."

She cringed and kept walking. Pity she could not take credit for such a memorable deed. It might be the only thing she would be remembered for in the Crimea.

On the way back to the ward, she begged a pint of beef tea from Sister Mary Francis. The feisty little nun ran the kitchen like a fortress, forbidding a crumb of food or drop of soup to be issued without a diet roll order. But during their crossing of the Mediterranean, Josie had helped the seasick sister, and the nun now proved she had not forgotten the kindness.

****

Over the next few days, in an effort to better his

chances of recovery, Josie fed Mose fluids every hour. She slept in a chair by his bed at night and spent as much time as possible by his side during the day. Dr. Cowper did all that was possible too, but it wasn't enough—Mose continued to languish.

By the third afternoon, Josie knew Mose was not going to survive. His pulse grew weaker, and his sunken eyes robbed his face of its youth. He was plagued by agonizing leg cramps that set him to screaming in the night, but he never complained and he always thanked her for even the smallest attention.

"Nurse Posey?"

Josie leaned forward in her chair and rested her fingertips on his forearm. "Yes, Mose."

"I'm right scared a dyin'," he said, "but being dead won't be so bad."

Tears brimmed over Josie's lashes, and she choked back the words of denial she longed to utter. "What exactly do you mean, Mose?" It took every ounce of self-control she possessed to keep her voice steady under the weight of her sorrow.

"When I cross over," he explained, "I'll see all the men I know'd from here that's gone before me. And I'll be with my Ma. She died when I was born so I never even seen her face. I guess its time we met."

There was a peacefulness about Mose that unnerved Josie, and despite the fact that he was a mere lad, there was a profound wisdom and dignity in his reasoning. He proved out the theory that knowledge was not accumulated by longevity, and bravery was not seen only on the battlefield.

She wiped Mose's face with a cool wet cloth. His eyelids were near transparent and blue-tinged like a baby's, and his cheeks were soft and fuzzy as a peach. A few sparse whiskers bristled on his upper lip. He was so proud of them, always claiming that a mustache made a man more dashing and dignified.

"It got dark early tonight," he mumbled.

Josie's hand stilled as she glanced up at the bright shaft of afternoon sunlight streaming in through the skylight. Mose's condition was declining rapidly, and his heartbeat was frightfully irregular. He had a much more delicate constitution than his outward appearance had ever indicated.

She crooned him a lullaby, and her voice cracked with sorrow.

"Young Mose," Old Pauly said, as he maneuvered forward with his crutch in one hand and a sword in the other. "Take my saber, lad, I'll not be leading many a charge with only one leg. Besides you're the best soldier among us."

He laid the weapon at Mose's side and wrapped the boy's fingers around the grip. Then he saluted and hobbled away—tears glistening in his eyes. Soon the other men began to file by.

Each one presented Mose with whatever piece of military accouterment they could spare; a regimental cap, a powder flask, all the necessary items that a properly outfitted soldier needed to go to war. And each one saluted him proudly.

It was no secret that Mose wanted to be a soldier. Being an orderly had not been his choice, but being a kind gentle caring person had been, and the patients loved and respected him for it.

"Here's me favorite dagger, laddie," the last man stepped forward. "It's from the 42nd Highlanders. The Black Watch remembers you."

Mose smiled weakly barely able to keep his eyes open. Then he stiffened and although his eyes were open, he blindly reached out to her. "Nurse Posey will you light an annual candle for me?"

"Without fail," she promised and cradled his cold fingers in her hand. His respirations were labored and a gurgling sound issued from his throat as he fought for every breath.

"I used to light one every year for me mum. I'll have to ask her if she knew." He swallowed hard and sighed. "I bet she's as pretty as you."

His grip on her hand tightened. Then it went slack. The light in his eyes faded to a stony glazed dullness, and the air rushed from his lungs as he gave up his last breath on this earthly plain.

Josie clenched her jaw and clamped a hand over her mouth. A howl of pain tore at the back of her throat and sorrow, jagged as broken glass, ripped through her body. Young Mose, the most valiant of all her boys, was gone.

****

Garrick stepped from the curb onto the main street. His head ached, and his mind was foggy from too many hours in a smoke filled room. Gratefully, he inhaled a deep breath of cold clean early morning air.

He'd spent the entire evening at the gaming tables trying to ferret out a new lead for his article on the missing British supplies. Many an unguarded word slipped out under the influence of a free drink or in the heat of high bidding. It was an old strategy and usually a profitable one, but tonight his efforts had been in vain. He hadn't learned one thing of any value. At least he'd won enough money at the tables to cover the cost of the liquor.

Irritated with his lack of progress, he headed for the boardwalk as he formulated an alternate plan of action. After the New Year, he would seek out his contact in Constantinople. Tuco always knew the latest rumors circulating in the region. It would give him a new starting point. Resigned to this strategy, he shrugged off his discontent and reaching the corner, he turned left. Then two women walking up ahead caught his attention.

"Josie, please listen to me," the shorter female pleaded.

That was Gemma's voice. Garrick quickened his pace.

"Its madness to keep wandering the streets," the little blonde continued. "Tis near dawn. We've been at this all night."

At what? Garrick wondered with alarm. It was nearly four in the morning. These women were courting danger if not disaster. At least Gemma should know better than to be out at this hour.

As he gained ground, he shoved his angry thoughts into order. Josie was about to get a good piece of his mind. She had no business putting herself in such danger.

"Someone in this place of unending misery must have an ounce of pity left for the dead," Josie said.

"Perhaps we could speak with Miss Nightingale," Gemma suggested.

"Or perhaps you could speak to me," Garrick growled, breaking in on their conversation.

In unison, the girls halted and spun around to face him.

"Lord above, what are you doing out at this hour," he thundered. He opened his mouth to say more but the tears on Josie's cheeks and the quivering of her chin cut him short.

"What is it? What's happened?"

"It's Mose," she sobbed. Then she just stared at him.

He gripped her shoulders and gave her a little shake. "What about the boy?"

"He's, he's dead." There was disbelief in her voice as if she refused to acknowledge her own words.

Mose dead? How could it be? "What happened?"

"It was the cholera," Gemma explained.

Garrick clenched his jaw and stifled a groan. It didn't seem possible. He'd just seen the boy a few days ago. How the poor lad must have suffered.

Josie clutched at his arm. "I couldn't save him," she said, a far off look in her eyes. Then her face crumpled into a collage of grief and tears.

Heartache crushed in on him. He slid his arms around her, and she sagged against him. As her weeping lessened, he eased her away from his chest. "Why are you roaming the streets at this hour?" he asked.

"Mose was underage and not officially in the Queen's service," she said. "And even though he served as loyally as any soldier, the Army wants to relegate him to a common grave reserved for prisoners and the unknown. I would see him treated more kindly, with a decent marker to bear witness to his existence."

Garrick was silent. He hated this war and the helpless way it made him feel, and he hated himself for forgetting that eventually caring always brought pain. Pain like the kind that clawed its way through him now. He remember Mose as he'd been on Christmas day, all happy and childlike and wrapped in holiday cheer; full of life and mischief and blindly in love with Nurse Posey. That was the most precious thing Garrick had shared with the lad— their mutual love for Josie.

Tugging a handkerchief from his pocket he gently blotted away Josie's tears. "I know of a small church and graveyard on the other side of town," he said. "The cemetery lies beneath a hardy stand of trees with a clear view of the Sea of Marmara."

Josie remained mute, her eyes downcast, Gemma at her side.

"The priest is a friend," he added, trying to reassure both women, "and an honorable man. He would make sure the grave was well tended and undisturbed."

Josie glanced up and her expression progressed from desolate to encouraged. "Oh yes, that sounds perfect."

"I'll make the arrangements," he offered and pressed the handkerchief into her hands.

"We need a coffin as well," she added, "and a grave marker. That's why I brought this." She held out a small ratty damask bag which he assumed held coinage.

Gently he pushed her hand aside.

"I said I'd see to it," he repeated. "Mose was special to me too. I had hoped...well never mind. Just stay with him, I'll come for you."

Josie clutched the purse to her chest like a six year old hugging a rag doll.

He studied the expression in her eyes and it scared him. It held trust and appreciation and other sentiments he had no business getting mixed up with.

"Again you have appeared just when I needed you the most," she said, "only this time you have rescued me from the jaws of despair rather than the jaws of wild dogs."

She leaned forward and brushed a kiss upon his cheek. Her quiet touch rocked his senses and in the peach tinted shadows of the pre-dawn, it was excruciating to know such a tragic reason had brought them even closer together.

Suddenly, worry and anguish rushed back over her visage, settling in her eyes. "We only have three hours before the Army carries out its decree," she said.

"I'll be there in time. I never break a promise, remember?"

A weak smile pulled at her lips, and he wished he could hold her until all her pain faded to a dark memory.

Instead, he forced himself from her side and strode away. But a part of him stayed behind, right there in her arms. The part of him that now belonged to her.

"I never break a promise," he muttered.

And he never had, except for the one he'd made to himself about never falling in love.

Should auld acquaintance be forgot,
And never brought to mind?
Should auld acquaintance be forgot,
And auld lang syne!

~Robert Burns

Chapter Fourteen

Tonight, darkness arrived without fanfare and alone with her grief, Josie stared out the distorted windowpane of her room. Bleak recollections of the recent funeral blurred her vision and all she saw was the sorrow she felt.

Two days ago, she and Garrick and Gemma had buried Mose. The kindly parish priest had officiated, and several children from the nearby orphanage had fashioned cloth flowers to put on Mose's grave. They promised to plant real flowers for him come spring.

The cemetery had seemed a gentle place, a sanctuary for grave markers reserved strictly for the young. Like Mose, many of the children buried there had been destroyed by the war. Other lost little souls had simply been casualties of life, a more enduring battlefield where on a daily basis they fought to survive. But now Mose's suffering was over. How she wished she had done more for the boy who had come to mean so much to her. Was he with his mother as he had hoped he would be? Or was the Earth his mother now and he slept safe in the palm of her hand? Thanks to Garrick, the boy had been spared the anonymity of a mass grave. Now for all eternity, Mose would lay in repose with his feet pointing away from Scutari and toward the England he loved.

She pressed her fingertips firmly against her

temples. Her eyes burned, and her head ached from crying. Every time she dared to devote two consecutive moments to thinking about Mose, she started to weep again. She hadn't been able to save him—just as she hadn't been able to save Phillip. And the similarity of their deaths had unfettered her old grief, allowing it to combine forces with her newly acquired sorrow.

With a shuddering sigh, she stepped away from the window and turned toward the lopsided chiffonier that stood slumped against the adjoining wall. Last year's well-worn calendar glared back at her from atop the tattered dresser scarf. In a few hours it would be 1855, but she didn't feel like celebrating. The old year had ended in abject misery. What if the new one was equally as unkind? How could she endure such grief and despair twelve months running?

She sank onto the small wooden stool crouched before the old dressing table. She must focus upon all the joy Mose had brought into her life. Weeping continually and willing the dead back to life did not honor them or set them free to enjoy the glory that surely awaited those who crossed over. Mose had always tried to make the best of any situation, he would expect her to do the same. Perhaps her night out with Garrick would give her the strength to do just that.

Grabbing her brush, she dragged it through her hair. The uneven bristles raked her thick mane, and a mixture of pleasure and pain prickled along her scalp. Pleasure and pain, the same emotions she felt when she thought of Garrick. She longed to see him tonight which of course was the pleasure. But she dreaded the times they spent apart, the times when he was in danger, the times when he might not come back or perhaps not want to. That was the pain. And although she certainly knew Garrick somewhat better by now, he remained a difficult man to fathom.

She wondered if he was a frequent visitor to the far side of town where the funeral had been held. Only someone trusted and respected could have received such a quick response and full cooperation from the locals. Even more curious was the fact that the orphans from the almshouse appeared at ease and familiar with his presence.

A smile found its way to her lips. Garrick was so unlike the men she knew in London. He definitely lived *in* the world rather than *for* the world or its opinion of him. After all a man looking for acceptance did not run about in attire more suited to Natty Bumpo. She touched the dried rose he'd given her then reached for the music box and set it to playing. What rapture she had found in his arms as they had danced on Christmas morn.

Swaying to the tinkling melody, immortalized in her mind as *their song*, she gathered her hair atop her head and arranged it first one way and then another. Between each creation, she canted and postured trying to decide what would please Garrick most. Tonight he must find her irresistible. Tonight she wanted him to satisfy the craving that possessed her whenever he was near. She felt so empty since losing Phillip. Garrick had the rare ability to fill that void where other men only seemed to intensify it.

She lowered her arms and her coiffeur collapse.

Don't forget, she reminded herself, it's just for tonight.

Garrick was an adventurer, a man on the prowl with the world for his jungle.

She didn't care. One night of enchantment would have to be enough.

Taming her hair into a knot at the nape of her neck she pinned it into place. The high lace collar of her claret-colored dress softened the severe style, and she hoped it was the perfect combination of modesty and enticement.

Skimming her hand upward along her thigh, she raised the hem of her skirt and peered down at the white silk petticoat that peeked out from beneath it. The scalloped lace edges, trimmed with pink satin rosebuds, infused her with a secret confidence and daring. What would Garrick think when he saw her clad only in lace and ribbons? Did they have the same expectations? It was what she wanted, what she needed, what she was willing to defy the house rules for. All she had to do was keep her emotions safely locked away and no one would get hurt. She would not look beyond tonight, nor expect to find love. Once before, she had sacrificed all because she believed in love. Now she sacrificed the prospect of love because she believed in a man. A beautiful magical man.

The skirt slipped from beneath her fingertips, and with a silky sigh, washed back over the petticoat. The sensuous drift of fabric was like a caress against her skin. Sparks crackled between the layers of material, and the tingling quickened her pulse and fueled her anticipation.

Anticipation...

It was a positively indecent feeling yet glorious...so glorious.

She touched a drop of precious perfume to her wrists and the cleavage of her dress. The scent swirled about encouraging her romantic notions.

She was ready and more than willing.

****

The carriage skidded around a corner and Garrick braced one foot against the fore-wall to keep his balance.

He felt light headed with anticipation and the very idea irritated him. Wrestling his smile into a more somber expression, he decided there was no need for Josie to see him grinning like the fool that he was.

Yes, he freely admitted it. He was a dolt, an imbecile, an idiot. Or at least he would be if he gave in to the one emotion he had successfully avoided all his life. He was falling in love or more precisely he had fallen. He should be scared to death. Instead, he was intoxicated with the reckless danger the feeling inspired. It was the same way he felt when he followed the soldiers onto the battlefield or when he managed to get an exclusive on the most sought after story in town. It made him feel alive.

The coach lurched sideways and rattled over an upheaval of frozen mud.

The roads in Scutari were a disaster. And because of the foul weather, Garrick had suggested Josie dine with him in his newly acquired and conveniently located accommodations rather than a local eatery. Was the inclement weather the reason she had accepted? He couldn't help but consider the other possibilities presented by the situation.

The carriage slid to a halt.

"Wait here," Garrick called to the driver as he stepped down.

With a determined stride he ascended the steps to the north door of the nurse's quarters. Then a feeling of trepidation snared him around the throat, and he slowed his pace. What in the name of all that was holy was he doing becoming involved with Josie? She would expect more from him emotionally than he was willing to give. He'd end up hurting her and that wasn't his intention.

Damn good intentions. The road to hell was paved with them and so was the road to his past. He wanted her, and if she granted him another opportunity to share more than idle conversation, he wouldn't turn her down. Not this time. Josie was old enough to know what she was doing. Their ride home on the mule had made that perfectly clear. But what transpired between them tonight had to be by her design. And if the worst came to pass and she so directed, he would relinquish his romantic expectations and treat her with platonic restraint.

He raised his hand to knock and the door swung open. Josie stood before him, a vision in smoky burgundy, and he realized he would never be content to enjoy her from afar.

"Josie." He breathed her name softly as if speaking it too loudly might make her disappear. "Tonight your beauty evokes such warmth it should be springtime all over the world."

A rosy blush infused her cheeks. "Thank you," she said with a playful smile. "Regardless of the temperature, it's a lovely evening." She drew her woolen cape closer and rested her hand upon his proffered arm.

Descending the steps, he tore his gaze from her face and glanced up at the sky. She was correct. The heavens were studded with stars and not one cloud obscured the velvety black canopy. Having eyes only for her, he hadn't even noticed.

"Quickly," she said, urging him to a faster pace. "We dare not tarry or Martha may discover us. Lately, she's been scolded for turning a blind eye and for being much too lenient a housemother."

As they reached the carriage, Josie lifted her skirt to accommodate the step, and he caught a flash of shapely, stocking-clad ankle swathed in white lace and pink rosebuds. His heart lurched. Get a grip, he chided. You've seen many a frilly undergarment on an assemblage of women.

He climbed in beside her and settled back against the cushions. She slipped her hand into the crook of his elbow, gave a shiver, and cuddled closer.

His pulse bounded with an irregular beat, and he felt uncomfortable as he glanced at her from the corner of his eye. A part of him wanted to gather her closer and a part of him wanted to run before it was too late. But too late for what?

"Back to our prior location," he instructed and tapped on the side of the coach.

The driver clucked the horses into motion.

Garrick cradled Josie's hands between his and stared out the window and wondered what the evening would bring. Would he be cast as lover or friend? It hardly mattered, he decided, either way he'd be damned by his own emotions.

The driver finally slowed the team to a slippery canter then reined them to a halt at their destination.

Alighting, he reached to assist Josie. Settling her at his side, he reluctantly slid his hand from her to hand the driver the usual fee plus a goodly tip. "I appreciate your braving the roads tonight" Garrick said. "Happy New Year."

The driver counted the money. "This will help to make it so. One thousand thank yous, my friend." The man grinned and coaxed the horses into a skittish walk.

Garrick stared at Josie's upturned face. In the cold night air, her perfume surrounded them like the fragrance of a summer breeze—frozen in time and place. They should go inside but he didn't want to move. He only wanted to cheriesh the image of her standing there in the moonlight.

The powdery scent of lavender and lilac teased and excited his senses, and for one breathless moment she gazed up at him, her lips parted slightly, her eyes lit by star-shine and innocence. Then she shivered again and his concern for her comfort broke the spell of his fascination.

With a smile he took her arm and escorted her into the once opulent building where he let a small apartment. Broken chandeliers hung from the ceiling at cockeyed angles, and red flocked paper peeled from the walls.

Josie glanced around in wonder. "Exactly what was the purpose of this establishment prior to the war?" she asked.

Perhaps he should have warned her. "It was a....house of pleasure. It could be worse," he added, at her expression of disbelief. "It's much better than my previous accommodations, and I've a friend who recently arrived only to be relegated to a room above the morgue. It's much quieter there, of course, but not nearly as well appointed."

Josie rolled her eyes at his attempt at humor, but she issued a good natured laugh and he met no resistance as he steered her up the curved staircase to the second floor. She did not shock easily. Another trait he appreciated.

Key in hand, he unlocked the door and ushered her inside. Immediately she gravitated toward the cheerful blaze in the hearth. He took her cloak and added another hefty log to the fire.

"Please," he nodded toward the velvet love seat, "do make yourself comfortable. I'll get us a drink." He heard the rustle of silk as she followed his suggestion.

Shrugging free of his coat, he grabbed two glasses and a liter of whiskey. He'd tried to locate a good bottle of wine but despite his claim that money was no object, he was unable to procure one for New Year's Eve. "All I could purchase was Ankara Gold," he handed her an empty glass and stood ready to pour. "Is it too coarse for you?"

She tilted her head as if she'd been issued a challenge. "Having never tried it, I couldn't say. It sounds most refreshing." She smiled demurely and daintily held out the crystal-ware as if she were attending a lady's tea. She was too damn trusting. He filled the glass to the brim.

Straightening to his full height, he eyed the empty space beside her on the settee. Then not wishing to crowd her physically or emotionally, he reached for a hard-backed chair and dragged it closer to the fire and Josie.

He sank onto the uncomfortable seat, filled his own glass, and set the bottle within reach on the hardwood floor. He studied Josie with a veiled gaze. She was beautiful, guileless, intelligent, and irresistible. She was everything he wanted in a woman and nothing he deserved. He was a renegade by trade and by nature, and he enjoyed too many bad habits that he didn't care to break.

To prove a point he downed a healthy draught of whiskey.

Amazingly, Josie did the same. Then her eyes grew wide and her cheeks flushed pink. She exhaled as though she breathed fire. "Water," she croaked through a sputtering cough.

He leapt to his feet, grabbed his canteen, and pressed the uncorked opening to her lips. She gulped down three mouthfuls of water, fell back against the settee, and fanned her face with her free hand. He reached for the glass she still held in the other.

"Mercy that was good," she declared.

He stifled a laugh and lowered his arm to his side. Josie never seemed to miss an opportunity to take a bite out of life, or in this case, a good swallow.

Leaving the water at her side, he resumed his place. He was captivated by the way she seemed filled with wonder as she experienced aspects of the world that to him seemed old and jaded. It refreshed his enthusiasm and gave him a second chance at living. He supposed he hadn't done very well with his first opportunity.

"Care for more?" he asked, now that she had caught her breath.

"Perhaps in a moment," she said with a smile.

Using the toe of her foot, she slid off one leather slipper and then the other. "I do like the way it makes me hot all over."

Her choice of words made him rather hot in a particular area.

Garrick ran his hand across the back of his neck, then leaned forward resting his forearms on his thigh. "Are you hungry?" His appetite was up, but not for food. He wanted to know the flavor of Josie's lips. He wanted to savor the silky taste of her in his mouth and on his tongue. He wanted to...

"It mightn't be a bad idea," she said. "I haven't eaten since breakfast."

Thankful for something to do, he set his glass aside, rose, and stepped to the window. Throwing open the sash, he retrieved a wooden box from the ledge and blew the snow from the little crate. After closing the shutters, he sauntered back to her side. "We've smoked roast pheasant, ships biscuits, apricot preserves, and of course more whiskey." Proudly, he arranged the food before her. "I bartered a remarkably good pen for the bird—I hope it was worth it."

Before he had a chance to hand her a fork, she plucked a tiny piece of meat from the platter and sampled it. He winced with pleasure as she pouted her lips and sucked on the tips of her fingers.

"It's beyond delicious," she reassured.

With a sigh, he retired to his chair across from her.

"A pheasant for a pen," she mused, then suddenly straightened. A spark of inquisitiveness brightened her eyes. "Exactly how does one go about making such a trade? Was it through the black market?" she asked, in hushed tones as if someone might be listening.

Garrick's eyes narrowed as he reached for a slice of the tempting meat. What an odd question, but then she was full of curiosity about so many things. "Yes, it was a black market of sorts," he admitted, popping the morsel into his mouth. "But it was an innocent transaction with no malice intended and no one's honor at stake. Normally such negotiations are dangerous. I wouldn't recommend it for the inexperienced."

"But how do you know where to find someone wishing to sell a pheasant?"

He smiled at her naiveté. "You find a go-between. It's his job to know what's for trade or sale in the area and at what price. He sets up the meeting and then you're on your own."

"And how do you recognize a go-between?"

"They each have their own territory," he explained as he refilled her glass. "Why so many questions?"

"I just wish to know whom to avoid," she said, quickly turning her attention to spreading jelly glaze upon a biscuit.

"You don't have to worry about that unless you plan to visit Pasha Johnny's in Constantinople or you care to dine with Rashi at the local cafe here."

As if mulling over this information, she took another tiny sip of Ankara Gold and for a silent moment that felt like an eternity, she stared at the flames in the hearth.

He studied her profile. Her nose was too pert to be considered perfect but he liked it that way. He liked everything about her. At least what he'd seen so far.

She glanced up, and he felt guilty as if he'd been caught peering through the key hole of her bedroom door.

"Thank you again for making the arrangements for Mose."

"You're welcome, Josie."

She smiled, but there were tears in her eyes and

to his surprise she downed the rest of the whiskey and set her empty glass aside. Josie was about to drown in her sorrows. He should have notice the wistfulness about her sooner. He should have recognized the haunted look that beset her eyes. This war, this earthly replication of hell, had finally gotten to her. She'd held out longer than most men he knew.

Absently she stroked the nappy velvet of the seat cushion at her side. Then her expression hardened and she balled her hands into fists. "I'm so angry," she declared, grinding out the words as if each syllable was grist for a mill made of her hatred.

"At whom?" he asked in surprise.

"At England and the Queen and heaven help me, even God."

She buried her face in her hands and wept, and for one terrible moment he didn't know what to do. She was obviously bewildered by the feelings that raged in her heart. He supposed they were opposite of everything she had been taught. Maybe all she needed was permission to damn the world.

He rose from his chair and sat down at her side.

"It's all right to be angry Josie," he said, as he gathered her into his arms. "Anger can be a great source of inspiration. You can get mad but it's wise to remember you can rarely get even."

She splayed her fingers against his chest and angled back from him, and he loosed her from his embrace.

"If you don't accept that," he cautioned, "the world will defeat you by letting you defeat yourself. Believe me I know."

"But you are not defeated, you charge about, pen in hand, bringing to light one controversial issue after another. You turn crusader at the least provocation."

He frowned and leaned forward to retrieve the

glass from where he'd placed it upon the floor. "Oh I'm quite good at championing other peoples' causes, it was my own legacy that confounded me and drove me near to ruin."

"Whatever do you mean?" she asked and seemed sincere in wanting to know.

"I wasted my youth," he explained, "trying to get even with God and Fate and the world in general. And for some reason, I thought that required living hard and dangerously. I've seen it all and done it all. I've been to the four corners of the world, yet I'm a stranger to any place called home." He paused and studied her face. "I've spent too many years tearing things down rather than building them up. There's nothing permanent in my life, there never has been except Shamus, and he's getting old. Someday he'll be gone too."

"But what of your parents?" she asked.

A shiver snaked through him. He hadn't planned on revealing the most anguished chapters of his life. Josie seemed to have enough painful memories of her own to deal with. On the other hand, it might do them both good to share.

"I never knew my father," he began, "and my mother died when I was ten." He twisted the whiskey glass round and round and stared down into it. The bright little circle of liquid gold stared back at him, unblinking, like the eye of the tiger that hunted him still. "I killed the man who caused my mother's death. I committed an act that was at the same time horrendous and ineffectual. I had no choice yet it served no purpose. And I never got even, I only got older. Don't let that happen to you."

He snagged the neck of the whiskey bottle and refilled both their glasses. Other than Shamus, Josie was the first person to whom he'd ever entrusted this much of his *life's story*. He wondered what type of review his recital might elicit.

"Tell me more," she gently urged. "If you want to."

Oddly enough he felt compelled to convey to her the part of his past that controlled his present and loomed ahead in his future. Perhaps if he put a name to the demon by expressing his feelings in words he could conquer the beast. And if he planned to have a future with Josie, she deserved to know his past.

"My Father left before I was born," he said, daring to take her up on her offer to listen. "My Mother never said an unkind word about him, and even as a child I knew she still loved him and missed him and mourned the fact that he had run off with someone else. Someone younger, to feed his ego. Someone richer, to feed his gambling ways."

"To keep us from starving my Mother worked at the local bakery. Up before the sun, coming home after dark, her arms aching from kneading bread dough for pastries we couldn't afford to buy, her back tired from unloading bags of flour and sugar, her feet sore from standing all day and walking to and from work. It was a hard life. Yet she always made time for me and tried to show me that what counted in life was what was in our hearts not what was in our bank account."

He stopped to catch his breath. Josie gave him a hint of a smile and nodded her head encouragingly. He supposed he might as well go on. There was little point now in turning back.

"We lived in a rough neighborhood, of course being just a lad I didn't realize it at the time. One night a man broke in to rob us. What a laugh. He was dressed better then we were. Angry for having chosen so unwisely, the blackguard rampaged around the room breaking what little we did own. He drew a pistol and aimed it at the little china teapot that sat upon the mantle. The porcelain keepsake was chipped and it leaked, but it was the only material thing my mother truly treasured. My Father had given it to her as a wedding present. She pushed the man aside, and he dropped the pistol.

"Enraged at her interference, the bastard struck her a round-house blow that caught my Mother on the jaw. She tumbled to the floor in what seemed like slow motion. I'll never forget that image. Her hair fluttered gracefully about her face and shoulders as it did when we walked in the park on a breezy day, and her eyes were wide as if I had just surprised her with one of my childish poems. Then her hands grasped at empty air and I reached out to catch her but she was too far away. As she hit the floor, her head struck the flagstone hearth with a sickening thud.

"Looming over her, the big man kicked her and drew back his arm to strike her again. My frantic gaze fell upon the pistol half-hidden beneath a chair. I ran forward and grabbed up the weapon. It was cold and heavy and made me feel unafraid. Struggling to cock back the hammer, I pointed the weapon at the man and pulled the trigger.

"Fire belched from the muzzle, the flash of light so bright it momentarily blinded me, and the smoke that filled the air stung my eyes and burned my throat. I felt the thundering blast reverberate through the room, and I heard the sound of the man's body as it crashed to the floor. The burglar laid face-up and deathly still. A stain spread out around his head like a dark halo. It grew larger and larger never seeming to stop.

"I dropped the pistol and ran to my Mother's side. She smiled weakly, her cheeks as white as her nightgown. *"My brave little soldier,"* she whispered and touched my arm. *"Someday I pray you will find your Lady Gallant."* With a fragile sigh she closed her eyes, never to open them again. I held her hand until her fingers turned cold."

He heard Josie sob but he didn't look up. He had to finish, had to explain. "We used to play this game you see. She was the queen, and I was the brave knight come to save her from the dark tower or from a dastardly dragon. Then as a reward, she would grant me the hand of the fairest maiden in the land, the hand of my lady gallant. But I didn't save her that day and until now—there have been no fair maidens in my life."

He fell silent and gathered enough courage to gaze at Josie's face. Her look showed neither pity nor fear. And she didn't turn away. Then an expression of enlightenment softened her features.

She reached out and touched his cheek. "After that you were an orphan," she said. "That's why you knew the priest and the children at the almshouse. You've visited them before haven't you?"

"I've run across them a time or two," he admitted, as he captured Josie's hand and held it in his. "Usually when I had a shilling to spare."

"And you looked after Mose because he was all alone too."

Pain and regret knotted in the pit of Garrick's stomach. Mose's death had caught him totally off guard. Too late he had realized how fond he'd become of the boy. He had thought to sponsor Mose the way Shamus had found and sponsored him, passing on the torch as it were. He had dropped his defenses and defied the usual logic that governed his life. And what had it earned him? Nothing but sorrow. He stared at Josie. If he let down his guard where she was concerned, it would cost him even more. Maybe too much.

"Mose was a good lad," he said.

"But he never got to go home," she pointed out, her expression turning even more wistful.

"I'd say he was home. You saw to that, Josie.

You gave him love and encouragement—the likes of which he'd never known before. This wretched place was more a home to him than anywhere else. England failed him, Josie, not you."

She lightly brushed her lips upon his cheek, then his mouth, and he reached for her with a rough passion that flooded through him unchecked. The tart taste of liquor blended with the sweetness of her skin, and he lost himself in an embrace that made him sweat with urgency. A log shifted in the fireplace, breaking the silence, and he forced himself away from the haven of her arms to gaze into her eyes. Her trusting brown eyes, eyes that sparkled with passion.

"Josie," he whispered, and held her at arm's length, "sometimes the turmoil in our lives can distort our perception of what is right and—."

"I don't care anymore what's right or wrong," she interrupted. "I just know I want to feel something other than sorrow." She struggled to draw closer to him. "Please," she whispered, "just for tonight."

Garrick needed Josie with a passion he had never known before, but that did not make it right. He had to give her every chance to change her mind.

"Its not always wise to live just for the moment."

"I'm not," she insisted. "Come tomorrow, this night will be a part of me that will endure forever. Give me one bright and noble moment to remember amongst all these days and months of darkness."

She framed his face with her hands and traced the soft pads of her thumbs across his cheeks. He relaxed and she leaned closer, burning a lingering kiss on his mouth. Then she slid her arms up around his neck and held him, simply and gently. A long sigh escaped him. When was the last time he had felt so free of anguished and dire memory? Josie transformed his mere existence into effervescence, and she made his world a softer place with three dimensions and future visions.

She shifted closer, and the lace edging of her dress tickled his neck. He breathed in the scent of her and lost himself to the realization that she was really there, in his arms. Easing her head to one side, he nuzzled and nipped at the delicate spot beneath her right ear. As she melted in his embrace, he could taste the wanting on her.

In one more moment, he would be beyond caring about honor and protocol, but he refused to be responsible for anyone's heart. With great effort, he drew back from her one last time.

"Josie," he groaned. "You've just lost someone very special, someone you had grown to love and it's the Holiday Season. You're lonely and homesick. Are you sure it's the real you who wants to be with me tonight and not the overwhelmed little girl who came to Turkey to save the world?"

Her cheeks were flushed, and her chest rose and fell too quickly. "I'm sure, and Mose's death only serves to remind me how precious and short life can be."

He took a deep breath and glanced away. "You're so young." The words came out in a sad voice that he hardly recognized as his own.

"I had a lover once if that is your concern."

His gaze darted back to her face. So she wasn't a virgin after all. Was he jealous or relieved? The image of another man touching Josie twisted through his gut, and a primitive instinct of rivalry and possessiveness threatened to rule his logic. He was jealous.

"We were to marry," she said, with a wistful little smile as she took her turn at revealing the past. "We were so in love. Phillip was a physician you see, and he supported me in my endeavors to become a nurse. And against everyone's advice, the two of us labored to bring medicine to the backstreets of London—where it was needed most. Rather than worry about acquiring an ostentatious surgery, Phillip had only a small laboratory where he worked tirelessly trying to find cures for everything from anthrax to the zymotic diseases. But he worked too hard, stayed up too late, and ate too little and when the cholera struck him down, he had no defenses to save himself. And just like Mose, I could not save him either." Her words tapered off into silence and a far away look clouded her expression.

So, it was not only her family who had betrayed her but life itself. She looked so abandoned and forlorn. What could he possibly do to reverse the effects of such sorrow? He knew what a burden it was to carry nightmarish images around in one's mind. And although it was not a burden you could simply put down, it was a burden whose weight you could share.

"I'll make you forget the pain," he said gruffly, "and we can make new memories."

She glanced up and a glimmer of happiness brightened her expression, but regret seemed to hover nearby as well.

"Not memories to replace what you had with...Phillip," he reassured, "new ones to stand along side those."

As if she had waited a lifetime to hear such words, Josie gave a little cry of joy—then all but threw herself into his arms. Her skin was hot from the fire in the hearth and the fire that he felt mounting in her body. He drew her close and boldly explored her mouth with his tongue. Dreams of possessing the rest of her as fully drifted through his mind. What had he done to merit this moment? He dare not even ask.

Releasing her, he shrugged free of his wool

jacket and vest. She reached to loosen his cravat.

Taken off guard by her assistance, he sat motionless and studied her face. Even with her hair constrained into an unbecoming bun, she was beautiful. And despite what she had just told him, he still saw innocence in her. It was not a quality related to her enlightenment of men or to her scholastic knowledge. It was just a part of her nature and the way she perceived the world. And for all her bravado, he thought she was a bit nervous and unsure of herself. Her hands shook as she released the last button on his shirt.

Cool air seeped beneath his clothes and licked at his bare skin, and he yearned to discover her beauty still hidden from view. As if reading his mind, Josie shifted her hands to the neck of her dress, and in mind melting fascination, he watched her liberate first one pearly button from the fragile loops of thread, then another and another.

Inch by inch, her smooth white skin was revealed, taunting him as the neckline of her dress grew deeper and wider. White lace and a pink rosebud peeked out from beneath the dark burgundy fabric, and his breath caught in his throat.

At the sound, she hesitated.

Brushing her hands aside, he caught the open bodice and smoothed it back and down over her shoulders. Freeing her arms from the sleeves, the material fell softly to her waist.

She wore no corset only a camisole, and the curve of her firm breasts threatened to spill up and over the sleek fabric. Dazzled by the riotous accumulation of lace, roses, and ribbons, his gaze drifted lazily over her form, the combination of his prim image of Josie and the erotic under-things she wore exploded into a conflict of sensations— unexpected and delightfully unsettling.

"You're quite bold in your choice of fashion," he

pointed out with a smile, as he envied the silk that caressed her in places he longed to touch.

Doubt shadowed her expression. "Does it leave something to be desired?"

"Oh yes, I dare say it does."

"What?" she demanded petulantly.

"Only you," he reassured.

A naughty smile was her only reply. The expression didn't appear to be practiced or contrived, and he ached a little more with wanting her.

"You're so beautiful."

She glanced down almost as if embarrassed or unbelieving. He tipped up her chin, forcing her gaze to meet and mingle with his. "Take off the rest of your dress," he whispered.

Like a cat uncurling from a sweet dream, she rose to stand before him. Then she slipped her thumbs under the fabric that hung gathered about her hips and with a slight bit of encouragement, the quilted taffeta slid downward over the wonderful curve of her bottom.

The fabric billowed to the floor and pooled around her ankles. The glow of the fire blurred the edges of her silhouette. To Garrick she seemed a wingless angel in white camisole and petticoats. She reached up to unbind her hair, and her gleaming tresses, dark as mahogany, tumbled forward—giving sharp contrast to her cream colored shoulders. He stared up at her in wonder, and for the first time in his life, he felt like heaven might be within his reach.

Loosening the ribbon tie at her waist, she sent her silk petticoat the way of her dress and with a perfumed whisper it descended, leaving her clad only in the deliciously thin camisole and the sweetest most delicately embroidered pantaloons he'd ever laid eyes on.

With each layer of clothing, she abandoned,

Josie seemed more carefree and natural. And like a child who knew no shame, she stood before him unabashed.

He ran his hand upward along her thigh. With a smile, she held out her hands. She looked good enough to eat, and he could wait no longer for a hardy sampling. Gaining his feet, he reached for her, and without reserve, she filled his embrace—conforming to the hard plains of his body.

Roughly, he sought her mouth, seeking to make her his own, wanting to leave a mark on her that proclaimed her his custody. She was wet and inviting and easing his tongue between welcoming lips, he forced a more intimate union between them.

Emotions much deeper than the normal Saturday night lust enlivened him. He swept Josie up into his arms, carried her to the bedroom, and nested her into the downy softness beneath the canopy of the bed.

Quickly shedding the remainder of his clothing, he slid into bed beside her, seeking the comfort and passion he knew awaited. The counterpane, in counter point, was chilling as a winter wind. He gasped at the shock of cold then groaned with pleasure as Josie pressed her body against the full length of him.

Face to face they studied one another. She reached up and stroked his cheek as if in wonder, as if she too questioned the reality of the moment. Capturing a handful of her hair at the nape of her neck, he angled her head back and memorized the shape of her mouth, the curve of her cheek, the arch of her brow. She gazed back at him, anticipation shimmering in her eyes.

He slipped his hand beneath the gossamer fabric of her under garments. She unbuttoned her camisole as he reached lower, and the smooth rounded cheeks of her bottom flexed against his palms. He wanted to tear the remaining clothes from her body and bury himself inside of her. But that would be like gulping a fine wine. On this momentous night he would not be rushed, not even by his own needs.

Her camisole slipped sideways, exposing rosy nipples that seemed to beg for his attention. He kissed her lips then scooted lower. She riffled her fingers through his hair and cradled his head against the soft mound and hard peak of one breast. He razed his tongue across the tempting center. The bud was a currant berry waiting to be plucked and savored, and taking more of her into his mouth, he feasted upon her.

Josie moaned and arched against him. Encouraged by her reactions, he tugged open the tie at her waist and pushed the pantaloons down over her hips. With a frantic little wiggle she kicked free of the last bastion of thin fabric that separated their naked bodies.

Still captivated by the taste of her breast, he teased his fingers lower through silky curls and a more intimate sanctuary. Then giving in to the heat of his ardor, he raked his bare chest upward to face her once more. But his hand never left the smoothness between her thighs, and a dewy softness met his touch as he parted her with his fingers.

He kissed a path to her ear. "Tell me what drives you to exquisite madness, Josie," he coaxed as he delved deeper, "and I promise to assure your dementia."

She cried out and pressed closer, and he quickened the stroke. She was warm as fresh cream, and he was a cat died and gone to heaven.

"Garrick," she panted, "you are driving me dangerously near to the edge of reason." She eased onto her back and urged him to cover her body with his. "I want to feel you inside of me."

Her abandon revived his youthful exuberance.

He felt nineteen again and ready to conquer the world. Following her invitation, he cloaked her body with his. Her thighs parted in a welcoming embrace and in one slow continuous motion he took her. A whimper escaped her lips, but the demanding pressure of her hands on his buttocks inspired him onward and without hesitation, he claimed her fully.

Sheltered by darkness, they surrendered to one another. Josie wrapped those lovely long legs around him, and his imaginings became real. She matched his movements urgently and desperately, and his body was assaulted by an ecstasy he wished could last forever. The beauty of the moment matched the beauty of the woman who clung to him with such need—such desire. He held her fiercely as if she were an illusion that might disappear, and together they traveled through a personal time and space made only of this passion, this oneness.

Josie's frantic breathing transformed to lusty moans, and he drowned himself in the waves of delight that twisted through her body. Surrounded by the pulsing rhythm of her release, he spilled himself into her and ached at the realization of a dream as well as the fulfillment of their physical union. He had crossed a barrier that left no turning back and he was glad.

Spent and happy, they clung to one another and lights flashed and the bed shook. Saints above, he considered himself an ardent lover but this had never happened before. Then he heard shouts of "Happy New Year". It was midnight, and in celebration, the revelers were shooting off ammunition rockets. The bright wishes of a new year heralded by weapons of war. 'Twas an interesting use of mines and canisters but he liked his way of celebrating better.

He nuzzled Josie's neck and teased her with the remaining glory of his erection. "Happy New Year," he whispered in her ear. Rising up on his elbows, he gazed into her face and grinned. Her eyes were sleepy, and her cheeks were rosy.

"Perhaps it will be after all," she murmured.

Men love in haste,
But detest at leisure.

~Lord Byron

Chapter Fifteen

It was dawn, but the golden glow that peeked over the horizon did nothing to brighten Danford's foul mood, nor did it illuminate the general darkness of his character. He'd wasted half the night watching the building across the street and all the while his loathing had simmered, growing more potent and deadly. Uttering a growl, he flicked the smoldering cigar butt to the ground and crushed it beneath the toe of his boot.

Turning up the collar of his greatcoat, he slapped his gloved hands against the upper part of his body to try and generate some heat. No doubt the two of *them* were warm enough, or more likely hot and sweaty. Were they still abed entwined in one another's arms? What did she see in him? Nurse Posey had been up there for hours spreading her legs for a penniless war correspondent, a man who dressed like a barbarian, a man who couldn't offer her anything other than a good screwing. If indeed, Allen was proficient at that.

He could have given her the same and more. He could have satisfied her carnal needs and fulfilled all her worldly cravings and obsessions. Then again, perhaps it was for the best. The woman had a strange effect on him. After she had refused his Holiday invitation, he hadn't even bothered to go to Greece. And he'd felt oddly sad and dejected. She was one of the few good and decent persons he'd run across in his sordid life, and one of the few women who were bold enough to point out his short comings and expect more of him. He was definitely better off without her. Still it rankled that the Newsboy had managed to get his hands on that sweet-stuff and he had failed.

Now, now, Danford reminded himself, soon women by the score would be begging for his attention. Once he had possession of the Idol's Eye, the world would be his to command.

Yes, all in good time. There was really no hurry. He clasped his gloved hands behind his back and straddled his legs in a defiant stance. If there was one thing he had acquired over the years, it was patience—infinite patience and faith in Man's willingness to be corrupted. He had not, however, acquired a tolerance for those who interfered in his dealings, business or otherwise, and that brought things 'round full circle to the meddling Mr. Allen.

Danford needed a few weeks without anyone breathing down his neck, but lately the British Government was putting pressure on the Turkish authorities to expose the undercover operations running rampant in the area. No doubt the renewed fervor had been precipitated by Mr. Allen's controversial news articles. Damn it all, the man was becoming insufferably inconvenient. He needed tending. Then again, pawns should be used to their fullest extent before they were sacrificed for the good of the game.

He glanced at the clock tower. It was nearly 6:00 a.m. Nurse Posey should soon be on her way to hospital. What was keeping them? One more buck and tussle?

His gaze snapped to attention as he caught sight of the couple emerging from the building. He drew back into the morning shadows and watched as the Newsboy adjusted the hood of Nurse Posey's cape.

The reporter snuggled the wool at her neck and drew her forward to kiss her. She yielded willingly and only the noisy approach of an araba interrupted their nauseating display of groping.

Garrick hailed the vehicle and sent Nurse Posey on her way. Then he struck out on foot in the opposite direction.

Hot in pursuit, Danford kept to Garrick's heels. As the journey took them across the Bosphorus his pleasure doubled. It appeared the Newsboy's destination was Constantinople. Did that mean the strategy he'd concocted was being set into motion even more quickly than anticipated?

****

Sunlight brightened the far shore as Garrick headed for Pasha Johnny's. At night, the infamous bar and eatery boasted the wildest women, the most potent liquor, and the best source of underground gossip and hearsay in Turkey. Overflowing with local color and information, the controversial late night watering hole was worth a king's ransom to a newspaper man.

As he strode through the front door, his gaze swept the now empty room, and his stomach rebelled at the strong smell of garlic. At times the pungent odor seemed to permeate the entire north side of town. Crossing to the bar, he found Johnny himself behind the long polished expanse of mahogany.

"Good day, Johnny," Garrick began.

"Is it?" The man answered, noncommittal as usual. Johnny was the manager and muscle behind the establishment. But he wasn't the money or the brains. That was Tuco's domain.

"Tell your boss that I'd like to buy him a drink," Garrick offered amiably.

"Mr. Tuco, he ain't up yet."

"I don't believe it," Garrick jibed. "He's too much the adventurer and mercenary to sleep-in. He'd be

216

afraid something important might happen without him."

A dark-skinned little man materialized at Garrick's side. "You know me too well," Tuco said. His broad smile was conspiratorial, and his limpid brown eyes were alert but friendly. Besides owning Pasha Johnny's, Tuco found delight in keeping the local hearsay bubbling and brewing. He was also the most notorious go-between in the lawless territory west of Serasker Pasha Tower.

"I will have my usual," Tuco said, to Johnny.

"Make it a coffee for me," Garrick put in. That was the first time he'd ever turned down hair-of-the-dog. He shrugged. It was probably best to keep a clear head.

The bartender delivered their drinks then at Tuco's nod, the man discretely wandered off.

"Anything new regarding who's running the show around here?" Garrick asked.

"It is written on this paper," Tuco said, as he slid a scrap of parchment across the bar to Garrick. "Remember the information did not pass my lips."

Garrick's eyes widened as he read the names. "Is your source reliable?"

"It is hard to say."

"Then it is hard to pay," Garrick negotiated.

"Verify the information first," Tuco offered. "I trust you."

"A generous offer," Garrick said.

"And a safe one. I know where you live." The little man chuckled. "Besides, the fee is double if not paid at time of services rendered."

Tuco was a scoundrel, but an open-faced one.

"Your record at the track is good enough for me," Garrick said. "I'll pay now." He laid down the usual fee on top of the bar.

Tuco glided his palm across the coins, and they disappeared as if by sleight of hand.

They talked a few more moments in general terms regarding general topics then the Turk favored him with a stilted bow indicating their conference was at an end.

Garrick returned the gesture of respect, gulped down the last of the dark Turkish coffee, and took his leave.

Excitement wound through him like a living entity. If this information proved true, he had an exclusive that would set Parliament on its ear. He'd best send a telegram to Shamus and have him confirm the details in London. Meanwhile he'd investigate the two people here who were supposedly involved.

As he walked, a chill crept across his shoulders. He halted and turned around. Was he being followed? The only occupants on the otherwise deserted street were a three-legged dog and an old lady toting a laundry basket. Everything appeared normal and above suspicion, but he'd been around long enough to trust his gut instinct rather than his eyes. In Turkey, there were dangers greater than enemy bullets.

Shaking off the ominous feeling, he boarded a transport bound for Scutari. Why was he so edgy? He should have gotten a real drink at Pasha Johnny's, but he'd promised himself to cut down on the hard liquor. Besides, after last night, a drink would probably put him under.

Visions of Josie elbowed aside his concerns, and he smiled. It was a miracle he had enough energy left for anything besides twelve hours of sleep. It had taken all his will power to leave Josie this morning. If only they could run away together and forget the grim nightmare that surrounded them. But regardless of what he felt or wanted, he knew nothing could stop the reality of the war. At least not for longer than one night at a time.

As the little passenger barge made port, a sobering question commanded all his attention. Was the war the only reason that he and Josie were together? Was it only the confusion of the times that made them seek comfort and shelter in one another's arms? What would happen when the war was over? Would Josie's need for him fade away with the echo of the last rifle shot? No it couldn't be. What had happened between them last night was more than just the desperate uniting of two wounded souls trying to survive. At least he thought it had been.

He ran his tongue across his lips and tried to find a lingering taste of her. He couldn't and was almost glad. He had no business wanting to keep a part of her, no business thinking they could belong to one another. It seemed clear that she expected no strings attached to their relationship. *Just for tonight.* That's what she'd said. But he couldn't forget the feel of her body beneath his. He couldn't erase from his mind how it felt to be inside of her, and how her shuddering climax had delivered him to a world he yearned to visit again.

Leaving the dock he headed for the telegraph office. As he walked, erotic images of Josie blurred through his mind. Never in his life had he been so consumed by passion. He chuckled. Never in his life had he been so surprised by a proper lady's choice in undergarments. The sight of her so clad had been a sensual surprise. Everything about her had been soft and yielding and wonderful. And Josie approached sex like she approached everything else, wholeheartedly. The second time they had made love she had stormed his body and taken him, and he had been a willing captive unable to resist her. Yet at the same time, she had seemed in wonder of her own sexual appetite. Had he aroused new heights of pleasure and desire in her? If so, it had been a selfish labor on his part. Exciting Josie excited him.

He recalled their parting kiss. She had seemed reluctant to leave this morning and despite what she said about no attachments, he wondered if she didn't feel differently in her heart of hearts. That possibility sharpened his senses, and he realized he was leaping off a cliff of undetermined height. If he wasn't careful, he could break his neck falling in love. Maybe he'd get over the feeling. It probably wouldn't take more than a lifetime or two.

Annoyed by such maudlin feelings, Garrick shoved open the door to the shack that housed the telegraph equipment. The operator jerked his head up in surprise. Then disinterest reclaimed him and the man wearily returned his gaze to the papers that littered his desk.

Garrick scooped up a form from the little wooden tray which sat beside the waiting blotter, pen, and ink well. He paused to consider the content of his missive. It must express urgency, yet remain cryptic, for not even the telegraph operator could be allowed to know this information. Garrick wasn't sure whom to trust, and he didn't want an innocent bystander getting involved in the deadly game that might be unfolding.

He began to write but halfway through he hesitated. Was it just a coincidence that this significant information had shown up on the heels of his editorial about the missing supplies? It seemed a bit fortuitous. He shrugged and continued. Whatever the probabilities, he could hardly afford to ignore the tip.

Signing his name, Garrick handed the completed slip to the bland-faced soldier behind the counter. The fellow remained impassive as he read what was to be transmitted, and satisfied that the confidential meaning of his note remained intact, Garrick sat down to await the reply. Knowing it could take hours, he stretched out his legs and crossed them at the ankle. Perhaps he could catch forty winks. Settling his fur hat low on his brow, he laced his fingers together over his abdomen and closed his eyes. He sure hadn't gotten any sleep last night. A delightful sacrifice—one he would willingly make again.

****

"Mr. Allen. Your reply is ready. Mr. Allen?"

With a growl of irritation, Garrick dragged himself back to consciousness. "I'm awake, man. Stop jostling me." He opened his eyes, sat up, and adjusted his hat. Finally recalling where he was he reached for the written response. "Thanks," he mumbled and focused his attention upon the missive.

Nothing at first glance to report/will keep eye on wig/suggest you follow up at your end without delay/watch your backside/have grown accustomed to you the way you are, i.e., without any new bullet holes or saber wounds/ Shamus.

Garrick smiled. Shamus didn't usually waste so many words on sentiment. He must be mellowing with age. Will keep eye on the wig, meant Shamus would be watching the Minister of Parliament supposedly involved. Unfortunately, the rest of the message meant an immediate trip to the frontlines to tract down the officers supposedly in charge of running things over there.

What time was it? He stood and checked his watch. It was near three thirty in the afternoon. With any luck, he could still catch the last military steamer bound today for Balaclava.

Feeling guilty for having snapped at the telegraph operator, Garrick rummaged in his pockets for a coin but found none. He'd given Tuco the last of his money and was insolvent until his next stipend came through from *The Times*. Laying a fresh cigar on the counter he strode toward the door.

"Thanks, friend," he called out. "Have a smoke on me."

His hat jammed more securely into place, Garrick turned into the wind and hurried toward the docks. In the distance the Barracks Hospital loomed into sight, and its dark silhouette was drawn in sharp contrast to the snow covered hills behind it. He turned in that direction and his pulse quickened. Then convincing himself there wasn't time to stop and say good-bye, he turned away. The brooding image of the hospital dissolved, but it was harder to rid his mind of the vision of Josie.

Deciding to at least send her a note, he reached for his journal. This way was best. He would remember her as she had looked this morning, all contented and dreamy-eyed after their night of loving. Besides, he didn't know if he had the strength to leave her twice in one day.

He wrote as he walked and reaching dockside, engaged a young lad to deliver the note. As the boy stood waiting for recompense, he recalled he had no coins. Poor little pip, he must give him some sort of remuneration. Garrick reached for a cheroot then dropped his arm to his side. He supposed the children here were led into temptation often enough without his help. The little boy stood staring at the brass buttons on the front of his fringed leather coat. Garrick twisted loose the one cast like the head of a buffalo and handed it to the boy. The lad's wide-eyed smile assured him it was acceptable payment.

Not looking back, Garrick hurried to the gangplank and leaped aboard the last British Army steamer as it made ready to heave to.

****

"Good riddance," Danford said, as he watched the ship head for the open water of the Black Sea. The inspired rumor he had fed Tuco had found its intended home.

With a smirk, Danford ambled toward the boy to whom Garrick had given a paper. Purposely colliding with the lad, Danford knocked him down then with feigned concern hauled him back to his feet. "Careful, sonny. Are you hurt? I believe you've dropped something." He snatched the letter from the gravel path and noted the intended recipient.

"May I have it back please, sir?" the boy asked. "I'm to deliver it straight away."

"Yes I saw you with Mr. Allen," Danford acknowledged. "I know him personally and Nurse Posey as well. In fact I'm on my way to see her now. Why don't I deliver this for you? It would save you the bother."

The boy was silent as he cast a longing glance at the children playing nearby.

"I'm sure you've more amusing things to attend to and there's a shilling in it for you." Danford slipped the shiny coin from his pocket and held it up for display.

Fortunately for Danford, money turned a blind eye to age as it beguiled, and without further hesitation the child held out his hand. He deposited the promised silver in the tiny palm but oddly enough, the bounty didn't bring a smile to the little boy's face.

As the lad scurried away, Danford turned his back to the street and a rush of contentment streaked through him. Everything was falling into place quite nicely.

The Newsboy was out of town, Nurse Posey was busy saving the world, and soon he would take possession of the opium he'd been promised. Recently recovered from the bottom of the sea, this British commodity would be appropriate trade for the Russian artifacts being transported from Odessa. These antiquities, fashioned during the reign of Catherine the Great, were magnificent, yet they paled in comparison to the final prize. The ultimate treasure. His crowning achievement. Unfortunately, these transactions would take several days— perhaps weeks. And in the mean time, he must find amusement where he could. With a smile, he glanced at the note in his hand.

My dearest Josie,

Please forgive me for not coming in person to say good-bye. I've stumbled upon information which requires my unmediated attention at the frontlines. Keep thee safe my most beautiful lady and trust no one. Danger is afoot in all quarters. I will contact you immediately upon my return.

Your most humble servant and admirer,

Garrick

Danford shook his head. This missive would never do. He mangled the letter and cast it to the ground. The muddy water soaked into the parchment, and the poetic words of warning blurred and ran together.

The greater part of our happiness or misery depends upon our disposition and not upon our circumstances.

~Martha Washington

Chapter Sixteen

"Nurse Posey, Nurse Posey."

Startled by the unexpected sound, Josie flinched then exhaled a long slow breath. She had yet to grow accustomed to the voice of her new orderly. Setting aside her pen and ledger, she shifted in her chair and willed a smile to her lips. "Yes, Pete."

The freckle-faced lad snatched the woolen cap from his head, and the thatch of red hair captured beneath it sprang to life and stood on end. "Here's a note," he said and held out a folded piece of paper. "I ain't sure who it's for."

"Thank you," she said and reached for the missive.

"You're most welcome, ma'am. And I'm hopin' its good news."

He jammed his hat crookedly back into place and turned away to answer a summons from a patient.

Josie stared after Pete, but the image of Mose filled her mind's eye. In unguarded moments, anguished thoughts of the boy still fed the loneliness she felt for him. Then as memories of last night took precedence, the pain began to ease, her shoulders relaxed, and the smile on her lips reappeared without too much assistance.

What was Garrick doing right now? Absently she toyed with the paper in her hands. Then she noticed the letter she held was marked to her attention. Easing it open she read the contents, and her hands began to shake.

Dear Nurse Posey,
Thank you for a delightfully amusing evening. It was just the playful distraction I needed before returning to the frontlines. In my absence look to Danford for support. I've discovered he is not such a bad chap after all.
Expect me when you see me,
G. Allen

A delightfully amusing evening? Her cheeks burned and she clenched her jaw. A playful distraction? The bottom dropped out of her stomach, and a strangled breathless feeling crushed in on her chest.

The man was a journalist. Was that the best he could do to express the enchantment they had found in one another's arms? Not believing her eyes, she reread the note.

Hot anger twisted through her belly, and she curled her toes inside her shoes. Would she never learn? Like an enamored schoolgirl, she had spent the morning recalling the ecstasy they had shared and all the while Garrick was making plans to take his leave. She crushed the note into a ball then picked it open, and as if hoping the act of repetition would somehow change the words, she read it one more time.

It was heartless. He was heartless. Tears burned in her eyes, and her vision blurred. Oh bother, she'd be damned if she'd cry over him. She blinked several times and swiped the back of her hand across her cheeks. One determined tear escaped and fell upon the note. It ran down the length of the handwritten missive and before it reached the bottom of the crumpled paper, it turned into nothingness. Were Garrick's feelings for her just as fleeting and insubstantial?

This morning the emotion reflected in his eyes had told a different story. She had witnessed joy kindled by their night together and regret stirred by their parting. The passion between them had been fueled by a full night of loving. It was hard to believe that even in the midst of a Turkish winter such lusty tumult could have cooled so quickly. She folded and unfolded the paper. Something was wrong. Garrick would not be so uncaring.

"Pete," she said, "may I see you a moment?"

"Yes, ma'am," he replied and hurried to her side.

"What did the person look like who gave you this note?"

"Nobody give it to me. It be tacked to the door with a carpenter's nail."

"I see. So you've no idea who left it there."

"No ma'am. Did I do something wrong?"

"Of course not, Pete. You did just fine. Don't concern yourself. Go back to whatever it was you were doing."

"I don't rightly remember what that was. But I know we need more water. I'll go and fetch some."

"That's a good idea, Pete. I know you're trying your best."

At her praise, his mouth split into a toothy grin and whistling a tuneless melody, he went to collect two empty buckets. In the process he upset the broom and dustbin, and she winced as he banged his shin against the corner of a cot before he disappeared out the door.

Shaking her head in sympathy for the lad, she returned her gaze to the letter. This time she studied the contents with cold logic and an analytical eye, not hot anger or wounded pride, and her puzzlement deepened.

Why would Garrick encourage her to seek Danford's help or attention? The two men were all but sworn enemies. And if anything, there seemed to be a new possessiveness in Garrick's attitude toward her. She felt it in his mannerism, like his hand at the small of her back as they crossed the hotel lobby this morning. Or in the way he grabbed her without preamble and kissed her good-bye with a combination of roughness and need.

She drummed her finger on the table top and tried to recall the pattern of Garrick's handwriting. She'd seen it at their original interview and didn't recall it being so scrawly and hard to read. But then perhaps he had written this letter in haste. Or sadly, without caring.

Her hand tightened around the note, and she shoved the paper into her pocket.

It was unfair to judge Garrick without first speaking with him. Written words could oft' deceive. Last night he had been untiring in his efforts to please her, and in his arms she had found a new world that was safe from harm and sadness. It had not felt like mere amusement nor simple distraction.

She had bared her heart, body, and soul to Garrick. And he had done the same. Against all her better judgment, she had trusted him completely— surrendering herself to his mercy. If she now suffered deception and indignity it was her own fault. She had demanded no promises. That none were given nor observed should come as no surprise.

Still, she expected at least a modicum of heartfelt reverence shown for the memory of their night together. She'd not be considered a mere dalliance devoid of all feeling. When Garrick returned, she would set the record straight. In the meantime, she must stop wallowing in self-doubt and get back to work.

Her chair scraped along the floor as she stood.

Grabbing up her empty bandage tray, she stalked over to the supply cupboard. As she rummaged about on the shelf for tow, her hand brushed against the tiny kegs of caviar that Danford had sent over at Christmas. She'd yet to do anything with them. Why not take care of that business today? Thanks to Garrick, she knew to approach the negotiations through a *go-between*, and although she didn't dare to barter with Tuco in Constantinople, visiting Rashi at the local cafe sounded safe enough.

Gazing around the room, Josie mentally assessed each patient. They could manage without her for a few hours. Most of the wounded were on the mend, and the incidence of cholera had dropped dramatically once Miss N. had discovered their water supply was draining through a putrid horse carcass prior to reaching the distribution point.

Yes, going now seemed an excellent idea. She was just in the mood to haggle or more precisely, she was in the mood for a good fight. And although the words *black market* had an ominous ring, surely it was like any other market. She was very good at shopping. Even on Bond Street, she procured the best prices.

Josie gripped the door of the cupboard intent on closing it. Then the lacy stenciling on the caviar containers caught her eye. A sample of her wares seemed a good idea. She retrieved one of the tiny wooden casks and concealed it inside a small cloth sack.

"Pete," she called, "I'll be away from the ward for a few hours to check on provisions. If you need help, seek out Old Pauly and do exactly as he advises. Dr. Cowper has already made his rounds and there were no special orders." Pete stared at her as if he expected her to deliver the closing line of a poem. "That's all Pete. Do you understand?"

"Oh yes ma'am. Don't forget your cape," he

advised. "Its winter time you know."

She smiled at his childlike observation. "Yes, I know," she reached for her wrap, "and you keep the fire stoked."

Disobeying the rules once again, Josie left the hospital by the side exit. The weather was nearly pleasant today and as she crossed the courtyard, the brightness of the morning bolstered her enthusiasm. She would show them all, even Garrick. She needed no man to run her life or tell her what to do.

Procuring a fairly decent carriage, she relaxed back against the squabs, and as the driver urged the team into a steady pace, the thrill of danger revived her battered ego and excitement overshadowed her anger. This feeling of invincibility was soon put to the test as the araba hit a rut, and the wheels on the right side of the coach careened up off the ground. Caught unaware, Josie skidded sideways on the well-worn seat and slammed to a halt against the far door. Then she nearly pitched head first onto the floor as the carriage shuddered and heaved back down onto all four wheels.

She reached out to steady herself, and a pang of loneliness speared through her. The seat beside her was noticeably cold and empty. Today's ride was quite unlike the one she'd shared last night with Garrick. Damnation. Despite the possibility that he only toyed with her affections, she still wanted him desperately.

Oh she was such a fool where matters of love were concerned. The logic of her mind and the emotions of her heart lived by vastly different rules. Too late, she realized that one night with Garrick would never be enough. Only a lifetime would suffice.

As the carriage veered onto a connecting avenue, sunlight streamed in through the window. She edged closer to the light, but it did not touch the place in her heart that was frozen with doubt. Only Garrick could renew life back into that part of her being. Renew it or kill it forever.

The coach slowed. She stared out the window, and her eyes grew wide. The scenery had changed and not for the better.

This section of the town was not only in disrepair, it was unwholesome and feral. Crumbling houses lined the dusty street. Ragged curtains fluttered outward through windows where the glass was missing, and broken flower pots lay abandoned on stoops. The once gay market place was dirty and forlorn, and even in their idleness, the men who stared back at her from the boardwalks appeared tough and rowdy and ready for misadventure.

Her gaze swept the street. There wasn't another woman in site. Indecision pounded in her chest as the coach drew to a halt.

"Kind lady," the driver questioned, "are you most positive this is the place you desire?"

Ignoring his obvious concern for her safety, she forced herself to exit the conveyance. "Yes. Thank you," she searched her purse for the money to pay him. "Will other coaches be available for my return trip?"

"A few," the driver replied, as he counted the coins she deposited in his hand, "at least until nightfall. After dark only the very brave and the very foolish frequent this boulevard. You'd best be gone by then."

Without further ado, he clucked the team into action and left her to stand alone on the ramshackle porch of the public house. Nervously, she glanced over her shoulder then studied the building's facade. The original name of the cafe, scrolled in squirming Turkish letters, was overlaid with a makeshift sign that read *The White Horse Inn*. The local people were clever at capitalizing on the homesick British.

Many Turks had even managed to conquer halting English in their attempt to profit. Although mercenary in motivation, you had to admire their adaptability and perseverance.

Mustering her courage, she eased closer to the entryway. The door was slightly ajar, and with her hand flat against the wood, she gently widened the gap. The hinges creaked as if they adorned the portal of a long forgotten crypt. She cringed and waited. Seemingly desperate to escape to the outside world, the stale air from inside the café rushed past her. The haze of cigar smoke burned her eyes, and the smell of sweat and spilled whiskey tingled in her nostrils. She was almost afraid to inhale the sinister atmosphere.

Most of the floor space was covered at random with clusters of tables and chairs, and a long narrow bar hugged the far wall. Displayed behind this expanse of gleaming mahogany was a large faded painting featuring a voluptuous woman who frolicked naked in a Garden of Eden. Two people appeared to be the only occupants of the establishment; a shabby looking old man affecting interest in sweeping the floor, and an ebony haired young woman who filled lamps and trimmed wicks as if by rote. Since neither seemed especially threatening, Josie slipped inside. Then she hesitated and took a step backwards. It might be prudent to remain close to the door.

The dusky skinned female glanced up, and her eyes narrowed as she slinked out from behind the bar. Crossing the room, she approached to within a few feet of Josie. The large golden hoops that pierced her earlobes clanked in counterpoint to the bangles on her wrists. She looked Josie up and down, and her red gash of a mouth tightened into a flat line. "What do you want little girl? We need no more barmaids and I am the only dancer."

Josie swallowed hard. "I came to see Rashi," she said, with a lift of her chin. Her fingers shook as she loosened the clasp on her cape. The gray wool parted and the woman's dark gaze flickered over Josie's uniform.

"So you are a nurse from the hospital," the girl observed, with a toss of her head.

"Yes," Josie acknowledged, "I need supplies you see, and I was told Rashi could help."

The woman's mouth softened and her stance relaxed. Apparently, nurses posed no threat to her world—only dancers.

"We are the same you and me," the girl declared. "Each in our own way we ease the pain of the soldiers." Her lips curled into a tawdry smile, and she toyed with a lock of her thick black hair. "Sit down," she offered, "I will fetch the man you seek."

The girl turned and strutted back across the room. Her movements were exaggerated as if she practiced her walk for later when the bar would be crammed with lusty men vying for her attention.

Josie sank down onto the nearest chair. The seat was hard and uncomfortable—granting no hospitality. Afraid to touch anything, she kept her hands in her lap and clutched the cloth bag that held the keg of caviar.

What was taking so long? As thoughts of leaving skittered through her mind, a shadow fell across the filthy tabletop and she felt a presence looming over her shoulder. She craned her neck sideways, and her gaze climbed upward finally coming to rest upon the face of a man who could only be described as formidable. He appeared seven feet tall, and Bedouin style, he was swathed from head to foot in a flowing white robe. His eyes glittered like chips of black coal, and a thin dark beard and mustache accentuated the grim set of his mouth.

He shifted his stance and rested one hand upon

the hilt of the curved sword that hung from his cloth belt. Josie gasped and drew back from the shiny well-honed blade.

"I am Rashi," he said.

Her gaze snapped back to his face.

"And Rashi is always available for a beautiful woman." With a secretive smile, he bowed and touched the fingertips of one hand to his forehead, lips, and bosom. Straightening he gestured toward the chair across from her. "May I?" he asked.

"Yes of course," she croaked. She licked at her lips, but her mouth was so dry the effort had little effect.

"What might Rashi do for such a charming lady as yourself?" His voice was rich and dark as Turkish liqueur.

Unsure of how to begin, Josie just stared at him. Honesty was generally the best policy, but illegal trading no doubt had its own set of protocol and etiquette. She decided on the direct approach. "I would like to make an exchange," she said in her most business-like voice, "on the black market."

Rashi's eyes widened ever so slightly then he began to laugh. It was a great reverberating sound that seemed to well up from deep inside of him.

Josie gritted her teeth in indignation. The last thing she had expected was to be laughed at. Rummaging around in the cloth bag, she liberated the wooden cask of caviar and tossed it onto the table.

Rashi's laughter slowed then waned completely, and he reached for the container. Turning it over, he examined it carefully, and his brows arched upward. "Ah," he crooned, "Khavyar. And from the Steppes of Astrakhan."

"How much for one hundred of those?" she asked.

"What do you wish in return?" he replied, neatly

234

avoiding her question.

"I need linen for bandages and chamber pots, as many as you have."

He set the wooden keg back upon the table. "I cannot get those for you."

"But why not?"

"Such items are not common trade commodity."

Josie's shoulders slumped. She hadn't anticipated that possibility. Now what? In a panic, she racked her brain for an alternative choice in trade items. Nothing came to mind.

"Would 20 lbs. of opium be sufficient compensation?" he asked.

Josie's heart skipped a beat. It had not occurred to her to try and trade for anything as precious as medicine. She twisted her hands in her lap. She'd have a lot of explaining to do. The unexpected appearance of linen and minor pieces of equipment was one thing, but the sudden surfacing of drugs was rather a different matter altogether. Was this part of the lost shipment from the *Prince*? Had the medicine somehow been retrieved from the sea by the ambitious Turks? If so, she would be reclaiming supplies that had originally belonged to the Army. What could be wrong with that? Besides, she could worry about the consequences later. There always seemed time for regret—if not repentance.

"Yes. All right," she said, before her good sense could intervene. "I will accept the medicine. I could bring the rest of the caviar tomorrow."

"I admire your enthusiasm. Unfortunately we will not have the opium for another three weeks."

Three weeks. That was a disappointment. Still the black market service was more timely than the Army Purveyor's Office.

"That would be fine," she said. "Should I come back here?"

Rashi shook his head. "As much as I would enjoy

once more partaking of your loveliness, I must advise otherwise." His gaze flamed from hot to sizzling, and Josie wondered how she could feel so naked with all of her clothes on.

"In exactly three weeks from tomorrow," he continued, placing emphasis on each word, "you must go to the church on the far side of town. You are familiar with this place?"

"Yes, I know of it," she whispered, recalling Mose and the newly turned grave he rested beneath.

"Good," Rashi said. "At exactly twelve o'clock noon, you will see a man walking in the garden. His name is Vlad."

She started and sat forward. "A Russian?"

"Do not be alarmed. Vlad is any nationality that best enhances his purse. He will have the opium. The rest is up to you and him."

With veiled eyes, Rashi rested one hand on the table palm up.

Oh dear, she hadn't considered that either. Obviously, he expected to be paid for being the go between. The money in her pocket would barely cover her fare back to the hospital. She had nothing to offer him.

His gaze drifted languidly down the front of her uniform then back up to her face. Surely, he would not try to take liberties for services rendered?

The sun went behind a cloud, and the cafe was plunged into deep shadow. The girl at the bar no longer appeared sympathetic, and the man who cleaned the floor paused to lean on the handle of his broom. Both occupants watched her with no more compassion than if they attended a local cockfight.

Josie leapt to her feet, her gaze locked on Rashi. "Keep the caviar," she said, as she pressed the keg into his outstretched hand.

His face cracked into a grin, and his large ivory teeth gleamed brightly in contrast to his dark skin.

As she fled to the door his booming voice followed. "Your smile would have been payment enough little dove. But I thank you for the additional bounty."

Heart pounding triple time, she could barely catch her breath, and lurching across the porch and into the street, she gasped in a lungful of clean air. The clamor of horses' hoofs sounded at her back and she spun around. Afraid the driver of the approaching araba might not stop for her she stepped farther out into the street and waved her arms.

The coach careened to a halt, the front wheels missing her toes by inches. Without waiting for assistance, she scrambled on board. "To the Barrack Hospital, quickly," she called from the open window.

The carriage pitched forward into motion, but it wasn't fast enough to suit Josie. She could not distance herself from this place quickly enough.

Around a shuddering breath, she issued a prayer of thanks and willed herself to relax. There was no need for alarm, she was safe now. The hospital was just up ahead. A great sigh of relief escaped her lips. She felt dizzy after her brush with the Turkish underworld as well as giddy with her success. Not only had she bargained away the useless food, she had traded up from chamber pots to medicine.

Her troubles were over.

Her smile faded.

Her troubles had just begun. A thousand things could go wrong. Three weeks from tomorrow they could trick her.

They could wait for her at the church and rob her of the caviar without giving her anything in exchange. Who knew what they might do? Life was cheap here. Scenes of being kidnapped and forced into the white slave market blurred through her mind.

She leaned forward and buried her face in her hands.

What had she gotten herself into?

Even she was not so naive as to believe there truly was honor among thieves.

...and he smelled the battle afar off,
the thunder of the captains, and the shouting.
~Old Testament: Job, XXXIX, 25

Chapter Seventeen
The Crimean Peninsula

Thick white fog sashayed uninvited through the British field camp. It curled around the soldiers asleep in the dirt, and like a hard working whore, it offered a cold embrace and no excuse as it stole their warmth and promised nothing.

Garrick stepped around a stockpile of ammunition, shoved his freezing hands into his coat pockets, and walked on. As he halted before the officers' quarters, the ethereal mist spiraled about his boots. "I'm here to see Lord Pagent," he said, and peered around the bulk of the soldier who stood between him and the entrance to the General's tent.

"General Pagent is not available."

Of course he was. He could see the man from here. He stared pointedly past the guard, but the sentry remained impassive.

Having spent the last seven days in transit, with little food and less sleep, Garrick was feeling anything but cordial. Biting back a surly remark, he took the opportunity to study the General from afar. Drawn and wan the man lay propped up in bed, his arms resting listlessly atop the covers. It would appear black marketing was exhausting business.

"Would you at least tell Lord Pagent I'm here?" Garrick requested.

The sentinel looked him up and down. "Well just who are you?"

"Garrick Allen," he answered as calmly as possible, "special correspondent for *The Times.*"

With a grunt that showed how unimpressed he was, the soldier pivoted and stepped through the inverted V in the canvas. He stood close to the General and spoke so softly Garrick wasn't able to catch what was being said.

The conversation was short and ended with a salute.

"The General suggests that you return in two weeks for your interview," the guard stated, as he resumed his post. "Lord Pagent also said, and I quote, 'By then I shall either be cured or dead'."

"What ails him?" Garrick asked, and to his surprise the sentry granted him an answer.

"A shoulder wound that will not heal, the Crimean fever, possibly cholera. He's been bedridden for months but refuses to leave his men or the frontlines. Print that," the soldier said gruffly.

"I just might." Garrick cast another glance toward the marquee. The man inside was doubled over in pain, but he never uttered a sound.

He reconnoitered the camp, speaking with the noncommissioned lads who were awake now and going about their early morning chores. Each one corroborated the guard's story. Lord Pagent had been out of action for over two months. He couldn't possibly be the man behind the smuggling activity. The last incident had occurred only a few weeks ago. Of course that left the lesser officer who had been named as a conspirator in the illegal operations, but he had a feeling this would also turn out to be a fabrication.

He dragged the fur cap from his head, plowed his hands through his tangled hair, and then resettled the hat back in place. His fortuitous lead was beginning to smell like a red herring. He wondered if Shamus had come to the same conclusion in London. Was the real mastermind behind the operation feeding them false information? Was he worried they were getting too close? He needn't be. They had only one other pitiful scrap of information upon which to base their theory. This tidbit, procured from his source in Varna, proclaimed a fellow named Vlad was involved on the Russian side of the operation. *A Russian named Vlad.* That should nicely narrow his search down to about ten million men. He might as well be looking for a Swede named Sven or a Frenchman named Pierre.

Lost in thought, Garrick crossed the compound to join a group of bedraggled soldiers huddled before a small campfire. The dismal flames reflected the downcast atmosphere and little heat. No one spoke or even glanced up at him. They all appeared too tired and pensive for mindless chatter or idle curiosity, and without comment, Garrick joined their silent vigil.

Suddenly, the oppressive silence was shattered, and the dreary morn was rocked by a thunderous explosion. Grapeshot rained down from above and bounced along the ground like hot black hail. A cannon ball from a six-pounder tore through the tent on his right. The hurtling orb went straight through the canvas unhindered. Then it smacked into the dirt plowing up a ten-foot furrow before coming to rest.

What was going on? They were miles from Sebastopol and out of fixed cannon range.

The soldiers sprang into action, grabbing for their rifles and the Queen's cold steel. Armed with paper, pencil, and pistol he fell in line with what was left of the Royal Fusiliers. As they rushed into the roiling fog, he lost sight of the man on either side of him, and with each step he took into the forbidding wall of white, Garrick feared to either fall off a cliff or walk into the waiting arms of the enemy.

Innocent sounds turned menacing as they echoed through the swirling vapors. Points of origin became indistinguishable, and he jumped at the chink of a horse's bit or the clatter of a soldier's weapon against his ration tin. His gaze darted to the right. What was that?

A short distance away three men stood crouched and at the ready. Were they friend or foe? His guts tightened into a knot as he peered through the frosty haze. Then he relaxed his grip on the pistol and his shoulders sagged in relief. They weren't men at all, but a group of bent saplings poorly attired in scrub brush.

He choked in a breath of air and resumed his course. The acrid taste of spent gunpowder drifted on the breeze and already the sanguine smell of the dead and injured wafted through the air like a repulsive cheap perfume.

Reaching a barren ridge, the battalion halted and regrouped, and word came 'round that under the cover of the fog the enemy had forayed well beyond the normal lines of demarcation. No one knew how many Russians were out there, but with Ukrainian reinforcements arriving daily, the last count set the ratio at six to one, their favor. Not the best of odds.

A fresh barrage of gunfire severed Garrick's thoughts. He took shelter beside a rocky escarpment as the foliage around him burst into flames. The inferno was both beautiful and unholy in its intensity. It roared and crackled, sending ash and embers arching upward. In contrast to this blinding bit of brightness, another nearby bush smoldered and spewed black smoke. It mingled with the white fog turning the world a fearful grey.

As these vivid images filled Garrick's mind, he opened his journal and concentrated on transforming what he was witnessing into words. As he wrote, the chaos that screamed at him from all sides seemed to fade to insignificance. Then a mortar exploded on his left, spattering dirt and rock across the page upon which he wrote. The back of his hand turned to fire as a few stray pieces of stone embedded into his flesh. Damn. He gritted his teeth and dislodged the fragments with the stub of his pencil. The pain seared deeper and drops of blood welled up to fill the depressions where the gravel had been.

He grabbed a handful of the snow that lay hidden in a shadowy nook and pressed it to the back of his hand. Then loosening his cravat, he tugged it free, brushed the snow aside, and tied the tattered fabric around his injured hand.

As he reached again for his journal, a mortar struck a cypress ten yards to his right. It hit the trunk low and dead center, and the huge tree shattered as if it were made of glass. Nettles and branches hurtled in all directions. He threw his arms up to protect his head. For a man who did not sanction war, he could not be more embroiled in one.

Great chunks of the tree hurtled back to the earth. They crashed onto the ground with a terrible thud, but the sound couldn't mask the thumping of his heart as it pounded in his chest. He began to sweat. Only last week William Russell had been wounded. Was it his turn today? He was getting too old for this kind of excitement. He didn't enjoy going one on one with the devil any more. But if he hadn't come to the Crimea, he never would have met Josie. Despite the layer of grit that coated his face, he smiled. Who would have thought to find an angel like Josie in this dark corner of hell?

The bugler sounded the advance, and the soldiers scrambled to their feet. Garrick shoved his journal and pencil inside his coat and levered up off the ground to join them.

The men, in loose formation, crested the ridge and began to traverse the mist covered down-slope. Then an unexpected rush of cool air rippled the fur on the hat that he wore. The wind was up and the ill fated breeze tore away the protective curtain of fog. He watched in horror as the wispy veil dissipated. The plateau down below hazed into view—revealing an inhospitable landscape dotted with a full compliment of Russians all firing at will.

One after another, the British soldiers succumbed to the enemy barrage. Like tin soldiers, they slumped to their knees and tumbled down the hill. The few troops still at the top of the ridge, dug-in behind tufts of earth and fragmented gabions. Garrick hit the dirt beside a pile of rubble that had once been a corncrib. As he came to rest on his belly, dirt ground into the makeshift bandage on his hand, and jagged stone dug into his hip. Reduced to crawling on his belly, he inched forward and gained a more tolerable position.

Flying debris smashed into the ground a foot from his face. It kicked up a cloud of dust that stung his eyes and burned his throat. Coughing and choking, he retrieved his journal. This could be his last chance to make an entry.

He took stock of his surroundings and studied the men who fought at his side. They bore ordinary faces, fixed into extraordinary expressions. He saw courage and resignation and even fear, but he didn't see hate. He was glad for that. In this atmosphere of confusion and disorder, he saw peaceful men thrown by the hand of Fate into the bubbling caldron of war. He saw the will to live, the need to survive, but no satisfaction nor joy in destroying. Was that mankind's redeeming quality? He could kill with compassion.

Another spate of gunfire raked the area. He

couldn't see what was happening. Shifting onto his side, he edged forward to peer around the rubble. Fifty yards to his left, the Highlanders were assembled in rank and file two men deep. Dressed in their kilts and cherry-colored coats, they were all that stood between the advancing Russians and the road back to Balaclava and the British supply port.

"Remember, lads," Sir Colin Campbell's voice rang out, "There is no retreat from here. You must die where you stand!" Each soldier remained silent and stood a little taller.

Enemy horse artillery opened fire, and the British forces lay down under the guns. Then the canons grew still.

Over four thousand Russian cavalry men advanced on the thin red line, and a pall descended on the plateau, the stillness broken only by the steady tromp, tromp, tromp of the approaching enemy.

Garrick scribbled madly, the words coming fast and furious.... *Grim expectation hangs in the air, more potent and pungent than the smell of gun powder. Foggy apparitions ring the battlefield, wispy phantom soldiers from wars fought long ago. They watch in silence. Who will join their ranks today?*

The enemy came into range. Garrick's hand stilled. The ghostly wail of bagpipes screamed across the plains, and the hair on the nape of his neck stood on end. The Scots rose up from the ground, bloody red specters in perfect parade drill formation. They faced the advancing army with calm deliberation as they directed one well placed volley and then a second.

The Russians hesitated, as if they suspected a trap, and their fear was their undoing.

At the third salvo, the Muscovites turned and ran.

Although greatly outnumbered, the Highlanders

surged forward—the desire for a full-fledged charge plainly etched upon their determined faces. "Ninety-third! Ninety-third! Damn all that eagerness!" Sir Colin ordered, keeping the men in check.

The Russians fell back to the trenches, and the sound of retreat was heard as they relinquished the newly gained territory.

Awed by the spectacle, Garrick entered another line of tribute. *Discipline and unbound courage conquered raw brute strength, as a fearless handful of men held back an army.*

The Cossacks withdrew to the safety of Fort Nicholas, and Garrick studied the maze of ditches that protected the land surrounding the stronghold. The miles of man-made dikes resembled the canals of Venice or the winding streets of Cairo, and each gully was filled with mud and a thousand blindly obedient Muscovites.

A perimeter checkpoint was established, and in ragged victory, the remainder of the British troops returned to the field camp. Garrick followed along, helping to search for survivors. On mounds of grass and in puddles of water, the fallen men lay like twisted dolls—their arms and legs akimbo. Most were dead or barely clinging to life.

A groan floated through the air and caught his attention.

"Stretcher bearer," he hollered, as he scrambled over a boulder and shoved through a thicket.

Receiving no response to his call for assistance, he glanced back over his shoulder. The main body of the army was already past. He was alone in a small-secluded area where minutes before the enemy had stood.

Spotting an injured man lying near a fallen tree, Garrick hurried forward and knelt down beside the British soldier.

The fellow was old, with white hair and wise

features. His face was pale, and his eyes were bright with pain. Fiercely he clutched at a side wound. The blood ran down between his fingers darkening the foreign soil he had fought to defend.

"Let's have a look," Garrick said.

As gently as possible he loosened the fellow's grip. Then he fought to remain expressionless as his gaze fell upon torn flesh and exposed rib bones. Wadding up his kerchief, Garrick pressed the pad to the wound and the flow lessened. No bubbles issued forth with the blood, he guessed the shot had missed the lung. Wondering if the ball had gone all the way through, he slid a hand beneath the soldier and felt for an exit wound. When he drew back his hand, it was covered in blood.

He needed more cloth for a bandage. He removed his leather coat and tossed it aside then tore the sleeves off his shirt. Folding the fabric into a thick square, he eased it under the soldier.

The man stared up at him. The flicker of life dimmed in his translucent blue eyes, and his lips were ringed with a whitish pallor. "I'm so c-cold, sonny."

Garrick snared his coat with one hand and dragged the wool-lined leather over the shivering man. "Just lie still," he advised, "We'll make it back to camp."

Gaining his feet Garrick glanced around. Not a single person stirred on the hills around him. He was on his own, and that meant transporting this man back to the Army field doctor in a travois of some sort. He searched the nearby brush for suitable branches. The thorny tangle of scrub tore at his hands and caught on his pants, but it yielded nothing useful.

Straightening, he hurried over to a more promising area. There were no usable tree limbs there either, but he did come across a leather haversack. That was good luck. He could cut strips from it to use as thongs.

Suddenly, a bright agony seized the right side of his head. In the back of his mind he imagined the faraway sound of a rifle shot. Twisting around, he tried to look in that direction but his knees buckled, and he fell to the ground.

He lay there amongst the brush unable to move, and it felt as if the weight of the world crushed down upon him. Unblinking he stared up at the sky. The fog had lifted completely, and the color reflected back was so blue it hurt his eyes.

He thought of Josie. He really must take her on another picnic. Little Josie Posey. Her name echoed through his mind. Because of her, he had learned to dream again. Maybe he was dreaming now. Red hot pain stabbed through his head. This did not feel like an illusion.

Involuntarily, his right hand tightened around the leather strap of the pouch he'd found. Then his grip went slack and he was floating, drifting, going beyond the misery.

A searing white light flooded his mind—only to transform into a numbing black void.

...treachery and violence are spears pointed at both ends. They wound those who resort to them worse than their enemies.

~Emily Bronte, *Wuthering Heights*

Chapter Eighteen

"Step aside, now," the Quartermaster ordered, "step aside."

Danford stifled an ill-mannered retort then relinquished his position beside the main entrance of the Barrack Hospital.

The Russians had been busy at Eupatoria north of Kalamata Bay, and another shipload of British wounded was being received. But Danford wasn't interested in the soldiers or their plight. He watched for only one man who may have been on the transport, Garrick Allen.

Many days had past since he'd maneuvered the Newsboy into heading across the sea to the peninsula, but sooner or later, the deception was bound to come to light, and sooner or later, the tenacious bastard was bound to head back to Scutari. Damn the meddling fool, if he would only stay away a while longer.

When Allen did return, he was sure to head straight to Ward C and Nurse Posey's welcoming nest. The girl made excellent bait. At times he almost felt pity for the girl. She believed in the mercy of a new dawn, while most humans were ruled by the heartless pleasures of the night. Of course it still rankled that the silly twit had spurned his affections. That's what had prompted him to write such a mean and insensitive note in place of

Mr. Allen's missive. Had it been cruel enough to cause her a good measure of well-deserved heartache?

It was disgusting and down right irksome to admit a woman could create such havoc in his life, disrupting his schemes and causing him to second-guess himself and his motivation. Nurse Posey set his mind to considering the other side of life, the side that he'd never seen nor wanted to know. The side ruled by kindness and love and other driveling and useless emotions. His parents hadn't taught him about those feelings, and neither had anyone else. And no woman, not even Nurse Posey, was worth the effort of changing now.

A blustery voice rang out, interrupting his mawkish contemplations.

The booming utterance filled the foyer as it cut through the din of shuffling feet and moans of pain. Ah, there was the source of the disturbance. It was General Middlemarch, the Superintendent of the Heavy Cavalry.

"Keep up the good work, lads," the man praised, as he forced his way out of the building in opposition to the stream of incoming wounded.

A stylish young woman clung to the General's arm. As the officer drew near, Danford nodded in acknowledgement. The short stocky General strutted by, his chest puffed out like a plump guinea fowl. He grunted a perfunctory response but didn't bother to stop for polite conversation.

Danford's gaze slid sideways to the General's wife.

She blushed and glanced away.

He had seen that same high color in her cheeks last night as he had spilled his prurient interest into her. Danford's mouth twisted into a smile. The General was a pompous ass, and his wife a good piece of one.

The ill-matched couple continued toward the exit. Danford directed a look of contempt toward the man's overfed backside then refocused his attention on the sweet seduction of the woman's swaying hips. The general's wife was bored silly, and needy to the point of refusing him nothing regardless of how imaginative he became. With a self-satisfied smirk Danford deliberated over what he would do with her tonight. Evil mischief could be wrought on so many levels and on a grand scale if properly planned and executed.

Then his thoughts came back around to Garrick Allen and his smile withered. The man was the last of a dying breed. Didn't he realize that chivalry was dead and the days of the hero were numbered? Heroes, what nonsense. Childishly intrepid in the face of danger, they defied the normal logic of the world as they rushed in without thinking to perform foolish acts. He despised heroes. They gave credence to the more extraordinary and exalted side of man. But on the brighter side, heroes did not always live to tell their tales. Perhaps such a fate would claim Mr. Allen.

Untouched by the grisly display before him, Danford slouched back against the wall and watched the endless parade of wounded. It intrigued him that people were so quick to label the soldiers as valiant and lionhearted. They just obeyed orders. They were toys, pawns really, used in the games that politicians and diplomats played. Games that spanned continents and altered the course of civilizations. Did the face of destruction look the same, regardless of time and place? He wondered then shrugged. Just like the God of Peace, the Deities of War would always exist.

Two orderlies approached with yet another litter, but as the men drew near Danford's interest quickened. The unmoving patient who lay upon the stretcher was covered with a familiar looking coat. By Lucifer, it was the Newsboy's.

"Gentlemen," he said, and stepped forward, "a moment please. I believe you bear a friend of mine." At his approach the men paused and wearily glanced off into space. Danford angled the unconscious man's head around to more easily identify him. Disappointment followed on the heels of his surprise. It was Allen's coat all right, but a withered old man lay beneath the garment not the reporter.

"Where was this soldier, I mean my friend, when he was wounded?" Danford asked.

"The plateaus 'afore Sebastopol," replied the man in front.

"He was lucky," the lad at the back put in. "The battlefield was heavy with thickets and gorse, and I hear tell they didn't find him 'til the last reconnoiter."

Danford mumbled an appropriate response as he fingered the worn leather. "What a shame his favorite coat has become soiled and bloodied. I'm sure he would wish me to keep it from further harm." Without awaiting a reply, he seized the garment.

One man opened his mouth as if to protest.

"I assure you," Danford challenged, "I do not desire this coat for selfish purposes. As you can see it hardly runs to my taste."

The man looked him up and down then snapped his mouth shut.

"Carry on," Danford suggested, by way of dismissal. "Do not linger at my friend's expense."

Accustomed to taking orders the men obeyed.

Danford ambled off in the opposite direction. Curiosity surged through him but a few troubling questions squelched his desire to celebrate.

Reaching a secluded offshoot in the hallway, he halted to examine the coat more closely. It seemed odd that the reporter would be separated from his trademark attire. Maybe Allen really was dead. Now there was a cheerful possibility. He checked the pockets. They were empty. He ran his hands over the leather but found no bullet holds nor bayonet slashes. Some of the blood on the jacket was sticky and fresh, some appeared days old and crusted over.

But whose blood was it? The old man on the stretcher, the reporter's, or both?

****

Perched precariously upon the edge of his cot, Garrick struggled to remain upright. He remembered being on a plateau searching. Searching for what? Sticks, no branches, something with which to make a travois. Yes, that was it. He'd found an old man wounded and he was trying to help him. And then what? He couldn't remember.

Bleary-eyed he glanced around. His jumbled gaze skidded sideways, coming to rest upon two men who appeared to be the only other patients in the field hospital tent. The men were hunched over in their chairs playing Ecarte or All-Fours, Garrick couldn't tell as they were too far away. One fellow's head and left eye was bandaged, and the other lad had rib splints and his arm in a sling. They were both much younger than the old soldier he'd been trying to help.

As he concentrated harder, a jagged piece of memory painfully gouged its way to the surface of his mind. He'd been shot. Gingerly he ran his fingertips along the four inch wound on his right temple. It throbbed unmercifully but seemed well approximated and not too swollen. He was fortunate to be alive.

His vision went all blurry again, and he closed his eyes and cradled his head in his hands. Where were all the other injured men? Surely more then the three of them had survived the battle. And why did there seem to be so many guards stationed at the entrance to the tent?

At the rustle of stiff canvas he glanced up. An orderly bearing an arm-load of kindling was admitted. The man lumbered forward and dumped the fuel beside the stove then turned to leave.

"I say friend," Garrick called out, "might I have a word?"

The orderly started in surprise then drew closer to the bed. "So you're finally back amongst the quick and the conscious," he said with a grin, "and British to boot."

"Of course I'm British," Garrick replied somewhat confused by the man's statement. "How long have I been here?"

"A week, maybe two. Time has a way of slipping by unnatural like around here."

"And my coat" Garrick said in a sudden panic. "Where is my coat?"

"I don't recall you was wearin' one when they brung you in. All you had with you was a haversack and that's over with General Richardson. Good thing you finally come to your senses," the orderly added, "we was about to transport you to the prison compound along with them two boys."

"But that's absurd," he exclaimed. "I'm Garrick Allen, special correspondent for *The Times*."

"Well in all fairness," the orderly defended, "how was we to know that. Turns out the bag you was totin', contained papers written in Rooskie. And seein' as you weren't wearin' no recognizable uniform, we kept you here rather than shipping you back to Scutari with the British wounded."

Garrick glanced again at the men playing cards. Despite closer inspection they simply appeared tired and worn like any soldier from any country, but as he listened more intently he now realized they were in fact speaking Russian. That explained the guards.

"I found that haversack on the battlefield," he declared as another memory made itself known. "Were the contents of any importance?"

The orderly chuckled. "Them fancy generals was hoping it would be. But when they finally had it translated, it turns out they was just a sheaf of stories and poems or some such nonsense. You could probably get it all back if it ain't been burned. It'd make a dandy souvenir."

Poems and stories. How extraordinary. A man in the trenches across from him, an enemy by place of birth, was out here just like him writing verse and prose in the midst of chaos and death.

'Yes, I would like the pouch and papers back," Garrick said. For some reason he felt obligated to save the literary collection. He pictured the pouch and recalled there had been a set of initials etched upon the front of it. "Did they discover the name of the man who wrote the stories?"

"I believe so," the orderly puzzled. "It was Louie or Leo. Yeah, that's it. Leo, Leo Tolstoy."

At the mention of the name the enemy soldiers glanced up. They talked excitedly for a moment then broke into a heartfelt song.

"Pipe down over there," the orderly shouted. The men quickly obeyed but a flame of rebellion burned in their eyes where before only dull acceptance had lived.

The orderly turned to leave.

"One more thing, please," Garrick said. "There was an old man with a chest wound. He was on the field near me. Did he make it?"

"You know his service number?" the orderly asked.

"No."

"Then I can't help you. Without a number or a death record you can't get any information from the Army. Now I got work needs doin'." The man headed towards the door. "I'll inform the guards that you're one of us" he called over his shoulder. "I doubt those two will give you any trouble, but I'll send someone in to watch your back."

Garrick swung his legs up onto the cot and cautiously slumped back against the straw filled ticking. His head felt split wide open. As his vision wavered again, he closed his eyes preferring to see nothing rather than a dim blur. How long had he been unconscious? The orderly had said one week, maybe two. He rubbed his hand across his cheek, noting a healthy growth of beard. He'd guess no more than twelve days.

His stomach gave a resounding growl. He should have asked the orderly for some food. Then a shiver ran through him and once again, he regretted the loss of his coat. It was some consolation to think it covered the old soldier. He supposed it was silly to be so attached to an inanimate object, like a child with a favorite blanket, but during his life he'd kept few mementoes. The loss of even one keepsake took a great toll on his meager inventory.

He raised one arm and draped it across his eyes. The soothing darkness deepened, and he let his mind wander. How pitiful that his life could be summed up in half a lorry load of trinkets and old leather. Yet he knew it was his own fault as he had purposely abandoned or thrown away most things associated with deep feelings or sentiment.

With an unusual degree of sentimentality, he ticked the items off in his mind that he had retained. There was his coat, his trunk of books, an ostrich plume from the costume of a particularly beautiful dancing girl in Tangiers, and until recently, the red rose from his mother's coffin bouquet. Josie had the flower now. Did she cheriesh it as much as he had? Wherever he had traveled he'd kept that fragile bloom safe from harm. Yet giving the dried flower to

Josie had seemed the most natural thing in the world. It was as if he had saved it all this time just for her.

Josie...

He lowered his arm to his side. It seemed an eternity since he'd seen her sweet face. He open his eyes and stared up at the sagging roof of the tent. He hadn't meant to be away this long. Did she think he had abandoned her? If only she were here now. No, he recanted that wish. He didn't want her to see him injured and barely able to care for himself. And he didn't want her here, neck deep in the bloodiest part of the war.

New energy coursed through his body. He wished now he'd told her that he loved her. The blood drained from his head and he felt nauseous.

"It's true," a familiar voice taunted in the back of his mind, *"you're in love."* The very idea still frightened him. And why shouldn't it? He didn't trust in happiness. The world didn't work that way. Dame Fortune had given him nothing in the past to make him expect anything in the future. That's why he surrounded himself with irony, dark humor, and sarcasm—emotions with which he was familiar. He didn't know about tenderness, and sharing, and putting someone else first.

Was he willing to learn?

That grand possibility held promise.

Did he have a choice?

That realization made his hackles rise. Garrick didn't like being backed into a corner, even if he had carved the niche by his own design. He massaged his aching brow. Now was probably not the proper time to examine his feelings for Josie. He couldn't think straight. If he wasn't careful, he might start believing that he couldn't live without her or that she needed him as desperately as he needed her.

He curled his hands into fists and fought to cling

to his common sense. Josie's image dimmed in his mind, but the vision would not fade away completely. He sighed and ran his parched tongue across his cracked lips. What he wouldn't give for a shot of whiskey. Someone around here must have a bottle. Now there was a sensible reason for getting up and about.

Once again he forced himself upright and onto the edge of the bed. The act took less effort this time. That was encouraging. Gritting his teeth, he levered off the bed and onto his feet. That was more like it. With a cocky smile, he stood erect—feeling quite smug and proud of himself.

Then his smile transformed into a grimace, and he dry-heaved and reeled backwards onto the bed.

****

Josie examined the next new patient. He was an elderly man with a nasty chest wound. Thankfully the bleeding had stopped and his lungs did not seem affected. He was unresponsive, however, and deathly pale and she feared his chances for survival were slim.

Leaning closer, she prepared to cut away his soiled bandages. A crackling noise sounded where her arm brushed against his shirt. There was something beneath the garment. Probably his enlistment papers or a letter from home.

Recently, a new procedure had been instituted, and now when a patient was picked up on the battlefield, the pockets of his outer clothing were emptied and the contents transferred to the inner folds of his shirt. The practice had become a necessity as the injured soldiers were frequently separated from their coats. The men still able to fight were more in need of the outerwear, and the ill were too weak to protest. The frail man shivered. Poor old fellow. Somehow, she must procure an extra blanket for him.

Setting aside her scissors, she gently rummaged about inside the frayed shirt. Her fingers curled around a small journal and a few blood stained parchments. She eased them free, set the ledger aside, and spread the parchments flat upon the bed. Were they letters from his wife or a daughter?

She gave the matter little concern as she busied herself cleaning his wounds and applying fresh bandages. "You're safe in the hospital now," Josie said as she worked, "and your only task is to get well." Regardless of their degree of consciousness, she always talked to her patients. She'd been taught that they could hear voices, even if they couldn't respond. How frightened they must be.

As she gathered her supplies to move on to the next patient, she casually perused the missive that lay beside the old man, and her name leaped out at her from one of the pages. Surprised by this revelation she read the paper from top to bottom. It was a copy of a newspaper article proclaiming the nurses the Joan of Arcs of the Crimea. And along with the journal, there was a poem entitled *Promise to the Light Brigade,* signed Garrick Allen, Special Correspondent, *The Times.*

She stared in wonder at the papers, then glanced at the unconscious soldier. Why was this old man carrying Garrick's ledger, poem, and dispatch? If indeed, they were Garrick's.

But of course they were. His signature was there plain as day. She traced her finger across his name. Something nagged at the back of her mind...the handwriting. She tightened her grip on the ragged edge of the paper, and weak-kneed hurried to the supply cupboard. Reaching inside, she retrieved the note Garrick had written to her on New Year's Day. Heart pounding, she compared the two missives and her thoughts spun out of control. The penmanship and signatures were completely different.

Any man's death diminishes me, because I am involved in Mankind.
Therefore, never send to know for whom the bell tolls, it tolls for thee.

~John Donne

Chapter Nineteen

The lamplight flickered, and legions of shadows marched across the wall of Josie's bed chamber. Inching closer to the insubstantial light, she stared once more at the papers in question. Which was the forgery, and which was real? These words, and a battalion of worries, paraded through her mind. Her heart dictated that the article and verse were authentic. They appeared to be penned with the fervor and earnest emotion of someone who suffered the pains of the world. In stark comparison, the content of the brief note was cold and illogical and uncaring.

Leafing through the journal, she had discovered the last entry had been made upon the field of battle. This revelation did nothing to ease her concerns and as she smoothed the edges of another tattered document, her throat tightened and an even more disturbing question harangued her. Whose blood darkened the page, the old man's or Garrick's? He'd been gone for so long. Where was he?

Last evening after her shift, she had searched for Garrick in every ward at the Barrack and General Hospitals. Her emotions were torn between hoping and yet not hoping to find him among the newly arrived wounded.

Somehow learning of her quest, Miss N. had

queried the Generals with whom she was on speaking terms. But not one person on this side of the Black Sea appeared to know where Garrick might be. She had petitioned the British Ambassador, but he'd been of no assistance. Garrick's crusade for the truth in the Crimea had won him few friends in the upper echelons, and the Viscount Stratford de Redcliffe made it clear he was not interested in the whereabouts of one rebellious reporter.

She inhaled a shuddering breath. If Garrick wasn't among the wounded, did that mean that he was dead? She wrung her hands and clung to the belief that he was still alive somewhere on the peninsula.

Directing her logic down a different path she reconsidered her patient, the old soldier. How did he fit into the scheme of things? Although stronger, he remained unresponsive, and it could be days or weeks before he could provide any clue as to why he had been carrying Garrick's personal papers. And if the article and the poem were genuine, that meant the note she had received on New Year's Day was counterfeit.

But who would do such a thing and why?

Danford Smythe came to mind. His name was mentioned in the missive. Such a scurrilous act was not beyond his warped sensibilities.

Josie slumped back against the chair and glanced out the window.

The rosy breath of dawn now touched the far horizon.

She had fretted and pothered the entire night away, yet succeeded at resolving nothing. She was not one step closer to pinpointing Garrick's location—nor confirming his safety.

Exhausted, her head nodded forward then she jerked awake. She should get ready for work...no it was Sunday and she and Gemma had been granted their turn at a day of leisure. Rotating by groups and agreeing to cover for one another the nurses had worked out a schedule approved by Miss N. Gemma had sneaked out last night and would most likely be gone another twenty four hours before returning to the room they shared. That suited. Now she could follow through on her clandestine intentions without fear of interruption or the need for explanations.

She rubbed her hand across her tired eyes. In addition to worrying over Garrick, she was anxious about tomorrows meeting with Vlad. It would be difficult to steal away from the ward during the noon hour, and she could not afford to get lost on her way to the little church. That's why she had decided to make a practice run today.

But that was later. She gave a great sigh and yawned...much, much later.

****

Josie's eyes snapped open with a start.

The sun was high in the sky and bright light streamed in through the window. She must have been asleep for hours.

Levering up from the hard chair, she massaged life back into one hip and shuffled over to the chiffonier. What time was it? Eleven twenty five. Oh dear, she was off to a bad start with barely enough time to reach the church by twelve noon.

Not bothering to comb her hair, she slipped on her simplest wool frock, grabbed up her cloak, and hurried outside to hail a carriage.

"St. Mary's church," she instructed the driver, "as quickly as possible please."

As the coach jolted from one pothole to the next, Josie faithfully recorded the sequence of streets that comprised the route, and when the araba drew to a halt she consulted her pocket watch and noted the time. The ride had taken twenty three minutes.

Longer than she had anticipated.

Stepping down from the coach, she paid the driver and turned toward the cathedral.

Noon Mass was about to begin and the narrow street bustled with late comers. She hurried along with the flow of the crowd, but at the church vestibule, she unobtrusively angled off to the right and followed the overgrown footpath to the back of the rectory.

The nearby cemetery, where Mose now rested, was separated from the cathedral by a large herb garden. The withered vines and unruly bushes sprawled in wild and wintry disarray.

She paused to study her surroundings.

Two men meandered the lane up ahead, and even though the temperature today was almost pleasant, they were both bundled up tight, nearly consumed by their greatcoats. One man carried a dark blue velvet box, the other a leather valise.

The man with the box glanced over his shoulder, his darting gaze nervous and furtive.

Instinctively Josie ducked beneath a grape arbor.

These men seemed somehow out of place in the desolate garden. Did they clandestinely meet here today as she planned to do tomorrow?

Sobered by such a thought, she gripped the lattice work and peered through the twisted remnants of brown stems and leaves. Dried vines poked at her cheek and snagged her hair as she canted her head to keep the men in view.

They halted at the far side of a rosemary patch. Their lips moved but she could not hear their words.

Curious beyond good sense, she slipped from the bower and scurried across the overgrown path to the shelter of the bell tower. Her back against the cold rough bricks, she inched along sideways to the edge of the north wall.

"I will miss our fortuitous partnership," said the smaller of the two men. The man's speech was wrapped in a Russian accent heavy enough to crush set mortar.

"Yes," came the reply, "it has been a profitable enterprise, but now it is time to call it a day. Nothing good lasts forever." The second man stood with his back to her, his voice muffled by the collar of his coat.

"These Russian jewels are magnificent," the foreigner said, as he held up the velvet case. "And the furs await you at the appointed place. You will not be disappointed in either commodity. They are more than a fair trade for the opium."

Josie stifled a gasp. Opium! This must be Vlad, the man she was to meet with tomorrow. If so, who was the Englishman? Her eyes narrowed as she stared at his back. If she didn't know better she'd think it was Danford.

"You look worried," the Muscovite said.

"It has nothing to do with our arrangement."

"Ah," the Russian said and nodded his head knowingly, "the reporter still rankles you. I see it in your eyes. My comrade is still available for hire to eliminate your problem. He can do more than just spread rumors and lies."

"No," the taller man replied. "Mr. Allen has caused me many a dark hour, but I'm quite capable of dealing with the situation my self."

Josie tensed and strained forward. They were conversing about Garrick.

The Russian clucked his tongue and shook his head. "I think you must hate this man very much."

"With a grand passion," the other replied. "But I'll soon have what I want, then it will no longer matter if Mr. Allen remains at the front, returns here, or drops off the face of the earth."

Josie's mouth went dry, and her stomach

seemed to leap up and coil in her throat. Garrick must still be on the peninsula. She balled her hands into fists, and for the first time in her life Josie wished she were a man. A wild primitive anger coursed through her body. She wanted to leap from her hiding place and beat the living hell out of this terrible person who plotted against the man she loved. She had her suspicions as to who this man might be, and she must learn more regarding his intentions. Relaxing her clenched hands, she forced herself to concentrate on the rest of the conversation.

"Have you found a buyer for the opium?" the Englishman asked.

"Yes, a woman." The Russian snorted out the reply as if it were a ludicrous idea. "She trades for caviar of all things. The food is not worth the shipment of medicine, yet Rashi said to take the loss and I owe him. I think he was attracted to the little English nurse, and he feels pity for her cause."

"The woman is an English nurse?" Wariness honed each of the larger man's words.

"Yes as I said. A pretty flower, fair of skin, with dark radiant eyes. And with curves a man could get lost in. Or so Rashi describes her."

The taller man glanced over his shoulder.

Josie's heart skipped a beat then tripped forward at a furious pace. It *was* Danford.

She swallowed hard and pressed back against the wall.

"My dear Vlad," Danford said. "You promised to sell the drugs outside of the country. I cannot run the risk of having this shipment traced back to me. Remember, no loose ends."

"I have no choice," the Russian protested.

"There is always a choice," Danford said, as he took a step forward, "although it may not be to your liking."

Without warning the church bells above Josie clamored into life. The cacophony of sound washed over her like a tidal wave. Her back levered against the wall, she slid to the ground, squeezed her eyes shut tight, and covered her ears. The earth trembled beneath her. The timbre and resonance surged through her body and pounded in her brain. Then the last toll of the bell drifted away into nothingness and a jarring silence took its place.

Her breath came in ragged gasps. She opened her eyes and clinging to the craggy wall, dragged herself upright to search for the men.

Only one remained in sight. Danford. He carried both the valise and the blue velvet box as he hurried from the garden and disappeared into a far stand of trees.

Josie waited for what seemed an eternity. Then convinced that Danford was not coming back, she stepped away from the bell tower and sprinted forward. As she reached the spot where the two men had stood, she stopped short and bit back a scream.

Vlad lay upon the ground, face up and unmoving, his complexion white as chalk powder. Blood covered the front of his clothing, and along with his life, disbelief slowly drained from his open staring eyes. He appeared to have been shot.

Gritting her teeth, she knelt at Vlad's side and although it seemed a wasted effort, she palpated his neck. His skin was cold and smooth as marble. No life sign could she find. There would be no purpose in returning here tomorrow.

Nausea crept around her stomach and up the back of her throat. She retched then wondered at her response. By now she should be accustomed to seeing the dead and dying. But at the hospital it was different; not so swift and unexpected. Not murder.

Gaining her feet, she stumbled backwards through the prickly patch of herbs. *Rosemary for remembrance.* The childhood ditty skipped through her mind. She would not soon forget the dreadful sight of Vlad nestled amongst the blood-spattered winter foliage.

Turning she ran toward the church and a tangible fear, greater than anything she had ever known, rose up and strangled every other emotion.

In the blink of an eye Danford had murdered Vlad. Was Danford now on his way to kill Garrick?

Go to God's infirmary and rest awhile.
                              ~Florence Nightingale

Chapter Twenty

A chill draped itself across Josie's shoulders as she hurried along. Was every section of the Barrack Hospital cold and drafty? Or was it just her impending interview with Miss Nightingale that made her shiver?

And what had she done to warrant such personal attention? Perhaps it was about the wooden spindles she'd stolen, or maybe Dr. Dennison had finally made good his threat to report her. Yet these incidents had taken place months ago. It must be something more immediate. Could it be regarding her un-chaperoned excursion to the White Horse Inn, or even worse what she had witnessed at the church yesterday?

Reaching Miss N's apartment, Josie lightly tapped upon the door.

A pale thin assistant with a surprising amount of energy answered the knock. "Very good," the woman began brightly, "and right on time. Well do come in Nurse Posey, the open door encourages the influx of cold air and our leader is ailing enough as it is."

Josie slipped in through the opening. The assistant slipped out, closing the door behind her.

"Come forward, please," Miss Nightingale requested, "and take this seat on my right. Forgive me for receiving you from my bed, but this morning it is the best I can manage."

Indeed, today their mentor did appear very ill,

yet her tired eyes still reflected the fire of her crusading nature. "It has come to my attention," she began, "that the recovery rate throughout the hospital has increased most dramatically."

"Oh yes," Josie acknowledged, thankful that the topic of conversation was general and not personal. "I believe your timely discovery of the horse carcass in the water supply has turned the tide. Unfortunately, while the incident has helped the lads tremendously, it has also proven to be another blow to the pride of the medical staff."

Miss Nightingale issued a rather unladylike sound, seemingly a cross between a snort of derision and a sigh of resignation. The silence that followed made Josie fidgety and the unintentional display did not go unnoticed by the older woman.

"I imagine," her leader acknowledge, "you are eager to learn the true purpose of our little meeting. It is not in regard to Dr. Dennison."

Josie gave a start and began to speak.

Miss Nightingale raised a hand to silence her. "No need to defend yourself my dear. The man may have been a satisfactory surgeon, but he was also an insufferable idiot. Were we not in such dire need of qualified staff, I would rejoice at his leaving. Besides, no one knows better than I that there are always two sides to every story. In addition," the older woman continued, "my request to see you has nothing to do with your assignation with a certain newspaper reporter."

Josie's mouth went dry, and her heart pounded at a furious pace.

"Your search for him among the wounded told the tale," Miss Nightingale explained. "I have a feeling," she added, with a far away look in her eyes, "that you did not enter into the encounter lightly." Then the woman's face became unreadable. "Lose your heart, but not your head," she advised. "That is what counts in the long run."

Josie sat mute and wide-eyed.

"You are an intelligent woman, Nurse Posey, or I would not have allowed you and your friend, Miss Winslow, to join our ranks. I also know who your father is, and I can only guess what it cost you in money, pride, and commitment to become a nurse. You do not seem prone to hysterics, nor do you back down from a fight, which is precisely why we are having this conversation."

Josie didn't know whether to be flattered or fearful of such an in-depth character analysis.

"I wish for you to make a short trip to the peninsula," Miss Nightingale continued. "Someone must record the ambulance techniques used by the French nuns. I had intended to oversee the task myself, but due to health reasons it was necessary that I cut short my tour of the hospital at Balaclava."

"To the peninsula," Josie murmured. "That is within the war perimeter."

"Yes. Quite," Miss Nightingale acknowledged. "In the thick of it as they say. Of course this request is purely voluntary."

This was an unexpected opportunity, in truth the perfect answer to her dilemma. Josie was sure Garrick was somewhere near the frontlines. But it would also be a very dangerous venture. Conquering her fears before they could rear up full-blown, she readily agreed to go.

"When do I leave?" she asked, leaning forward with unabashed eagerness.

"On the morrow," Miss Nightingale informed her. "I will send Agnes to you this evening with further details and your traveling papers."

Tomorrow! Just as well, that way there would be less time to worry and fret. And the quicker the better if she was to reach Garrick before Danford.

"While visiting the nuns," Miss Nightingale continued, "you will please take meticulous notes and render drawings when necessary. The information will be invaluable to the advancement of our nursing theories. We've no one to spare to escort you, but the soldiers will respect your uniform and aid you along the way. So," she added, "other than the obvious concerns, have you any questions?"

"No, Miss Nightingale. Thank you for this opportunity. I won't let you down."

"That is why you were chosen," her leader said, with seemingly heartfelt enthusiasm. "That will be all then," she said ending their conversation.

Josie rose and stepped toward the door.

"Oh, there is one more thing, Nurse Posey."

She halted and turned once more to face her superior.

"It is my understanding that the Army has never determined who was responsible for stealing the spindles from the Doctors' staircase. Have you any ideas regarding the matter?"

Josie swallowed hard. "No Miss Nightingale."

"I thought not," the other woman said. Did a smile twitch upon her lips? "It was quite a daring undertaking," she added, "and while I'm sure well intentioned, not an act of resourcefulness that I wish to see repeated."

By way of dismissal, Miss Nightingale picked up a memo and studied it.

Josie turned and fled the premises.

One word frees us of all the weight and pain in life. That word is love.

~Sophocles

Chapter Twenty-One

"What do you mean open this in case of your demise?" Gemma asked and waved the sealed envelope in Josie's face.

"Exactly that," Josie tightened her grip on the valise and made to step around her friend, but the girl nimbly blocked her move.

"But Miss N indicated the tour of the hospital at Balaclava would not be unduly dangerous," Gemma argued.

"I'm sure it won't be," Josie agreed, "And I'll be surrounded by armed soldiers ready to protect me at all cost." An image of Vlad in the rosemary patch flashed through Josie's mind, and her bravado dimmed. It was Danford she feared, not the incidents of war. But that was information best kept to herself. "Still I will be much closer to the frontlines," she added. "Who knows what might happen?"

"Bloody hell, Josie." Gemma's words were barely able to squeeze past the angry set of her mouth. "Why did you have to volunteer for such a dangerous assignment?"

Josie stared at her friend. She owed Gemma the truth. "There's another reason I was willing to go out on the inspection tour," she admitted. "I'm still trying to locate Garrick."

Gemma's brow furrowed then her expression softened. "What do you mean?"

"I wired *The Times*," Josie said, "Garrick's editor hasn't received a dispatch from him in over three weeks, and no one on this side of the Black Sea seems to know where he is. I have to find him, Gemma. I know he's in danger, and I love him."

These last three words came out in a whisper. It was the first time she had uttered the declaration aloud. Until now the words *I love him* had only existed as an echo in her heart. But now, having spoken the words once, she yearned to shout them from the rooftop. She yearned to call them into the wind, loud enough for Garrick to hear them wherever he might be.

Gemma relaxed her bulldog stance. "What makes you think he's in danger?" she asked.

"It's all rather complicated," Josie hedged, "and hard to explain. It has to do with Danford Smythe, and the black market, and a dead Russian spy."

Gemma's mouth gaped open.

"I've written it all down in the letter," Josie nodded toward the envelope.

"But you must tell the British authorities at once," Gemma advised. "They will help you."

"Why should they? The Army doesn't care one wit what happens to Garrick. He's been a thorn in their side ever since his arrival. To them his disappearance would be considered a boon. Besides, I can't just march into Military Headquarters and declare Danford Smythe, British spy and wealthy gentleman extraordinaire, a thief and a murderer. At best they would accuse me of being an hysterical female. At worst they might detain me against my will. That would leave no one to help Garrick."

Gemma reached for her cape. "I'm going with you," she said.

Josie stayed the girl's motions, and the love she felt for her friend welled to a painful knot in the back of her throat. "Someone must be here in the advent of Garrick's return," Josie said. "He may not even know he's in danger, and he'll want an explanation as to where I've gone and why. I can't trust anyone but you."

The stubborn expression returned to Gemma's face. "I don't like this," she protested.

"I know," Josie said softly, "but truly there is no other way."

****

As she stood on the bow of the steamer, Josie held tight to the tattered wool blanket she wore over her cape. The weather was freezing cold, and she was chilled to the bone, yet these miserable conditions topside were preferable to the dank and stifling realm below deck.

Frosted with foreboding, the inhospitable water had betrayed her mission for five days running. Black in temperament, as well as name, the ebony sea had fought the ship's forward progress with unrelenting stamina and hour upon endless hour they seemed not to move at all.

She stared at the dark choppy waves. This heartless tarn, a horrifying work of nature, was the watery grave of countless men. Tossed by hurricanes and riled by storms, the inland ocean cruelly separated the British soldiers from their supplies and the healing comforts of Scutari and she had come to hate this never changing dark visage.

As if aware of her disparaging accusations, an angry wave surged upward and smothered the bow. The vessel shuddered and lurched to starboard. Barely able to maintain her footing, Josie grabbed a metal strut with both hands. With icy indifference, the gale battered the prow. It snatched away her breath and froze her tears upon her cheeks, but the weeping in her heart continued to flow freely.

She gripped the rail until her knuckles turned white. What if she were too late? Garrick's image haunted her night and day, and every moment it took to reach him seemed to stretch into infinity, and forever was a weighty foe beneath which to labor.

She closed her eyes and still saw his face. She must find him. He was her second chance at life, at love, at happiness. How had she survived this long without him? She remembered what true love felt like, what it could do to a woman's heart and soul, and she wanted to feel that way again. She wanted to be loved by Garrick. Phillip would have wanted it too.

Opening her eyes, she glared in defiance at the dark smudge of land on the far horizon. Did it appear somewhat closer? Yes, they were finally making headway. At that realization, Josie's heart raced then her palms began to sweat. What was she to do once they reached the Crimean Peninsula? After completing her assignment for Miss Nightingale, she couldn't just wander about willy-nilly looking for the war. She should be making some sort of a plan to find Garrick and the forbidding frontlines.

She knew the main Russian stronghold was at Fort Nicholas in Sebastopol, and the Allied Army would be close at hand. But what reason could she possibly offer the French nuns for wanting to travel in that direction?

Out of habit, Josie patted her uniform pocket, and the parchments cosseted within crinkled reassuringly. She'd left the journal safe in her room, but carried Garrick's poem and newspaper commentary, in effect a part of him. She knew in her heart he had not written the New Year's Eve missive. But he had touched these pages with the very same hands that had held her with equal passion. He had pondered over each word written upon these precious papers. Keeping them near made her feel closer to him, and she thought somehow this special connection would lead her in the proper direction.

****

The countryside careened past in a blur of sepia fringed in white. Josie clutched at the open framework of the transport vehicle and braced her feet against the floorboards. "Is it prudent to run headfirst into a war rather than trying to sneak up upon it?" she asked, hoping the driver would slow their madcap pace.

"Do not worry, Cherie. The axles and wheels are quite sturdy, and most of the Muscovites are civilized enough not to fire upon a medical supply wagon."

Most? That was reassuring. At least she was no longer aboard that damnable steamship. Of course, arriving at the French field hospital alive would be helpful to her plan.

As they rounded a curve the driver leaned against her. "Mon petite chuette," he said. "You are much too pretty and soft to be British, are you sure you are not from Bordeaux or Poitiers?"

"I am British," Josie assured him, "to the core. You however, leave no doubt as to heritage. Only a Frenchman would be so bold as well as daring."

At her double-edged compliment the man threw back his head and laughed then he urged the mules into an even more breakneck speed.

By the time they reached the perimeter of the camp, Josie's bottom felt more bruised than the last melon on Chelsea's fruit day. And her hands were numb from the death-grip she had maintained the entire distance.

Reining in the team, the driver sent the vehicle into a skidding halt before a large marquee tent. Two nuns scurried forward to great them.

"The chaplain told us to expect you, little one,"

the older woman said. Her English was sweetened by a melodious French accent. "We are sorry that Miss Nightingale and the others have taken ill. Our prayers are with them."

Josie thanked her and cautiously crawled down from the wagon.

"Would you care for a cup of chamomile tea, dear?" the smaller nun asked.

Josie nodded and relaxed the fist she held clenched against her midsection.

"When you ride with Etienne," the woman added, "you throw caution to the wind as well as your stomach."

The Frenchman gasped at the remark and feigned a hurt expression.

"But he is the most courageous ambulance driver in all of the Crimea," the nun added.

At such praise, a look of pride replaced the man's frown and he grinned and drove away.

Josie followed the nuns into the tent where she carefully eased down onto the one chair at the table that sported a cushion. Even with the padding, it hurt to sit.

As one Sister steeped tea, the other presented her with a mountain of statistics, documents, and scaled down sketches of ambulances. Josie felt her hand spasm at the thought of copying all this information. Mercifully, some of the material had already been duplicated for her.

With the image of Garrick hovering in the back of her mind, she immersed herself in the information heaped upon the table and by late afternoon, she knew more about French ambulances than Napoleon III knew about French women.

"Dear ladies," Josie said, as she finished tracing the last sketch. "You are indeed ingenious in your approach to treating the victims of war. Miss Nightingale will be forever grateful for your generosity in sharing such knowledge."

At her accolades the nuns fairly glowed and beatific expressions shimmered upon their faces. "In the name of God," the elder said, and made the sign of the cross, "we all fight the same battle in caring for the sick and injured. Use the learning to save lives. That will be our reward."

Josie stood and rubbed the small of her aching back. "Are there any British soldiers or citizens in your field hospital?" she asked, as casually as possible.

"Of course not, dear. They would be at the British camp or on their way back to Scutari by way of Balaclava."

Eyes downcast Josie organized her notes and drawings. "How far is it to the British base camp?" she asked.

"I believe it to be seven kilometers east by northeast. Is that not correct Sister Clarisse?"

The other nun nodded in agreement.

Seven kilometers. Josie exhaled slowly. With the main roads churned to mud it might as well be on the moon. Why in heavens name weren't the two allied armies bivouacked beside one another? Nothing in the military ever made sense. Yet there must be a way of getting there. She'd come too far to turn back now.

"May we offer you supper before you depart?"

Josie's gaze darted to the nuns. They expected her to leave immediately but she knew the transport ship waiting to take her back to Scutari would not embark for two more days. This was her opportunity to strike out on her own.

"No thank you," she said, "although I do appreciate your hospitality". Her stomach grumbled as if in protest to her decision, but her desire to be out from under the watchful eyes of the kindly nuns outweighed her need for food.

Scooping up the sheaf of notes, she shoved them into her bag. "I would, however, like to stretch my legs a bit before facing the return trip. I will have one of the soldiers direct me to Etienne when I am ready."

Both sisters opened their mouth as if to protest her plan, but before they could voice their opposition to her intentions, Josie ducked through the opening in the tent.

Did one of the nuns call her name? Pretending not to hear she kept walking.

Several paces up the path, she deposited her parcel of notes in an area where they were sure to be found. That way if something untoward should befall her, the nuns could forward the information back to Miss Nightingale at Scutari.

Skirting the barracks, Josie angled across the compound to the supply depot where lorries weighed down with ammunition and gunpowder were being unloaded.

If only she could stow away on one of them.

Excited by the prospect she quickened her pace. Then she paused. What was she thinking? None of the French supply wagons were likely to be heading to the British camp. Now what?

Nearby, a bedraggled collection of donkeys and other work animals milled about in a makeshift pen. A jumble of small drays stood beside the arena. Perhaps she could go it alone.

Her back stiff with desperation and determination, she circled around to the left. Nothing was going to keep her from reaching Garrick. She'd walk to the British lines if necessary.

"Halt mademoiselle."

She jumped in surprise as a perimeter guard stepped from between two tents to block her path.

"No one is allowed beyond this point," he said, in his native language.

Frantically she worked to recall her rudimentary French. "I'm a British nurse," she explained. "Sister Clarisse sent me to observe your method of cataloging supplies." Did the lie sound convincing?

He studied her face and contemplated her figure.

She smiled and tried to slow her rapid breathing.

"You may proceed then, but via the main entrance," he instructed, and nodded over his shoulder.

"Merci," she said and moved to follow his directions.

He snared her elbow as she passed.

The pulse in her neck jumped as she stared up into his face. It was all she could do not turn and run.

"I am free from duty at five o'clock," he said, with a grin.

She smiled with relief and disengaged his hand from her arm. "I only have time for wounded soldiers," she said, and stepped around him.

"For you, cherie, I would gladly shoot myself in the foot."

"Please don't go to such trouble," she called over her shoulder. "I'm not staying long."

He gave her a good-natured laugh. "I miss you already."

Not looking back, she boldly picked her way over the uneven terrain. She was sure the sentry's gaze was still focused on her backside, and reaching the refuge of the supply tent, she gratefully slipped inside.

Three small lanterns with soot-coated mantles comprised the only source of light, and to her good fortune, the soldiers who unloaded the supplies were too preoccupied to take notice of her.

Keeping to the shadows, she ducked behind a towering wall of barrels and crates.

By sense of touch, she felt her way along the row of provisions. A splinter gouged her hand. Biting back a yelp of pain, she gritted her teeth, yanked the wooden shard free, and raised her palm to her lips to suck away the blood. Then at the sound of voices, she angled her head to one side and peered through a gap between two barrels. Her minor injury forgotten, Josie eavesdropped upon the men. Straining to hear, she mentally labored to convert the rapidly flowing foreign words into English.

A French officer appeared on the scene. "You are to deliver these cases of champagne to the Duke of Cambridge," he ordered and tapped his riding crop against the wooden crates stacked beside a small wagon.

"But the Duke is at the British front at Mamelon," a soldier of lesser rank complained.

"That is the whole idea," the Officer said. "The wine is a gift from General Pelissier to celebrate the British taking the area and advancing to the trenches at Malakoff."

"Seems they could use gun powder and blankets more than sparkling wine."

"Oui, I agree," the third Frenchman put in. "His royal highness, the Duke, can afford his own spirits. Why not leave this for us. We fought as hard today as the English."

"It's a matter of politics and upper class back-scratching," the man in charge explained. "General Pelissier sends the wine and in the next big attack, the Duke will assign the vanguard to the French. Glory and honor bought with a bottle. It happens all the time."

"I'd rather have the glory of the bottle directly," the man loading the wagon said.

"Just do as you are told, Bertrand," the officer

ordered. "Toot de sweet," he called over his shoulder and he took his leave.

Josie nearly squealed with delight. She could not believe her good fortune. Here was her transportation, ready to depart and headed in the proper direction.

"Orders, be orders, Bertrand," the smaller man finally said. "If we hurry we can be there by dawn. Bring along a cartouche of bayonets," he whispered, "we've extras, but the Britishers are low on them. We'll trade for a bottle once we get there."

Bertrand grinned. "A little low-class back scratching. I like the way you think, Michele. You would do well in politics."

The two men secured the load and scrambled aboard. As the driver urged the team into a walk and through the gaping tent flaps, Josie darted from the shadows and eased up onto the back of the open wagon. She shoved her way between two crates, settled in for the long haul, and wrapped her cape around her body and face.

Exhausted she closed her eyes, but too nervous to sleep, she soon opened them again. Her stomach grumbled, and she shivered. Was Garrick cold and tired and hungry too? Please, God, she prayed, let him be alive and safe.

To keep up her nerve, she pictured Garrick in her mind and recalled the night they had made love. His silken kisses had sweetly aroused every part of her body. A memory of that fire flared deep inside of her then quickly died away—leaving her feeling even more empty. She knew why. Their unnamed magic had been forged by a shared experience. She could never recapture that magnificence alone. It could only be rekindled in Garrick's arms. Without him she was incomplete, like a violin without strings, or a flower that held no fragrance. As loneliness hardened to a cold lump in the pit of her stomach, she hugged her cape closer and tried not to cry.

The horses labored uphill, and although it seemed impossible, the wagon slowed to an even more snail like pace. The moon had crossed the sky hours ago, would they never reach their destination? Then as they crested the ridge her anticipation was renewed. A jumble of sounds met her ears, and the smell of wood smoke filled the air. Above the whir of a grindstone, and the ring of a smithy's hammer, she heard men's voices and they were speaking the Queen's English.

Shivering with expectation as well as the cold, she peeked out from beneath her woolen cloak. In the soft light of the burgeoning dawn, she saw the hazy outline of tents and the neat rows of picketed horses. This had to be the British field camp.

Gathering her garment about her, she scooted to the far edge of the wagon and eased down to the ground. They were moving faster than she had anticipated and she stumbled to the side of the road, nearly losing her balance. Hood jammed into place, she careened to a halt and cautiously perused her surroundings.

In every direction, the convoluted terrain was dotted with soldiers as they rose to meet the day. Men on ridges were silhouetted against the purple haze of the morning sky, others were grouped in small clusters, some silent, some singing sad songs, some rowdy and scuffling. A tangled forest, ravaged for the wood it once promised, loomed just beyond the glow of the furthest campfire.

She edged along the side of the muddy road, and her gaze drifted over the miles of tents and fabricated buildings. It could take days to search the entire camp for Garrick. There must be a more logical approach for her to employ. She would begin with the hospital tent. If he wasn't there, she would demand assistance from the officer in charge of the command post. Yes, that was a good plan.

Reaching a fork in the road, she bore to the right, keeping the parade commons and flag pole in view. Every tent looked the same. It would be easy to become lost in this city of soldiers.

Sidestepping a deep rut, she paused and a familiar figure caught and held her attention. But it wasn't the man she loved, it was Danford Smythe. Did he also seek Garrick? The jumble of nerves in her stomach tightened. She must not lose sight of him.

He crossed beyond the perimeter of the camp and entered the woods, and as the distance between them lengthened, panic squeezed at her heart. She hitched up her skirt to avoid the mud and rushed into the forest after him.

A drizzling rain began to fall. It blurred the world around her. Where had he gone? He seemed to have disappeared right before her eyes.

In a dither, she halted and turned around full circle. The scraggy underbrush appeared the same in every direction and each tree mirrored the next. Fright kicked at her stomach and she felt like a six-year-old separated from her parents at the county fair. Chiding herself for her stupidity, she wandered first one direction then the next.

Thickening clouds continued to hold the sun at bay and while watching for signs of Danford, rather than paying attention to her footing, she met her doom.

A patch of wet leaves betrayed her step. She skidded sideways and pitched over the lip of a small ravine. Arms reaching, hands grasping, she sought to slow her descent, but the hillside was devoid of brush or anything viable with which to break her fall. She tumbled downward—nonstop—her trajectory culminating in an abrupt halt at the bottom, where she lay stunned and breathless. Every muscle and joint felt imprinted with the rocky terrain recently covered, and she felt as if she'd been trampled by a coach and four.

As if taking pity upon her, the rain ceased and the sun came out to comfort her aching body, and a delicious sleepiness blanketed her senses. She closed her eyes, just for a moment, and surrendered to bruised exhaustion.

While there's life there's hope.
~Miguel De Cervantes

Chapter Twenty-Two

"There, there, child, you're safe now, Mother's got you."

The soothing voice and reassuring words slipped through the darkness to draw Josie back to the conscious world. Her eyes fluttered open, and she stared up into the face of the woman in whose arms she was being held.

The dark-skinned female gave her a comforting hug and smiled down at her like an old friend. "That's better," acknowledged the portly woman seated upon the ground at her side. "You're doing quite nicely now. Just rest a spell longer and catch your breath."

Having dispensed this advice, the stranger gently assisted Josie into a more upright position. Silently they studied one another. Josie hadn't felt this cosseted and protected since she was a very little girl. A child often left alone to view the world from between the starched folds of Nanny Everette's white smocked apron. A smile eased across her lips. The woman before her wore a faded yellow dress and a floppy blue hat, sporting red ribbons. Nanny would have loved that notion.

"I'm Mary Seacole," the woman said, by way of introduction. "But most of the lads call me Mother Seacole."

"I am Nurse Posey and my friends call me Josie. Where am I?" she asked and glanced around.

"Well lamb, at present you're at the foot of a

rather nice cypress tree. And I'd say we're approximately half a kilometer from the Russian lines."

A lump of fear, fiery and caustic, rose up in the back of Josie's throat. But it was not the proximity of the enemy that filled her with such unease. She grabbed at Mother Seacole's dress and twisted her fingers into the soft fabric. "The man I was following. Where is he?"

"You were alone when I came upon you," Mother assured her. "I saw no one else,"

She groaned inwardly. Danford had eluded her. But if he was in the vicinity, it was possible Garrick was nearby as well. "Perhaps you know of another man I seek," Josie began. "He's tall with dark hair. You could not mistake him for another as he usually wears high black boots and a fringed leather jacket."

"Sounds a bit like a free-trapper I met down in Panama," Mother Seacole said with a chuckle. "He was from the Americas," she reminisced, a far away look in her eyes, "and as fearless a man as ever there was. At least in most instances," she rambled on. "Then one night he suffered a knife wound while fighting over the favors of a woman, and as I stitched him up, he fainted dead away. Men become children when they fall ill or injured," she declared. "That's why simple mothering is usually what the poor dears need most."

"Yes, yes, I believe that to be true as well," Josie agreed, breaking in on the other woman's musings. "But the man I spoke of, it's imperative that I find him."

"He may have made his way to Spring Hill," Mrs. Seacole suggested. "I've been gone since sun up, but as the crow flies it's not far from here. Why don't we head that way ourselves? Upon our arrival we can search for your friend and you may refresh yourself and take nourishment."

Josie glanced around. The night truly was drawing nigh. She must have lain asleep for most of the day. Maybe it would be a good idea to go to this Spring Hill. The name sounded safe and somehow familiar. Concentrating harder she remembered why. "You're the sutler who runs the *British Hotel.*"

"That I am." Mother Seacole beamed at the recognition. "And along with convalescing gentlemen officers, I serve a darn good mess. My mince pies and comestibles are much sought after."

"I've heard about you," Josie conceded. "Several wounded soldiers at Scutari have spoken of you with great fondness."

Mrs. Seacole's smile broadened. "Hopefully the lads haven't divulged all the details of my exploits. One day I plan to write a book about my wonderful adventures, and if my escapades are common knowledge, who will pay the purchase price?"

Suddenly, and with unexpected agility, the older woman gained her feet and then reached down to assist Josie. "Come along girl. Are you able to stand?"

"Yes. I believe so." Accepting the outstretched hand, she levered up off of the ground and after being assessed for permanent injuries and none being found, the two of them headed off into the countryside on a path that was to Josie indiscernible.

"What in heaven's name are you doing wandering about on your own, Miss Josie?"

"I was on assignment for Miss Florence Nightingale," she explained "to study the methods used by the French nuns in treating the wounded in the field."

"I see," Mother said, as she guided Josie over a stony ridgeback. "'Tis true these women are good examples for us all. They're intelligent and full of no nonsense. And Miss Nightingale, is she still ailing?"

"Unfortunately, yes. Do you know her?"

"Not really," Mrs. Seacole said with a wistful expression. "We met but briefly when I passed through Scutari. It was many weeks ago, but I shall never forget walking through those fearful miles of suffering."

"You were at the Barracks Hospital?" she asked, in surprise. "I'm sorry to have missed you. Why did you not remain with us? We certainly could have used your helping hands, and in Scutari you would not have been in mortal jeopardy on a daily basis as you must be out here."

"It sounds a good plan doesn't it?" the woman said softly, "but although I was not told in so many words to move on, neither was I asked to remain."

"But this is shocking news," Josie said. According to her patients, the skills of this Jamaican woman were legendary. They declared she performed medical accomplishments that bordered upon the miraculous. Some called her the yellow woman and precious as gold was her knowledge of herbal cures and remedies. How could the authorities shun her offer of help?

"Please," Josie urged, curious to know more about this stalwart woman, "tell me how you came to be here and how you dared to entertain such an undertaking as the *British Hotel*".

Mother Seacole gave a weary sigh as if the act of looking back reminded her of just how arduous the self imposed journey had been. Then she brightened noticeably and launched into a tale as remarkable as it was entertaining.

"I had just come home to Kingston town," the woman began, "to help with the yellow fever epidemic of 1853. Many of the English stationed there were stricken down with the deadly foe. Sometimes," she pointed out as an aside, "the Motherland pays dearly for her colonial possessions, and this time the price was the death of many soldiers."

"About eight months later, it became necessary for me to return to the Isthmus of Panama to wind up the affairs of my hotel there. But before I left for Navy Bay, word came 'round that Britain had declared war against Russia. Several of the English regiments I had known so well in Jamaica had already left for the front. I longed to join their ranks and would stand for hours staring at my tattered world map studying the area where someone had chalked a red cross to mark the location of the Crimea. I've always had the wanderlust," she admitted with a mischievous grin. "A trait acquired from my wayward Scottish father."

"I realized it would not be an easy journey, but I had endured much during my time in Cuba and Panama, and having survived those tribulations no worse for wear, I reasoned I could accomplish this as well. Wherever the need arises, and on whatever distant shore, I asked no higher or greater privilege than to minister to the soldiers."

Mother Seacole stopped to take a breath and Josie glanced at her in wonder.

"Upon finally reaching London," the woman continued, "I eagerly inquired at the War Office. But my request for an interview with Lord Panmure was refused. At this stage, being naïve and still optimistic, I transferred all my energy and attention to the Quartermaster General's department. There I was at least granted an interview, but the results were equally unsatisfactory. It was suggested I apply to the Medical Department which I did. But again, no luck. All this required many more days than I had anticipated, which broke my heart as I was desperate to reach the lads, and it was none too easy on the purse I might add. Yet day after day, I was forced to sit idle—watching and waiting as my time and finances eroded away with equal vigor."

"Blind fools," Josie said, without thinking.

"It was not entirely unexpected" Mother Seacole said soothingly. "In my country, a medicine woman would be much sought after, especially in times such as these. But in England, despite my references, they merely laughed at my suggestion."

"But there must have been a mistake or some confusion regarding your experience and purpose," Josie said.

The older woman favored her with an indulgent expression. "It's highly unlikely dear. I carried letters of introduction from two British Army physicians, both of whom I worked with in Kingston. I imagine it was simply due to the color of my skin. It makes a difference to some folks. Of course the soldiers never seem to notice. They just care that I've a gentle hand and a bit of tried and true knowledge when it comes to tending their wounds and ills."

Josie was shocked by this information then she wondered why she should be. After all, if the Army was reluctant to accept the aid of English nurses, how much more difficult it must be for this Jamaican woman to plead her case.

"Please," she prompted, "do go on."

"Well, when necessary I can be remarkably stubborn, a trait acquired from my Jamaican mother along with her healing skills. And since Miss Nightingale and the rest of your lot had already left for the Crimea, I decided to offer myself as a recruit directly to Mrs. Sydney Herbert in London. I was sure more nurses would follow your group, but my presence before the door of her outer office was duly ignored and again I sat vigil alone and in vain. I confess," she said with a shake of her head, "my dreams were dashed to a new low. They were to reach an even lower depth when one of Mrs.

Herbert's companions finally took pity to inform me that no position was currently available nor was anything likely to open up that would be suitable for a *woman of my type*. In other words I was summarily dismissed."

"That night, feeling utterly dejected, I wandered along the London docks, and as I stood in the cold misty darkness, I cried and prayed and wondered why. Why was I called to serve and then denied service? "

"How," Josie declared, "could you possibly keep going under such circumstances?"

"How could I not?" Mother Seacole returned. "I knew the lads needed me. And no doubt, they were suffering more than I. So after a good night's sleep, the answer came to me. If I could not go as a nurse, I would simply go as a friend. I could at least bring them a bit of the hearth-fires and home cooking. I sent word on ahead to raise interest and clientele then I boarded the screw steamer *Hollander* and here I am."

"And you met with Miss Nightingale when you arrived in Turkey?"

"Yes, although this happenstance did nothing to alter my course of action. Following a courteous but brief conversation with your leader in Scutari, I was obliged to spend the night in the washerwomen's quarters. Then the next day I went to Constantinople and on to the Peninsula and here I am."

Josie blinked several times as if the action would clear her mind, yet she could think of nothing appropriate to say. She would have expected more fair minded consideration from Miss Nightingale. "I'm sorry," Josie said, not quite sure for whom she apologized. "It was very foolish of them to refuse your offer of help, and it was very brave and magnanimous of you to forge ahead on your own."

"I don't know about being brave," Mother Seacole said, with a smile. "I leave that to the soldiers. And as far as forging ahead on my own well, when the British Government turned me down in London and Miss Nightingale turned me down in Scutari, I was given no other choice. Besides," she added, "I like the freedom of doing things my own way. I've a feeling I wouldn't have lasted a fortnight being told what to do and when to do it."

As they proceeded in silence, Josie mulled over this bundle of extraordinary information. Then the stillness surrounding them was interrupted by an oddly yet not unmusical woofling sound. Rounding a clump of trees Josie saw the source of the curious noise. Up ahead stood a little brown donkey, harnessed to a small dray.

"There's a good girl," Mother Seacole said. As they drew near, she scratched the long eared animal's shaggy neck. The whimsical beast continued to *sing* and huffle while Mother retrieved a biscuit from her pocket.

"You're a good pip to stay put this time and not wander off," she praised, as she fed the treat to the little burro. The endearing animal seemed to smile up at her, then in search of another reward, the donkey soundly nudged Mother's ample thigh. The woman laughed good-naturedly and promised the beast more treats upon their return to the hotel.

Josie glanced at the contents of the cart. There were blankets and bandages and glass jars of crushed herbs, and several containers of mysterious looking ointments. All were neatly stored within wooden crates. A barrel of water filled the remaining space, and an armload of fresh flora lay off to one side. Particles of dirt still clung to the roots of the greenery, and they smelled freshly harvested. Evidently, Mother Seacole had been out seeking a bit of native plant-life to add to her stores as she scoured the countryside for any forgotten soldiers.

"Well," Mother said to the little donkey, "that explains it. Now I see why you did not follow your nose back to your pen."

Josie glanced in the direction Mrs. Seacole indicated. The heavy cart had sunk into the mud, anchoring the cart and small animal into place.

"I know it's a lot to ask," the older woman said, still referencing the donkey, "but you're strong for your size and we must all do the impossible while we're here. Walk on girl," she commanded, giving the animal an encouraging slap on the rump.

The plucky beast strained against the traces. Josie helped Mother push the cart from behind. There was a sucking sound as the conveyance lurched forward and the uneven wooden wheels escaped the clutches of the mud.

"Go, go, go." Mother encouraged as she ran ahead to take hold of the donkey's halter. In mass, they sprinted forward until they reached a rocky patch where they could slow their pace without fear of sinking back into the mud.

"Good show," Mother gasped happily between breaths. "The worst is over then. It's mostly down hill from here."

****

The *British Hotel* was a vision out of time and place. It stood proudly in the middle of nowhere and appeared to grow directly up out of the ground. If the surrounding landscape had sported fewer trees and a bit more sand, the remarkable structure would have qualified as a mirage.

A truly inspired concept, it offered succor to officers in various stages of recovery. This was evidenced by several men who now lounged upon the porch. Some played cards, others simply sat soaking up the last rays of the setting the sun. Josie stepped around a man smoking a long stemmed pipe. The aroma of tobacco wafted pleasantly through the air.

The interior of the rustic structure was neat and clean and equally appealing, and as she entered the establishment, the wooden floors creaked out a welcoming hello. Great shelves lined the walls, crammed to overflowing with all manner of supplies and staples. Pairs of boots in various sizes filled one whole section, and a smoked ham flanked by braids of fresh garlic hung on a timbered upright.

Several of the soldiers straightened and took notice as she crossed the room.

Mother shepherded her over to a vacant chair. "What is the name and rank of the soldier you seek?" she asked.

"His name is Garrick Allen," she said. "But he is not a soldier," she hastened to explain. "He's a correspondent for *The Times*." Would this latter information aid her search or hinder it? Not everyone appreciated Garrick's role in bringing news to the people back home.

Mother's expression brightened and she seemed appreciative rather than taken aback by the revelation. The older woman calmly made a circuit of the room, stopping to speak quietly with each man. They all listened attentively but each in turn shook his head in a negative response.

Josie's shoulders slumped. She knew without being told no one had seen Garrick. Tears burned at the back of her eyes. Where could he have gone?

"I'm sorry, love," Mother said, as she took to the chair at Josie's side. "No one has seen your friend. But there is a packaged tour arriving tomorrow from Constantinople. Perhaps someone amongst that group will have seen your friend."

"A packaged tour?" Josie echoed.

"Yes. Can you imagine? Travel and accommodations, London to the battlefields, all for five pounds. Ghastly isn't it? The people who organize these escapades provide their clients with horse races, dog hunts, and cricket matches. And I provide the food."

Josie studied Mrs. Seacole in surprise.

"Well why not?" Mother defended. "If these rich women and traveling gentlemen are hardhearted enough to come here for their entertainment, I'm glad enough to take their money. And the funds go back into helping the lads, so where's the harm done?"

"None of course," Josie agreed. She thought again of Garrick and a great sigh of sadness escaped her lips.

Mrs. Seacole took her hand and patted it reassuringly. "He means a great deal to you doesn't he?"

Afraid to speak less she break down and cry, Josie simply nodded.

Everyone thinks of changing the world,
but no one thinks of changing himself.
~Leo Tolstoy

Chapter Twenty-Three

Artillery officer Leo Tolstoy lay in the field camp and stared up at the starlit sky.

Did beauty equal to the ugliness spawned by war still exist upon this mortal coil? Of late it seemed an impossibility. War was so unjust and futile. All who waged it must be driven to stifle the voice of conscience within themselves. And this evening, Leo realized he was no different. Heaven help him, his heart held not one ounce of pity for the anguish of the world. Tonight it was a personal grief that plagued him.

He rolled his head from side to side, overwhelmed by anger and disbelief. How could he have been so careless? He supposed being chilled to the bone, half starved, and shot at had something to do with it. Yet to leave his haversack behind was a very great loss, and the resulting sorrow he felt was more crippling than any physical pain he had suffered thus far in battle. The months, nay years, of meticulous notes and vivid impressions were gone to him forever. Or could these literary labors, born in his brightest moments and his darkest hours, be accurately reconstructed? To his weary mind and body, the task of recapturing such fleeting gifts of inspiration seemed improbable at best.

He shifted his gaze and studied the Russian camp. It was deathly quiet on the 4th bastion, and like lumps of hard coal, the soldiers lie scattered and frozen in place upon the unyielding ground. What a contrast to the mind-shattering chaos that would most assuredly erupt with the advent of the dawn. And come tomorrow afternoon, he would be transferred to the battery on the River Belbek. That circumstance would take him closer to his brother but many miles farther away from his lost treasure. Tonight was his last chance to take action.

His time and patience were running out, and although he recognized these icons as the strongest of all warriors, tonight they were his greatest enemies. Perhaps the here and now was the only time that really counted. It is the most important time because it is the only time over which we have any power.

Emboldened by his own rhetoric, Leo eased from beneath his tattered blanket, rolled onto his side, and levered into a crouching position. As he prepared to creep silently from camp, a hand snaked out and seized his arm.

"What do you contemplate?" Mikhail whispered.

Leo held his position and quietly observed the face of his friend. "I thought you were asleep," he replied.

"That is not an answer," the other man insisted, his tones hushed and flavored with concern.

Leo remained silent, and his lack of response spoke volumes to his comrade.

"You are returning to that field of destruction to look for your wretched knapsack aren't you?" Mikhail accused. "If our soldiers catch you retreating, you will be shot for a deserter," he warned, "and should you be captured by the British or French your fate will most likely be the same."

Leo smiled reassuringly. "It is my life's blood upon those pages, Mikhail," he explained, slipping free of the other man's grasp. "And should I die trying to retrieve them, it is of little consequence.

For without them I am just as dead."

****

Adjusting the strap of the haversack more comfortably on his shoulder, Garrick again questioned the wisdom of his decision.

Perhaps his head injury had done more damage to his brain than he realized. In his heart, he knew he should not be returning to the Russian front, but this damnable bag full of another man's dreams drew him like a magnet back to the field where he had first stumbled upon the leather albatross. He wondered if his own journal were in the hands of someone who gave a damn about the written word.

On the positive side, it was because of this ill advised literary mission that he had come to realize the leads he followed on the peninsula were complete fabrications. While speaking with the British field commander regarding the return of the leather pouch, he had overheard another conversation, one that refuted everything Tuco had told him.

Lord Pagent had been absolved of any wrong doing by the illness he suffered, and he now knew the other officer supposedly involved had been killed weeks ago. It was back to square one in determining who was behind the stealing and selling of Allied supplies. His money was on Danford. But why the misleading information? Simply to cover his tracks? Or was it just for sport? Either way you had to give the man credit for being as ingenious as he was dangerous. And either way, resuming the investigation would mean locating Danford as soon as possible.

Groping his way through the lackluster foliage, Garrick forced his attention back to the present. On the eastern plains, the sun crept slowly over the horizon. And today, as the great burning orb grudgingly appeared, it seemed to lumber into place with a heavy heart.

Cresting a small rise, he paused and studied the terrain. This section of oblivion seemed somewhat familiar. He was sure this is where he had nearly lost his life. Now what? Should he just toss the bag upon the cold ground in the likelihood that some Russian straggler seeking his division would blunder upon it? That seemed a bit chancy.

At the sound of someone approaching, Garrick's decision was made for him. The French or British would not be coming from that direction. It could only be a Muscovite.

He looped the strap of the haversack over a nearby tree branch, and with his flagging energy renewed by chance of discovery, he plunged into the underbrush and secreted himself behind a large boulder.

Once again the bracken rustled and Garrick peered from his place of concealment to see who, besides himself, was mad enough to be wandering this deserted battlefield.

A Russian soldier, thin and tired, stumbled into view. The man poked about the landscape with a large stick as if he searched for something. Garrick glanced up at the leather bag. It still swayed to and fro where he had placed in the tree.

The slight movement caught the attention of the enemy soldier. As if stunned by the discovery, the man halted dead in his tracks. Then his expression transformed into that of wonderment. He tossed the stick aside and reached for the pouch. Gently he disengaged it from the limb and clutched the worn knapsack to his chest as if he cradled a well-loved child, and in a reverent manner, he raised his gaze heavenward. Then suddenly, as if remembering where he was, he glanced around and quickly retraced his steps in the direction from which he had come.

Garrick studied the retreating figure, and an odd feeling of sadness washed over him. The man he'd watched was his sworn enemy, yet in another time and place, perhaps they could have called one another friend.

Two men look out through the same bars:
One sees the mud, and one the stars.
~Fredrick Langbridge

Chapter Twenty-Four

Nerves all a jangle, Josie glanced over her shoulder. It was twilight and very eerie, and the possibility of ogres and demons did not seem all that outlandish. Perhaps she should have waited until morning. But in her heart she felt time was of the essence.

For two precious days, she had remained with Mother Seacole at the *British Hotel,* and not one of the pretentious travelers on the package tours had seen or heard of Garrick. That left one logical path to follow. Her best chance of finding Garrick was to find Danford. Those two men were destined to cross paths, and the Lord only knew what disastrous consequences would result from such an encounter.

She had spent most of the day convincing Mother Seacole to guide her back to the area where she had last seen Danford. It hadn't been a debate easily won, but the dear woman had finally relented, realizing that Josie's love for Garrick was a force that engendered action first and sound reasoning second. So here she was once again, alone in the woods, beyond the perimeter of the British field camp. But this time, as she trekked through the newly fallen snow, she had taken note of several landmarks, ensuring a successful return to camp should the need arise.

Where, she wondered, had Danford been hurrying off to on the day she had seen him. Most likely to another clandestine meeting. As if to confirm her suspicions, the dim outline of an old cottage wavered into view. Had this been his destination? Was he there now? Smoke curled from the lopsided chimney indicating someone was inside or at least near at hand.

Before deciding whether to boldly advance or reconnoiter the area first, a rustling noise sounded in the underbrush. Vivid memories of the wild dogs she'd faced near Danford's villa tore through her mind, and she stood frozen in place. It's just a deer or a horse strayed from the picket she silently reassured herself

The foliage quaked more vigorously and with a bellicose grunt, a wild boar trotted into view. He was enormous, with reddish eyes and shiny white tusks. Like medals of honor, well-healed battle scars were displayed upon his thick brown hide. Black spiky bristles of hair rippled along his back

Josie took one step backward. The beast followed—stopping when she stopped, moving when she moved. The end of his snout twitched as if he'd caught her sent and relished a more thorough sampling.

Careful to move only her eyes, Josie glanced around. The cottage was too far away to make a dash for it, and she choked back the impulse to call for help. Any abrupt noise might set the animal to the attack.

A branch snapped behind her. She jumped and so did the boar. A second noise sounded. Without warning, the hoary creature hunched his back legs, dug his feet into the dirt, and lunged forward.

With a scream, she turned to run but something blocked her retreat. A solid form clothed in brown leather brought her up short. She caught a fleeting glimpse of a man's hand wrapped around the butt of a large pistol. In one smooth motion, he cocked the hammer and squeezed the trigger.

Bright light and a thunderous noise erupted from the barrel of the revolver. The percussion threw her up against the man's rigid chest, and his free arm surrounded her—keeping her upright.

Ears ringing and senses reeling, she peeked sideways. The acrid smoke dissipated and swirled upward. The fearsome beast was gone.

With a sob of relief, she buried her face against the man's shoulder and clutched at the lapels of his coat. The softness of leather beneath her fingertips brought her comfort, and she studied the garment more carefully. It was Garrick's. Once again, he had come to her rescue. He was her guardian angel, her champion, always there when she needed him most. Heart pounding she responded to his embrace, and with a thrill in her heart and a sigh upon her lips, she reached up to stroke his cheek. Then her smile froze and she strained back in shock and disbelief.

It was Danford. His pale hair lay feathered around his face and the collar of the coat that belonged to the man she loved. She shoved at his chest. "Let me go," she demanded.

Danford shifted his hand to tightly grasp her upper arm. "My, my, such an ungracious attitude."

Her gaze flickered once more over his attire. "Why are you wearing Garrick's coat?"

He glanced down. "It's rather a good fit don't you think?"

She felt the blood drain from her face. "Where is Garrick? What have you done to him?"

"Nothing...yet. And if he stays away from here tonight, we might all make it out of this God awful country alive."

"What happens tonight?" she blurted, not stopping to evaluate the consequences of actually knowing.

"I imagine you shall find out soon enough.

Unfortunately, you have a most remarkable penchant for being in the wrong place at the wrong time. Now," he ordered, "come along to the cabin."

"I'll do no such thing," she retorted and kicked at Danford's shins.

Her well aimed blows merely glanced off his high-topped boots. Then he held her at arms length and watched her with an expression totally lacking in emotion. She clawed at his hand and twisted in his grip feeling like a child struggling against a Goliath. Finally a look of impatience enlivened his features, and he twisted her arm up behind her back. "I suggest you behave yourself," he growled. "And wipe that look of self-righteous fury from your face."

She flinched in pain then schooled her expression into a wooden stare.

Without further conversation, Danford pivoted and marched her stumbling to the cottage. He kicked open the door and shoved her inside.

She scrambled across the room, and with her back to the far wall, she assessed her surroundings. The large antechamber served as entryway, kitchen, and sitting room. Sparsely furnished, the little shack was draped with cobwebs and abandonment, and though some areas were scuffed clean by recent foot steps, dust layered the majority of the floor. The door was bracketed by two shuttered windows. To the left was an adjoining alcove that appeared to be a bedroom. She saw no other exit.

Flames licked at the logs in the fireplace, casting a ludicrous rosy glow on the ceiling and floor. The room looked more like a romantic hideaway than a newly relegated Bastille.

Her head snapped up as Danford slammed the door shut. He barred it from the inside and crossed the room to stand before her. "Don't try to escape," he brandished the pistol in her face. "It will be dark soon, and I've no intentions of spending my evening rescuing you from the wilds. Next time I'll champion the boar instead of you."

The tone of his voice seemed to lack conviction, but she wondered at his brutish statement. "You're mad," she dared to whisper aloud.

As soon as the words were out she regretted them. Danford's eyes grew cold as blue ice. Then he smiled. "Madness often stands toe to toe with genius."

"It would seem madness also stands toe to toe with arrogance," she spat back at him.

Danford raised the revolver and eased the tip of the barrel under her chin, forcing her to tilt her head back. "Don't press your good fortune, Nurse Posey. Beauty only goes so far in compensating for a sharp tongue and a disagreeable disposition."

She gritted her teeth and balled her hands into fists. The motion did not go undetected and Danford forced the cold metal a little harder against her jawbone. She yearned to strike out at him and smash the mocking grin from his face. But getting herself killed wouldn't help. She must escape and warn Garrick—for if he were headed toward this cabin, she had a feeling it could be a fatal mistake. She relaxed her hands.

"That's a good girl," Danford lowered the gun. "I would hate to have to tie you up. Unless it was to the bedpost of course."

Her eyes widened at his innuendo.

He laughed and chucked her under the chin with his free hand. Then he strode from her side, added another log to the fire, and flopped down into a nearby chair.

"Make a pot of tea," he commanded, as he laid the pistol on a small table at his side.

As if in a dream Josie stepped to the sideboard and retrieved two cups, a teapot, and a container of loose tea. Using a singed rag that hung nearby, she pulled the old kettle from the coals.

Like a self-assured old tom with a cornered mouse, Danford watched her every move, and she hated feeling vulnerable and helpless, especially in front of a man like this. Her hand faltered as she poured the boiling water into the pot. Then her temper flared and hoping to annoy Danford, she took her time steeping the brew.

Slowly she filled the cups and the idea of dashing the scalding drink in his face crossed her mind. But that would probably only infuriate him, adding to her precarious position. Yet there had to be some way to outsmart Danford.

Resigned to biding her time, she crossed the room, and set the chipped cup and saucer beside the loaded pistol and candle lantern that also occupied the table.

He reached out, but not for the tea, his hand coming to rest upon her thigh. She gasped and stepped backward beyond his reach.

"We could have been so good together," he said pensively. Then as if they were simply attending a Sunday social, he calmly picked up the tea and took a sip. Lowering the cup slightly, he again watched her over the rim. His well-honed stare scraped back and forth over her until she felt worn thin beneath his scrutiny.

"Why are you here?" she asked, hoping to prod him into revealing some useful information.

"I suppose there's no harm in telling you," he replied, with an egotistical toss of his head. "It's quite a fascinating story really. I'm about to make the business transaction of a lifetime." He took another sip of tea, as if granting her a moment to contemplate the magnitude of his words. "By the time the moon rises tonight, I shall be one of the richest men to whom Great Britain has ever laid

307

claim."

She picked up her cup, edged across the room, and slipped into a chair beside the fireplace. "More black market dealings I presume," she said, hoping to steal some of his prideful thunder.

"Of course," he cheerfully agreed without a hint of guilt or shame.

"Is the opium you killed Vlad for part of the trade?"

He slammed his cup down sloshing the remaining contents over the rim and into the saucer. Then he smoothly recovered his surprise. "I don't know what you mean," he countered and smiled.

Why turn back now? "I saw you, at the church, in the herb garden."

He raised a brow but still admitted nothing. "And to whom have you related this imaginative tale?"

"No one," she said, not sure whether she lied or not. She had written it all down in the note she'd given to Gemma. Had her friend opened the letter yet? Knowing Gemma, the girl had probably read the missive before Josie had been halfway to the dock in Scutari.

"You had best be telling the truth," Danford said, a far away look in his eyes.

"I don't see how stealing pain medicine from the soldiers will make you rich," she said trying to draw Danford back into conversation.

"No, of course not," he admitted. "If you must know I left the opium at the front door of General Hospital."

There was a surprise.

"It was a momentary lapse in judgment," he clarified, as if it were necessary to justify the act of mercy. "Besides, the Russian furs and artifacts I had bartered for were worth far more, and soon I shall take possession of the Idol's Eye."

The Idol's Eye? She'd never heard the term before.

"I assume from your expression you are not familiar with the gem, or surely you would be more appropriately impressed."

She cocked her head to one side inviting him to continue.

"The Idol's Eye is magnificent," he began, appreciation rather than greed seeming to brighten his expression. "70 carats, large as a bantam's egg." He waited again for some reaction or a sign of comprehension. "It's a Golconda diamond, you senseless woman," he said in exasperation. "It was once set in the eye of an idol, hence its name. And being pear shaped with a slight bluish tint, it was a perfect fit. Then the sheik of Kashmir was forced to ransom the prize to save his daughter, Princess Rasheetah. She was being held captive by a Turkish Sultan. Personally I would have kept the stone," he said thoughtfully. "One can always get another daughter. Regardless, that is the path by which one of the most remarkable gems in the world has come to this land, and soon it will be mine."

She sat stunned, not because of the Arabian Night's tale that she had just heard, but by the idea that a woman long ago had been kidnapped, men had died, and her soldiers had temporarily suffered without proper medicine, all for a stone that had once adorned a statue. It was insane.

"Nothing to say?" Danford queried. "I see the idea of being uncommonly rich still does not sway you around to my way of thinking. You are an unusual woman, Nurse Posey. Unusual and unfortunately also an encumbrance."

A pounding at the door brought them both up short.

Was it Garrick? How had he managed to find them? As Danford seized the pistol and leaped to the door, she changed her mind and prayed it was anyone else but her beloved. Yet she couldn't take the chance. She gained her feet and opened her mouth to call out.

"Not a word out of you," Danford growled, "or it shall be the last you utter."

He drew closer to the portal his hand upon the crossbar. "Who's there?" he called.

"Merhaba. It is Hasad."

Her shoulders relaxed and she exhaled, realizing she had been holding her breath. It wasn't Garrick!

Danford turned in her direction. "You," he ordered in hushed tones and a wave of the revolver, "hide in the other room." She hesitated. "This man really would kill you," he added.

As this information struck home, she fled to the bedroom and eased the door shut leaving it opened a crack so as to watch what was to transpire.

The pounding sounded once again. "Quickly, quickly. All has gone bambok."

The man sounded desperate. Danford raised the bar and opened the portal. The Turk burst into the room, turned, and slammed the door shut.

"What's wrong?" Danford asked, quickly replacing the bar. "Have you the jewel?"

"I am lucky to have my life," Hasad growled, as he tore the wolf-skin hat from his head and paced back and forth.

"What happened?" Danford demanded.

"There are two Russians in the woods."

"Russians? Are they still there?" Danford asked.

"Evet, yes, and yakin, very near. Only a few paces to the south, off in the trees."

"And the diamond," Danford asked, for the second time. "Where is my diamond?"

"They are very agitated," the Turk said, as if he had not heard the question. "I think they mistook me for you. They said they had taken care of a man named Vlad, and now it was my turn. Or as the case may be, your turn."

Here was another unexpected revelation. Josie had been wrong. Danford hadn't killed Vlad. It had been the Russians meting out punishment for the man's traitorous activities.

"Playing both sides is a dangerous game," Danford sneered.

"You are telling me? I cursed them for the dogs they are and when they heard my words uttered in Turkish, it took them by surprise. That is when I fought them off and made my way to the cabin."

With a complete lack of concern for the other man's tribulations, Danford focused once more upon his main objective. "The diamond," he insisted, his voice deadly calm, his pistol now leveled at other man's chest. "Where is the diamond?"

"It is here," the Turk reassured, as he patted his pocket. Then his hands wandered over the front of his body as if they had a mind of their own. Suddenly his actions turned frantic. He stood stock still and stared at Danford. "It must have fallen out when I struggled to free myself from the Muscovites."

The blood drained from Danford's face, but the mask of white made him look cold and menacing rather than weak with distress.

"I was fighting for my life," the man said in an attempt to justify his mistake.

"You fool," Danford yelled. "That jewel was worth a thousand men like you."

The Turk took a step backward as if he realized his life was not much safer inside the cabin than it had been outside with the Russians.

There is no stronger bond of friendship than a mutual enemy.

~Frankfort Moore

Chapter Twenty-Five

Garrick approached the cabin with caution.

Undisturbed snow blanketed the patch of ground behind the cottage and the land, flat and white, taunted him like the purest piece of paper. A blank page waiting to be written upon and he had a feeling tonight's story was about to unfold.

Concealed amongst the trees that edged the glen, he studied the dilapidated structure. A light glowed from within and despite the gathering gloom, he detected intermittent puffs of smoke escaping the chimney. Someone was definitely at home. Was it Danford?

The British soldiers at the field camp confirmed the fact that Smythe had recently taken up residence here. It was surprisingly bold of Danford to be so blatant about his whereabouts and activities. He must be quite sure of himself or planning to leave the area in the very near future. Garrick had plans too. He intended to apprehend Danford while he was in possession of the stolen merchandise. Then there would be no opportunity for the man to weasel out of admitting he'd been playing a dirty little game at many other peoples' expense. And, Garrick admitted with a twinge of personal ire, he wanted his damn coat back. How Danford had come by the garment he didn't know, but according to the lads, the man he sought was said to be sporting attire that could be no other.

Keeping to the shelter of the trees, he edged forward. Then he heard the voices. Oddly, they seemed to emanate from outside the cottage not from within. Even more curious, they were speaking Russian. And they sounded angry. Just another clandestine meeting, or was there something else afoot? It seemed rather risky business for the Muscovites to stray this far from their own camp. He wended his way closer, and the men came into view. There appeared to be only two of them. Rather a meager showing for a military maneuver.

While the Russians were engaged in their heated discussion, Garrick gained cover on the far side of the little hovel. He eased the homemade fladdermine into a depression in the dirt, carefully arranged several short logs beside the explosive, and securely staked the wood in place. Tying an old rope he had brought along to the upright, he played out the hemp, and retraced his steps back to the protection of the trees.

He never dreamed he would be thankful for the existence of such a terrible instrument of destruction. On the other hand, a well timed explosion gave a man a nice edge. Of course, his piecemeal creation wasn't likely to harm anyone, just make a good bit of noise and throw shot in all directions.

As he hunkered down out of the wind, he recalled the night several months ago when he and William Russell had discussed the making of such weapons. For three abysmal days they had been pinned down near Canrobert's Hill, forced to take shelter in a tent that was much too small for two grown men, and much too leaky to be called a place of refuge. The mud had run in rivulets between their boots and around the upended stumps they had used as chairs. Luckily, the fermented Raki had flowed as freely as the mud. Lacking all other forms of entertainment, they had discussed everything under the sun—from the unfathomable intricacies of a woman's mind to the abominable genius of the mind of Man. And while women labored to bring new life into the world, the male of the species seemed to labor over developing ways of killing his brother.

The fladdermine he had just planted was a prime example. The Germans had used the explosive devices for at least 150 years, *what did Prince Albert think of that?* At least the British had not followed through with their threat to use a mixture of sulfur and coke to smoke out the Russians at Fort Nicholas. No doubt, the use of lethal gas would one day become commonplace.

Shaking the fragments of memories from his mind, he dragged his attention back to the present and contemplated the odd gathering of characters introduced into this impromptu play. It seemed a tale flung heedlessly into the face of the last winter winds. And where the story would alight and how it would end, left few scenarios to his liking.

As he watched, the two Russian soldiers appeared to have finally reached an agreement and together they approached the cabin. Armed to the teeth, they boldly headed for the door. Then realizing that discretion was the better part of hotheaded recklessness, they took up positions on either side of the portal. One man leaned forward, and employing the butt of his rifle, pounded upon the old wooden structure. "Danford Smythe," he called, "open up, you are surrounded."

Garrick glanced in all directions. He hadn't seen or heard anyone else. The Muscovites were bluffing. That was the ploy he'd been intending to use. This state of affairs was transforming from interesting to fascinating. Without thinking, he reached for a cheroot then stilled his hand. He dare not strike a match. Instead, he twisted a small twig from a nearby tree trunk and chewed on the spindly stem.

"What do you want?" came the muffled reply.

It was Danford's voice all right. Garrick smiled with satisfaction. His luck was holding.

"You have betrayed the Motherland," one of the soldiers declared. "Now, like Vlad, you pay."

Garrick harbored a new regret upon hearing that bit of information. Apparently Vlad had been eliminated. So much for following up that avenue of information.

Silence continued to reign for what seemed an eternity. Then having grown impatient with waiting, one of the Russians raised his rifle and fired point blank at the old wrought iron hasp.

The door flew open. A man flung himself through the portal and stumbled and fell to the ground.

"Bloody fool," the words rang out from within the cabin. Then the door slammed shut.

"Don't shoot," said the man, who lay sprawled in the snow. "The one you seek is inside. He has only one pistol."

The Cossacks scrambled about and seized the man. A vehement dissertation of Russian and Turkish filled the air. Obviously this man was not Danford. Then in the blink of an eye, one of the Muscovites pulled free his pistol and shot the Turk. Never uttering a sound the man fell to the ground to lay unmoving.

Garrick stifled a curse and swallowed hard. He hadn't been expecting that. It would appear these Russians were dead serious about killing Smythe and anyone else who might get in their way. Danford had much to answer for, yet an execution style death carried out by an enemy of the British Empire seemed somehow inappropriate. Parading Smythe before the courts thus ridiculing him publicly and ruining his reputation would be a far more painful and lasting punishment.

The Russian soldiers stepped over the inert form of the Turk and headed once more for the cabin.

It was getting dark and Garrick guessed it was the appropriate time to make his offstage entrance into this little drama. Pistol at the ready he yanked on the hemp rope. The stake uprooted freeing the logs. The wood crashed forward. He held his breath. Would the handcrafted devise even work? In his mind's eye he saw the flintlock igniter trip forward. With any luck, it would fire off the main charge; that is if the powder had remained dry. Two heartbeats later a grand explosion ensued. He grinned and stifled a cheer of success. Shot rained down on the shack, clattering against the rooftop and dripping off the eaves. It also struck a few of the trees in the forest rattling the branches, disturbing the snow that for months had lain cradled in the twiggy arms.

"Move in on the left, sergeant," Garrick shouted, using the Russians' strategy against them.

The Cossacks fired blindly in all the wrong directions.

Garrick leaped sideways and hit the ground rolling. He returned fire—striking the man on the left. The other soldier reached down, dragged his comrade to his feet, and together they scramble off into the woods. For good measure, Garrick fired off three more rounds.

Several seconds passed as muffled cries of pain faded away into the darkness. Then all was utterly still. He gained his feet and edged forward, and his left foot came into contact with a small parcel lying in the snow. Retrieving the bundle, he unwrapped and opened it.

By the light of the moon, he examined the contents of the velvet drawstring bag and his eyes widened in appreciation. Was this the true reason the Russians had come here tonight? He could see where it would inspire men to murder, and it came as little surprise that Danford would somehow be embroiled in the transaction.

He crossed the short distance to the man lying in the snow. The Turk was beyond help. Garrick shook his head and kept walking toward the cabin. "You can come out now, Smythe" he yelled. "The Cossacks are gone."

The door opened a crack. "Is that you, Newsboy?" Danford called back. Garrick could visualize the sneer that accompanied the words.

"Yes," he answered coolly, "and I believe I've something you want. It's the biggest damn diamond I've ever seen in my life. "

The pause that followed told him he was right. Then he heard a scuffling noise from within and what sounded like a woman's voice. "That makes us even," Danford called back. "I've something you want as well."

"Garrick, don't come any closer. Danford has a gun."

With a shock, Garrick realized it was Josie's voice. What was she doing here? His heart seemed to stop—then it tripped forward and thudded in his chest triple time. Heaven help him, he would never have set off an explosive mine near the cabin had he known she was inside. Smoke billowed up from behind the cottage. The red hot shrapnel had set the tinderbox of a cabin on fire. The front door suddenly opened wide and coughing and choking Danford careened through the opening.

Garrick took shelter beside a small woodshed, pistol cocked, a moving target almost in range. His finger tightened around the cold steel of the trigger then he slackened his grip and turned the gun aside.

Danford held Josie by one arm using her as a shield.

"Throw down your weapon, Allen, and come

out," Danford ordered, "We wouldn't want dear Nurse Posey getting caught in any crossfire." He raised his revolver and skimmed the side of the barrel along her cheek. The subtle action was both murderous and sensual.

Rage exploded in Garrick's belly and burrowed deeper into his gut but his need for action turned impotent as his fear of injuring Josie took precedence.

"Run, Garrick," Josie cried. "He's mad. He..."

Her sentence was cut short as Danford jerked her arm—forcing her to silence.

Garrick stared at Josie's face. The wild terrified look in her eyes drove through him like a lance. Legs braced, he waited and held his position.

Danford glanced to left and right. "No hordes of soldiers at the ready?" he jeered. "Your theatrics were amusing, but I think you are alone."

Garrick gritted his teeth to hold back a retort. At least he had drawn Danford out into the open. That evened the odds a little. The cabin now burned with vigor, and as the glow of the conflagration steadily grew brighter, he studied his adversary more closely. The brazen blackguard really *was* wearing his fringed coat.

"All in all," Danford chortled, "it's quite apropos don't you think? A beautiful girl held captive, a diamond of unimaginable worth offered for her freedom, and history repeats itself."

Garrick groaned inwardly. Now what was Danford rambling on about? Their lives hung in the balance and the scale was tended by a philosophical lunatic. "What do you want?" he asked evenly.

"The diamond, of course," Danford said, "and safe passage back to Ankara."

"Release Josie and I'll give you the gem," Garrick countered. He dangled the drawstring pouch out in front and the weight of the large stone made the velvet bag sway enticingly from side to side.

"I'm not as trusting as the Sheik of Kashmir," Danford said. "Besides, your proposal leaves too many loose ends."

"I'll come out and relinquish my pistol, Smythe," Garrick negotiated, "just leave Josie here with me, unharmed. You would be well on your way to safety before I could walk back to camp and return with help."

"I think not," Danford said. "Although I hate to admit it, you are much too resourceful. The girl goes with me."

Josie's face turned white as Irish linen, and Garrick feared she was about to do something desperate and dangerous. He felt the same way. He couldn't let Danford leave with her. When it came to self-preservation Danford would always attend to his own needs first, and if that meant abandoning Josie along the way he'd do so without thinking twice.

The wind blew cold but he started to sweat. He still had the diamond. The one thing that Danford wanted most. He liberated the gleaming jewel from its velvet cocoon and leisurely tossed it up and down. "I'll throw this in the woods before I allow you to take Josie away from here," he called out.

Danford's eyes widened with alarm then narrowed in anger.

Time passed as if in a dream and everything seemed to be happening in slow motion. The timbers of the cabin snapped and groaned as the fire consumed them. A tower of sparks spiraled lazily up into the air, and the surrounding snow-covered field glowed red like a corner of hell.

Smythe cocked the hammer back on the pistol he held at the ready. "You're bluffing," he snarled, shifting the muzzle of the revolver away from Josie's ribcage and toward Garrick. The movement seemed to push Josie over the edge. She screamed and shoved at Danford then stepping between the two men, she ran toward Garrick.

A shot rang out.

Josie hesitated, her eyes grew round with surprise then she fell backward toward Danford who stepped forward to catch her.

"You son of a bitch," Garrick yelled, running forward.

"I didn't shoot her," Danford hollered. "The shot came from the woods." He thrust Josie into Garrick's arms. "We're not alone," he added.

The diamond and velvet bag slipped from Garrick's fingers. He gathered the woman he loved against his chest, picked her up, and headed for the far side of the charred cabin. A moment later, Danford followed.

Unknotting the Holland scarf from around Josie's shoulders, Garrick used the cloth to staunch the blood issuing from her shoulder wound.

Danford shed Garrick's leather jacket and draped it over her unmoving form.

The two men sought shelter behind what was left of the cabin. "If she dies I'll kill you Smythe," Garrick gritted, from between clenched teeth

"I told you, I never fired my pistol. The Russians must have returned. They're terribly tenacious bastards once they get hold of an idea."

Since Josie had fallen backwards toward Danford and not away from him, Garrick had to consider the logic of this explanation. But now what? Would the sound of renewed fighting bring the soldiers from the British field camp? The blazing cabin hadn't initiated a response, nor had the previous explosion and exchange of gunfire. He had a feeling they were on their own.

Josie moaned and turned her head from side to side.

"Josie." He breathed her name as if it were the

first time and the last, then he gathered her in his arms and held her tight. "Open your eyes love. Look at me. You're going to be all right."

"Garrick?" she murmured. "Oh, darling. I came to warn you. I feared Danford was going to kill you."

Garrick glanced at Smythe.

Danford shrugged. "The thought has crossed my mind on occasion."

"But he didn't kill Vlad, the spy," she ramble on, in a barely audible whisper.

"Never mind that," Garrick said. "Don't talk. We'll get you out of here as soon as possible." He checked beneath the linen cloth. The bleeding had lessened but her cheeks remained ghostly pale.

"It's your fault she's out here, Smythe," Garrick accused.

"No more than yours, Newsboy," Danford retorted.

The truth of Smythe's words made him feel all the worse as he watched the woman who had come to mean the world to him bleeding in the snow. They must get to a secured area and find medical care for Josie. His soul would never withstand the horror of another woman he loved dying right before his eyes.

He eased Josie to the ground. Thankfully, the heat from the burning cabin helped to keep Josie comfortable, but it also shed light on their tenuous position. More shots rang out from the direction the Russians had taken earlier. Both men returned fire.

"How many do you think there are?" Danford asked as he shifted about pressing closer to the ground.

"At least three, maybe more," Garrick said as he reloaded his revolver. He knew there was only one logical course of action to take. One of them should remain with Josie, and one of them should circle around and come up from behind the enemy. But who would go and who would stay? He didn't trust

Danford to carry out either mission.

"I'll go," Danford said, as if he too realized this was the only way out of their situation.

Garrick stared at Danford trying to fathom his true intentions. Would the man simply fade into the forest and not look back, leaving them to fend for themselves?

"Keep them occupied until I'm clear, Newsboy," he sneered as if reading Garrick's mind. Holding at the ready, he waited for the shifting clouds to blot out the light of the full moon. Then he crawled off into the shadows.

Garrick emptied six rounds in the direction they had last seen gunfire. Quickly reloading again, he noticed there was not much ammunition left. The noise from the pistol shots roused Josie from her semi-conscious state. "Garrick," she called out. "Garrick, where are you?"

"I'm right here," he said and reached over and took her hand in his. It was cold as ice. "There's nothing to worry about," he lied. Nothing other than the fact that their lives depended on the scruples of an egotistical robber baron. Of course without the diamond Danford would be reluctant to desert them. He patted the pocket of the coat he wore then groaned inwardly. He must have dropped the gem when Josie had been shot. Still it was probably nearby and Danford would never easily relinquish such a fortune.

Gunfire erupted again. But this time, the sound came from behind the Russians. Garrick breathed a sigh of relief. Smythe had kept his word after all. The moon shrugged its robe of clouds and as light filtered down through the trees, he detected several stealthy figures moving about. Reinforcements. Danford was about to be severely outnumbered, which meant he'd have to go after him and bring him back. They would have to take their chances defending their position from here.

Retrieving a small derringer from the pocket of the borrowed coat, Garrick pressed the weapon into Josie's freezing fingers. She stared at him in confusion.

"You must stay awake and alert until I return," he ordered. "Can you do that?"

"Yes," she answered, with a slight nod of her head, her eyes wide with fear. "I love you," she added in a whisper.

"I love you too, Josie." He leaned forward and kissed her forehead. A tear slip from her eye and trickle down her cheek. "I'll come back" he reassured her and wiped it away with his thumb. "I've waited my entire life to find my lady gallant and I'll bloody well not lose you now."

He tore himself from her side and followed the path Danford had made in the snow. The wet terrain muffled his approach, and he came up behind the other man undetected.

"Psst, Smythe," he hissed, when he was near enough to be heard.

Danford jumped and spun around.

"It's me, Garrick," he quickly identified himself.

"Christ you gave me a start," Danford swore.

"We have to fall back to our original position," Garrick began. "There's more Cossacks approaching from the North and soon there'll be too many of them for us to handle."

"Bad luck," Danford retorted, "just when I was growing accustomed to playing the hero." He nodded toward a small pile of firearms heaped beneath a nearby tree. "I eliminated the two soldiers who were harassing us and appropriated their pistols and rifles."

Garrick was impressed by the other man's show of fortitude and ability. "Well done," he grudgingly acknowledged, although he had little doubt

Danford's enthusiasm was inspired mostly by concern for his own life. "We can use the guns and ammunition. Now we'd best be on our way."

They divvied up the weapons and made haste to return to the cabin. As they rounded the far side they saw Josie propped up on her good arm, derringer shaking but pointed in their direction. When she recognized them, she gave a great sob of relief, dropped the weapon, and slumped back to the ground.

"Take heart, Josie," Garrick encouraged. "We're going to fortify our position."

Setting the newly acquired Russian armaments within easy reach, they labored to arrange the charred debris into a redoubt high enough to give them some protection on the far side.

They had barely finished the makeshift construction when the shooting began in earnest. A bullet struck a nearby rock, sending a stone fragment ricocheting off in Danford's direction. The man swore and fell backward. Garrick crawled over to him and examined the wound. "It only grazed your cheek," he reported.

"Feels like it damn near took the side of my head off," Danford groused, a dazed look in his eyes.

Garrick shoved Danford back to a position of safety. As he sought to return to Josie's side, a support beam from the old cabin broke loose. It crashed to the ground and tumbled end over end, headed straight for them. Trying to redirect its path, he flung himself in front of the onrushing column of charred wood. The beam knocked him down, then came to rest full weight on his left thigh. The pain was dreadful, and a broken bone seemed a good possibility. As Danford shifted the weight from his leg, agony exploded like a nine-pounder, and he feared he was going to pass out.

Josie watched in horror then inched her way

over to his side. She packed snow over the singed clothing and burned flesh. Then she stopped to press the scarf against her own wound, now open and bleeding anew.

Danford gave a bark of sarcasm. "The three of us don't even make a decent pair," he said, with a quirky smile as the blood ran down one side of his face.

Garrick wondered if the man would now show his true colors and abandon them to their wounded fate. He felt around on the ground and located his revolver. He'd be damned if he'd let that happen. As he tightened his grip on the firearm, he noticed an eerie dead calm had claimed the night. Then he heard the sound of marching feet. Many, many, marching feet and voices calling out into the night. He couldn't make out the words, but they were growing ever closer. It seemed as if half the Russian army was advancing upon them. But they were coming from the south, the wrong direction.

The troops grew increasingly boisterous. "Nurse Posey? Mr. Allen? Where are you?"

"They're speaking English, Josie, we'll be all right now," he tightened his arm around her shoulder.

"Time for me to take my leave, old man," Danford announced.

Garrick glanced at the man who had fought at their side. "Too bad you lost the diamond, Smythe," he pointed out. "Especially since you nearly sacrificed all our lives to acquire it."

Danford reached inside his shirt, pulled the gem free, and held it up admiringly. "I saw you drop it when Nurse Posey was shot," he said, and grinned like a little boy with the finest toy.

Smythe could have left at any time, but he hadn't. This was a revelation to boggle the mind. Neither man moved. Garrick lowered his pistol. "See you around, Smythe," he said.

"Not if I see you first, Newsboy." His old demeanor fully recovered, Danford gave a condescending laugh and disappeared into the night.

Still holding tight to Josie, Garrick levered his pain-wracked body upright and peered over the barricade they had created. A smile pulled at his mouth. "Here comes Gemma," he described, "followed by a brigade of British soldiers, a grey-haired priest, and two French nuns." He shook his head in amazement.

"Leave it to Gemma," Josie put in, "to inspire a rescue mission comprised of the British army and a French legion of God,"

Josie's wound had stopped bleeding, so he commandeered her bloodstained white shawl and waved it over head. "Over here," he shouted, "here we are." The search party, responding to his call, changed course and headed in their direction.

Suddenly Garrick felt exhausted, and he slumped back upon the ground. Then he felt dizzy, but it was fear not pain that gripped him. Only now did he realize how close he had come to losing Josie.

She reached over and gently stroked his cheek.

He captured her hand and kissed her fingertips. Josie filled his heart with hope and his soul with light. These past few weeks, her absence from his life had been a penance of dark loneliness, something he never wished to suffer again.

"Will you marry me?" he asked, the words tumbling out before he realized what he was saying.

The expression in her eyes gentled but she remained silent.

Panic rippled through him. Was she undecided? Even the Fates could not be so cruel as to give him a taste of heaven and then condemn him to a living hell without her. He searched her face for an answer.

"And just why should I marry you?" she demanded in a weakened version of the no-nonsense tone he had come to cheriesh. "Not one bit of flowery prose nor haunting ode has passed your lips to win my heart."

He gave a bark of laughter. "Poetic pentameter and sorrowful sonnet have nothing to do with my motives," he said. "I have considered this quite thoroughly and 'tis simply a matter of chivalry. After all, what kind of man would I be if I allowed you to go through the rest of your life with a name like Josie Posey. Marry me," he coaxed, and eased her closer. "Become Josie Allen."

"I thought you reporters knew all the details," she chided and angled her head back to stare into his eyes.

He raised a brow. "Exactly what does that mean?"

"Your honorable intentions are appreciated," she said, "but your facts are incorrect. Josephine is my middle name. My first name is Ellen." Her eyebrows knit in consternation but a smile twitched upon her lips. "Now I must face the remainder of my life with the name of Ellen Allen."

He laughed and smoothed a stray lock of hair back from her face. "A rose by any other name," he said softly, his lips brushing hers.

How do I love thee? Let me count the ways...
I love thee with the passion put to use
In my old griefs, and with my childhood's faith.
                    ~Elizabeth Barrett Browning

Epilogue
London, September, 1855

Ensconced in his favorite easy chair, Garrick set aside his newspaper and watched the morning sun wander in through the parlor window. He had come to love this time of day. It was full of possibility. And he loved Josie, *his wife*. Even now, those words sounded odd to his brain, probably because he was hard pressed to believe he was fortunate enough to have her in his life

"Another cup of tea, dear?" she asked.

"Yes, if you would, please." Blanketed in serene contentment, he watched as she retreated into the next room to fulfill his request.

Seven months had passed since their leaving Turkey. First, they had convalesced at the Kaiserwerth Hospital in Germany. Miss Nightingale had insisted. Then, still unable to resume their duties in the Crimea, they had married in Brussels before returning to England. Now, blissfully at peace with one another, they felt somewhat guilty as the war continued to rage on without them.

After much consideration, Garrick had decided to continue working for *The Times*. How could he possibly leave Shamus or the occupation he so loved? But he refused to take assignments other than in Great Britain. And in the between times, he wrote sheaves of poetry for Josie and was halfway through the first draft of his second novel. As for the love of his life, she was making great strides in reconciling with her family and she kept perpetually busy supporting Miss Nightingale's causes on the home front.

Of course, there were those rare occasions when life in the city became a bit too tame for either one of them. Then they would open a bottle of Ankara Gold, spend hours recounting their memories of the war, and talk about naming their first son Mose. Following that ritual, they would make mind blistering passionate love. And if that did not succeed in curing their wanderlust, they made love again.

Teapot in hand, Josie returned to his side.

"They've offered me a most tempting assignment in Nepal," Garrick said, keeping his tone as nonchalant as possible.

Josie glanced at him with an innocence that still sent him over the edge. Then she set aside the tea, smiled seductively, and reached for the Turkish whiskey and two crystal goblets.

Garrick grinned and reached for Josie.

Promise to the Light Brigade

At thirty and four,
I was sent off to war,
For *The Times*, St. George, and the Queen.
But all truths were laid bare,
Pain and death waited there,
Foolish pride and man's greed intervened.

Was it just for the key,
To the church by the sea
That men died so brave, and so young?
With blind faith, each one fought.
Precious freedom they sought,
And their courage shall not go unsung.

I witnessed it all
As they went to the wall,
As they charged up that valley outnumbered.
I'll let no man forget
The dark hell that was met.
By the honored, the gallant, six hundred.

~Garrick Allen
Special Correspondent, *The Times*

Historical Note

Roger Fenton, photographer at large, did not arrive in the Crimea until March of 1855.

Florence Nightingale, who returned to London following the war, never fully recovered from the Crimean fever. Undaunted, she fought from her bedside as an advocate for patients' rights and she changed forever the future of nursing by founding the Nightingale School and Home for Nurses. She was the first woman to receive the British Order of Merit.

Mrs. Mary Seacole did establish the *British Hotel* but not until the spring of 1855 and generally she traveled with two mules, not a donkey. After returning to Britain she published her book *Wonderful Adventures of Mrs. Seacole in Many Lands* and William Russell wrote the introductory preface.

The beautiful Idol's Eye diamond truly did exist and mysteriously appeared at a Christie's sale in London in 1865. It re-emerged after World War II and reportedly became part of a priceless collection of gems owned by Mrs. May Bonfils Stanton, who was the daughter of the publisher and co-founder of the *Denver Post*.

According to my research, the reports sent by the war correspondents to *The Times* were called despatches. For ease of reading the spelling was changed to dispatches.

A word from the author...

History being my passion, and having worked as a registered nurse for eleven years, I have always been intrigued by the legend of Florence Nightingale and the controversy surrounding the Crimean War. These elements became the inspiration for my book, *Lady Gallant*. I hope you enjoyed reading it as much as I enjoyed writing it. If you've a moment to spare, please come visit my website, www.ginirifkin.com, where you can learn a bit more about me and take a step even farther back in time with my medieval romance, *The Dragon and The Rose*.

My thanks to you
and
May all your ever afters be happy ones.